The frightening story of a disaster
that could happen here!
THE TOWER

"One of the tightest suspense novels I have ever
read."—Frank G. Slaughter

"Imperceptibly we pass from incredulity to interest, from interest to concern, from concern
to excitement—until, well, we find ourselves . . .
thrilled."—New York *Times*

"The suspense is kept very taut . . . comparisons
with *Airport* and *A Night to Remember* are, for
once, appropriate."—*New York* Magazine

"Remember *Day of the Jackal?* Well, here is its
successor, a sure fire winner of a suspense novel."
—Des Moines *Register*

"A marvel of suspense."—Hartford *Courant*

The Tower

Richard Martin Stern

WARNER
PAPERBACK
LIBRARY

A Warner Communications Company

For D.A.S. with love.

"It is the world's tallest structure, and the most modern, an enduring tribute to man's ingenuity, skill, and vision. It is a triumph of imagination."
—GROVER FRAZEE at the World Tower dedication ceremonies.

"A monument to Mammon, product of man's insatiable ego, an affront to the gods. That so much treasure should have been poured into the construction of this—this monstrosity while poverty, yes, and even hunger still stalk the land, is an abomination! There will be inevitable Divine retribution!"
—THE REVEREND JOE WILLIE THOMAS in a press interview.

"Eyewitness accounts and expert testimony are at such variance that it is difficult, if not impossible, to know where the truth concerning this disaster may be found."
—OFFICIAL REPORT OF THE COMMITTEE OF INQUIRY.

Part I

For one hundred and twenty-five floors, from street level to Tower Room, the building rose tall and clean and shining. Above the Tower Room the radio and television spire thrust sharply against the sky.

By comparison with the twin masses of the nearby Trade Center, the building appeared slim, almost delicate, a thing of fragile-seeming grace and beauty. But eight subbasements beneath the street level its roots were anchored deep in the bedrock of the island; and its core and external skeleton, cunningly contrived, had the strength of laminated spring steel.

When fully occupied, the building would house some fifteen thousand people in its offices and studios and shops; in addition it would accommodate twenty-five thousand visitors a day.

Through its telephone, radio, and television systems operating at ground level, broadcasting through the atmosphere or via satellite, its sphere of communication was, quite simply, the earth.

It could even communicate with itself, floor to floor, subbasement to gleaming tower.

Level by level it had risen, a marvel for all to see.

The great cranes hoisted steel into position and held it while the bedlam clamor of rivet guns gave proof that it was being secured; then, their work at one level completed, the cranes, like sentient monsters, hoisted each other to new positions to repeat the process.

As the structure grew, its arteries, veins, nerves, and muscles were woven into the whole: miles of wiring, piping, utility ducting, cables and conduits; heating, ventilating, and air-conditioning ducts, intakes, and outlets —and always, always the monitoring systems and devices to oversee and control the building's internal environment, its health, its life.

Sensors to relay information on temperature, humidity, air flow and content; computers to assimilate the data, evaluate them, issue essential instructions for continuation or change.

Are the upper ten floors, still exposed to the setting

11

sun's heat, warmer than optimum? Increase their flow of cool conditioned air.

Are the first ten floors above street level now cooling too rapidly in the dusk? Reduce their air-conditioning flow, and, as necessary, feed in heated air.

The building breathed, manipulated its internal systems, slept only as the human body sleeps: heart, lungs, cleansing organs functioning on automatic control, encephalic waves pulsing ceaselessly.

Dull silver was the building's basic color—anodized aluminum curtain panels covering the structural steel; the whole pierced by tens of thousands of green-tinted tempered-glass windows.

It stood in a plaza of its own, by its height dominating the downtown area. At its base three-story arches enclosed a perimeter arcade. Great doors led into the two-story concourse, to the elevators in the core structure, the stairs and escalators and shops in the lobbies themselves.

Men had envisioned it, conceived it, and constructed it, sometimes almost lovingly, sometimes with near hatred, because, like all great projects, the building had early on developed a character of its own, and no man intimately associated with it could escape involvement.

There is, it seems, a feedback. What man creates with his hands or his mind becomes a part of himself. And there, on this morning, the building stood, its uppermost tip catching the first rays of sunrise while the rest of the city still slept in shadow; and the thousands of men who had had a part in the building's design and construction were going to remember this day forever.

1

The police barricades had been stacked in the Tower Plaza since dawn that Friday morning. Now city employees were setting them out in neat straight lines. As yet no crowd had gathered.

The sky was clear, blue, limitless. A gentle harbor breeze swept the plaza, salt-smelling, fresh. The plaza flags rippled, Two on-duty patrolmen—more would be arriving during the next hour—stood by the arcade.

"At least," Patrolman Shannon was saying, "we've nothing political to cope with today, thank God for that. A political rally—" He shook his head. "The way some people in this country get stirred up over politics is a sin and a shame and a waste." He glanced upward at the towering, gleaming building. "It reaches almost to Heaven," he said. "Way above men's little squabbles."

Patrolman Barnes said, "Dig the uninvolved man." Patrolman Barnes was black. "To hear him tell it, all Irishmen are peaceable, loving, patient, unexcitable, kind, considerate, and totally nonviolent." Barnes had his master's degree in sociology, was already marked down for promotion to sergeant, and had his sights set on a captaincy at least. He grinned at Shannon. "Those love-ins they stage over in Londonderry, friend, are not what you might call church socials."

"Only when provoked," Shannon said. He allowed himself a faint answering smile. "But I'm not saying that sometimes the provocation doesn't have to be looked for. Sometimes it hides, like a mouse in a hole." The smile disappeared as a man approached. "And where do you think you're going?"

13

It was established later that the man's name was John Connors. He carried a toolbox. In testimony Barnes and Shannon agreed that he had worn work clothes and a shiny aluminum hard hat and the kind of arrogance a skilled workman is tempted to show toward those who ask silly questions.

"Where does it look like I'm going? Inside." Connors paused. His smile pitied them. "Unless you're going to try to keep me out?" There was challenge in the question.

"There's no work today," Barnes said.

"I know it."

"Then?"

Connors sighed. "Where I ought to be is home. In bed. A day off for everybody while they make speeches here and go upstairs to drink champagne. Instead, here I am because the boss called me and told me to haul my ass down to the job."

"To do what?" This was still Barnes.

"I'm an electrician," Connors said. "Would you understand what I'm supposed to do if I told you?"

Probably not, Barnes thought. But that was not the governing factor. The trouble was orders, or lack of them.

"You and Shannon," the duty sergeant had said, "get on down there and keep an eye on things. They'll be setting up the lines and we don't expect any trouble, but——" The sergeant had shrugged with a you-know-how-it-is expression.

And they did know how it was these days: every gathering seemed to generate its own unrest. All right, they would keep an eye on things, but that scarcely included keeping a workman away from his work.

"Do you carry a union card, friend?" Barnes said gently.

"So what are you?" Connors said. "An NLRB inspector? Yes, I carry a union card. I'm no scab." He pulled out his wallet and waved it. If it contained a card, it could not be seen. "Satisfied?" Connors put the wallet away again.

Shannon's temper was rising fast. "Let him go."

14

Still Barnes hesitated. As he testified later, he had had no reason for the hesitation, merely a feeling, and actions based on feelings are always suspect.

"Well?" Connors said. "Make up your goddam mind. Just standing here, I'm already costing the boss—"

Shannon said, "Beat it." There was a vein throbbing in the side of his neck. He looked at his partner. "We don't have any orders to keep people out, Frank. Let the son of a bitch go. Maybe he'll electrocute himself."

That was the way they remembered it, and told it later.

Months in advance the date for the dedication ceremonies had been set. It has always been so, and there is no other way, because building-completion dates are elastic; and the invited guests for the ceremonies were coming from Washington and from state capitals, from City Hall, from the UN, from head offices of radio and TV networks and worldwide wire services; those who wanted to appear and be seen, and those who would rather have stayed away but had been caught by the inexorability of an early invitation.

In Nat Wilson's office, facing the walls covered with thumbtacked drawings of the great building, Will Giddings said, "There are fifty things I want cleaned up. A hundred."

"So do I," Nat said. Simple truth. You live with a job for a matter of years, and, as with an artist completing his master work, you see here and there little touches you would like time to make. But there was no time today.

"And, goddammit," Giddings said, "I don't want stuffed shirts wandering around like a flock of goddam tourists." He paused. "We aren't ready. You know it. I know it."

When the opening-night curtain goes up, Nat thought, is there always this lament? Where had that thought come from? "We aren't ready," he said. "Agreed. So?" He was the younger man, architect-engineer, middle-sized, solid, rarely voluble.

"The hundred and twenty-fifth floor," Giddings said,

15

"just under the mast. Drinks, backslapping, congratulations, and a view of how many hundreds of square miles of water and country, and it can't be postponed because the characters who are coming are so goddam important, senators, congressmen, the governor, the mayor, UN types, movie stars, that kind of crap?"

"That kind of crap," Nat said.

Giddings was a big man, sandy-haired, blue-eyed, filling that ancient position of clerk of the works, owner's representative on the job. He was in his early forties. Somewhere, probably in the back of a forgotten drawer, he had an engineering degree, and now and again over their years on the job Nat had seen him, slide-rule in hand, doing his paperwork, but he always seemed more in character in his hard hat, riding an open hoist or walking a steel girder or prowling tunnels and subbasements to see that the job was done right. "I don't drink cocktails," he said, "and I don't eat little things with toothpicks in them. Maybe you do." There was tension in him plain to see.

"Beside the point," Nat said. "Grover Frazee set the day. Your boss."

Giddings sat down at last. He stretched out his legs, but there was no relaxation in the movement. "My boss," he said, and nodded. "We have to have businessmen, but we don't have to like them." He was studying Nat. "You must have been still wet behind the ears when you started on this job—how long ago? Seven years?"

"Close enough," Nat said. Back at the start of preliminary design, the conceptual thinking, he following but also flying along with Ben Caldwell's soaring visions. He could not resist glancing out the window at the distant Tower itself, clean and pure and beautiful against the sky: the result of those years of work. "So?"

"My building, sonny, goddammit," Giddings said. "Oh, it's part yours too, but I watched the start of excavation that went down eighty feet to bedrock, and I watched them top out the steel fifteen hundred and twenty-seven feet above grade, and I know every grillage, every column,

16

every truss, every spandrel beam as well as I'd know my own kids if I'd ever had any."

There was nothing that required comment. Nat was silent.

"You're a self-contained son of a bitch," Giddings said. "Is it a case of still waters running deep? Never mind." His eyes went briefly to the distant tower. "I lost some friends too. On any big job you always do." He looked back at Nat. "Remember Pete Janowski?"

Nat shook his head faintly.

"Walked out into air sixty-five floors up and splattered himself on a concrete ramp down in the bathtub."

"That one," Nat said, remembering.

"Big Polack," Giddings said, "a good man, never seemed to hurry, but he got the job done the right way, the safe way, and that was what shook me. When you can't put a cause to it, that's when you worry."

There was something in Giddings's voice, his manner—uptight was the word. Nat said slowly, "Are you making a point?"

It was as if he had not spoken. "Usually," Giddings said, "you can figure out why a man does something. I read where somebody robs a bank, and I think, 'The poor silly bastard wanted the money, maybe had to have it, and couldn't see any other way.' That's not an excuse, but it is some kind of explanation." He paused only briefly. "Take a look at these."

He took a manila envelope from the inside pocket of his corduroy jacket, tossed it on the desk, and then sat expressionless while he watched Nat pick the envelope up, open it, and spill its contents onto the blotter. Folded papers, the crisp paper of Xerox reproduction, covered with lines and figures and neat engineering lettering.

Nat looked up.

"Take a good look," Giddings said.

One by one Nat studied the papers. At last he looked up. "Design-change authorization," he said. His voice was quiet and he hoped that his face showed nothing. "My signature on all of them." Surprisingly his voice held steady. "All electrical changes. Not my baiiiwick."

17

Giddings said, "But nobody would question your signature. Caldwell Associates, Supervising Architects—you're their man on the job, you say something's okay, that's the way it is." He heaved himself out of his chair, walked two paces, and went back to drop into the chair again. He watched Nat and waited.

Nat still held one of the change orders. His hands were steady; the paper did not even tremble, but it was as if his mind had gone numb. "Were these changes made?"

"I don't know. I never saw those before last night."

"How did you miss them?"

"I can't be every place at once," Giddings said, "any more than you can. I have records, work signed off as done according to spec. Where there are deviations from original specifications I have legitimate approvals." He paused. "But I don't have those or any others like them, and I'd have raised hell if I'd seen them."

"So would I," Nat said. The office was still.

Giddings said at last. "That means what?"

"Not my signatures," Nat said. "I don't know who signed them or why, but I didn't."

Giddings got out of his chair again, walked to the windows, and stood looking downtown at the jagged skyline dominated by the Tower. "I figured you'd say that."

Nat's faint smile was crooked, unamused. "Of course." After the initial shock, your mind begins to work again, clearly, logically as it has been trained -like a bloody little computer, he thought. "If I had signed those changes, naturally I'd deny it, at first anyway. I didn't sign them, so I deny it too, but for a different reason. Either way my answer has to be the same, doesn't it?"

Giddings had turned back to face the desk. "Logical bastard, aren't you?"

Behind the shock now came the beginnings of anger. "I'll carry it further," Nat said. "Why would I have signed them? What reason would I have had?"

"I don't know. That," Giddings said, "is why I'm not beating the truth out of you right here and now."

"Don't even try," Nat said. His voice was quiet. With a

18

steady hand he picked up one of the papers, looked at it, dropped it again on the pile.

Giddings said in a new, quieter voice, "What kind of rot have we got buried in the walls of my building? How many corners did we cut without knowing it? How deep does it go?"

Nat's hands rested on the desktop. "I don't know the answer," he said, "but I think we'd better try to find it."

Giddings took his time, his eyes steady on Nat's face. "You try your way," he said at last. "I'll try mine." He indicated the papers. 'Keep those. I had copies made." He paused. "Your boss already has a set, in case you were wondering whether to plug him in." He walked to the door and stopped there, his hand on the knob. "If I find out those are your signatures," he said, "I'll be coming after you." He walked out.

Nat stayed where he was and looked again at the papers, poked them idly with one forefinger. The signatures were plain enough: N H Wilson. Nathan Hale: the names had been his father's idea. The original Nathan Hale was hanged. And from the looks of things somebody was trying to hang this one too. Well, if they thought he was going to walk meekly up the gallows steps, they were mistaken.

He picked up his phone and called Jennie at the switchboard. "Give me Mr. Caldwell's office, honey." And to Mollie Wu, Caldwell's secretary, "Nat here, Mollie. I have to see the boss. It's urgent."

"I was just going to call you." Mollie's voice held nothing. "He's expecting you."

Caldwell's office was the corner room, immense, impressive. Caldwell himself was a small man, slight, with slicked-down sparse gray hair, pale-blue eyes, and small, almost dainty hands. He was neat, quiet, precise, and in matters having to do with art, engineering, or architecture implacable. He was standing at the windows, facing the downtown skyline, when Nat knocked and came in. "Sit down," Caldwell said and remained at the windows, motionless, silent.

Nat sat down and waited.

"The great lighthouse at Alexandria, the Pharos," Caldwell said. "For almost a thousand years it guided ships into the Nile." He turned then to face the office. Backlighted by the windows, he was merely a shape, small against the immensity of the sky. "I met the captain of the *France* one day a few weeks ago," he said. "He told me that the first bit of America they see on their westward crossing is the top of that tower building we designed and supervised during construction. He called it the modern Pharos." Caldwell walked to his desk and sat down. His face now was clearly visible, expressionless. On the blotter in front of him Xerox copies were strewn. "What have we done to it, Nat?"

"I don't know, sir."

Caldwell indicated the papers. "You have seen these?"

"Yes, sir. And I've talked to Giddings." Pause. "Correction: I've listened to Giddings." Another pause. "For the record, those are not my signatures. I wouldn't have messed with electrical changes without Lewis's approval." Joseph Lewis & Co., Electrical Engineers. Nat had the absurd feeling that he was talking to himself.

" 'Wouldn't have,' " Caldwell said, "is a meaningless phrase in this context. Theoretically, nobody would have made changes without Lewis's approval. But somebody wrote those change authorizations, and on the face of it, it was with the authority of this office as supervising architects." Clear, logical, precise.

"Yes, sir." Like a small boy in the principal's office, but what else was there to say? The anger was banked now, a strong, steady force. "But why my name?" Nat said.

Caldwell studied him quietly. "Explain that question."

"Why not Lewis's or one of his people's? It would be more logical, less open to question."

"According to Will Giddings," Caldwell said, "there was no question. These"—he pushed at the pile of copies—"did not come to light until now."

"Then," Nat said, "we don't even know that the actual changes were made, because if they were, a change authorization would have had to be shown—"

" 'Would have,' " Caldwell said, " 'wouldn't have.' I

repeat: the phrases are meaningless." He was silent for a few moments, thoughtful. "I agree," he said at last, "we don't know that the changes were actually made. Neither do we know how serious they might be." He was watching Nat's face. "We would do well to find out, wouldn't we?"

"Yes, sir. Nat paused. "And there are other things to find out, too."

"Such as?"

"Why these change authorizations were written in the first place. Why my name was put on them. Who—"

"Those are questions that can wait," Caldwell said. "I appreciate your personal concern, but I don't share it. My concern is for the building and the integrity of this architectural firm." He paused. "Is that understood?"

It was almost like a chanted response: "Yes, sir," Nat said.

He walked out of the great office and past Mollie Wu's desk. Mollie watched him, tiny, pretty as a doll, bright and quick. "Problems, friend?"

"Problems," Nat said. "In batches." The implications were beginning to appear now, the almost endless possible permutations and combinations that could arise from deviations from the impeccably considered and intricately woven electrical design. "And at the moment," he said, "I don't know where to begin solving them." Simple truth.

"The longest journey begins with but a single step," Mollie said, "and whether that's Confucius or Chairman Mao, I haven't the foggiest notion, but I offer it for what it's worth."

Nat walked back to his own office and sat down to stare at the drawings thumbtacked to the wall and at the heap of design-change-authorization copies lying on his desk. The two formed an explosive mixture, and whether he had signed the changes or not was unimportant. What was important was that they had been issued and perhaps followed, corners cut, as Giddings had said, where no corners ought to have been cut, substitutions made where no substitutions ought to have been allowed. Why?

Wrong question, he told himself. Right now his concern

21

was properly with effect, not cause. And there was only one place where the effects could be discovered, and that was not here at his desk.

He gathered the change-order copies, stuffed them into the manila envelope, and tucked the envelope in his pocket. Out at the reception desk he paused only long enough to tell Jennie where he was going. "To the Tower, honey. I doubt if you'll be able to reach me. I'll call in."

2

10:05–10:53

The sun was high enough now to penetrate the cluster of downtown buildings and reach the floor of the Tower Plaza where the police barricades were in place, breaking the area into two great halves separated at the center by a passageway from the temporary platform against the arcade to the street.

"Where the VIPs will get out of their cars," Patrolman Shannon said, "and smile at the little people and walk like kings and queens to the platform—"

"Where the speeches will all be the same," Barnes said. "They will praise motherhood, the United States of America, and man's unquenchable spirit. One or two of the pols will slip in a little pitch for votes—" He stopped. His smile was apologetic.

"It's only," Shannon said smiling to himself, "that you are against kings and queens and such, and I glory in them. Think how it would be if there were only little gray people, no giants to dream and to do, no great tales to remember, no grand buildings like this one that even shut out the sun. What about that, Frank?"

"Maybe better."

"You," Shannon said, "have seen the insides of too

22

many books, and in them too many confused ideas." His gesture took in the entire shining building. "How would you like to have had a hand in building this? A great gleaming tower reaching to the sky, and your name on the bronze plate to say forever that you were a part of it? How about that?"

" 'General Contractor,' " Barnes read, " 'Bertrand Mc-Graw and Company.' " He was smiling again, this time with open amusement. "The Irish do get around, don't they? Do you suppose McGraw worked his way up from hod carrier honestly?"

"Did you work your way up from slave honestly, you black rascal?"

"Yassuh, boss." They smiled at each other.

"I have met Bert McGraw," Shannon said, "and a fine gentleman he is. On Saint Pat's Day on Fifth Avenue—"

"Playing his pipes, no doubt."

"Skirling," Shannon said. "You skirl pipes. You play pianos and fiddles and other lesser instruments." He paused. "Bert McGraw will be here this afternoon. In his place I would be too, to take my share of the glory."

"I think I'd go somewhere and hide," Barnes said. He paused. "I'd be afraid of hubris."

"You and your big words."

"A challenge to the gods," Barnes said, "and the feeling that they might lower the boom. The same thing that makes you knock on wood when you talk of something good that's going to happen."

For a moment Shannon was thoughtful. Then he smiled. "Like I said, Frank, the insides of too many books. What could your gods possibly do to this lovely structure?"

The building is alive, John Connors thought, its *presence* is almost palpable. His footsteps echoed in the empty hallways and corridors, and only black closed doors stared at him as he passed; but through the air-conditioning ducts he could hear the building's respiration, and deep in its core he could feel the life force throbbing, and he wondered if in its heart of hearts the living building was afraid.

Of him? Why not? It was a pleasant concept; it lifted

23

his spirits. He was only a tiny speck against the immensity of the structure, but the *power* was his, and he savored the knowledge as he walked, toolbox in hand, hearing the echoes of his own footsteps and the turbulence of his thoughts.

Nat walked the thirty blocks from the Caldwell offices to the World Tower building, in the exercise finding some relief from anger and stress.

"I guess some men play games for the same reason," he had told Zib once, "to get their minds off a problem and let it churn around down in the subconscious. I walk instead. I'm not anti-game. It's just that when I was growing up, we did other things. We fished, we hunted, we packed into the mountains on foot or on horseback; in the winter we skied and snowshoed." The sense of not belonging here in the East still made itself felt. "A primitive life," he said. "All the things you had, I hadn't. I'm not a very good swimmer. I don't know a thing about sailing. No golf, no tennis."

And Zib had said, "Maybe those things were important to me once, but they aren't now. I married you for other reasons. Maybe because I was sick and tired of the prep-school stereotypes I grew up with." She smiled suddenly, devastatingly. "Or maybe it was because you didn't try to get me into bed on our first date."

"Backward of me. Would you have gone?"

"Possibly. No, probably. I found you attractive."

"I found you stunning and a little frightening, so very sure of yourself here in your own surroundings."

True then, still true after almost three years of marriage.

He walked steadily, pausing only for traffic. He disliked the city, but it was where, as they said, the action was; and if the dirt and the noise and the crowding, the snarling, snapping attitudes, the unhappy faces were all around, why, so were the ferment and the excitement, the satisfaction of finding and being able to talk with your peers.

But most important, there was Ben Caldwell with his artist's eye and his infinite attention to detail which some called genius. The seven years spent under that man made up for anything else.

Oh, one day Nat would leave the city; that knowledge was sure and deep. Back to the big country where he belonged. And when that time came, he wondered, would Zib go with him or choose to stay behind in her own familiar scene? Hard to tell, and not pleasant to contemplate.

There were police scattered in the Tower Plaza. Nat looked at them with surprise, which was foolish, he told himself, because of course in the city, where bombing threats and violence are not unknown, there would be cops to handle an event such as the Tower opening. It just went to show that he didn't think.

There was a black cop near the door, listening to a big uniformed Irishman. The black cop looked at Nat and smiled politely. "Can we help you, sir?"

Nat took out the badge he wore on the job. "Architect," he said. "Caldwell Associates." He nodded at the bronze plaque beside the doorway. "Just going in to have a look around."

The black cop was smiling no longer. "Is anything wrong?" His dark eyes were quick on the badge, and he added, looking up again. "Mr. Wilson?" He studied Nat's face.

"Routine," Nat said, and thought, for God's sake, that he sounded like nothing so much as a character straight out of *Dragnet*.

"It was right then that I really began to wonder," Patrolman Barnes said later, "but it was still only a kind of hunch that maybe we ought to have stopped that fellow with the toolbox. And you know what a stink that kind of unauthorized action can cause. The Department exceeding its authority, throwing its weight around at innocent citizens, that kind of thing." Pause. "Still, I should have followed that hunch."

Now he said, "If there is anything wrong, Mr. Wilson— I mean, if there's anything we can do—"

"What he means," the Irish cop said, "is that we aim to please, we boys in blue. Never let it be said that we

25

refused to rescue a drowning man or help an old lady to cross the street. Be our guest," the big Irish cop said, and went on with what he was saying, which had to do with off-track betting—if you were a betting man, that was.

I am not a betting man, Nat thought as he walked inside. Another lack, he supposed, because Zib loved the horses and a point-spread bet on football games and things like tailgate picnics up at West Point before the game at Michie Stadium. I am a dull boy, Nat told himself.

Inside the concourse he hesitated. He had no real destination. Coming to the building where he had spent almost every working day during the last five days was an automatic act, arising from the kind of impulse that forces you to see for yourself the empty stall after you have been told that the horse is missing—not that there was really anything he could do until work crews were on the job again and specific change authorizations could be checked out by tearing into the structure to see what changes, if any, had actually been made.

But he was here, and the same impulse was still at work, and he walked the empty concourse around the core of the building to the banks of elevators and pushed the button for a fourteenth-floor local.

He heard the soft whir of the high-speed cable as the elevator began to move. Simultaneously the fourteenth-floor light showed on the indicator panel and floor by floor began to drop. Nat stepped inside as the doors opened, and there, his finger poised over the button, he stood motionless.

Faintly, within the hollow core of the building that housed the multiple elevator shafts, he could hear another cable whirring, an elevator rising or dropping at its swift pace.

The doors of his elevator closed automatically, and he was in total darkness. He found the light switch on the panel, turned it on, and stood for a few moments listening. The whirring of the cable continued to echo softly within the building's core. And then it stopped and there was silence.

All you can do is guess, he told himself; it could be anybody, and he could be on any floor between here and the mast, a hundred and twenty-five floors up. So? You are jumpy, Nathan Hale; those fake change authorizations have unstrung you. Forget it, he told himself. He pushed the button and the elevator began to rise smoothly.

He left the elevator on the eighth floor, and walked back down a single flight of stairs to the second of the building's five mechanical-electrical floors.

It was here, as belowground, and on the forty-fifth, eighty-fifth, and one-hundred-twenty-third floors, that even an unknowledgeable stranger would begin to comprehend some of the building's vastness and complexity.

Here the cables thick as a man's leg brought up from the bowels of the building primary power from the nearby Con Edison substation, fourteen thousand volts—far above electrocution strength.

And here the brooding transformers stepped down the voltage to usable levels for the heating, cooling, breathing, and electric-service needs of each of the building's vertical sections.

The odor of the walled-off floor area was the odor of a ship's engine room of heated metal and oil, of rubber and paint, of filtered air and wiring insulation and softly whirring machinery obeying the master, electricity.

Electricity made no sound—although transformers themselves gave off a faint hum—and it could not be seen. But it was the raw stuff of power, even more, of life itself for the building.

Without electricity the great structure for all its cunning complexity was merely a lump, a dead thing composed of hundreds of thousands of tons of steel and concrete, of tempered-glass windows and aluminum column covers, of cables and ducting and wiring and mechanisms complicated beyond belief—useless.

Without electrical power the building was without heat, light, ventilation, operable elevators or escalators, computer monitors and their overseeing controls.

Without electrical power the building was blind and deaf, unable to speak or even to breathe—a dead city within a city, a monument to man's ingenuity, vanity, intelligence, and doubtful wisdom; a Great Pyramid, a Stonehenge, or an Angkor Wat, a curiosity, an anachronism.

Nat stared at the main electrical cable neatly spliced to give off its enormous power here and yet carry that same power, undiminished, to the next higher mechanical floor, and so on to the building's top. Here was the building's life center exposed—open-heart surgery came to mind.

He was conscious of the envelope with the bogus change authorizations in his pocket, and again his anger was steady and deep, pushing at his thoughts.

He could understand Giddings's controlled rage because its roots were in him too, and for the same reason a job of work was a sacred thing.

Oh, many people, perhaps most people these days, didn't see it that way—Zib for one—but what those people thought in this area was unimportant.

To those who conceived and built the enduring structures—buildings, bridges, aqueducts, dams, nuclear power plants, massive stadia—the form was not important; to them the work was its own reward and it was not to be flawed, profaned by carelessness or, worse, by intent. It was to be as nearly perfect as man could make it or it was not a finished job, and what ought to have been a source of pride became instead a matter of shame.

Thinking of this now, for the first time even in his thoughts Nat let the anger loose. "Some son of a bitch," he said slowly, quietly to the great spliced cable and the brooding transformers, "has messed with this job, and whether what he did is serious or not, we'll have to find out, and we will. And we'll find him too, and hang him up by his balls."

Talking to inanimate things was silly, of course. Talking to trees and birds and chattering squirrels or soaring hawks was silly too, and he had done that most of his life. So I'm silly, Nat thought as he walked back to the

28

stairs; but somehow, the promise given, he felt a little better. He took the elevator to the next mechanical-electrical floor.

He found nothing; he had expected no more. His visit to each ship's engine-room area was merely a gesture, automatic as a householder's stroll in his patio each night. The floors between were empty and echoing; they smelled faintly of the newness of their materials—tile, wall paint, varnished wood door surfaces—as a new car driven from the showroom smelled of its new-car odor.

As he rose within the building, local elevator after local elevator, the city's skyline began to drop beneath him until on the hundred-and-twenty-third floor he could look down on even the flat tops of the twin Trade Center towers nearby.

He went on, stepping out at last into the Tower Room on the top floor, just beneath the communications mast. The elevator doors closed and immediately he heard the whir of the high-speed cables as the elevator began to drop. He frowned at the lighted DOWN arrow, puzzled. Summoned by whom? he wondered, and found no answer.

He watched the red light and listened to the cable's whir as he tried to estimate how many floors the elevator dropped before the cable was silent. Ten? Fifteen? Impossible to tell.

He listened as the cable sound resumed. This time there was a long period of waiting before the cable was again silent. All the way to the concourse? So? Forget it, he told himself again, and turned away.

The view from this top floor was unobstructed. There lay the harbor, the Narrows Bridge, the shining ocean beyond. Nat thought of what Ben Caldwell had told him: the first piece of America an incoming ship sees is the shining communications mast directly above this floor. He could understand the sea captain's thinking that had jumped immediately to the ancient Pharos, for a thousand years guiding ships into the Nile.

Northward the city lay in its even rectangular pattern of streets and avenues, the midtown towers from this distance and height looking like building blocks in someone's tabletop model. Unreal, even after all this time of familiarity.

He turned from the windows as the faint sound of an elevator started up again. This time the green light over the doors was on. He watched it and waited, wondering at his sudden sense of tension.

The cable sound stopped. The green light went out. The doors opened and Giddings stepped out. Behind him the doors closed quietly, but no light went on. "I wondered if I'd find you here," Giddings said.

"And why not?"

Giddings shrugged. He looked around the Tower Room. Tables were already set out along one core wall. Trays of canapes, bottles, glasses, bowls of nuts and chips, all of the paraphernalia of the standard cocktail party would be along shortly, together with waiters and bartenders, maids to empty ashtrays and take away dirty glasses while the talk went on and on and on. Giddings looked again at Nat. "Looking for something?" Giddings said.

"Are you?"

"Look, sonny—" Giddings began.

Nat shook his head. "Not that way. If you want to ask a question, ask it. If you want to say something, say it. I've just decided that after five years, I don't much like you, Will. I don't think I ever did."

"And now," Giddings said, "since I waved the change authorizations at you, you've found a reason, is that it?"

"Is that what you think?"

"And if it is?"

"Then screw you," Nat said.

Giddings's expression turned reflective. "Not very elegant language for an architect," he said. His voice was mild.

The moment of conflict was past. But, Nat thought, it would return; it was inevitable. "I wasn't always an architect." Horse wrangler, paratrooper, fire jumper, student. In the meantime, "You just came up from the concourse?"

Giddings took his time. "Why?"

"Were you in the building before?"

"I said why."

30

"Because somebody was." All along it had puzzled him; now he brought it out in the open for examination. "I heard elevators," Nat said. He paused. "Cops all over the plaza. Did they stop you?"

Giddings was frowning now. "They did."

"They stopped me too." Not strictly true, but there had been that conversation.

"And you're asking who else is in the building," Giddings said, "and why?"

"Exactly."

"Maybe," Giddings said slowly, "you made it up. Maybe there isn't—"

Giddings stopped and turned, and both men looked at the red light that had come on over the elevator doors; both heard the sound of the elevator moving. They looked at each other.

"I don't make things up," Nat said.

"This time," Giddings said, "I believe you."

"Remember it next time too."

All the way down to the empty concourse and out into the plaza. Nat found the same black cop with his big Irish mate. Giddings stood by watching, listening. "He and I," Nat said, pointing at Giddings. "Anyone else go in while you've been here?"

Barnes, the black cop said, "Why do you ask, Mr. Wilson?"

Shannon, the Irishman, said, "Big building. Other doors." He shrugged. "Maintenance men, other poor working stiffs."

Nat said, "Did anyone go in?"

"One man," Barnes said. "An electrician. He said there was a trouble call."

"Who made it?" This was Giddings.

"I thought of that," Barnes said. He hesitated. "Maybe a little too late.' He paused. "Is it important, Mr. Wilson?"

"I don't know." Simple truth. He was conscious again of the change-order copies in his pocket and he knew that it was the fact of their existence that was making him jumpy. But there could be no connection between them and whoever had gone into the building because the

31

change orders applied only to work in progress, and work was finished, or near enough. "He's riding the elevators," he said.

Shannon's face opened in a huge grin. "Now where's the harm in that, will you tell me? A man gets the yearning to ride an elevator, does the sky fall like Chicken Little said?" The brogue was heavy.

Giddings said, "An electrician. What was he carrying? Anything?"

Barnes said, "A toolbox."

Shannon said, "Oh, no, Frank, you forget. It was a bright shiny atomic bomb." He spread his hands to show its size. "Green it was on the one side and purple on the other with sparks shooting out, lovely to see——"

"Easy, Mike," Barnes said. He spoke to Nat. "Just a toolbox. And he was wearing his hard hat."

"Has he come out?"

"If he has," Barnes said, "it was by a different door." He hesitated. "And they are locked. Right, Mr. Wilson?"

"If they aren't," Giddings said, "they damn well ought to be." He looked at Nat. "We'd best check.

The doors around the great building were locked. Nat said, "No watchmen? No security people?"

"On any ordinary day," Giddings said, "by now this place would be crawling with work crews. As you damn well know. And anybody who didn't belong in the building——"

"I wonder," Nat said. At least he was thinking again. "I never thought of it before, but in something as big as this, with as many people milling around——" He shook his head. "Fish in the sea, inconspicuous." He was silent for a few moments, staring up at the arched vaulting of the concourse. "It never even occurred to me," he said at last, looking again at Giddings. "Don't you see it?"

Giddings shook his head slowly. "I don't even know what you're talking about."

Nat said slowly, "We design a building to be open, for people to come and go easily."

"So?"

"So," Nat said, "by its very nature it is—vulnerable."

32

"To what?"

Nat lifted his hands and let them fall. "Anything. Anybody."

3

For John Connors riding the silent elevators was an interesting, even pleasurable business; slick smooth-functioning machinery had always fascinated him. And if anybody was looking for him, as sooner or later they would be, riding the elevators and sending empty cars up and down the multiple shafts was probably the best way to confuse a search.

He was familiar with the building by day—ordinary workday. that was. What he had not realized was what the building would be like empty and echoing, just himself and the living, breathing structure.

It was like a cathedral when nobody else was there—only more so. He tried to think of an analogy. Imagine an empty Yankee Stadium, he told himself.

Hearing only his own footsteps echoing in a corridor, looking out of the rows of windows, the world beneath him, and seeing only the immensity of the sky, thinking that he had one chance and only one to do what had to be done, was like being on his knees in prayer, just himself in His presence, and echoing through his mind the hush and the expectation of something great about to happen.

Something he had heard once, perhaps at a rally, he didn't really remember, but the statement had stuck in his mind: "A few determined men changing the course of great events." He liked that. It had a grand ring. Determined men. Heroes. Like hijacking a plane and getting

33

clean away. Like terrorizing the entire Olympic Village. A few determined men. Or one man alone. They listen to you then. Trudging along corridors with his toolbox, riding the elevators—it was almost like being inside an immense funhouse.

Electricity, of course, was the key here. Electricity seemed to be the key to everything these days. Connors remembered that grid blackout a few years back, and how everything, but everything, had come to a full stop and some people had even thought the end of the world had come. Not everybody, of course, because nine months later almost to the day there had been that crush in the city's maternity hospitals to testify that some had spent the darkened hours profitably. But at first there had been near-panic, and that was the thought to cling to.

He was no electrical engineer nor even an experienced electrician, despite what he had told that black cop, but he had worked in the building and he knew in a general way how the power distribution was handled. On each of those electrical-mechanical floors was what is called a splicing chamber, and whenever he could, Connors had spent a little time watching the subcontractor's men at work, peeling back the steel-wire armor encasing the electrical cables and then peeling back the vinyl jacket under that, and finally getting to the heart of the matter, the big inside wires that actually carried the current.

He knew that through step-down transformers each mechanical-electrical floor furnished usable electrical power for a vertical section of the building, and that each also passed along in original strength to the next higher mechanical-electrical floor the electricity coming in from the substation outside the building. He didn't know what the strength of that primary current was, but it had to be high, maybe as much as five hundred volts, because why, otherwise, would they bother to step it down?

His first thought had been to attack the electrical installation that serviced the upper stories of the building, thereby isolating the Tower Room, where the reception was to be held. He had in his toolbox an eighteen-inch wrecking bar and some stolen plastic explosive, and with

34

them, he figured, he could stir up a considerable fuss and send sparks flying all over the place just like the Fourth of July.

But the more he thought about it, the more he wondered why he limited his efforts to the top floors. Why not attack the basic installation down in the bowels of the building where the power cables led directly in from the substation? Why bunt, when a triple would clear the bases? It was an appealing thought.

In the meantime, all he had to do was stay out of sight, and that ought to be easy. But just in case luck played him foul, it would be well to be prepared.

He opened the toolbox and took out the wrecking bar, hooked at one end, splayed and canted at the other. It was a weapon a man could use, and he had no qualms about using it if necessary.

They were setting up the low platform for the ceremony in the plaza when Nat and Giddings came out of the building. Giddings looked at it with distaste. "Speeches," he said. "The governor congratulating the mayor and the mayor congratulating Grover Frazee and one of the senators saying what a great thing the building is for humanity—" He stopped.

"Maybe it is, at that," Nat said. He was thinking again of Ben Caldwell's reference to the Pharos. "A world communications center—"

"That's crap and you know it. It's just another big goddam building and we already have too many of them."

It was a love-hate relationship Giddings had with the building he had helped create, Nat thought. Well, as far as that went, he vacillated himself between pride and admiration on the one hand and on the other a resentment that the inanimate structure had long ago taken on a personality of its own, dominating all who served it. "You stay here and swear at it," he said.

"And where are you going?"

The friction between them was threatening to break out into open hostility. Well, let it, if that was what had to be, but Nat would not precipitate it. "Where somebody ought to have gone earlier," he said. "To see Joe Lewis about these changes." He walked off across the plaza, unpinning his badge as he went.

This time, in the interest of speed, he took a subway uptown to Grand Central, walking only the two blocks back along Park to the Architects Building, and rode on the elevator to the tenth floor, where the sign on the glass door read: JOSEPH LEWIS, ELECTRICAL ENGINEER. The offices and drafting rooms occupied almost the entire floor.

Joe Lewis was in shirtsleeves in his big cluttered office. He was a small man, quick, sharp, direct. "If it's a new project," he said, "tell Ben I'm up to my ass in work for the next six months. If he can wait—"

Nat tossed the manila envelope on the desk. He watched Joe look at it, pick it up, and empty the change-order copies onto his blotter. One by one he read them swiftly, dropped them as if they were live things. He looked at Nat at last, anger plain. "You issued these? Who in hell gave you the right?"

"I never saw them before this morning?"

"That's your signature."

Nat shook his head. "My name, but somebody else wrote it." Like a word too often repeated, the truth was beginning to lose its meaning. I'll end up not believing it myself, he thought.

"Then who?" Joe said.

"I haven't any idea."

Joe tapped the papers with his finger. "Were these changes actually made?"

"We'll have to see." It was a conversation without point so far, but the groundwork had to be established.

"And what do you want from me? I gave you the drawings, the whole electrical design. If the job was done according to them, and not these—"

"Nobody's blaming you." At the moment, Nat thought, but nobody is really in the clear yet. "What I want from you is an order of priority. Which of these do we look at—"

"All of them. Every single goddam one, even if you

have to tear the building apart. I'm going to insist on it. Damn it, man, the electrical design of that building is in my name."

"And ours. I realize it." Why couldn't intelligent people see what was right in front of them? "But which do we look into first? And second? And so on? You're the expert. Give us a list in order of importance and we'll get McGraw's people on it."

Lewis sat down abruptly. "McGraw," he said. "Bert wouldn't have anything to do with this. He shook his head. "Impossible. You try cutting corners on a Bert McGraw job, fishing for kickbacks, bribing inspectors—and you get your head handed to you on a platter."

Nat sat down too. "I had heard that, but I had no way of knowing whether it was true." It could put a different light on matters.

"Next to building highways," Lewis said, calmer now, "there is probably more room for hanky-panky in the big building construction business than any other. The rackets boys have moved in and out for years. Longer. Usually, but not always, public buildings. Over in Jersey——" He shook his head. "Certain Jersey counties, I wouldn't take an electrical-engineering job if it had diamonds hanging on it. Over here is better. Most times. Far as I know, the fast-buck boys only tried once on a McGraw job." He smiled. It was a bitter smile, strangely contented.

So Joe Lewis was one of those to whom the job was sacred. Nat thought, one of the good ones. He said, "What happened?"

"They sent around some persuaders," Lewis said. "All McGraw said was that he wouldn't deal with small fry. The big boy or nobody." He paused: "It was a big building, lots of money that might be plucked, and maybe only a beginning, so the top boy came himself." He paused again. "McGraw took him up where they could talk in private—up as far as the steel had gone, forty, forty-five floors, nobody around, and the street a long, long way down. 'Now, you son of a bitch,' McGraw said after the rackets bum had had a good look and hadn't liked what he saw, 'do you want to ride back down in the hoist and walk away and never come back, or do you want to go down the fast way, right off the steel, right now, and they pick you up off the street with blotting paper? Make up your goddam mind.'" Lewis paused a third time. "They never bothered him again. Some men you can't push, you know, and it isn't worthwhile even to try."

Food for thought. Nat sat quiet for a little time, setting what he knew of Bert McGraw against the tale he had just heard. It fit. There was in the old man an instant willingness to shoot the works, roll the dice for whatever was on the table. It showed, unmistakable. The racketeer may have been as close to death on other occasions, but Nat was willing to bet never as openly. Leave McGraw out of the puzzle.

"Have you ever worked before with Paul Simmons?" he said.

"Ever since he married McGraw's daughter and McGraw set him up."

"Is that how it was? I never knew."

"Paul's a bright boy." Lewis stared thoughtfully at the change orders. "You think he might have issued these? Put your name on them?" Slowly he shook his head. "It doesn't figure. Sooner or later these would turn up, as they have, and then everybody asks, 'Who benefits?' The electrical subcontractor is the obvious man: he gets his bid price for doing substandard work, money in his pocket. But it's too obvious, too easy. And why does he need it anyway? He's got a going business and Bert McGraw as a father-in-law, and an obvious Ivy League pedigree, so there was probably money to begin with. Why mess with something like this?"

"So," Nat said, and his smile was without amusement, "nobody else had any good reason to issue change authorizations—and my name is on them. Dandy. Will you have that list made out for me? First things first, no matter how deep we have to go. It's got to be right."

Again he walked; it was the automatic reaction. Up Park to Forty-second, across to Fifth, and again uptown. He saw none of those who passed him; he saw only traffic lights and automobiles that might threaten. And he saw his thoughts.

The change orders were real. That was point one.

Either they had been acted upon—substitutions had been made and work avoided, with substandard performances the result—or they had to be ignored. That was point two.

Computers, using binary numbers, break a problem down the same way—either/or, yes/no—at each step. The method is almost foolproof—assuming that the right questions are asked, the right steps taken—but the difficulty is that the steps multiply exponentially, and the simple harmless-looking 1,2,4, series rapidly turns into a horror whose possibilities run into the millions.

And that, he thought almost angrily, is precisely why they have computers, which did him no good at all. It was the kind of random thinking that frequently interfered when you tried to concentrate.

He crossed Fifty-ninth Street into the park, and at once for him everything changed. His pace slowed and lengthened, his mind seemed to ease, and he began to notice his surroundings. Here there were trees and grass and bare rock, and even the sky seemed different, bluer, less tortured by civilization. Oh, there were no vistas such as he had once known, no distant mountains perpetually snow-capped, no clear dry air to breathe, no real silence. But it was better, and his thoughts ran more easily.

If the change orders had never been acted upon, then there was no reason for their existence—true or false?

Not necessarily true, because they could have been issued, could they not, for a different purpose from the obvious one of cutting corners? Such as? Such as pointing a finger of suspicion at one Nat Wilson. How about that?

Why? Nat had no idea. As far as he knew, nobody would want to go to that length merely to discredit him.

Was he so sure of that?

He stopped at a vending wagon and bought a bag of peanuts. Then he walked on, away from the zoo area, into the depths of the park. He sat down on a rock and waited with a mountain man's patience until one of the park squirrels came over to check him out. "Here you are," Nat said and tossed a peanut. "You're welcome," he added as the squirrel dashed off with his loot.

Was he so sure that nobody would try to booby-trap him? It was, he told himself, a pretty damn big assumption.

He had come, in effect, out of nowhere, the mountain West, with no friends here in the big time, no letters of introduction, no handles to grasp for leverage. And he had walked in with his portfolio and waited until he could see Ben Caldwell—it took four days—and had walked out with a job any number of young brushed-up well-recommended architects would have given their eyeteeth for. Seven years ago, the preliminary thinking just beginning on the World Tower.

The squirrel was back. He sat up and studied Nat. Nothing happened. Cautiously, he lowered his forepaws, rushed forward eighteen inches, and sat up again.

"Okay," Nat said, "it's a good act. Here." Another peanut.

"Did I step on toes then?" Nat asked aloud. "Have I stepped on toes since?" And the answer was probably, even if he hadn't realized it. So the possibility existed that the change orders had been issued merely to point a finger at him. Uncomfortable thought.

But suppose they had been acted upon, something he could not know until work of investigation actually began.

Then, of course, the immediate inference was the profit motive: reducing the quality of material and workmanship, thus increasing the profit margin between cost and payment for someone. Who? Paul Simmons was still the obvious candidate. But if Simmons had all going for him that Joe Lewis had mentioned, why would he take the chance of exposure? Nat had no answer.

There was a third possibility. Suppose the orders had been issued (by whom?) and acted upon, but innocently? What if Paul Simmons or his people had thought that these change orders represented an actual change in thinking on the part of the architects and engineers, and, theirs not to question why, they had gone ahead without

40

any taint of avarice? That kind of thinking led in different directions.

Nat cracked, opened, and ate a peanut. It tasted good. It occurred to him that he had had no lunch. He ate another peanut and then was aware that the squirrel was back, with a friend, and both were sitting almost at his feet, watching, waiting, "Sorry, fellows," Nat said, and tossed down two peanuts, left and right.

One more possibility, he told himself, and this one he had apparently tried to push down into the ooze of his subconscious in order to forget it, but here it came bubbling to the surface. What if the changes were aimed not at him and not at profit, but at the building itself? Did that make any kind of sense? Unfortunately, nauseatingly, it did. Or could.

Without calculations, which Nat could make but Joe Lewis and his people, the experts, could make faster, there was no telling how vital, or lethal, the changes were.

Buildings were not designed, as aircraft or space vehicles were, right down to the ultimate tolerances of their materials. Rather, because weight was not the basic problem, there was a safety factor calculated into every structural member, every cable, every wiring specification. Programmed right into the design calculations were remote contingencies such as winds of 150 miles an hour, far in excess of anything the city had ever known, or massive surges of electrical power almost impossible to conceive.

Because of the Tower's height, lightning strikes were accepted as normal; the mammoth steel skeleton would carry the charge harmlessly into the ground, as it had already done often enough during construction.

Earthquakes were the remotest of possibilities: no fault area lay nearby. Nevertheless, the foundations of the building went down to bedrock, that tortured schist that is the city's backbone, and with its firm grip on the solid base and its strong flexible structure, the building could ride out a quake of more than moderate intensity without damage.

In short, every menace that could be imagined had

41

been anticipated, and defenses prepared. Computerized calculations had been made. Models had been built and tested. The great building, as designed, was as durable as man's ingenuity could make it.

AS DESIGNED.

But change a little here, a little there in the wrong places—and durability, function, even safety can become mere illusion.

Why would anyone threaten a building's integrity in that fashion? Nat had no idea, but in a world where violence seems to be the norm and irresponsibility is exalted, mere sabotage of a building seems far from impossible.

The two squirrels were back again, and here came a third, zeroing in on the easy human mark. "There are times," Nat said, "when I think we ought to give the world back to you fellows. Like lemmings, we could walk into the sea. Here." He emptied the bag of peanuts at his feet and stood up.

4

12:30 P.M.

Bert McGraw was in his office high above the street with all those windows looking out at the city's buildings, a number of which he had had a hand in constructing. Usually he enjoyed the view. Right now he was not sure, because sticking up in the center of the skyline was the World Tower, and what Giddings had been telling him and showing him about that structure was enough to curdle a man's enthusiasm even on as bright and shining a late-spring day as this.

McGraw glared at the copies of the change authorizations on his desk. He looked again at Giddings. "Just what do we *know*?" he demanded. He had a deep-seated feeling that his hope was forlorn; that if examined carefully, the unpleasant appearances would not go away. But all a man could do was try. "Pieces of paper," McGraw said, "and not even originals at that."

"You're fancy-footing, Bert," Giddings said, "and it isn't like you. Those are honest Xerox copies of hankypanky that's been going on under your nose—and, yes, I admit it, under mine as well. How many of the changes were carried out I don't know yet. How serious they are I don't know yet. Why the changes were issued I can only guess."

McGraw heaved himself out of his chair and went to stand at the windows. Time was when he might have taken a thing like this in stride, or near enough. Now it was like a sneak punch to the kidney, and the world he looked out at tended to blur. It was not the first such experience, and it worried him.

"You're overweight," his Mary had told him, "and overworked and you aren't as young as you were, and that's what's the matter with you, Bert McGraw. Once upon a time, you could spend all night drinking and being a terrible grand fellow and come home bright as a daisy, almost. But you aren't that young any more. Neither am I, more's the pity. So stop your worrying."

The world swam back into focus. McGraw turned away from the windows. "Young Nat Wilson's name," he said. "Did the damn fool actually sign them?"

"He says no."

"And what do you say?" There was force in the old man yet.

"I don't see why he would," Giddings said. "What does he gain? He can stand by the drawings and say no changes allowed and be well within his rights. So why would he stick his neck out?"

McGraw walked to his chair and dropped into it. "All right," he said. "At least what we've got is confusion. On the face of those pieces of paper, the building, that great goddam beautiful building isn't up to specifications,

43

and that puts a foot in the door for all sorts of trouble—even, God help us, legal trouble."

"And work," Giddings said. "Walls are going to have to be opened up. Circuits are going to have to be checked out." He shook his head.

"We'll do what has to be done," McGraw said sharply. He paused, and the belligerence disappeared. "It isn't that I'm thinking of." Was he being mystical, even superstitious, as Mary, bless her, sometimes said he was, the bog Irish in him coming out? "You've seen it yourself," he said. "Little things go wrong on a job, accidents happen, shortages hold you up, weather turns bad, you're caught by a strike—" He spread his hands and rolled them into fists, studied them as if they were enemies. "And sometimes," he said at last, "the string of bad luck doesn't end. It's as if, God help me, some kind of bad spell has been laid on and not even a priest's blessing can lift it." He paused again. "Do you know what I mean, Will?"

Giddings was thinking again of Pete Janowski walking off the steel at the sixty-fifth floor for no reason at all. "I know what you mean," he said.

McGraw sighed heavily. "I hate to admit it," he said, "but there are two buildings in this town—I won't put a name to either one but I built them both—I wouldn't even walk into, let alone ride an elevator in." He shook away the thought. "Let it go. It's neither here nor there." He sat up straight in his chair and his voice turned brisk. "Why the changes were issued you can only guess?" he said. "All right, guess away."

"You aren't going to like it," Giddings said.

"Be damned to that." It was honest anger the old man felt now, solid and deep and strong. "We've been diddled, you for the owners, me for myself. By God, I want to know who and why."

Giddings shrugged. "The changes are all electrical."

"So?"

"With what I've seen," Giddings said, "all the changes call for lesser material or simplified circuitry." He paused. "What does that say to you?"

There was no hesitation. "That somebody was trying

44

to save money," McGraw said. He heaved himself out of
his chair again and walked to stare at a blurred world
through the windows. Over his shoulder he said, "And
the man who saved money, you're saying, are you not,
is the man who holds the electrical contract?" As before,
the world swam slowly back into focus. McGraw turned.
He kept his hands behind his back lest they demonstrate
the tension that was in him. "Paul Simmons—it's him
you're pointing a finger at, is it?"

"I told you I was just guessing."

"So you did."

"And," Giddings said, "I told you you weren't going
to like it."

"No," McGraw said in a new, quiet voice, "I don't like
it. I don't like you thinking it, and I don't like thinking
it myself." He brought his hands into view at last, fingers
spread and hooked, and he studied them for a long time in
silence. When he looked at Giddings again, his face was
almost gray. "We'll find out, Will," he said. "If I have to
pick him up with these two hands and bend him until he
breaks, we'll find out. I promise you. In the meantime—"
The words stopped suddenly as if the old man had forgotten what he was going to say. He rubbed one hand wearily
along his jaw.

"In the meantime," Giddings said as if he had seen no
lapse, "I'll try to find out what has to be done."

McGraw lowered himself into his chair. He nodded.
"You do that, Will. And let me know." He took a deep
breath. His voice was strong again. "We stand behind our
jobs. We always have."

"I never doubted it," Giddings said.

McGraw sat motionless in his big chair long after
Giddings was gone. He felt old and tired and reluctant to
do what had to be done. Time was when he would have
gone roaring out of his office at the merest whiff of suspicion that someone had been doing the dirty, whoever
it was, in-law, kin, saint, or devil. But age changes a man,
some of the certainties become less sure, the boundary
lines blur, and McGraw's temptation was to refuse to

believe that someone near, someone in the family had transgressed.

The old man was proud of Paul Simmons, his son-in-law. For one thing, Simmons was what used to be called a gentleman—Andover, Yale, that kind of thing, not McGraw's breed of alley cat at all. And Patty fit right into Paul's circle too, and that was further cause for pride.

McGraw and Mary lived still in the house in Queens that McGraw had bought with the earnings from his first sizable construction job thirty years and more ago. Paul and Patty lived in Westchester, only a few miles but an entire culture away from the McGraw house. You cherish the American Dream that your children will have it better than you ever did. And when it happens, you get down on your knees and thank the good Lord for His favor.

Now, McGraw told himself, pick up the phone and call your grand son-in-law a cheat and a thief. Bitter thought.

The copies of the change authorizations were still on his desk. He pushed at them with one big hand. They rustled like dry dead leaves.

It couldn't have happened, McGraw thought, not on one of his jobs, not under Giddings's nose, or Nat Wilson's. And how about the inspectors? Bought? Or simply diddled by the bogus engineering changes?

But it *had* happened. He knew that in his bones. Oh, it wasn't the first time on a big construction job that somebody had thimblerigged his part of the work, shifted things around like the man at the carnival with the half-shells and the pea that is never where you thought it was.

Invoices and bills of lading, work orders, specifications, even drawings themselves can all be altered or faked and work signed off that was never done, money passed under the table or left sticking to somebody's fingers—there are tricks galore, and at one time or another McGraw had encountered them all, and somebody had left the job at a stumbling run with his ass kicked right up between his shoulder blades and maybe a few teeth loosened in the bargain.

The telephone on the desk roused the old man, and he

stared at it with distaste for a moment before he picked it up.

"Mrs. Simmons is calling," his secretary said.

Patty couldn't know, McGraw told himself. And, goddammit, neither did he know yet for sure that Paul was the kind of scum who would foul up an honest job of work. That, like they said, remained to be proved, and a man was innocent until the proof was in. The hell he was. "Hi, honey," McGraw said into the phone.

"You wouldn't like to buy me lunch, would you, Daddy?" Patty's voice, like Patty herself, was young, fresh, enthusiastic. "I'm at Grand Central, and Paul's all tied up with a business appointment."

"And none of your friends are available," McGraw said, "so finally you think of your old man, is that it?" Just the sound of her voice brought a smile to his mind to counteract some of the mental pain.

"That will be a day," Patty said. "You know I would have married you myself if it hadn't been for Mother." And I almost wish I could have, she thought, but left that part unsaid. "Don't be stingy."

"All right, honey," McGraw said. "I have a couple of phone calls to make." One, anyway. "You get a table at Martin's. I'll be along shortly."

"I'll have a drink waiting."

McGraw hung up and buzzed for his secretary. "Get me Paul Simmons, Laura." He made himself wait quietly.

The secretary came back on the phone almost immediately. "Mr. Simmons is busy on the phone. I'll try again in a few minutes?"

Reprieve? McGraw thought. Nothing of the goddam sort. It can't be put off, he told himself. "No," he said, "let me talk to his secretary." And when the new pleasant voice came on, "Tell Paul," McGraw said, "that I want to see him here in my office at one-thirty sharp."

The secretary hesitated. "Mr. Simmons has a rather full schedule, Mr. McGraw. He—"

"Honey," McGraw said, "you tell him to be here." He hung up, hoisted himself out of his chair and started for the door. A short pleasant time with Patty, he thought,

and then—what was the current word that was so popular?—confrontation. So be it. He squared his shoulders
automatically as he walked through the doorway.

In his office Paul Simmons, on the phone, was saying,
"I've booked a table and I've told Patty I had a business
engagement, so I do think you owe me your company at
lunch."

"Do you indeed?" Her name was Zib Wilson, Zib
Marlowe-that-was. "I was expecting a call from Nat."
Not quite true: she had been hoping for a call from Nat.
"But," she said, "I suppose he's all tied up with the
Tower opening." She paused. "Come to think of it, why
aren't you?"

"I'm not wedded to my work the way some are. Your
loving husband, for example." Simmons paused. "Lunch,
my sweet. Over the first drink I'll tell you how much I
love you. Over the second I'll tell you in whispers what
I'm going to do to you the next time I get you into bed."

"It sounds fascinating." There were piles of manuscripts on her desk, the August issue of the book was not
yet locked up, nor could it be until she had at least one
more piece of usable fiction. On the other hand, a BLT
and a cup of bad coffee at her desk did not appeal.
"You've convinced me," Zib said. "Where? And when?"
Funny, she no longer even thought about Nat and what
his reaction would be if he knew she was straying from
the fold. Bad fiction, she thought as she jotted down
restaurant name and address. "Got it," she said. "*Ciao*.
And I'll pay my share. As usual."

Governor Bent Armitage, down from the capital for the
Tower opening, met Grover Frazee for an early lunch at
the Harvard Club on Forty-fourth Street. Over his martini
the governor said, "The corporation reports you've been
sending out haven't really said much, Grover. How are
rentals going at the Tower, or is it too early to tell?"

When he chose, Frazee thought, the governor could
put on a diffident, baffled, bucolic act that would fool
almost anyone. What was it they had called Wendell

Wilkie? The barefoot boy from Wall Street? Same thing. "The picture is still a trifle confused," Frazee said.

The governor sipped his martini with appreciation. "It used to be," he said, "that when you ordered a martini, that was it. Now you have to fill out a questionnaire: on the rocks or straight up? vodka or gin? olive, onion, or twist?" And then, with no change of expression, "I asked a question, Grover. Stop serving up ambiguities."

It was a sore troublesome point. "Rentals," Frazee said, "are going as well as can be expected under the circumstances."

The governor could smile like a Disney wolf, white fangs showing. "Twelve words that say exactly nothing. You'd have made a splendid politician. Rentals are not going well. Tell me why."

"A variety of factors—" Frazee began.

"Grover. You are not addressing a formal stockholders meeting. You are talking to one interested stockholder in the World Tower Corporation. There is a difference. Prospective tenants are staying away in droves? I want to know the reasons. Too much space available? Rentals too high? Money tight? Uncertainty in the business community?" The governor was silent, watching Frazee's face.

Frazee hesitated. The governor was a self-made man, and there were times, as now, when he set aside his jovial friendly front and allowed you to see some of the force that had carried him, almost, to the presidency of the United States. "All of those reasons," Frazee said. He hoped that his unconcerned shrug was convincing. "Things will change. They have to. The Trade Center is feeling the same pinch."

"The Trade Center," the governor said, "is Port Authority. Do I need to list the Port Authority's other assets? For them a less than full building complex can be tolerated almost indefinitely. We are a private corporation, and I keep thinking back to the Empire State Building sitting half-empty during the Depression."

Frazee said nothing.

"What it means," the governor said, "is that we seem to have picked a piss-poor time to build our shining great goddam building, no?" He finished his drink. "I promised myself two martinis," he said, and crooked his forefinger at the nearest waiter.

Frazee sat quiet, vaguely depressed. He was not a fearful man, nor did he consider himslf less than responsible. When problems arose, he was accustomed to dealing with them and not, like some, sweeping them under the rug. On the other hand, he did not rush into trouble as the governor was prone to do, because if you do not deliberately seek it, sometimes trouble passes you by. The rental situation in the World Tower was not happy-making, but neither was it critical. Yet.

"Cost overrun in construction?" the governor said.

There at least Frazee was on solid ground. "No," he said. "We've held very tight to estimtes." It was a source of pride. "Careful design, careful planning."

"All right. That's a plus." The governor smiled suddenly. "An unexpected plus. It gives a little room for maneuver, no?"

Frazee did not see how. He said as much with some asperity. His depression had turned to resentment at the apparent implication that he was overlooking the obvious.

"In some circles," the governor said, "it is called wheeling and dealing. In others it is considered merely sensible accommodation to the facts of life. First, you survive, Grover. Remember that. It is true in politics and it is also true in building management. Since we have not run over in construction costs, we can afford to take a little smaller income on our rentals without hurting ourselves, no?"

"We have published our schedule of rates," Frazee said stiffly. "We have signed leases on the basis of those rates."

"Good-o," the governor said. "Now where you think it expedient, let our agents sign some leases at a little less than our published rates and suggest to the tenants that they would do well to keep their mouths shut about it."

Frazee opened his mouth and shut it again carefully. The governor produced that wolf grin. "You're

shocked? It's what comes of a Racquet Club background."
He beckoned the waiter again. "We'll order," he said,
"while I still have a little martini left. Its going to be a long
dull afternoon." He consulted the menu, wrote out his
order, and leaned back in his chair. "There are a lot of
marbles involved, Grover," he said. "Maybe you don't
care about yours, but I do care a great deal about mine.
Gentlemanly ethics are all very well in yachting and golf
and other harmless pursuits, but we built that building to
make money." He paused. "Let's get on with it."

5

1:05

Paul Simmons was already in a small booth in the rear of
the restaurant when Zib arrived. He rose as she came
toward him smiling, skirt short on regal legs, long hair
gleaming, unbrassiered breasts jouncing gently. She slid
into the booth with the grace he always associated with
her. "I shouldn't be here," she said, and brushed the long
hair back with both hands. "I ought to be going through
piles of slush to try to find a piece of fiction we can use
without too much shame." She wrinkled her nose in
distaste.

"So I am all the more flattered." Paul beckoned the
waiter and ordered drinks—gin martinis, straight up, very
dry, very cold, with a twist. Then he leaned back and
smiled at Zib. "When am I going to see you?"

"You are seeing me."

"Not the way I want to. Shall I explain that?"

"You are a male chauvinist pig."

"And you love it."

Her smile was secret, inscrutable. It lifted the corners

51

of her mouth and brought tiny lights into her eyes. "There is more to us than sex," she said.

"Is there?"

Zib smiled again. The subject of sex was pleasurable, fun to spar about in a civilized way. It had been so as long as she could remember. "You're running true to type," she said.

"There are times when I wonder what my type is."

His secretary had caught him on the way out with Bert McGraw's message. He had listened and said easily. "Call him back, honey, and tell him I'm tied up—"

"I tried," the girl said. "But all he said was, 'Tell him to be here.'"

And what in the world did that kind of peremptory summons mean?

Now, "Once," he said, "I thought I was a pretty average sort of fellow—school, college, then probably some corporation where I could serve my time without too much strain."

Zib watched him steadily. "And?" Her voice was quiet.

The drinks arrived. Paul lifted his in salutation and sipped slowly. "You haven't met my father-in-law, have you?"

"Nat speaks of him."

Simmons set his glass down and studied it. He nodded slowly and looked up. "Nat would speak of him. They're not unalike. Bert is a brawling two-fisted Irishman—"

"Nat isn't. Nat is a lamb, sometimes too much of a lamb." Zib frowned. "Dont look at me like that. He is."

"The last thing I want," Simmons said slowly, "is to quarrel with you."

"Then don't say things like that."

"We're touchy today, aren't we?"

"He's my husband."

"And you know him well." Simmons nodded. But the fact is, he thought, she doesn't know her husband well. In Simmons's opinion, she didn't know him at all, which was, perhaps, all for the best. "So," he said, "we'll stick to Bert McGraw, my revered father-in-law."

52

Zib had one of her rare flashes of insight. "You're afraid of him, aren't you?"

He sipped his martini while he considered the question and at last said, "Yes." He had no wish to appear heroic; there was more to be gained by appearing otherwise, in effect throwing himself on Zib's mercy. It was an approach he had used before with success. "You and I," he said, "are anachronisms. We were raised to believe that all men were gentlemen and all women ladies. No cheating, no gouging, no butting in the clinches, life played strictly by Marquis of Queensberry rules." He was silent, watching for effect.

Zib was not sure that she understood exactly what he meant, but she was flattered that he would speak seriously to her about serious matters. Few men did. And she and Paul did come from similar backgrounds, so with that at least she could agree. She nodded. "Go on."

"I think kids today see it more clearly than we ever did," Paul said. "They listen to the Golden Rule and the Ten Commandments and they say they're crap because nobody believes them any more. Well, that isn't exactly true, but the people they point to, the ones we look up to, the ones who have been what we call successful, it is true that they haven't always played by those rules if they've ever played by them."

Zib thought she followed him now. "Your father-in-law?" she said.

"Exactly. Bert is a street fighter in a gutter neighborhood; he's that much in tune with his environment. He's in a tough trade, and because he's tougher than most, he gets along fine."

Zib looked across the table with fresh interest. "And you don't?"

He shrugged, modest now. "I stagger along." His smile was appealingly wry. "With Patty pushing me every step of the way."

In a sense, he thought, he had been accurate when he said that he wondered what his type was. He was and always had been a chameleon, with a chameleon's ability to blend into his surroundings. He had brains, technical competence—it would have been surprising if he had lacked technical competence after the education that had been provided for him—and he was long on charm, but there the list of assets seemed to end. Sometimes it seemed to him that an essential ingredient had been left out of his particular formula, a hardening agent perhaps, and the result was that he had never coalesced into a firm recognizable entity.

"I like Patty," Zib said.

"You're welcome to her." Again he smiled. "That isn't as far out a suggestion as it sounds. I wouldn't be surprised if Patty decided to play both sides of the street. She's unsold on men. Or me." He paused. "Shocked?"

"Hardly."

"The emancipated woman?"

"We face things as they are."

The worst part about any aspect of Women's Lib, Paul thought, is that it is taken so seriously that its disciples can speak only in clichés.

Zib studied her martini. She looked up. "I don't really know you at all, do I?" She paused. "Sometimes I wonder if I really know anyone. Do you ever get that feeling? You know, that you're—locked out?"

"Frequently." Paul gestured to the waiter for another round of drinks. If he was going to face Bert McGraw, he thought, he wanted inner support.

"What you said about Nat," Zib said.

"I said he was not unlike Bert McGraw."

"And what did you mean by that?"

Paul smiled. "He's a character out of the Wild West. He covers it well, but every now and again a little of it shows. 'When you say that, smile, podner!' That kind of thing."

Zib shook her head. "You're wrong. I told you. He's a lamb and I wish he weren't." Because if he weren't, she thought, I wouldn't be carrying on with you, or anybody else. So, in a sense, it was Nat's fault. Comforting thought.

"Sweetie," Paul said, "let me tell you something. Don't ever push him too far. Now, let's order. I've been summoned to the presence."

Patty was at a table for two at Martin's when Bert McGraw walked in. Martin himself, menus in hand, scurried up in greeting and led the way across the restaurant. McGraw bent to kiss his daughter, not on the cheek, but squarely on the mouth; for the McGraws a kiss was a kiss and not a vague gesture.

Then he sat down. His whiskey was waiting, as promised, a generous hooker of bourbon on ice. He tasted it, sighed, and smiled at the girl. "Hi, honey."

"You look peaked, McGraw."

"Maybe I am, but seeing you makes it better." Simple truth. Patty was a long generation removed from his Mary, but there was a similarity between the women that never ceased to amaze him, a quiet warm steadiness that certainly had not sprung from his rough genes. In her presence he could relax. "Between you and the whiskey I'm feeling fine."

Patty was smiling too. "Liar. You're tired. They put too much on you on the big jobs, and there's never been a bigger than the World Tower."

"Your mother's been at you."

"She didn't need to." Smiling still. "I have eyes in my head. You need a rest. Take Mother away. Take that trip to Ireland you've always talked about." Patty paused. "Why haven't you ever done it, Daddy?"

Why indeed? "There's never been the time."

"That isn't the reason."

McGraw smiled. "If you're such a smart whippersnapper, tell me what the reason is." He shook his head then. "No, that isn't fair, is it? I'll tell you the reason, honey. It's because Ireland isn't a place to me, it's a dream, and I'm afraid the dream would be damaged if I actually went to look at it." Confession. He finished his whiskey.

Patty was smiling fondly. "I believe it all but one part," she said, "and that I won't swallow. You afraid? Of anything? Ever?" She shook her head. "I don't think so."

There were times when his feeling of closeness to her equaled, in different ways even surpassed, his feeling of closeness to Mary. Wife and daughter were not the same

55

thing: each had her domain where she ruled supreme. "Afraid of many things, honey," McGraw said. "Afraid from the moment I saw you through the hospital window that one day you would go away, as you have—"

"I haven't gone away, Daddy."

"In a way you have. I don't know how mothers feel about their sons who marry, but I know how a father feels about his daughter." He forced himself to smile. It was uphill work. "The finest man in the world isn't good enough for her."

"Do you think Paul is the finest man in the world?"

Right up to you, McGraw. How do you answer that? Smiling, "I've known worse." Have you? After your talk with Giddings, do you still think so?

Patty's smile was gone. "I wonder if you mean that."

"I said it, didn't I, honey?"

Patty said, "You're a woolly bear, Daddy, and, I've been told, a very fine poker player." She shook her bright head. "I don't see how, because sometimes you're so transparent. I always thought you liked Paul."

"And what changed your mind?"

"The look in your eye. Daddy, what's happened?"

McGraw took his time. He looked up as a waiter approached.

"Another drink, sir?" the waiter said.

"Yes." It was Patty who answered. "For my father, but not for me." And when the waiter was gone, "It's bad?" she said.

"Bullied by my own daughter," McGraw said. He tried to keep it light, but he wasn't sure it sounded that way. "I don't know, honey. There may be—things to do with the World Tower."

"What kind of things?" And then, contractor's daughter, subcontractor's wife, she answered her own question: "Shenanigans? Paul? But how could—" She stopped. She said quietly, "He could, couldn't he? I've heard your tales—kickbacks, false invoices, bills of lading—" The words came easily to her tongue. "Is that it?"

"I don't know anything for sure, honey. And I'm not going to badmouth a man until I do know."

The fresh drink arrived. McGraw looked at it, picked it up, and made himself sip it slowly. What he needed, he thought, was not a drink in a glass, but a bottle. And cronies, as in the old simple days. Frank and Jimmy and O'Reilly and McTurk--the names ran through his mind like a litany. Drinking and brawling and laughing together—a long time ago.

"Yes, Daddy."

Good God, was he talking aloud? He noticed that his hand was unsteady as he set the glass down.

"I've heard you talk of them all," Patty said. "I wish I'd known you then."

He had himself under control again. "I was pushing forty, honey, when you were born."

"I know."

"Mary, bless her, only a year younger."

"I know that too. It never mattered that you were older than other parents. You weren't really."

"I don't know," McGraw said. "The young days were gone, and there you were." He smiled. "We wanted you bad, honey. I went down on my knees and thanked the good Lord when you arrived healthy and whole." He picked up the glass again. "Let's order a meal."

It was as if Patty had not heard. "What happened to them, Frank and Jimmy and O'Reilly and—was it McTurk?"

"It was. A big black Irishman with shoulders like a truss bridge." McGraw was silent. "What happened to them? I don't know, honey." Today was filled with confessions and reminiscences. "I had a dream once. I was climbing a mountain with friends. Up and up we went, into the mists. I lost the sight of them, and even the sound of their voices, and there was nothing to do but climb on." He paused, looking far beyond the girl, beyond the walls of the restaurant, into the past. It took an effort to bring himself back to the table. "At the top of the mountain," he said, "I came out into bright sunshine. I searched, but I was all alone. I never knew what happened to the others. I don't think you ever know. At the top of the mountain

57

you are always alone." He started to beckon the waiter and then stopped. "What was that you said?"

"I'm leaving Paul, Daddy. Or I was. But if he's in trouble—" She smiled, mocking herself. "I don't mean to sound noble. I detest noble women. Their—nobility spoils everything they do." Pause. "It's just that if Paul's in trouble, then this isn't the time to walk out on him, is it?"

"I don't know, honey. I don't know what the reason is." McGraw hesitated. "Do you want to tell me?" How many times had he asked that question, knowing that the answer was yes or the subject, whatever it was, would never have been brought up? He watched the girl quietly and waited.

Patty smiled again. "I guess I'm transparent too. Maybe we'd better not play poker together."

McGraw said nothing.

The reason," Patty said, "is the usual sordid reason. Or maybe it isn't usual these days. Maybe to most people a little wife-swapping doesn't matter. But it does to me."

McGraw sat quiet, fresh anger under tight control. He said at last, "It does to me too, honey. And to your mother."

"I know." Patty was smiling gently. "You gave me old-fashioned standards. I'm glad."

McGraw was silent for a time. He said at last. "Do you know who it is?"

"Zib Wilson."

"Does Nat know?"

"I haven't asked him."

There was silence. "Maybe," McGraw said slowly, "if you'd had children. I know that's old-fashioned too."

"We can't, Daddy. That's another part of it. Paul had a vasectomy. He didn't bother to tell me about it for a long time, but there it is." Patty picked up the menu. She smiled brightly. "As they say, so what else is new? I think some food for you, McGraw. Unless you're going to drink your lunch, you drunken lout?"

God, he thought, if only we could take on their problems, their pain. But, of course, we can't. "You sound just like a nagging wife," he said.

Patty's eyes were very bright, too bright. "And you,

Daddy, sound—" She stopped. Tears appeared. She got Kleenex out of her purse and swabbed viciously. "Oh, damn!" she said. "Damn, damn, damn! I wasn't going to cry!"

"Sometimes," McGraw said, "it's that or break something. I'll order for you, honey."

Zib took a cab from the restaurant back to the magazine. In her office she plumped down in her chair, kicked off her shoes, and ignoring the pile of manuscripts on her desk, stared unseeing at the wall.

She did not for a moment really believe what Paul Simmons had said about Nat: that he was a character out of the Wild West she would do well not to push too far. She had her own view of Nat.

On the other hand, how well did she really know her husband? How well could anyone know another? The question recurred constantly in the fiction she had to read, and there just might be something to it after all.

She had lived in married intimacy with Nat for almost three years now, and while that wasn't long as some marriages went, it was certainly long enough to develop familiarity with at least the man's approach to the more common daily activities, and were not these indicative of basic character traits?

Nat emptied his pockets carefully each night and hung up all of his clothes. He put trees in his shoes. He squeezed the toothpaste tube from the bottom instead of the top, and Zib was convinced that he counted silently to himself as he brushed his teeth for exactly thirty seconds, or was it forty-five? One chimpanzee, two chimpanzee, three chimpanzee . . .

Zib was a restless sleeper. Nat, on the other hand, settled himself on his back and did not stir. Nor did he snore. And although he was not one to sing in his morning shower or otherwise behave in a manner abominably ebullient so early in the day, he was cheerful over fruit juice, egg, and coffee, and in the preparing of them never seemed to have things go perversely, maddeningly wrong.

His morning run in the park and his walks to and from the office plus a regimen of daily floor exercises kept him in splendid physical condition. The running and the walking Zib supposed she would in any case have been able to bear, but the floor exercises would have been just too much if Nat had not explained that they were necessary because of an old spine injury sustained when he was thrown from a horse on some monster mountain out in the West.

He was even-tempered and did not swear at waiters or cab drivers. He was punctual. He preferred bourbon to martinis, which at first had seemed odd, but now seemed quite ordinary. He looked with approval and an artist's eye at pretty women, but Zib would have wagered heavily that looking was as far as it went. Their own sex life was pleasant, varied, and without the compulsions some seemed to have these days.

Where in all that was the character Paul Simmons pictured?

And why was she so suddenly concerned anyway? Could she actually imagine Nat in the outraged-husband role, confronting her with the fact of her infidelity and, if Paul were to be believed, taking some kind of retaliatory action? The kind of thing that turned up in the *Daily News* or, for that matter, in probably half a dozen of the manuscripts sitting right here on her desk? Nonsense.

If there was one quality Nat lacked, it was aggressiveness. She remembered talking about that lack one night. She had said, "You're better than you think you are. Ben Caldwell knows it. Why else would he have pushed you along the way he has?"

"Nobody else around." Nat smiled. "Next question?"

"That," Zib said, "is one of the most annoying things about you. You won't be drawn. You know, I've never seen you lose your cool."

"It happens sometimes."

"I don't believe it." And then, groping for words to clothe the idea, "Respect," she said. "That's the thing that counts."

"Important," Nat said. "Agreed. So?"

60

"How can you respect somebody who doesn't have even a trace of bastard in him?"

Calmly, "Or bitch?"

"Right."

"Would you rather I had temper tantrums? Threw things?"

"That isn't what I mean. But in this world either you push or you get walked on, don't you see that?"

"It's a big-city attitude."

"This is a big city." She paused. "Why did you ever come here?"

"Because I don't belong, you mean?"

"That isn't what I mean and you know it. All I'm asking is why you came here in the first place."

"To find you."

"Be serious."

"All right." Nat was smiling again. "Because Ben Caldwell was here, and I wanted to work with, work under the best. Simple as that."

"And you have." Zib nodded. "When the World Tower is all finished, wrapped up, just another big building, then what?" She hesitated. "Back to your mountains?"

"Possibly. Probably. Will you come with me?"

"I'd be out of place. As much—" She stopped.

"As much as I am here?" He shook his head, smiling again. "You will fit wherever you are. You're a social creature."

"And you?"

Nat shrugged. "Sometimes I wonder," he said.

No trace of temper, Zib thought now; never a trace of temper showing. Oh, not emotionless; not that. With her he could be a passionate man, lover. But other times, in ways Paul Simmons had hinted? No way. Paul was wrong. That was all there was to it.

Then why the small nagging doubt? Answer me that, Elizabeth.

6

1:30–2:10

Bert McGraw was back in his office after lunch, and
Paul Simmons, clearly uncomfortable, sat low in one of
the leather visitor's chairs. The old man, Paul thought,
was like a bear with a sore paw, and it behooved him to
tread warily. He looked at his watch. "One-thirty," he
said, "on the dot." He paused and, daring, added, "As
specified."

"I had lunch with Patty," McGraw said. He had himself under control, but how long the temptation to hammer on his desk and shout could be restrained he had no
idea.

"I was busy for lunch," Paul said. Along with his
chameleon abilities went an actor's voice. "Business is
good."

"Is it now?" Deliberately the old man picked up the
manila envelope of change-authorization copies, looked
at it, and then, with a sudden flipping motion, scaled it
to land accurately in Paul's lap. "Have a look," McGraw
said, and heaved himself out of his chair to walk to the
windows, his back to the room.

In the big office only the faint whispering of the papers
in Paul's hands disturbed the silence. Paul said at last,
"So?"

McGraw turned from the windows. He stood square,
his hands behind his back. "Is that all you have to say?"

"I don't understand. What else is there to say?"

"Did you make those changes?"

"But of course."

"Why *of course*?" The old man's voice was rising.

Paul scratched an eyebrow. "I don't know what to say. Why wouldn't I make the changes?"

"Because," McGraw said, "you're not some dumb working stiff. If somebody says, 'Do this,' you don't just do it without question. You—" McGraw stopped. "Say it," he said, "whatever it is."

Simmons's voice had taken on a faint edge. "I'll try not to make it irreverent," he said, "because you don't like that."

"Say it however you goddam well please." The old man was back in his big chair, holding tight to the arms.

"All right," Paul said. "It goes like this. Most times if somebody says, 'Change this,' I want reasons. But when Jesus Christ Ben Caldwell or his anointed disciple Nat Wilson give me the Word, then I tug at my forelock and say, 'Aye, aye, sir,' and the change is made. Not for me to question why. Does that answer the question?"

McGraw said slowly, "Don't be flip with me, young fellow." Automatic response. He sat quiet, thoughtful, puzzled still. He said at last, "You're sayin', are you not, that it was Nat Wilson himself who signed those changes?"

Paul's face showed surprise. "I never thought different. Why would I?"

"And," McGraw said, "because the changes, as far as I've seen, stand to save you a little money here, a little there, all of it adding up to quite a bit, then you had even more reason to take what was handed you without question, is that it?"

"I think I recall you suggesting," Paul said, "that the teeth of gift horses are best not examined." He tapped the papers in his lap. "If this was the way they wanted their building wired, and as you say, I saved money by doing it their way, why should I raise any kind of a fuss?"

McGraw said slowly, "Nat Wilson says he didn't issue those changes."

Paul's face altered, but he said merely, "I see."

"And what, goddammit, do you see? Will Giddings doesn't believe Wilson issued those changes either. Neither does Ben Caldwell."

"And what do you think, Father-in-law?"

63

The office was silent again. McGraw looked at his hands spread flat on the desktop. "What I think," he said slowly, "would call down penance in confession." He was looking straight at Simmons now. "I'm thinking that the knave-or-fool judgment applies. You're carrying on with the man's wife—"

"Patty told you that?"

McGraw sat silent, watching still.

"Okay," Paul said at last. "That's how it is." He spread his hands. "You can't understand it—"

"That I cannot. Nor can I forgive." The black fury was rising, irresistible. "I'm an old-fashioned working-class fool, and you're young, bright, educated, decently bred, and all—and the stench of you is in my nostrils like the stench of something dead that's been out in the sun too long."

"Look," Paul said, "I've taken enough—"

"You haven't begun to take," McGraw said. "Move from that chair before I'm done and I'll break your back." He paused. His breathing was audible now. With effort he forced his voice down. "Why would Nat Wilson issue those changes? Tell me that. They gain him nothing. He is the architect. He and Ben Caldwell, Ben mostly of course, but that changes nothing. Between them they approved Lewis's electrical drawings, his design. Why should Wilson make any attempt at change?"

Simmons sat silent. He wanted to stand up and walk out, and was afraid. The old man behind the desk was, as he had told Zib, a fearsome old man, quite capable of the physical violence he had threatened.

"I asked you a question," McGraw said.

"You asked several."

"Then answer them all."

Simmons took a deep breath. "Nat Wilson is a subtle man," he said.

"And what, goddammit, is that supposed to mean?"

"He resents me."

McGraw was frowning now. "Why?" And then, "Because you're carrying on with his wife, is that what you mean?"

64

Simmons nodded. It was better, he thought, not to speak.

"I don't believe it," McGraw said. "I know the man. If he knew you were sneaking behind his back, he'd brace you with it and take a few teeth out of that Pepsodent smile. He—"

"And he is playing with Patty," Paul said.

McGraw opened his mouth. He closed it again, but it reopened despite him. And then it closed once more. And opened. No sound emerged. His face had lost its color and his breath came now in great gasps that were not enough. His eyes protruded as he tried to make a gesture with one hand, and failed. He slumped deep in his chair, gasping still like a fish on the bank.

Paul got up quickly. He stood for a moment indecisive and then walked to the door and threw it open. To Laura outside he said, "You'd better call an ambulance. He's —I think—he's having a heart attack."

Grover Frazee took a cab back to his Pine Street office after his lunch with the governor. He had known Armitage a long time, and in the usual meaning of the words they were, he supposed, good friends.

But in the governor's world, and as far as that went in Frazee's too, friendship was a fine-sounding word that had very little to do with business. Business was conducted on its merits, period.

If a man produced you backed him; if he failed, you did not.

Oh, he hadn't failed. Not yet. But in the foreseeable future the building was going to be damned near empty. There was the rub.

You could lay the blame to general business conditions or that administration down in Washington with its three-steps-forward-and-two-and-a-half-steps-back policies.

But placing the blame accomplished nothing. Explanation rarely helped, and in this instance, today at lunch, explanation hadn't even softened the governor's attitude.

"You're the man in charge, Grover," the governor had said, "which means that you get the brickbats as well as

65

the bouquets. I know the feeling and the position." He grinned bitterly as he stirred sugar into his coffee and watched the liquid swirl. He looked up at last. "How bad is it? Give me some figures." He watched Frazee steadily.

Frazee gave them to him—percentage of rented floor space, and of possible new rentals, certain and hoped-for income versus basic maintenance and carrying costs. Discouraging. "But it can't last," he said.

"The hell it can't." The governor's voice did not rise, but it had taken on a new note. "Unemployment hasn't dropped and inflation hasn't been whipped. I don't think there's a chance of our going into a thirties-type depression, but neither do I think that all of a sudden everything is going to be ginger-peachy, particularly in the big cities."

"Bob Ramsay—"

"Bob Ramsay hears voices. It's a wonder to me he hasn't come down from the nearest hill with new tablets. He thinks we're going to put the whole state to work for his city, and we aren't. He thinks maybe he'll make the city into the fifty-first state, and he isn't going to. He thinks Congress is going to roll over and wave its paws in the air after giving him a blank check, and it isn't going to work that way either."

Privately, Frazee entertained similar views, but he said nothing.

"He loves this city," the governor said. "I'll give him that. And he's held it together almost with his bare hands. But the fact of the matter is that too much business is moving out, into the suburbs, more than is coming in. The big time, the big apple, the place where it's at—that concept has lost its appeal. What is left here is turning rapidly into a place for the very rich and the very poor, and neither group rents office space in big buildings."

Well, Frazee thought now in the quiet of his own office, Bent Armitage was probably right. He usually was.

The phone on his desk buzzed quietly. He opened the switch. "Yes?"

"Mr. Giddings to see you," Letitia's voice said. "He says it is urgent."

First Armitage at lunch, now Will Giddings obviously

with some kind of trouble; there are times when they seem to come at you from all sides. "All right," Frazee said in resignation. "Send him in."

Giddings came straight to the point. "Time to plug you in," he said, and tossed an envelope filled with change-authorization copies on Frazee's desk.

Frazee shook them out, looked at one or two, and then looked up at Giddings in mild puzzlement. "I'm not an engineer," he said. "You're supposed to be. Explain."

Giddings explained, and when he was done, he sat back and waited.

The big office was still. Frazee pushed his chair back slowly, got up, walked to the window, and stood looking down at traffic. His back to the room, "You didn't know about the changes," he said.

"I didn't know. I'm at fault, along with Caldwell's people—Nat Wilson in particular—and Bert McGraw. We're all responsible."

Frazee turned back to the room. "And now what?"

"We check out each one of these to see if the changes were actually made and what effect there might be."

"What kind of effect?"

Giddings shook his head. "I won't even guess. It could be trivial. It could be serious. And that's why I'm here."

Frazee walked back to his desk and sat down. "You want what?"

"To call off that nonsense this afternoon up in the Tower Room." A big man, serious, forceful. "I don't want people up there."

"Why?"

"Goddammit," Giddings said, "do I have to spell it out? The building isn't finished. Now we know, or at least have reason to believe, that there may be electrical flaws in what is done. We don't know how serious the flaws are, and until we do know it doesn't make sense to have an indoor garden party, for God's sake, when right in the middle of it—"

"The lights might go out?" Frazee said. "Something like that?"

Giddings studied the backs of his hands while he calmed

67

himself. He looked up at last and nodded. "Something like that," he said.

"But you can't be sure, can you?"

He was no match for Frazee at this kind of thing, Giddings told himself. He was no fluent, smooth business type; he was an engineer, and at the moment, with those pieces of paper lying on Frazee's desk, he was almost prepared to admit that he wasn't even a very good, that was to say careful, engineer. "I can't be sure," he said. "That's why I want time."

Frazee was thinking of Governor Armitage. "You're the man in charge," the governor had said, "which means you get the brickbats as well as the bouquets." True enough, but why not duck and let someone else take the brickbats?

"I don't see how we can call off the arrangements, Will," Frazee said. He smiled.

"Why the hell not?"

Frazee's manner was patient. "Invitations went out months ago and were accepted by people who might now otherwise be in Moscow or London or Paris or Peking or Washington. They have put themselves to some trouble to appear here for what amounts"—Frazee's smile spread —"to a launching, Will. When a ship is launched, it is not complete either: months of work remain. But the launching ceremony is a gala occasion, set far in advance, and one simply does not call off that kind of affair at the last moment."

"Goddammit," Giddings said, "you can't equate a striped-pants cookie-push with the kind of trouble we might have, can't you see that?"

Frazee sat quiet, contemplative. He said at last, "I can't see it, Will. What kind of trouble concerns you so much?"

Giddings lifted his big hands and let them fall. "That's the hell of it. I don't know." Giddings was thinking now of Bert McGraw's theory that some buildings were accursed, and while he didn't believe it for a moment, he had known jobs on which nothing ever seemed to go right, and try as you could, you could find no solid explanation. Then there was that one other thing today, only a little time ago: "Somebody's running around inside the building, and I don't like that either."

Frazee frowned. "Who?"

"I don't know, and we'll play hell finding out without a floor-to-floor search with an army."

Frazee smiled. "Ridiculous. Why is the man even important?"

Giddings said, "Look, there are too many things I don't know, and that is just the goddam trouble. I'm responsible to you for that building. I've lived with it and sweated over it—"

"No one could have done more, Will."

"But," Giddings said, "things got by me and by everybody else too, and now all I'm asking is time to find out how serious those things are. Is that too much to ask?"

Frazee picked up a gold pencil and studied it thoughtfully. Suppose things did happen during the reception in the Tower Room? What if there were some kind of electrical failure, what harm? Would it not, by showing up flaws within the building, in a sense take the monkey off his back, give him more time to find tenants, by following the governor's cut-rate suggestions if no other way; in a sense, by shifting blame to McGraw and Caldwell, contractor and supervising architect, would he not place himself in the position of saying that circumstances beyond his control delayed the rush to occupy the splendid facilities of the brand-new World Tower communications center?

Giddings said, "At least you're thinking about it. That's something."

Frazee put down the pencil. "But I'm afraid that's all it is, Will." He paused. "We cannot cancel the arrangements. I'm sorry you don't see that, but you'll have to take my word for it. We cannot make the building a laughingstock right at the beginning."

Giddings sighed and stood up. He had, really, expected no more. "You're the boss. I hope to hell you're right and I'm wrong, seeing things, shadows, thinking about a big Polack who walked off a steel beam for no reason at all

—no, he doesn't have a goddam thing to do with this, it's just the kind of thing that sticks in my mind and I don't know why." He walked to the door and paused there, his hand on the knob. "I think I'm going over to Charlie's Bar on Third Avenue. I think I'm going to get drunk." He walked out.

Frazee sat on at his desk, motionless, thoughtful. His own thinking was sound, he was convinced, but another opinion was frequently a good idea. He picked up the phone and said to Letitia, "Get me Ben Caldwell, please."

The telephone buzzed. Frazee picked it up and spoke his name. Ben Caldwell's quiet voice said, "Something on your mind, Grover?"

The papers were strewn on the desk in front of him. "These—things," Frazee said. "I don't even know what to call them—papers changing design—you know about them?"

"I know about them."

"Your man seems to have signed them."

"He says no. For the moment I believe him."

"Are they important, Ben?"

There was no hesitation. "We will have to see."

No trace of anxiety, Frazee thought, and found relief in the concept. "Will Giddings wants me to call off today's opening."

Caldwell was silent.

Frazee, frowning, said, "What do you think?"

"About what?" This was the unworldly side of Caldwell.

"Should I call off the opening?"

"Public relations is not my line, Grover." There was a hint of asperity in the quiet voice.

"No," Frazee said. "Of course not."

There was a short silence. "Was that all?" Caldwell said.

"That was all." Frazee hung up and reflected that of all the men he knew, the governor included, only Caldwell had the power to bring back boyhood memories of leaving the headmaster's study after an unpleasant interview.

Well, one thing was settled: there was no need to change plans for the afternoon.

7

2:10–2:30

The governor was of two minds, but as usual his practical side prevailed. There was nothing that said that he, governor of the state, must check in with the city's mayor when he came to visit. On the other hand, why raise hackles unnecessarily? And Bob Ramsay's hackles were notoriously easy to raise. "I'm still at the Harvard Club," the governor said on the phone to the mayor. "Is that turf neutral enough for a Yale man? If it is, come up. I'll buy you a drink. We can go over to Grover Frazee's hoedown together."

Mayor Bob Ramsay was fifty-seven years old, in splendid physical shape, in his second term as mayor of the great city and loving ever minute of it. In the mayor's lexicon the word challenge was set in capital letters.

Deep in a leather chair in a corner of the club lounge, a snifter of cognac at his elbow, "What are you going to talk about?" the governor said. "Brotherhood of man as symbolized by the World Tower?"

It was a favorite theme of Ramsay's. But Bent Armitage had a way of souring even the most lofty thoughts, and the theme immediately lost its savor. The mayor sipped his black coffee. "I haven't thought much about it," he said. It was a mistake.

The governor's grin appeared. "That's crap, and you know it, son. Like Mark Twain, you spend a great deal of time preparing your impromptu remarks. We all do. Why not admit it?"

"What I intended to convey," the mayor said stiffly,

"is that I haven't yet decided exactly what remarks are called for."

The governor switched the subject smoothly. "What do you think of the building?"

Ramsay sipped his coffee again while he examined the question for booby traps. "I think we are all agreed," he said, "that it is a lovely structure, one of Ben Caldwell's best, if not his crowning achievement."

"I'll go along with that," the governor said.

"And it brings additional space—"

"—which the city needs like a broken head."

Ramsay finished his coffee deliberately. He set the cup down. "Not fair and not true. What the city needs is all the fine facilities it can have—and this is one—together with the kind of aid that every large city in this country must have or perish." It was a matter of faith with him. He looked at the governor in challenge.

"Maybe," the governor said. He looked at his watch. "We have a little time. Let's kick it around a bit. Suppose I offer the idea that cities of over-a-million population are as out of date as the dinosaur? What do you say to that?"

The mayor breathed hard and said nothing.

"I'm serious," the governor said. "What about an abundance of one-hundred-thousand-population cities, each containing all the necessary services and surrounded by the necessary industries and enterprises to provide employment, but without the helpless slums and the gigantic welfare rolls and the crime problems that come out of them? Would you go along with that concept?"

"And you," the mayor said, "are the one who is always accusing me of seeing visions, looking for pie in the sky."

"A little different," the governor said. "You're looking for manna to keep your pet dinosaur alive. I'm looking for a new kind of livestock we can live with." He paused and grinned. "That's a piss-poor analogy, but maybe you'll see what I mean. Call it a modern-day version of Jefferson's ideal bucolic civilization, to replace the monster-city environment we've created in which nobody's happy." He paused again. "Except maybe Bob Ramsay."

The mayor had been doing his arithmetic. "We would

have to break this metropolitan area up into a hundred and thirty separate cities, each going its own way—"

"Independent as hogs on ice," the governor said. He nodded. "There's nothing wrong with tug-and-haul. That's what it takes to hammer out policy."

"I rarely know," the mayor said, "whether you are serious or your tongue is pushing hard at your cheek. Do you know yourself?"

Again that grin, directed inward at the governor's own foibles. "This time," he said, "I am perfectly serious. Your city is breaking up anyway, new poverty is moving in and solid middle-class support moving out. In not too long you'll have left only people living in penthouses and riding in limousines, and people living in slums mugging each other in the streets and subways." The governor paused, unsmiling. "Can you deny it?"

The mayor could not. "But you make it sound hopeless, and it isn't. Give us back some of the taxes the state takes from us, the federal government takes from us, and—"

"And," the governor said, "you'll provide more low-income housing, more welfare, more indigent hospital care, more slum schools." He paused for emphasis. "And you'll simply attract more people who need those things. So you'll be digging your hole deeper and compounding your problems, and that means you'll need more police to cope, and firemen, and courts, and, inevitably, *more* low-income housing, *more* welfare, *more* indigent hospital care, *more* slum schools—ad infinitum." He paused again. "You're beyond the point where you can even hope to catch up."

The mayor was silent, depressed.

"What I'm saying," the governor said, "is that our brand-new shining beautiful World Tower isn't a sign of progress at all; it's a sign of retrogression, just another dinosaur stable." He finished his cognac and sighed. "So let's go down to it and tell everybody that the building we dedicate today is a symbol of the future, man's hope, the greatest thing that has come along since the wheel." He stood up wearily. "What the hell else can we say?"

8

Assistant Fire Commissioner Timothy O'Reilly Brown was tall, redheaded, and intense, with a low boiling point. He did not know Nat, but he knew Ben Caldwell by soaring reputation, and if there was anyone in the entire city who did not know of the World Tower building, Tim Brown had no idea who it might be, so he was not on entirely unknown ground. Nevertheless, "What you're telling me," he told Nat now, "is a purely internal matter. I've no desire to mix into it. You and Bert McGraw and the owners can straighten it out between you."

"You know better than I do, of course," Nat said, "but aren't fire regulations sometimes relaxed or maybe overlooked when a special event has to go through on schedule?" He was being as tactful as he knew how. It was uphill work.

"No."

"Never?"

"You heard me."

Tact be damned. "That," Nat said, "is horseshit, and you know it. *Most* firemen, fire inspectors, are honest, just as most cops and building inspectors and most contractors are honest and most mistakes that are made are honest mistakes." He paused. "But some aren't, and you know that too."

Tim Brown said, "The door is right behind you. I don't know what kind of shenanigans you're trying to pull, but I'm not even going to listen to the pitch. Out."

Nat made no move. "Suppose," he said, "just suppose—"

"I said out!"

"I don't think you're big enough to put me out," Nat said, "and think of the stink there'd be if you tried and something did happen at the Tower building." He paused. "It would look like Assistant Commissioner Brown had his fingers into something, wouldn't it? Or don't you even care about that?"

Tim Brown had half-risen in his chair. He sat down now. The nightmare of every public official, of course, was the possibility of merely being accused of misprision whether innocent or not. He hesitated.

"I'm not accusing anybody," Nat said. "I'm not hankering for a slander suit. But what I am saying is that apparently changes in electrical design have been made, and maybe those changes reduce or even eliminate the designed safety factors, and *if* certain leniencies in fire regulations were allowed in order not to stop this scheduled opening, then if anything were to happen in that building, there might be hell to pay and no pitch hot." He leaned back in his chair. "I may be jumping at shadows. I hope I am. Then you can call me a fool and I'll apologize for taking up your time."

Brown was silent still, thinking hard. He said at last, "What do you want me to do?"

"It's your department, but—"

"That's no help. You come in here shouting 'Fire!' and then wash your hands of all knowledge. You—"

"If and when you climb down off your high horse," Nat said, "maybe we can make some kind of sense, but not before." He stood up. "I've tossed it in your lap." He started for the door.

"Hold it," Brown said. "Sit down." His face was suddenly weary. He took a deep breath to regain control. He said slowly, "I've got a sick wife and an ulcer and an understaffed fire department in a city full of people who don't give a shit about the kind of protection we try to give them, who think alarm boxes are for games—do you know that I lost two men this last week, two men *killed* answering false alarms?" He shook his head. "Never mind. My problems." He opened a drawer, got out a pack of cigarettes, shook one loose, broke it in half and threw

75

it angrily into the wastebasket. He tossed the package back into the drawer and slammed the drawer shut. "That's fourteen today I haven't smoked," he said. He made himself sit quietly. "Now let's talk sense." He paused. "What exactly have you got?"

Better, Nat thought, and ticked items off on his fingers. "First," he said, "a batch of copies of design-change authorizations with my name on them that I didn't sign. We'll have to assume somebody wanted the changes made. Joe Lewis, the electrical engineer, is checking the changes now to see how deep they go."

"How do you know they were even made?"

"We have to assume they were. Isn't that how you people think? You assume the worst can happen and you try to prevent it? Not all oily rags ignite spontaneously, but you call all oily rags fire hazards."

True enough. Brown, calmer now, nodded affirmation.

"It's out of my field," Nat said, "and I'm just guessing, but I can think of a dozen things your people *might* have overlooked, knowing that the building isn't really occupied and knowing too that today's doings were planned months ago and can't be postponed." He paused. "Pressure in the standpipes, floor hoses actually in place, fire doors operable and not blocked, sprinkler systems checked out, standby generators checked and ready—how much is your department's job, and how much belongs to building inspectors, I don't know; you've always seemed to work together."

"We do." Brown smiled wearily. "Or we try. We try to work with the cops too—"

"And that's another thing," Nat said. "The plaza's crawling with cops. I assume that's because somebody is worried about something." And, face it, he told himself, that makes you a little more uptight too. "So am I," he said, "even if I don't know what." He was thinking of the blinking elevator lights, the soft whirring of the high-speed cables as somebody moved around in the empty building at will.

"These days," Brown said, "with nuts throwing bombs or shooting into crowds for no reason at all, everybody

76

is always worried about everything." He paused. "Or ought to be." He sighed. "All right. I'll see what I can find out. And I'll see that the building is as well covered now as a building that size can be."

The words started up again a train of thought already half-forgotten. "A building that size," Nat said, and paused thoughtfully. "Despite every safety factor we design into it and every care we take with it and every possible threat we anticipate and plan for—it's still vulnerable, isn't it?"

Brown opened the desk drawer, glared down at the cigarette package, and then slammed the drawer shut again. "Yes," he said, "your big building is vulnerable. The bigger they are, the more vulnerable they are. You just don't think about it."

"I'm thinking about it," Nat said.

He walked again, back to the Caldwell offices. Ben Caldwell had already left for the ceremonies at the Tower building. Nat walked into his own office and sat down to stare at the drawings thumbtacked to the wall.

He told himself that he was being frightened of shadows as when, a time not easily forgotten, backpacking alone somewhere above the thirteen-thousand-foot contour, he had come across the largest bear tracks he had ever seen showing plainly the long front claws that spell grizzly.

Grizzly bears were extinct, some said; or near enough. Near enough was no consolation. One grizzly bear was more than ample: one grizzly bear was entirely too much.

Black bears were one thing: you left them alone and, unless it was a mother with cubs, they would not bother you. But the big fellow, *Ursus horribilis*, played by no rules except his own: what grizzly wanted, grizzly took, and his temper was short.

He could outrun a horse and he could kill a thousand-pound steer with a single blow of his forepaw. Searching for goodies like marmots or pikas, he could overturn with a flick of a paw rocks that two men together could not lift. When you hunted grizzly, or his cousin the big Alaska brown, you never, never, never fired unless you were above him; otherwise, those who knew assured you, no

77

matter what weight weapon you were firing, he would get to you, and then it was Kitty-bar-the-door. And Nat wasn't even carrying a gun.

All of this brought to mind by a few footprints on a windswept mountain slope high above timberline.

The balance of that afternoon Nat had had the feeling that he wanted to look in all directions at once; and that night after dark, in his sleeping bag, staring up at the stars and at occasional clouds that moved across their patterns, it had been worse: every night sound, every rustle of wind in rocks or stunted Alpine growth, sounded an alarm, and despite his fatigue from the days tramping, sleep was a long time coming.

When he awakened shortly after first light and reluctantly climbed out of the warm sleeping bag into the brisk mountain air, the grizzly was not immediately in his thoughts—until he saw the fresh tracks only feet from where he had slept. The great beast had obviously come to see what this strange animal was; for all his bulk quieter than the night itself, curious, fearless—and in the end, uninterested.

Nat never saw the bear, but he never forgot it. Now, sitting in his silent office, "I never saw the man in the building either," he said aloud, "and probably I'll never see him, and maybe he is harmless too, but I don't for a moment believe it."

He sat up and put through a call to Joe Lewis. "Anything yet?"

"We're not magicians," Lewis said. "Some of those changes we're going to have to put into the computer and see what happens if: *if* we have a circuit failure here or an overload there; that kind of thing you don't expect but you've got to consider." He paused. "You aren't usually jumpy."

"I am now," Nat said, "and if you ask me why, I can't tell you. Call it a hunch."

There was a short silence. Lewis said, "When did these changes turn up?"

"This morning. Giddings brought them in."

"Where did he get them?"

"I don't know." Nat paused. "Maybe I'd better find out."

There was no answer at Giddings's telephone at the Tower building. Nat called Frazee's office. Frazee had already gone to the festivities. "Can't have a program without the MC," Letitia Flores said. "My boss man is starting the talkfest right about now." Letitia was plump, fluent in four languages, efficient as Joe Lewis's computer. "Anything I can do?"

"Giddings," Nat said. "Do you know where he is?"

"Charlie's Bar on Third Avenue." Letitia gave the address. "Next question?"

"If he calls in," Nat said, "tell him I'm looking for him."

"Shall I tell him why?"

Strangely, Nat thought, there was no need. On this problem, their previous frequent differences notwithstanding, he and Will Giddings saw eye to eye. "He'll know," he said.

Again he walked, without thought of the exertion, without any sense of physical fatigue, by the turmoil that was building in his mind compelled into activity. This time he noticed his surroundings.

Just in the years he had known it Third Avenue had changed. He had come too late for the El, which once had rocketed down through the Bowery, a summer-night excursion, he had been told, with open lighted tenement windows showing humanity in most of its usually private activities. But just in the last few years the change in the avenue seemed to have accelerated, and what once had been *neighborhood* was now impersonal shops and apartment buildings, sidewalks filled with strangers, hurriers-on, passers-through. Like himself.

Charlie's Bar was a throwback: swinging doors with the name etched in heavy glass, heavy dark wood bar and booths and tables, the smell of pipe-smoke and malt, and the sound of quiet male talk. It was a bar where customers were known and a man could still while away a quiet afternoon over a few mugs of beer and talk. Zib, for all her Women's Lib, Nat thought, would come in here and

79

immediately twitch to get back out again though no word of unwelcome would be spoken.

He found Giddings at the bar, a shot glass of whiskey and a full mug of beer in front of him, and the bartender leaning on an elbow in friendly conversation.

Giddings was not drunk, but there was a glint in his eyes. "Well, well," he said, "look who's here. Wrong side of town, isn't it?"

"You can do better than that, Will." Nat gestured at the drinks on the bar. "I'll have the beer, but not the shot." Then, again to Giddings, "Let's take a booth. Talk."

"About what?"

"Can't you guess? I've talked with Joe Lewis. His people are going to the computers. I've talked with a fellow named Brown downtown."

"Tim Brown?" Giddings was alert now.

Nat nodded. He accepted the filled mug of beer, reached for his pocket.

Giddings said, "No. On my check." He slid down from his stool. "Charlie McGonigle, Nat Wilson. We'll be over in the corner booth, Charlie." He led the way, drinks in hand.

The beer was good, cool, not icy, soothing. Nat drank deep and set the mug down.

"Why Tim Brown?" Giddings said. He ignored the boilermaker in front of him.

It was beginning to sound like a record too often played or a word become meaningless. Nat wished it were. "Too many mistakes," he said. "You're an engineer. You understand that. Something goes wrong. It ought to stop right there because we've designed in safety devices that ought to function immediately." He paused. "But suppose the safety device has been bypassed? Or it isn't functioning because the fire department people or the inspectors let it go just for now?"

Giddings shook himself like a dog on a hearth. "Maybe," he said. "But if you went to Tim Brown, you're thinking fire. Why?" Bert McGraw's mention of jinxed buildings was very much in his mind. He wished he could shake the thought.

"Electrical changes," Nat said, "all of them. You can fuse steel with a hundred and ten volts. I've done it: a knifeblade shorted out in an electric toaster once."

Giddings's nod was almost imperceptible. His eyes were steady on Nat's face.

"We bring power into that building," Nat said, "at thirteen thousand eight hundred volts, not a hundred and ten—"

"You're thinking of whoever it was riding the elevators?" Giddings paused. "But why? Tell me, man, for the love of God, why?"

"I don't know." Simple truth, but the hunch that was almost conviction remained. "You're a big man," Nat said. "You ever been in a bar fight?"

Giddings smiled faintly, without amusement. "One or two."

"Has it ever been because some little man was liquored up and looking to show what a ring-tailed wonder he was and he picked on you because you were the biggest man in the bar?"

Giddings was silent, thoughtful. "Go on."

"I don't know what's going on," Nat said. "I'm an architect. I also know horses and I know mountains and I know skiing and—and *things*. I don't think I know much about people."

"Go on," Giddings said again.

"I'm no shrink," Nat said. "But if somebody can't get anybody to pay attention to him even when he goes around like a freak, and decides that, say, a bomb is the only answer, where does he plant it? In an airplane gets lots of attention—but they don't plant bombs in little airplanes, do they? It's always a big shiny jet. Or it's a crowded airport that's known around the world—it isn't at Teterboro or Santa Fe."

Giddings picked up the shot glass and set it down again untouched. "You've flipped," he said. And he added, "I hope."

"I hope so too." Nat felt calmer now, almost resigned, which was strange. "That building of ours," he said, "is the biggest. And today is the day everybody is looking at

81

it. Look there." He pointed to the color TV set mounted behind the bar.

The set was on, the volume turned down. The picture was of the World Tower Plaza, the police barricades, the temporary platform now partially filled with seated guests. Grover Frazee, a carnation in his buttonhole, smiled and extended his hand as more guests mounted the platform stairs. A band was playing; the music reached only faintly across the barroom.

"You didn't want the opening," Nat said. "Neither did I. Now I want it even less and I can't say why." He paused. "Look there."

The television camera had swung from the platform and the guests to the crowds behind the barricades. Here and there a hand waved at the lens, but it was on scattered handheld signs that the camera focused. "STOP THE WAR!" one sign read. "STOP THE BOMBING!" urged another. The signs waved angrily.

The camera moved on, paused, and then zoomed in to focus on a new sign: "MILLIONS FOR THIS MONSTER BUILDING! BUT HOW ABOUT WELFARE?"

"All right," Giddings said. "The natives are restless. They always are these days." He picked up the shot glass and knocked the drink back, his good humor restored.

The camera had returned to the platform steps where the governor and the mayor paused to wave at the crowd. Watching, "I always have the feeling," Giddings said, "that politicians will gather to dedicate a whorehouse if there's publicity to be had." He was smiling now. "But, then, whores vote too, same as anybody else."

Nat said quietly, "Where did you get those change orders, Will?" He watched Giddings's smile disappear.

"Are they real, do you mean?" Giddings said. There was truculence in his tone.

"You've shown me copies," Nat said. "Where are the originals?"

"Look, sonny—"

Nat shook his head. "I told you: not that way. If you're afraid to answer the question, just say so."

"Afraid, hell."

82

"Then where are the originals?"

Giddings turned the empty shot glass around and around on the table top. He said at last, "I don't know." He looked up. "And that's the stupid simple truth. What I got in the mail yesterday was an envelope of Xerox copies." He paused. "No return address. Grand Central Station postmark." He spread his large hands. "No note. Just the copies." He paused again. "It could be somebody's idea of a joke."

"Do you think that?"

Giddings shook his head slowly. "I don't."

"Neither," Nat said, "do I."

9

3:10–4:03

Watching the arriving guests and the still orderly crowds behind the barricades, considering the waving signs in all their shades of meaning or non-meaning, Patrolman Barnes said, "Security. Ten years ago, Mike, did you ever hear the word?"

"The name of the game," Shannon said, as if the cliché explained everything. He was a fine figure of a man and conscious of it. In front of the barricades he did not exactly strut, but neither did he try to make himself inconspicuous. "You not only read too much, Frank, you think too much."

" 'Free the Russian Jews,' " Barnes read from a nearby waving sign. "The last time I saw that sign was in the UN plaza."

"With today's prices," Shannon said, "you save what you can to use over and over again. At the ballpark you see the same banners game after game."

"Not quite the same," Barnes said. He was smiling. He

and Mike Shannon got along fine, and if there was disparity between them in education or even quickness of intellect, well, what of it? Other factors, like ease, rapport, and loyalty, were far more important. "Have you been inside this building at all, Mike?"

Shannon had not. It was not exactly that a building is a building is a building, although some of that concept did color his thinking: it was rather that in the city there are so many buildings, as there are so many neighborhoods, that a man could drive himself daft trying to keep up with them all and did best to mind his own business in his own familiar areas. He said as much. "But you," he said, and shook his head, "you take in too much territory, Frank. It isn't healthy." He paused. "What about the inside of this building? What sets it apart?" He paused again and looked heavenward. "Aside from its size?"

"A central security desk," Barnes said. "There is that word again. It's a command post in touch with every floor. There's a computer center that controls temperature and humidity and heaven knows what all throughout the whole building. The fire doors to the stairwells are locked electronically, but if there is an emergency, they automatically open from the stair side. There is a double fire-alarm system that can be activated from any floor—" He was silent, smiling faintly.

"And what is funny?" Shannon said.

"I heard a story once," Barnes said. "The airplane of the future. It takes off from Heathrow Airport near London. It tucks up its flaps and gear and swings its wings into supersonic position. Then a voice comes on the loudspeaker: 'Welcome aboard, ladies and gentlemen,' the voice says. 'This is Flight One Hundred, London to New York. We will fly at an altitude of sixty-three thousand feet, at a speed of seven hundred twenty miles an hour, and we will arrive at Kennedy Airport at precisely three-fifty-five New York time. This is the most advanced aircraft in the world. It is entirely automated, and there is no pilot aboard. All operations of the aircraft are handled electronically, all contingencies have been anticipated, and nothing can possibly go wrong go wrong go wrong . . . wrong.' "

Shannon shook his head. "I don't know where you get them," he said.

Grover Frazee, that fresh carnation in his buttonhole, waited hatless and smiling at the foot of the platform steps in the Tower Plaza, as automobile after automobile drew up in the cleared street lane to discharge its passengers. Every one of them wore, Frazee thought, the expression that is reserved for weddings, parliament or legislature openings, to dedications. Oh, yes, and for funerals. Now where did that thought come from?

He stepped forward, hand outstretched. "Mr. Ambassador," he said, "how generous of you to take the time to come here today."

"I vould not have missed it, Mr. Frazee. This huge beautiful building dedicated to man's communication with man—" The ambassador shook his head in admiration.

Senator John Peters had shared a taxi from LaGuardia with Representative Cary Wycoff. They had flown up from Washington together on a shuttle, and part of their conversation stuck in Cary Wycoff's mind. The conversation had begun idly enough while they were still on the ground at National Airport.

"Time was," the senator had said as they fastened their seat belts, "when it was the railroad or nothing. Back before the war. You don't remember that, do you?"

Cary Wycoff did not. He was thirty-four years old, in his second term in Congress, and even the Korean War was before his time, let alone World War II, which obviously Jake Peters was referring to. "You are pulling rank on me, Senator," Cary said.

The senator grinned. "Pure envy. I'd like to be your age again, just starting out."

"Now," Cary asked, "or then?" He had never thought of it before in quite this way, but was the wish for renewed youth pure nostalgia or simply a desire to stick around and see what came next? Sheer selfishness or intelligent curiosity?

"Now," the senator said with emphasis. "I have no hankering for the past. I went down to Washington in thirty-six. Depression is only a word now. It was a pustulating sickness then, and no matter how much we told ourselves we were making progress in curing it, actually all we were doing was feeding the patient aspirin and putting Band-Aids on his open sores and hoping to God he wouldn't die on our hands."

Against this kind of elder statesman talk Cary always felt defensive. "We have problems today," he said. "You won't deny it?"

"Oh, hell, son, you know better than that. But the difference is that today we have the means to improve things. We have the knowledge, the wealth, the production, the distribution, the communication—above all, the communication—and what we had then was damn little more than hysteria and despair."

"The knowledge?" Cary said. "It seems to me—"

"I used the word advisedly," the senator said sharply. "Knowledge we have. The question is whether we have the *wisdom* to use it properly. That's why I'd like to be your age again, just starting out, but in a world that could be a better world than it's ever been since Eve gave Adam that apple. Only I doubt if it was an apple; I never heard of apples in Mesopotamia, where the Garden of Eden is supposed to have been. Ever think of that?"

Cary had not. Thinking about it now, he was amused, not so much by the question as by the senator's adroitness in bringing it up and thereby switching the conversation without even seeming to shift gears.

Jake Peters was an anomaly: he spoke with a big-city working-class accent that was almost the "dese," "dem," and "dose" type, but his erudition in astonishing areas could rock you right back on your heels. If you argued with Jake Peters, as a long list of his Senate colleagues could testify, you did well to have your homework letter-perfect.

The senator was already off on another subject. "I don't know about you," he said, "but I almost didn't come today." He smiled. "Ever get hunches, son?"

Cary Wycoff did, but disliked admitting it. "Now, Senator," he said.

"Oh, I'm not clairvoyant," the senator said. He was smiling. "And I've known Bent Armitage a long time and this means a lot to him." He paused. The smile faded. "At least I think it does. I never asked him."

"I should think," Cary Wycoff said, "that it means a lot to many people. A new building means new jobs, new businesses attracted into the city, more taxes—"

"You see it black-and-white, don't you?" the senator said.

It was a sore point. Cary Wycoff regarded himself as liberal in view and political position, and yet to his dismay occasionally, as now, the charge of tunnel vision cropped up and he did not know how to refute it. "I don't try to stifle dissent, Senator," he said. And he added, "As some do."

"If you think you're sticking your finger in my eye, son," the senator said easily, "think again." There was an air of circuit-rider righteousness in young Wycoff, as in other congressmen and even presidential candidates the senator could name, and he had long ago decided that argument with them was futile. A man totally convinced of his own rectitude saw only heresy in any other view.

"If a man believes in what he says or does," Cary Wycoff said, "I believe he should be allowed—"

"To do what? Commit violence? Destroy records? Set bombs?" The senator watched Wycoff's indecision.

"Our own revolution," Cary said at last, "was violent dissent, wasn't it?"

"It was," the senator said. "But if those who launched it and carried it out had lost instead of winning, they would have had to take the consequences, however noble a document the Declaration was and is. They were laying their heads on the block and they knew it."

"Then," Cary said, "morality is decided by whether you win or lose? Is that it?" There was scorn in his voice.

"That," the senator said, "has been argued for a long time, and I don't pretend to know the answer." He smiled. "What I do know is that when somebody takes the law

87

into his own hands and because of it somebody else is injured, I don't hold with total amnesty."

"You don't believe in turning the other cheek?" Cary was sure he had scored a debating point.

"I've known times," the senator said, "when all that got a man was two black eyes instead of one—and he still had to fight." He leaned forward to poke a bill over the cab driver's shoulder. "Hunch or not, here we are."

They stepped out of the taxi and walked between the barricades toward the platform. Signs waved. A few voices began an unintelligible chant.

"Cops all over the place," Cary Wycoff said. "You'd think there was a threat of some kind."

"I would have thought," the senator said, "that you would call them fuzz." And then, "Grover," he said, "you picked a fine day for it."

"Welcome, Jake," Frazee said. "And Cary. You're in good time. We're about to start the teethclicking."

All three men smiled.

"Up you go on the platform," Frazee said. "Sort yourselves out. I'll be right up."

"I take it," the senator said, "that you want brief mention of God, motherhood, and man's future—without political overtones?"

Frazee smiled again. "Precisely."

The building was equipped with a closed-circuit television net that could scan every floor, every subbasement. But on this day, the building not yet open to the public, the security desks were unmanned and the television systems were dead.

The point had been argued, but economy had carried the weight. The World Tower, it was said, was no Fort Knox with untold wealth in gold piled high for the taking. Not yet.

Later, when the building was occupied, fully tenanted (Grover Frazee had winced at the thought and at the use of the manufactured word), security would become a problem, as it is in all of the city's large buildings, and the expense of that security would be accepted as a matter of routine.

Later, all of the security desks would be manned day and night, and the closed-circuit television would maintain its ceaseless vigil. But not yet. Not today.

But even today, as for many months since the building's skeleton of structural steel had begun to be fleshed out and clothed, the computer center was manned. Consider the analogy of the heart beating in the fetus, well before birth supplying nutriment and life force to the developing organism.

Here at the semicircular desk facing the blinking lights, the rotating spools, and the rows of instrument dials, one man watched over the health of the great structure.

Floor 65, northwest corridor, required additional cooling air—was there a leak of some kind allowing outside heat to enter? A question to examine tomorrow, in the meantime, more washed, cooled air to the northwest corridor.

Floor 125, the Tower Room, in anticipation of the flood of reception guests with their concomitant BTUs, each human a walking heat machine, was already cooled two degrees below normal.

The pressure of the electric current into the building from the Con Edison substation held steady. The flow would fluctuate as automated systems turned on and off.

From the step-down transformers, all voltages were steady within their normal limits.

Elevator No. 35, local floors 44–54, was still shut down for repair; it showed dead on the panel.

In the subbasements automated systems functioned, motors hummed softly, standby generators waited with their massive built-in patience.

All systems normal. All systems go. The man in the padded swivel chair facing the great panel could relax and almost doze.

His name was Henry Barber and he lived in Washington Heights with a wife, Helen, three children, Ann, 10, Jody, 7, and Peter, 3, and Helen's mother, 64. Barber had a degree in electrical engineering from Columbia. His hobbies were chess, pro football, and the old movies shown at the Museum of Modern Art. He was thirty-six years old. He never became any older.

Mercifully, he never knew what hit him: the blow from the eighteen-inch wrecking bar shattered his skull, he was almost instantly dead and therefore totally insensitive to what happened later.

John Connors stood for a few moments, studying the blinking lights of the control panel. Then he left the quiet room and went on down the stairs to the subbasement where the electrical cables entered the building from the nearby substation. There, door closed, secure from interruption, he sat quietly, from time to time glancing at his watch.

The question he had asked himself earlier was still in his mind, answered satisfactorily now. He repeated it over and over again with pleasure as he studied the massive electrical cables and the brooding transformers: Why bunt, when a triple would clear the bases?

"Swing away," he whispered. "Swing for the fences."

In the plaza the band played "The Star-Spangled Banner" and protest signs waved to the rhythm.

Rabbi Stein prayed that the building with its communications potential be an instrument of peace for all mankind.

In a corner of the plaza, subtly contained by a few uniformed police, a mixed group, Arabs and non-Arabs, chanted for justice in Palestine.

Monsignor O'Toole blessed the building.

Signs calling for birth control and nationwide legalized abortion sprouted like crocuses in early spring.

The Reverend Arthur William Williams called for celestial blessing, peace, and prosperity.

Signs appeared demanding taxation of church-owned property.

The Reverend Joe Willie Thomas attempted to climb the steps to the platform microphones and was restrained. From the foot of the steps he denounced idolatry.

Grover Frazee acted as master of ceremonies.

The governor spoke. He praised the buildings purpose.
The mayor spoke in favor of brotherhood of man.

Senator Jake Peters praised progress.

Congressman Cary Wycoff spoke of the benefits the building would bring to the city.

A ribbon across one of the concourse doors was cut in full view of television and still cameras. It was hastily replaced and cut a second time when it was learned that NBC-TV had missed the shot.

The invited guests flowed through the door and into two automated express elevators for the less-than-two-minute trip to the highest room in the tallest building in the world where the bar tables were already set up, candles lighted, canapes set out, champagne was chilled and ready, and waiters and waitresses stood by.

Part II

"The important thing to remember is that with high enough temperatures, anything will burn, anything!"
—ASSISTANT FIRE COMMISSIONER
TIMOTHY O'REILLY BROWN,
speaking to the press

10

In the Tower Room, drink in hand, "I have absolutely nothing against holy men per se," the governor was saying to Grover Frazee, "but some of them do take the bit in their teeth and go on and on and on."

"Would you care to have that quoted to the state electorate?" Frazee said. He felt better, easier, more relaxed than he had all day. Will Giddings had depressed him; there was no denying it. But with congratulations coming in now from all sides, the sense of depression had faded and then disappeared altogether. Looking contentedly around the room, "Might cost you some votes," he said.

"You know," the governor said, "I'm not sure I'd give a damn. I have a ranch out in the mountains in northern New Mexico. The ranch house sits at eight thousand feet on a green meadow. There's a trout stream, and from the ranch house porch a view of thirteen-thousand-foot mountains that never lose their snow." He too looked around the crowded room. "The ranch looks better and better all the time." He caught the eye of a passing waiter. "Bring me another bourbon and water, son, if you please." And then again to Grover Frazee. "I've even switched from Scotch." He smiled as the mayor walked up. "Ah, Bob," he said.

"I thought it went quite well," the mayor said. "Congratulations, Grover."

"Your remarks on the brotherhood of man laid them in the aisles, Bob," the governor said. "As I pointed out earlier, it is those carefully prepared impromptu comments that do the trick." There were times when the governor felt almost ashamed baiting Bob Ramsay; it was, as they said in his adopted West, as easy as shooting fish in a rain barrel, too easy. "Where's your good lady?"

"Over by the windows." The mayor's voice was fond. "Admiring the view. Do you know that on a clear day—"

"Do we have clear days any more?" the governor said. And then, "Strike that. I'm thinking of something else." Of limitless blue skies and mountains clearly visible a hundred miles away, turning purple in the dusk; of vast quiet and a sense of peace. The governor felt suddenly sentimental. "You've been married how long, Bob?"

"Thirty-five years."

The mayor examined the statement for barbs. There appeared to be none. "I am." He glanced in his wife's direction.

"And who is that with her?" the governor said.

"One of your boosters, a cousin of mine. Her name is Beth Shirley." The mayor was smiling now. "Interested?"

"Lead me to her," the governor said.

She was tall, this Beth Shirley, with calm blue eyes and auburn hair. She nodded acknowledgment of the introduction and then waited for the governor to set the conversational pace.

"All I know about you," the governor said, "is that you are Bob Ramsay's cousin and you vote the right ticket. What else should I know?"

Her smile was slow, matching the calm of her eyes. "That depends, Governor, on what you have in mind."

"At my age—" the governor began. He shook his head.

"I don't think your life has stopped yet," Beth said. The smile spread. "At least that is not the picture I've always had of you. Don't disappoint me, please."

The governor thought about it. He said at last, his smile matching her own, "You know, I think the last thing I want in this world is to disappoint you." Strangely enough it was true. It was, he decided, the old goat in him coming out. "And," he added, "if that sounds ridiculous, why, let it. I've ben ridiculous before. Many times."

Talk swirled around them, but for the moment they were alone. "Your ability to laugh at yourself," Beth said, "is one of the things I've always admired in you."

Man's capacity to absorb flattery, the governor had always thought, is without limit. "Tell me more."

"Bob Ramsay cannot laugh at himself."

"Then he ought not to be in politics. The President of the United States can't laugh at himself either, and we're all the losers for it."

"You might have been President. You came close."

"We used to say," the governor said, "that close only counts in horseshoes, and then you have to be damn close. The presidency is a spin of the wheel. Few men ever get a first chance and almost none a second. I had my shot at it. There won't be another, and that's that." Why was he thinking so often today of that trout stream winding through the foot of the meadow, and the scent of evergreens in the high clear air? "Do you know the West?"

"I went to the University of Colorado."

"Did you, by God!" Whoever arranged these chance meetings, the governor thought, probably knocked themselves out laughing at man's conceit that he controlled his own destiny. "Do you know northern New Mexico?"

"I've skied and ridden in the mountains."

The governor took a deep breath. "Do you fish?"

"Only trout fishing. In streams."

It was then that Senator Peters walked up, champagne glass in hand. "Always you've been against monopolies, Bent," the senator said, "but here you are monopolizing."

"Go away, Jake." The intimate spell was broken. The governor sighed. "You won't, of course. You never go away. You're a bad conscience in the middle of the night. Miss Shirley, Senator Peters. Now tell me what you want, and then go away."

"You've been picking on Bob Ramsay." There was a twinkle in the senator's eye.

"Only to the extent," the governor said, "of putting him in the presence of a new idea. It had to do with dinosaurs."

"Bob is uncomfortable in the presence of new ideas."

"Miss Shirley is his cousin," the governor said.

The senator smiled and nodded acknowledgment. "I apologize." He paused, and then, in partial explanation, "Bent and I," he said, "have known each other for a long time. We speak the same language, except that we don't always agree, and his accent is better than mine. We worked our way through the same college and law school, Bent a little later than I. I waited on tables and drove a crew launch. Bent was more imaginative: he set up a laundry business and lived like a prince."

"And," Beth said, "Bob's way through prep school and Yale was paid by his family." She nodded her understanding of the implications.

"Bob loves this city," the senator said. "I honor him for that. He's as proud of this building as if he'd put it up himself."

"And you are not, Senator?"

"My dear," the senator said, "I'm an old-fashioned practical idealist. And if that sounds contradictory—"

"It isn't," the governor said. "In the trade union movement they call what Jake wants for his constituency pork chops—higher wages, benefits." He paused. "Not fancy buildings, am I right, Jake?"

The senator nodded. "Bob said you mentioned dinosaur stables."

The governor nodded in his turn, wary now. "Does that offend you, Jake? It's your city too."

"No offense. You fought this building, but you own a piece of it too."

"If you can't whip them," the governor said, "it is a good idea to sign on with them." He showed his fangs. "And Grover can be a persuasive fellow."

"How are rentals going?"

"As far as I know, very well." Only a slight untruth; the governor said it with ease.

"I hear different."

"You can hear what you want to hear, Jake. Nobody knows that better than you."

The senator hesitated. A waiter passed and the senator stopped him. "Take this stuff," he said, "and let me

98

have some honest whiskey." He set the champagne glass on the tray. "I never can hold my pinky right for champagne drinking," he said.

The governor said, "What's really on your mind, Jake?"

The senator hesitated again. "There's Cary Wycoff, bright-eyed and bushy-tailed, concerned about mankind's ills, which is fine. I told him we had today the means to cure them." His sudden gesture took in the room, the people, the bar and the circulating waiters and waitresses, the talk and the laughter, and, quiet accompaniment, piped-in music playing through concealed speakers above the air-conditioning's soft hum. "This is what we use our means for, a building to make a few people a lot of money. Or for a war, weapons to kill more people."

"I recommend two Alka-Seltzer," the governor said.

The senator smiled faintly. "I deserve that, Bent. I admit it. But I can't shake it. 'And doomed to death, though fated not to die.' In school I never knew what Dryden meant by that. Today I think I do."

"Maybe two Alka-Seltzer *and* a Di-Gel," the governor said. "You've got to break up those gas bubbles."

The senator was not to be distracted. "What you were saying to Bob Ramsay today," he said to the governor. "You probably have a point. Look." He gestured this time at the broad expanse of windows, looking out and down on lesser but still giant buildings in the foreground, the gleaming water of the river and upper harbor, the land of the far shore drifting off into industrial haze, smog.

The governor said, unsmiling now, "It's a mess, isn't it?"

"It is time we handed over, Bent," the senator said.

The governor's chin came up. "To young Cary Wycoff? To the paraders and protestors, those who are only *against*, never *for*?" The governor shook his head. He was looking again at the countryside spread before them, the rich, innovative, powerful, plundered countryside. "We've messed it up," he said. "I won't deny it. But in messing it up, we still have constructed something strong, durable, something around which we've built a nation." He smiled suddenly at Beth. "Do I sound like a politician? Don't answer that. I am."

"I'll vote for you," the senator said. He was smiling. "Good solid campaign oratory, Bent."

And Beth said in protest, "But I think the governor means it."

Jake Peters nodded. "He does. We all do, my dear. At least most of us. And there is the tragedy: the gap between belief—conviction—and performance." He looked around. "Where is that waiter with my whiskey? I'll go find him."

The governor and Beth stood quiet, together, and it was again as if a curtain had been drawn, shutting them off from the rest of the reception guests. Both recognized the illusion, neither questioned it.

"I was married once," the governor said. It seemed a perfectly natural thing to say. "A long time ago."

"I know."

The governor's eyebrows rose. "How do you know, Beth Shirley?"

"Your *Who's Who* entry. Her name was Pamela Brown and she died in nineteen fifty. You have a married daughter, Jane, who lives in Denver. She was born in nineteen forty-six—"

"Which," the governor said, "can't have been much after your birthdate."

"Is that a question?" Beth was smiling. "I was born ten years earlier." She paused. "And you won't find me in *Who's Who*, so I'll tell you that I was married once too. It was a disaster. I was warned, but warnings are usually worse than useless, aren't they? I think more times than not they produce the opposite effect. I married John at least partly because I had been warned, and I got what they had told me I would—a thirty-five-year-old son instead of a husband."

"I'm sorry," the governor said. He smiled suddenly. "Or maybe I'm not. I like it the way it is, your standing here talking to me." He saw Grover Frazee making his way through the guests, an unconvincing smile on his face. "Brace yourself," the governor said quietly. "We are about to be interrupted, damn it." Then, "Hello, Grover."

Frazee said, "I want to talk to you, Bent."

"You are talking to me." The governor's voice was

100

unenthusiastic. "Miss Shirley, Mr. Frazee. Grover's is the steeltrap mind behind the World Tower project."

"I'm serious," Frazee said. "We have a problem." He looked hesitantly at Beth. "I'd rather—"

"I'll leave," Beth said.

The governor caught her arm. "You will not. I'll never find you again." He looked at Frazee. "What's the problem? Spit it out, Grover. Stop mumbling."

Frazee hesitated. He said at last, "We have a fire. Somewhere on one of the lower floors. Oh, it isn't much, but there's a little smoke in the air-conditioning and Bob Ramsay and the fire commissioner are on the phone about it, so I'm sure it will be cleared up in no time."

"Then," the governor said slowly, "why tell me, Grover?"

Ben Caldwell walked up, small, almost dainty, precise. His face was expressionless. "I heard the question," he said. He spoke directly to the governor. "Grover is jumpy. He knows that there may have been certain irregularities in the building's construction. He is worried."

"And," the governor said, "you're not?"

The governor is a commander, Beth thought, watching, listening silently. He wastes no time in nonessentials; his questions probe.

Ben Caldwell said, "I don't make up my mind on insufficient evidence, but I am not worried, and I see no cause for worry. I know the design of this building, and a small fire—" He shrugged.

The governor looked at Frazee. "You want your hand held while you're told what to do? Very well. Take the fire commissioner's judgment, and if he thinks it is prudent to get this room evacuated promptly, then, by God, see to it, no matter what kind of press—"

It was then, without warning, with, some said later, an almost convulsive shudder of the entire great building, that the lights went out, the softly humming air-conditioning stopped, the music was silenced, and all conversation was stilled. Somewhere in the room a woman screamed.

The time was 4:23.

101

11

The fire sending the smoke into the air-conditioning ducts was small, and in the normal course of events ought to have been quickly and automatically extinguished.

It was in Suite 452, fourth floor, southeast corridor. The suite, already rented, was in the process of being decorated. Messrs. Zimmer and Schloss, the interior designers, did not believe in latex paint. There was something almost indecent in the ease with which a painter could clean his brushes in nothing more than soap and water. And the colors simply did not *sing!*

Suite 452 then, was being decorated with traditional oil-base paint. Gallon cans of paint thinner were on the floor in the center of the inner room beneath a plywood board resting on two sawhorses which the painters used as a table.

Oily rags igniting in spontaneous combustion were later believed to have started the blaze. A gallon of paint thinner apparently exploded from the heat and threw burning liquid in all directions.

The overhead sprinklers came on, but the plywood board protected the heart of the fire for a time while it gathered strength; and in any event water does not easily contain a fire of paint thinner, which like flaming gasoline merely spreads on the water and continues to burn. But without the protection of the plywood it is probable that the first tiny flames would have been smothered.

A warning light showed on the computer-control panel in the bowels of the building, but there was no one to see it.

The air-conditioning ducts in Suite 452 continued to

bring in a fresh supply of air to provide oxygen for the flames.

New paint on the walls caught fire. More paint thinner cans exploded from increasing heat.

The air-conditioning stepped up its efforts to control the temperature, thereby bringing in more oxygen. Smoke began to seep through the entire system and at length reached the Tower Room ducting.

But even at this point there was no real danger or even major problem.

Primary systems went into almost immediate operation; backup systems stood by against their need.

Automatic alarms sounded in the firehouse only two blocks away. Within less than three minutes two fire trucks were on the scene, working their way through thinning crowds in the plaza.

Promptly the crowds began to gather again, hampering the firemen's work. Police, Shannon and Barnes among them, moved the crowds behind the still-standing barricades. A kind of order was restored.

High up on the building's gleaming side a plume of smoke appeared, dark and ugly against the sky. Strangers in the crowd pointed it out to one another, not infrequently with glee; there is a kind of joy in discovering that the high and mighty have their problems too.

On the television screen in Charlie's Bar, the camera had begun the incredibly long climb up the building's face, floor after floor, the whole foreshortening as the angle steepened.

"Beautiful damn thing," Giddings said. "I hate to admit it to you, but it is. And we'll find out tomorrow about those goddamned change authorizations, run them down, get things straight. I've talked with Bert McGraw and he says he'll do whatever, and what Bert says, Bert does." He was feeling almost friendly now. "You're a prickly bastard sometimes, Nat Wilson, but I'll have to say, even if you do get funny ideas, that by and large you know your trade. You—"

Giddings stopped suddenly. His eyes were still on the

TV screen. The camera now had reached the tower. It paused there, shiny structure plain, blue, blue sky the backdrop.

Giddings said in a voice that was not quite steady, "What's that little plume of smoke? Just there. Below the tower."

"I see it," Nat said. He stared.

"Air-conditioning exhaust," Giddings said. "Somewhere there's smoke inside, and that means— Where do you think you're going?"

Nat was halfway out of the booth. Giddings grabbed a fistful of Nat's jacket and held it tight. "You son of a bitch," Giddings said. His voice was low now. "You knew too much. All along, you—"

Nat broke the big man's grasp with astonishing ease. He slid out of the booth and stood up. "I'm going to the job," he said. "Are you coming or are you going to sit there on your fat ass?"

In the center of the plaza a battalion chief with a white hat directed operations through a bullhorn. Hoses snaked across the pavement. Water was beginning to gather in puddles on the concourse floor.

At the barricade, "Nobody allowed through," Patrolman Shannon said. And then, "Well, what do you know? It's you again."

"Just get the hell out of the way," Giddings said, and started forward.

Patrolman Frank Barnes appeared, his dark face solemn. "Easy, Mike," he said to Shannon. And then to Giddings and Nat, "Orders. I am sorry."

And here came a new siren sound wailing up the street, a black limousine, red light flashing. Assistant Fire Commissioner Brown was out of the car before it stopped. He was hatless and his red hair flamed. He walked with the awkward stride of a long-legged animal; a stork came to mind, an angry stork. He stopped in front of Nat.

"Were you just guessing or did you know this was going to happen?"

It was a question that was going to be asked again and

again, Nat thought, and knew no way to stop it. "Does it matter now?" he said. "You've got a fire and we're here to do what we can."

"Which is exactly what?"

"I don't know, but between us we know this building better than anyone who isn't inside it." He was thinking of Ben Caldwell, of course, and Bert McGraw. But they were top echelon. He and Giddings were the men on the job with the intimate knowledge only day after day and month after month of living with the structure could provide. "And," he said, "maybe better than they do at that."

"All right," Brown said. "Come on, but stay out of the way."

Shannon opened his mouth to protest. Frank Barnes held him silent with a gesture. "Good luck," Barnes said. He paused. "I mean that."

Brown walked straight to the white-hatted battalion chief in the center of the plaza. "What's the story?"

"We haven't found where it started, yet. Third floor, fourth floor." The chief shrugged. "It had a start, just the hell of a start, too much of a start."

Giddings said, "Sprinklers?"

The chief looked at him carefully. "Sprinklers," he said, and he nodded. "They help. Most fires that start they contain. This one they didn't."

"And that," Nat said, "means what?"

"I wouldn't know what it means," the chief said. "When its all over, I hope, we may be able to find out. Sprinklers just make some fires worse. Potassium, sodium, electrical fires, gasoline fires—water can be bad."

Nat said slowly, "Potassium, sodium—that means a bomb?"

"Possibly." The chief raised his bullhorn. "More hose! Move it in!" He lowered the bullhorn. "The smoke's heavy and that could mean anything too."

Giddings said, "You said electrical fire was a possibility too." He looked at Nat.

"God knows," Nat said. "Third floor, fourth floor—"

He shook his head. "They're not mechanical floors." He was silent.

Brown said, "The Commissioner's up in the Tower Room. And the mayor."

"And," Giddings said, "more other brass than you can count."

Brown ignored him. To the chief, "Shall we bring them down? There's a phone. And just two of those express elevators will do it."

"It's a hell of a walk," Giddings said, "in case you're thinking of getting them down any other way. That building core where the elevators are is safe as anything can be."

They felt, then, rather than heard the sudden explosion almost beneath their feet. Sound, dull and distant, came a moment later, like a closet door closing hollowly with enormous force. The puddles of water on the concourse floor rippled gently. The interior lights were suddenly dead.

Giddings said softly, "Jesus!"

Brown looked at Nat. "That means what?"

Nat closed his eyes. He opened them again and shook his head to clear away the cobwebs of shock. He said slowly, "The guts of the building are down there, everything that drives it and makes it live."

"Down in those subbasements," the battalion chief said, "is where the primary power comes in, right?"

Nat nodded.

Giddings said again, "Jesus!"

"Right from the substation," the battalion chief said. "At eight, ten thousand volts." He raised the bullhorn and sent men scurrying down into the bowels of the building.

"Thirteen thousand eight hundred, to be precise," Nat said. "And I'm not an electrical engineer, but if somebody monkeyed with those big transformers, oh my God!" He was silent, motionless, staring into the concourse. "Come on," he said softly, "come on!"

Brown was frowning. "Come on who, what?"

"Standby generators," Giddings said. "If they function, we'll at least have power for the elevators."

Brown said quietly, "And if they don't?"

"Then," Nat said, "you've got a Tower Room filled with important people a hundred and twenty-five floors above a fire. And if it gets out of control—"

"It won't," the battalion chief said.

"It will," Giddings was looking at Nat. "What are you thinking?"

"That was an explosion," Nat said. "Bomb? Maybe. But what about an enormous short in a primary circuit? You've heard a hundred-and-ten-volt light fixture short out?"

There was silence. Giddings said, "Go on, goddammit, what are you thinking?"

"I told you I wasn't an electrical engineer," Nat said, "but, damn it, what about an overload because of a short? How long does it take with that kind of power to overheat wiring—particularly if it's substandard wiring?"

The battalion chief said, "Substandard?" He looked from one man to another.

"We don't know," Nat said. His voice was quiet, almost resigned. "I haven't heard a standby generator starting up. Maybe we wouldn't."

"And maybe we would too, and it hasn't functioned," Giddings said. "Maybe it was damaged too. Computer control should have—"

"Should have, shouldn't have," Nat said. He was thinking of Ben Caldwell's comment. "The words have no meaning."

A fireman came stumbling out of the nearest concourse door, vomiting. Once in the open air he stopped and stood wearily, bent almost double, retching helplessly. He saw the battalion chief, and he straightened up and wiped his mouth and chin with the back of his hand. "Bad down there." The words were almost incoherent. "The whole— like a ship's engine room—burning." He paused for another retching spasm. Black vomit dribbled down his chin. "We found one man," he said. "Fried like bacon." He paused. "And at what looks like a computer panel there's another one—dead."

An ambulance attendant led the fireman away.

Brown was looking at Nat. "What about that sub-standard wiring and a big short-circuit overheating it?"

"What he means," the battalion chief said, "is that instead of a fire in the subbasement and another on the above-grade floors that we know about, we may have a hundred potential fires from buried wiring that burst its insulation when an overload hit." He was looking at the building's gigantic face in awe.

"It couldn't happen," Brown said.

The battalion chief looked at him. "Yeah," the chief said. "I know. None of this could happen." He paused. He said slowly, "But maybe, just maybe, it has."

Brown looked again at Nat. His question was wordless, but plain.

"What do we do now?" Nat said. "We try to figure out what's happened. We toss ideas to Joe Lewis the electrical engineer and he does with them what he can. We try to figure out some way to get those people down even if they have to come down on their asses because their legs won't hold out. You people keep doing what you can, and we'll try to think." He spread his hands. "What else is there to do?"

4:23–4:34

Even with the fluorescent lights dead, there was ample light coming through the tinted windows in the Tower Room and the candles still burned. The governor said to Ben Caldwell, "What does it mean? No lights? No power at all?" His voice was steady, his tone almost accusatory.

"I don't know," Caldwell said.

"You're the architect. Find out."

The governor was the man in command, Beth Shirley

108

thought, and took comfort from the concept. What was that old song from *South Pacific*—"Some Enchanted Evening"? Listening to him in this moment of crisis as he took command without hesitation, it was difficult to control what she felt—like a schoolgirl with her first sudden crush. Well, so be it. She put her hand gently on the governor's forearm.

"It's all right," the governor said immediately. "We'll get it sorted out, whatever it is."

"I know you will, Governor."

"My name," the governor said, "is Bent. Don't ever use the title again." He took time to favor Beth with a swift grin. Then, to Grover Frazee who had not stirred, "Where is the Fire Commissioner? And Bob Ramsay? You said you have a telephone. Lead the way."

Across the broad, no longer silent room, on all sides conversation buzzing, Beth on the governor's arm, Grover Frazee leading the parade. Someone said, "What is it, Governor? Can you tell us?" And there was sudden silence in the vicinity.

The governor paused and raised his voice. "We don't know yet. But we'll find out, and when we do, you'll be told. That's a promise." Again that familiar grin. "Not a campaign promise," he added. It got a small murmur of amusement. They went on, following Frazee.

It was a pleasant office abutting the building's core, dimly lighted now by two candles. The mayor was at the desk, telephone at his ear. He nodded to the governor and said into the phone, "Then get him. I want a report from Assistant Commissioner Brown in person, is that understood?" He hung up.

Frazee said, "What do we do? Do we clear the room?" He spoke to the mayor and to the fire commissioner, who stood large and solid beside the desk chair.

"You heard the man," the governor said. "Before we do anything, we find out where we stand, how it looks from outside. We know there is a fire—"

"It wasn't the fire that shook this building," the fire commissioner said. There was truculence in his tone. "Unless there was an ammunition dump somewhere.

109

We've got other trouble and I want to know what before we let anybody go anywhere." ·

"Nobody's arguing," the governor said. "But there are some things we can do up here while we wait. Are the elevators operable? There should be standby power, shouldn't there?"

"There sure as hell ought to be," the fire commissioner said, "but I haven't seen any indication of it." His truculence had faded. He watched the governor and waited.

"Stairs," the governor said. "There are fire stairs, aren't there?"

"Two sets," the commissioner nodded.

"All right," the governor said. "Grover, have Ben Caldwell check the elevators. You check the stairs. Oh, yes, and have those waiters start passing drinks again. We don't want a bunch of drunks, but we don't want panic either. Get moving, man, and come back here before you tell anybody anything." He paused and looked down at the mayor. "It's your city, Bob. Objections?"

The mayor smiled faintly. "You seem to be in charge. Carry on."

If the governor felt the faint proud pressure of Beth's hand on his arm, he gave no indication. "It's probably nothing to get concerned about," he said, "but let's play it straight anyway."

Senator Peters walked in, nodded to the room in general, and leaned against the wall. "There was this young bank robber," he said without preamble in his normal voice and harsh accent. "His first job and he was uptight. He had his mask on and he rushed into the bank waving his gun. 'All right, you motherstickers,' he said, 'this is a fuckup!' "

Some of the tension went out of the room. The governor looked at Beth. She was smiling at the crudity. "That's our Jake," the governor said. "He can quote Shakespeare too, by the yard. He alters his repertoire to fit the situation." He paused. "You are getting a cram course in behind-the-scenes-and-the-speeches politics, aren't you?" He was smiling too. "Disillusioning?"

110

"No." She shook her head slowly in emphasis. "You are the people in charge. I am content."

"Lady—" the commissioner began, and stopped at the sudden ringing of the telephone.

The mayor picked it up, spoke his name, listened briefly. "All right, Brown," he said. "I'll put the commissioner on. Give him your report." He paused. "The whole report, no punches pulled, is that understood?" He handed the phone to the fire commissioner.

The senator said, "When somebody's on the phone and you can hear only his side of the conversation—" He shook his head. "I never know whether to look at him or stare out the window." Then, with no change of tone, "Quite a little party you people are throwing, Bent." He was remembering his vague hunch back in Washington.

"In case you were wondering," the governor said, "it wasn't planned quite this way."

"Understood," the senator said. "The topless waitresses failed to show, so you had to do something, no?"

Ben Caldwell walked in. He looked at the fire commissioner on the phone, glanced around at the rest, and nodded without expression. He said nothing.

The governor said, "Where's Bert McGraw? He ought to have been here."

"McGraw," the mayor said, "had a heart attack. That's all I know."

The governor closed his eyes briefly. When he opened them again, he said softly, "I always thought of him as indestructible."

"We're none of us getting younger, Bent," the senator said. "I haven't had any intimations of immortality for a long time." He was silent as the fire commissioner cupped his hand over the phone and cleared his throat.

"Brown says," the fire commissioner said, "that the fire above grade in the lower floors isn't good, but the battalion chief thinks it can be controlled. He's called in more units, equipment and men."

There was silence. Beth's hand tightened on the governor's arm. He covered it with his own.

"But the real problem," the fire commissioner said, "is

111

down in the mechanical-equipment basements. As near as they can figure—and one of your men is there, Mr. Caldwell—"

"Nat Wilson," Ben Caldwell said, "I hope."

"And," the fire commissioner said, "Will Giddings, clerk of the works, they're both there. Near as they can figure, like I said, some maniac got inside the building by pretending he was an electrician sent for some minor job. They found him down in the major transformer room, fried to a crisp. Somehow he managed to short out everything, near as they can tell, but the smoke's so thick they can't know for sure what happened except that there isn't any power."

Ben Caldwell said, "The standby generators?"

The fire commissioner raised his massive shoulders and let them fall. "There isn't any power," he said, "period."

Ben Caldwell nodded. He had lost none of his neatness or calm. "The elevators do not respond," he said. "I checked them all. There are the stairs, of course, and if the fire in the lower floors is in any way contained, as it ought to be, then the stairs will be perfectly safe. The fire doors are for just that purpose. I suggest that we start sending everybody down the stairs, half on one side, half on the other."

The governor nodded. "With marching orders," he said, "and a dozen or so men on either stairway to enforce them. No running. No panic. It's a hell of a long way down and there are going to be some who won't be able to make it on their own power and will have to be helped." He looked around the room. "It is a ridiculous way to run a railroad, I'll admit, but does anybody have a better suggestion?" He squeezed Beth's hand gently.

Grover Frazee started through the doorway and stopped. He was sweating. "The doors to the stairs," he began, and the words ran down. He tried again. "The doors to the stairs—are locked."

The fire commissioner said, "They can't be. You've got it wrong, man. There's no way—" He shook his head, raised the phone, and spoke into it. "Stay by the phone," he said. "We've got some looking to do." He hung up.

"Ben," the governor said to Caldwell, "you and the commissioner go see." He looked at Frazee. "And you come in here and sit down and pull yourself together, Grover." He looked at Beth and squeezed her hand. "I'm sorry for all this, my dear."

"In a way," Beth said, "I'm not. I don't think in any other circumstances I'd ever really have gotten to know you."

"The lady looks on the bright side of life," the senator said. "I applaud."

12

The building was in torment, gravely wounded. For a time, perhaps minutes, perhaps hours, many of its more serious wounds would not be visible, merely discernible, as in diagnosis, through sheer deduction.

There had been an explosion: that much was obvious. Much later bomb experts would assess the structural damage in the main transformer room and estimate the power of the explosive Connors had carried in his toolbox.

Plastic explosive is safe to carry: it is brownish-gray putty-like stuff that can be dropped or molded or otherwise pushed about without protest. It is set off by a probe inserted into its body and a small electric current sent through a wire to the probe. Its explosive force is almost unbelievable.

The main transformers had been badly damaged, and although the fire that started immediately after the explosion destroyed or distorted much material which might have been studied later, Joe Lewis's computers in a sense working backward from known results did a creditable job of reconstructing probable cause.

There had been a massive short-circuit in the primary

power, undoubtedly caused by the explosion. No other explanation fit the facts.

The resultant surge of uncontrolled power shot far beyond the cables thick as a man's leg designed to carry the voltage in safety, through the crippled transformers, and undiminished into wiring designed to transmit only such voltages as are required to light fluorescent fixtures or run electric typewriters.

The surge of uncontrolled power lasted only a matter of microseconds. That infinitesimal time was enough.

The result, as the battalion chief had feared, was immediate and catastrophic.

Wiring melted and in melting burst its insulation.

In some instances there were further short-circuits which, acting like arc-welders, threw the enormous heat of an open electrical spark against wall material, sound-proofing, insulation—all heat-resistant but never totally fireproof.

In the final analysis, nothing is. Far less than the ultimate heat of the sun's body will incinerate most substances. Witness Hiroshima, Nagasaki, or Hamburg.

Within the interior walls of the building, then, creeping fires developed.

Some of these would die for lack of oxygen, leaving only hotspots as their legacy.

But some would break into ducting or burst into open shafts or corridors, there to breathe deeply of fresh air, gather force and fury, and roar on, consuming paint, woodwork, fabric draperies, rugs, flooring, materials easily consumed, but also materials usually considered fire-resistant.

Overhead sprinklers, their fusible links quickly melted would come on and for a time stem the fires' spread.

But too much heat generates steam in waterpipes, which sooner or later burst, and then the sprinklers are dead.

The fires would be slowed here, slowed there, skirmishes, even battles against the multiple enemy would be won.

But from the beginning, as Joe Lewis's computers later showed, the outcome of the war was never in doubt.

114

Patty McGraw Simmons had always detested hospitals, probably, she admitted to herself, because they both frightened and embarrassed her. She was a healthy young woman and her feeling always in a hospital was that because of her obvious well-being she was resented. It was as if the silent eyes that watched her walk down the corridor were saying, "You have no right to be as you are when I am suffering. Go away."

But she could not go away this time, and that, somehow, made it worse. They had Bert McGraw in what they called the Coronary Care Unit in University Hospital, a room seen only when the door opened occasionally, a room filled with dials and shiny cabinetlike things whose use Patty could only guess at; and the bed her father lay in looking like some ancient torture rack with tubes and wires leading from it and him.

Oh, other people had heart attacks. You read about them every day. But not Bert McGraw, indestructible father and man. That concept was ridiculous, of course; it was just the Irish in her exaggerating. And yet there was more to it, at that, than could have been thought of other men.

Her first memories were of him, big and boisterous, shouting with laughter, treating Patty, as her mother said, "More like a bear cub, Bert McGraw, than like a tiny girl daughter. You'll break every bone in her body the way you fling her around."

And Patty herself had squealed denial to match Bert's "Nonsense. I'll not have her kept wrapped up in cotton wool. She loves it."

115

It was not the usual tomboy-father relationship, the way the books said. Once Patty had asked him point blank if he would rather she had been a boy. His answer, like all of his answers, was without hesitation, without guile, "Hell, no. If I had a boy, then I wouldn't have you, and that would make me a lonesome old man, it would indeed."

The door to the Coronary Care Unit opened and a nurse walked out. Patty had her brief glimpse before the door closed again without sound. A lonesome old man—the phrase was in her mind, and she could not have said why or how. A proud lonesome old man, lying helpless on a white bed.

When you are young, Patty thought, they do for you. They pick you up and brush you off and kiss you where it hurts; they are always there when you need them, and you take them for granted. Then their turn at helplessness comes along, and what can you do but sit and wait and wish that you could believe in prayer because a little simple faith would go a long way?

Mary McGraw, located at last among her good works in Queens, came walking quickly, breathlessly along the corridor. Patty rose and took her mother's hands, kissed her.

"There's nothing to say," Patty said. "He's in there." She nodded toward the closed door. "No one can see him. The doctor is a great heart man who'll tell me nothing, mabe because there is nothing to tell. Sit down."

Mary McGraw said, "He had been complaining of shortness of breath. I told him he was overweight and overworked. Maybe—"

"You'll stop right there," Patty said. "Next you'll be working it into being all your fault, which it is not." Maybe it is at least partly mine, she thought, for laying the burden of my troubles on him at lunch. And then a new thought occurred. "Paul was with him when it happened," she said. And where was Paul now?

Mary McGraw looked pleased. "I'm glad Paul was with him," she said. "He is such a fine boy, your Paul. He and your father get along so well."

116

What point, what purpose in saying otherwise? Patty was silent.

Her mother said, "Your father was always afraid you would marry some roughneck—like himself, he always said, which was not so, as he knew very well. Then when you brought Paul home, your father and I stayed awake half the night talking about him and wondering if he was the one for you. Do you remember the wedding? Of course you do. All those grand people on Paul's side and you on your father's arm—"

"Mother," Patty said, her tone almost sharp. "Daddy isn't dead. Other men have had heart attacks and recovered. You—you are talking as if he were already gone, and he isn't."

Mary McGraw was silent.

"We'll just have to see," Patty said, "that he doesn't work so hard, carry so much on his own shoulders."

Mary McGraw smiled. "Maybe Paul can help. He is young and strong, and doing very well, your father says."

"Yes." Automatic response.

"I just hope," Mary McGraw said, "that your father doesn't hear of the trouble they're having at the World Tower opening. He was to have been there, and he asked me, but I said no, all those important people, the governor and senators and congressmen and the mayor and the like, they just make me uncomfortable. But not your father. They don't impress him. He—"

"Mother," Patty said, and again her tone was commanding, "what trouble are they having?"

"It was on television. I heard about it on the T.V. when I passed through the lounge downstairs."

"We've been trying to reach you all afternoon." Unimportant now. "What kind of trouble?"

"There is smoke. A fire. Nobody seems to know." Mary was silent for a moment. And then, suddenly, "Bert! Bert! Please!" in a soft, urgent voice.

"He's going to be all right, Mother."

"Of course he is." There was quiet strength in her, now for the first time showing. Mary shook her head as if to

117

clear it, brushed back a strand of hair. "You've been here a long time, child."

"It doesn't matter."

"Waiting is the hard part." Mary smiled faintly. "It is a thing you learn." She paused. "I will stay with him now."

"You can't see him."

"He'll know I'm here. You go off. Have a cup of tea, go for a walk. Come back when you've rested a little. I'll be here."

"Mother—"

"I mean it, Mary McGraw said. "I'd rather be here alone for a bit. I'll say a few prayers for both of us." Her voice was stronger now. "Go along. Leave me with your father." Dismissal.

Outside gratefully into the bright sunlight, away from the place of, yes, think it, say it, the place of death. Not for you, Daddy, please, please. Oh, it will happen one day, but we don't think about that: we pretend that Death, that dark man, will stay in the shadows indefinitely, even when we know that he will not.

Where does one walk at such a time? To the park, greenery, trees in leaf? Where Daddy used to take you on Sunday Manhattan excursions to watch the monkeys at their antics, the sea lions enjoying themselves in their pool; to eat popcorn, too much popcorn, and perhaps ice cream as well? No, not the park.

Patty walked, and afterward had no memory of her route or direction, but compulsion of some kind must have been at work because suddenly here was the great shining World Tower she had visited so often during the years of its construction. But it was crippled now, a helpless giant, like Bert McGraw its builder; with a nasty plume of smoke standing out near its top, and here in the plaza fire hoses, so like the hoses and wires leading from Bert McGraw's bed, writhing through open doors into the concourse and disappearing in heavy smoke inside.

There were police barricades and gaping people staring like ghouls, spectators at a public execution lusting for

118

more blood, more terror. God! Patty wondered if she was going to faint.

"Are you all right, miss?" A policeman with a black face, polite, solicitous. Behind him stood another cop, scowling his concern.

"I'm fine," Patty said. "It's just"—she gestured vaguely at the tormented building—"this."

"Yes, ma'am," the black cop said. "A sad business." He paused and studied her. "Are you looking for someone?"

"I don't know who is here." Patty was conscious that her words were not making much sense and she tried to bring order out of confusion. "My father was supposed to be here. Up in the Tower Room."

"Your father, ma'am?"

"Bert McGraw. He built the building."

The big Irish cop grinned suddenly. "A fine man, miss."

"He's in the hospital with a heart attack." It was a conversation from Alice in Wonderland: each statement sounded wilder and less connected than the one before. "I mean—"

"And you're here in his place," the Irish cop said and nodded understandingly. "You see how it is, Frank." The grin was gone, wiped away by sudden solemnity. "His builing is in trouble and you've come in his place to give it support." He nodded again. "Would you be knowing the other two who are here? A big fella by the name of—" Shannon looked at Barnes.

"Giddings," Barnes said. "And an architect named Wilson."

"I know them," Patty said. "But they'll be busy. They—"

"I'll take you to them," Shannon said. He caught her arm in a hand as big as Bert McGraw's, led her past the barricade, and urged her across the plaza, past other cops, firemen, stepping over snaking hoses, avoiding puddles.

It was a construction-site trailer office, not far from the substation. Inside there were drafting tables and file cabinets, a few chairs, telephones, and the man smells

Patty had known on construction sites since memory began, now somehow comforting.

Shannon said, "Miss McGraw here—" He got no further.

Nat said, "Come in, Patty." He took her hand. "We heard about Bert. I'm sorry."

Giddings said, "He'll make out. He always has." And then, "Those goddam doors can't be locked. They can't."

Assistant Commissioner Brown and three uniformed firemen stood by, watching, listening.

Nat said, "We don't know. They can't be opened from the inside. Ben Caldwell verified that." He paused and looked at Brown. "The doors are fail-safe. For security reasons under normal circumstances they're locked by electromagnets from stairside. In an emergency, and God knows this is an emergency, or a power failure, they unlock automatically."

"It says here in the fine print," Giddings said. "But something's wrong, because they're never supposed to be locked from the inside and they are. Unless"—he shook his head almost savagely—"they could be blocked instead of locked."

"So," Nat said, "we send a man up each stairwell—"

"A hundred and twenty-five floors," Giddings said, "on foot?"

"In the mountains," Nat said, "you can climb a thousand feet an hour, more or less, on a trail. It's harder here because it's almost straight up. Say an hour and three-quarters, two hours. But how else?" He waited for no reply. To Brown he said, "Do you have any walkers? Give them axes and walkie-talkies and start them up." He nodded at the telephone at Brown's hand. "Tell them they're on the way."

"It's probably radio and television equipment for the mast," Giddings said. "Piled against the fire doors. I've warned them about that, but they don't listen. Heavy goddam crates, some of them are."

"Then," one of the uniformed firemen said, "give them halligan tools instead of axes."

"And tell them," Nat said, "to take it slow and steady,

120

settle right down at the beginning for the long haul." He seemed suddenly aware once more of Patty's presence. "Have you seen Paul?"

"Not since this morning." She paused. "Do you need him?"

"We need some information."

(On the telephone Joe Lewis, told of the mess down in the mechanical and electrical equipment subbasement, had said first, "Jesus! The whole thing gone?"

"There's no power at all," Nat had said. "There are two dead men down there, one of them, what's left of him, fried to a crisp, the firemen say."

"If he messed around with primary power, he would be." Joe had paused. "You're worried about buried fires in appliance circuits, that kind of thing? I can't tell you offhand, man. The way we designed it a power surge couldn't get through. There are circuit-breakers, grounds, all kinds of safety factors. The way we designed it. But if some of those changes were actually made, then I won't guarantee anything. What does Simmons say? He's the one who ought to know.")

Find Simmons.

"I haven't seen him," Patty said. "I'm sorry. He saw Bert after lunch. He was with him when he had his attack. But I don't know where he is now." She paused. "Unless—" She stopped.

"Unless what, Patty?"

Patty looked around the office. Everyone was watching her, and all she could do was shake her head in silence.

"Here," Nat said, and taking her arm, led her to a far corner. He kept his voice low. "Unless what? Where might he be?"

"You don't want to know." Her eyes were steady on his face. "I'm sorry."

"I don't want to know any of this," Nat said. "I don't want to know that there are a hundred people up in that Tower Room with no way to get out, and I don't want to know that there may be a hundred fires we haven't seen yet, maybe a thousand, about to break out of the walls—" He stopped with effort. "Patty, if you know where he

121

is, or even might be, then I've got to know because we have to know where we stand."

"Daddy might know."

Nat was silent.

"But even if he does," Patty said, "he can't tell us, can he? I'm not—thinking very straight. I'm sorry." She took a deep breath. "Maybe Zib knows where he is."

Nat made no move, but the change in him was plain, and deep. "Does that mean what I think it does?" His voice was quiet.

"I'm sorry, Nat."

"Stop being sorry and answer my question."

Patty's chin came up. "It means," Patty said, "that my Paul and your Zib have been, as they used to say, having an affair. I don't think it's even called that now. There is probably some in name for it. There is for everything else. I am sorry. For you. For the whole thing. But the point is, maybe Zib might know where Paul is. I don't."

Nat walked to the nearest telephone. He picked it up and dialed with a steady hand. His face was expressionless. To the magazine's operator, "Zib Wilson, please," he said, and there was nothing at all in his voice.

"May I ask who is calling?"

"Her husband." Was there angry emphasis there? No matter.

And here came Zib's light, easy, boarding-school-and-seven-sisters-college voice, "Hi, dear. What's up? Or is that a bawdy question?"

"Do you know where Paul Simmons is?"

There was the faintest hesitation. "Why on earth would I know where Paul is, darling?"

"Never mind the why right now," Nat said. "Do you know? I need him. Bad."

"Whatever for?"

Nat took a deep breath and held his temper firm. "We've got fires in the World Tower. We've got Bert Mc-Graw in the hospital with a heart attack. We've got a hundred people trapped in the Tower Room on the hundred and twenty-fifth floor. And I need information from Paul."

"Darling"—Zib's voice was the patient voice of a kindergarten teacher explaining to a backward child—"why don't you ask Patty? She—"

"Patty is right here with me. She said to ask you."

There was a pause. "I see," Zib said, and that was all.

The temper broke. "I'll ask you once more," Nat said. "Where is the son of a bitch? If you don't know where he is, find him. And get him down here. On the double. Is that clear?"

"You've never talked to me like this before."

"It was a mistake. I probably ought to have paddled your patrician ass. Find him and get him here. Is that clear?"

"I'll—do what I can."

"That," Nat said, "isn't good enough. Find him. Get him here. Period." He hung up and stood staring at the wall.

Giddings and Brown looked at each other and said nothing.

The walkie-talkie one of the uniformed firemen was holding came abruptly to life. "Chief?"

Chief Jameson raised the walkie-talkie. "Right here."

"Walters. The original fire started on the fourth floor. It's almost under control."

"Beautiful," Jameson said. "Beautiful." He was smiling.

"Not so beautiful," Walters said. "There are a dozen fires. More. Above us, below us." He coughed, a deep retching sound. "It's got to be wiring. Whatever let go down in the subbasement sent just a hell of a jolt through the whole building."

There was silence. Nat turned from the wall. He looked at Giddings. "Now we know," he said slowly. "From here on we don't need to guess."

Giddings nodded, an awkward, strained movement. "Just pray," he said.

13

4:39–4:43

In the office off the Tower Room the fire commissioner listened on the telephone, nodded, said, "Keep in touch," and hung up. He looked around the office. "They're sending men up the stairs." His voice was expressionless.

The governor said, "How long does it take to climb a hundred and twenty-five floors?" He waited, but nobody answered. The governor nodded. "All right, then we'd better try some things ourselves." He was silent for a moment, pondering the problem. "Ben, you and the commissioner commandeer three or four of those waiters. There are some husky lads. Start working on one of those doors." He paused and looked at the fire commissioner. "If we get a door open, we're in the clear, aren't we? A protected stairwell all the way to the ground?"

The commissioner hesitated.

The mayor said, "Speak up, man. Answer the question."

"It ought to be clear," the commissioner said. His tone was reluctant.

"Let's be plain," the governor said. "You're dragging your feet. Why?"

Beth Shirley stood quietly, watching, listening. Moment by moment, she thought, the governor was growing in stature, dwarfing other men in the room. Well, not entirely. Senator Peters in his own sometimes crude, sometimes erudite and understanding way bore up well under scrutiny too. It was a truism, of course, that in crisis you saw more clearly a man's quality, or a woman's for that matter, but she had never before realized how vivid the demonstration could be.

124

The commissioner was still hesitating, and now he glanced quickly at Beth. "The lady—" he began.

The governor's hand tightened on hers. "The lady," the governor said, "is just as interested in our predicament as anyone else. You haven't said it yet, but the implication is clear. The stairwells aren't the havens we thought them to be. Why?"

"The men on the stairs," the commissioner said, "have walkie-talkies. They're—reporting smoke."

The office was still. "That means what?" the governor said at last. He turned to look at Ben Caldwell.

"I couldn't say without more information," Caldwell said. He studied the fire commissioner. "What have you left out?"

The commissioner took a deep breath. "The first fire is contained. By itself it wouldn't have amounted to much. But what happened down in the main transformer room killed two men and apparently started fires"—he spread both hands—"throughout the structure."

Grover Frazee waggled his head in denial. "A modern fireproof building—that's ridiculous. How could it be? You heard it wrong." He looked at Caldwell. "Isn't that right, Ben? Tell him."

Caldwell said, "Fire*proof*, no. Fire resistant, yes. Now, be quiet, Grover. Let's find out exactly where we stand." He pointed at the commissioner. "Call them back. I want to speak to Nat Wilson."

Frazee said, "There. There's your proof. The telephone works, so we can't be out of electricity. Don't you see that?" He looked around at them all.

Caldwell said almost warily, "Telephones have their own power source. There is no connection." He accepted the phone from the commissioner. "Nat?" he said, and punched the telephone's desk speaker.

"Yes, sir." Nat's voice was hollow in the office. "You'll want a rundown. The fourth-floor fire is under control now. What happened down in the subbasement isn't clear yet, and there may not be enough left to find out ever, but whatever happened somehow managed to short out primary power, and we think, Joe Lewis, Giddings, and I, that the short sent a surge through the entire building and wiring overheated and burned through its insulation and conduit." Nat was silent.

"That." Caldwell said slowly, "could account for smoke in the stairwells?"

"We think so." Nat was unaware that he had dropped the "sir." "The men on the stairs report that in places the walls are too hot to touch. What's happening inside the fire doors is anybody's guess." Nat paused. "Only it isn't a guess. It's practically a goddam certainty. When Simmons gets here, we may know a little more."

Caldwell thought about it. "Simmons," he said, and was silent for a little time. Then, "Joe Lewis agrees that there could have been a current surge?"

"Yes." They were speaking in shorthand, implications plain.

"And you think Simmons—" Caldwell stopped. "Bert McGraw——"

"Bert's in the hospital with a heart attack," Nat said. Then, intuitively. "That may be Simmons's doing too."

Caldwell took his time. "The question here," he said, "is whether or not to try to break down the fire doors. If—"

"Are you getting much smoke through the air-conditioning ducts?"

"Not too much."

"Then," Nat said, "leave the doors alone." His voice was firm. commanding.

Another one, Beth thought, although she had never seen the man, who in an emergency would take charge. She looked up at the governor and watched him nod in understanding.

Ben Caldwell was hesitating.

Nat's voice said, "We know there's smoke in the stairwells. There's nothing to stop it from rising all the way to your floor. If you're more or less smoke-free now, keep it that way. Leave the doors shut."

"I think you are right," Caldwell said.

"Giddings," Nat said, "thinks the doors may be blocked by radio and TV equipment being taken up into the tower.

They've done it before, he says, and I've seen it myself. If that's so, the stairs may be blocked too."

Caldwell smiled his tight little smile. "Conditions scarcely anticipated in the design, Nat." He paused. "A concatenation of errors." He shook his head.

"We've got through to the Army," Nat said. "You'll see a couple of choppers around in a few minutes."

Caldwell's eyebrows rose. "Your idea?"

"Brown made the call. He's assistant fire commissioner, and they listened to him where they wouldn't bother with me." Nat paused. "I don't know what they can do, to be honest with you, but I thought it would be good if they had a look."

Again Caldwell smiled. "Keep thinking, Nat."

"And it might be a good idea to keep this line open."

Caldwell nodded. "I agree. I think that is all for now." He turned back to the room. "Comments?" He addressed them all. "Questions?"

"Just one," the governor said. "How did all this happen?"

CONSTRUCTION TIME

For some from the start it was one of those jobs you writhed in dreams about and awakened sweating. The sheer magnitude of the World Tower was frightening, but it was more, far more than that. The building taking shape seemed to develop a personality of its own, and that personality was malign.

On a cold fall day a freak wind whipped through the huge empty space where the plaza would be, picked up a loose piece of corrugation, and scaled it as a boy might scale a flattened tin can. A workman named Bowers saw it coming, tried too late to duck, and was almost but not quite decapitated.

The front tire of a partially off-loaded truck standing

perfectly still suddenly blew out with sufficient force to shift the untied load of pipe, burying three men in a tangle of assorted fractures.

On another cold fall day a fire started in a subbasement, spread through piled lumber, and trapped two men in a tunnel They were rescued alive—just.

Paul Simmons was standing outside the building, talking with one of his foremen, when Pete Janowski walked off the steel at floor 65. The Doppler effect accentuated the man's screams until they ended abruptly with a sickening *thunk* that Paul, not ten feet away, would never forget. He tried not to look, found it impossible, and promptly vomited on his own feet.

Was that the beginning of the end?

"These things happen," McGraw had said that night at the small house in Queens, Paul and Patty there for dinner. "I don't like them a goddam bit better than you do, but they happen."

"It seems to me," Paul said, "that there are too many of them that's all. I've been waiting ten days for transformers. Today we found them. Do you know where? Three thousand miles away in Los Angeles, don't ask me why, and nobody even bothered to ask what they were doing there." Men standing idle, because each day the transformers had been promised; labor costs mounting. "We order cable. It's the wrong size. We check out an elevator installation, and the motor won't start or the doors won't open because they weren't set right on the tracks. My top cable-splicer got tangled with his power lawnmower at home, for God's sake, and cut off three toes."

"You sound like it's getting to you," McGraw said. His eyes were steady on Paul's face.

Paul made himself slow down. "It is," he said, "and it isn't." The actor's confident smile. "But you'll have to admit, there have been a lot of strange ones on this job."

"I'll admit it, boy. But I wont let it grind me under either."

"It's almost," Paul said, "as if this were wartime with sabotage going on."

McGraw looked at him sideways. "You think that, do you?"

"Not really."

"It has happened," McGraw said. "I've known of it. And not in wartime either." He shook his head. "But not this time." He studied Paul carefully. "Are you trying to tell me something?"

Paul shook his head. He hoped his smile looked confident.

Because," McGraw said, "if there is something on your mind, now. not later, is the time to bring it out."

"Nothing to confess," Paul said.

McGraw took his time. "You're part of the family, boy, and kin have always had meaning to me. But we're in business, a hard business, and we have a contract, you and I, and I'll have to hold you to it. You know that."

"I never thought otherwise." The hell you didn't. But the actor's smile never faltered.

Patty had sensed that there were troubles, but she was unable to bring them to the surface. They were driving home from a Westchester dinner party one evening. "You and Carl Ross," she said to Paul, "seemed to be having a little problem." Their raised voices had dominated the evening.

"Carl," Paul said, "is pure unadulterated Westchester horse's ass."

In a way it was amusing, Patty thought, and tried to ignore the deep bitterness in his voice. "Pure Westchester." she said, "from Des Moines, Iowa."

"Everybody here comes from somewhere else. There's nothing new about that. Either they come from Des Moines, like Carl, or from South Carolina, like Pete Granger, or from some Western mountaintop, like that cowboy Nat Wilson—" Paul's voice stopped and they drove in silence.

Patty said, "What has Nat done? I've always thought he was a good man. Daddy thinks so."

"That whole goddam Ben Caldwell office walks on water. It's one of the requirements for employment."

Patty giggled. Keep it light, she told herself, but lightness was not easy these days. "If they get their socks wet, they're out? What about hitting a stray ripple?"

Paul's thoughts were already back on Carl Ross. "He," he said, "is one of those oh-by-the-way-today-I-heard-a-rumor boys. And the rumors are always vicious."

Patty said in a puzzled voice, "Nat?"

"What about Nat?" Paul's voice was sharp, defensive.

Oh God, Patty thought, are we this far apart? "I didn't know who you were talking about. Or is it whom? Who hears rumors?"

"Carl Ross, goddamm it. Nat doesn't hear rumors. Not ever. All he ever sees is what's under his nose, on paper, or built from drawings. He—"

"I always thought you liked him," Patty said. "And Zib."

There was a long silence. The night countryside swept past, a blur in the darkness. "People change," Paul said at last.

It was a temptation to point out that clichés had not always been Paul's stock in trade. Patty stifled the temptation. "So they do." She paused. "Nat has changed? Zib?" And then, answering at least one of her own questions: "I don't quite hold with the Women's Lib bit Zib considers so sacred these days. Of course, she has the figure for no bra, I'll give her that. But so do I, for that matter, and I don't choose to go around bouncing."

"Zib's all right." There was finality in the statement. It hung shimmering in the near-darkness.

In Patty's mind there was first stillness, then doubt, then sudden immediate conviction, almost a feeling of *déja vu*, a sense of I-have-been-here-before-but-only-in-bad-dreams; and finally, self-accusation, the charge of blindness, blame that she had not understood before that she had already joined the ranks of women with philandering husbands. Oh God, she thought, how—how dismal! But where was the deep hurt that should have been? Later, she thought, when I am alone and have time to absorb the enormity. Now she said, calmly enough, "So the change must be Nat."

"Yes." Merely that.

"In what way?"

"I don't want to talk about it."

"Why not, darling?"

The temper of the evening revealed itself. "Goddammit, why the inquisition? If I don't like the cowboy son of a bitch, do I have to give a bill of particulars to back it up?"

She had her own temper too. "What have you done to him," she said, "to make you dislike him so?"

"And what does that mean?" Paul paused. "Psychological reasoning from you?"

"You don't dislike anybody quite as much," Patty said, "as somebody you've done the dirty to."

"One of Bert's maxims, I suppose."

"I doubt if Daddy has ever done the dirty to anybody." Patty's tone was reasonable, but there was no mistaking her conviction. "He's beaten men into the ground. He's outdrunk them, outworked them, outfought them, yes, and outthought them. But it's always been right out in the open. He's never sneaked behind another man's back."

"Are you saying I have? Is that what all this is about?"

Patty took her time. She said at last in her calm voice, "Have you, darling? Is that where all the heat comes from?"

In the semidarkness of the automobile Paul's face was only a blur, all expression concealed. When he spoke at last, his voice was calmer. "Just how did we get into this anyway? I had a hassle with Carl Ross—"

"Hassles seem easily come by these days."

"All right," Paul said, "they do, they are. I'm uptight. I admit it. I'm right in the middle of the biggest job I've ever had, the biggest job of its kind anybody has ever had—do you realize that? There has never been a building like the one we're building."

"Is that all it is?" Patty said. "Just the job?" Make it so, she told herself, and knew that she would not believe it even if he said it was true.

But all Paul said was, "It gets to you. That's all."

"In what way?"

"I told you I didn't want to talk about it. You say you don't hold with Women's Lib. Okay, let's stay traditional.

131

You run the house. I'll take care of earning our living. You told me once you'd follow wherever I led. Okay, follow."

Figures do not lie. Oh, there are jokes about liars, damn liars, and statisticians. But when the figures were Paul's own, computer-verified, there was no point in arguing with them. And what the figures he sat staring at demonstrated brought a feeling of near-nausea to his stomach and to his mind.

He had figured too close in his original bid. Weather had been against him. Material delays had thrown all labor-cost computations into chaos. Accidents had slowed the job, and there had been a larger than usual incidence of work rejected and thus done over. He, Paul Simmons, wasn't as good at this business as he had come to consider himself. He had had sheer bad luck. God was against him. Hell, he could lay his hands on a hundred reasons (excuses) and none of them mattered a damn.

The facts stared him in the face, and the facts were that when he set percentage of the job on the World Tower completed against cost of the job so far, it was evident that he was not going to come out of the total job even financially alive, let alone showing a profit.

It was five o'clock. His own office seemed larger than usual, and very still. The outer offices would by now be deserted. Distant sounds of traffic reached him from the street thirty stories below. THINK, the IBM signs said. And some place he had seen a sign that read: DON'T THIMK, DRIMK. Why should that kind of nonsense run through his mind at a time like this?

He pushed back his chair, got up, and walked to the windows. It was an automatic reaction of McGraw's too; and why should that come to mind? That question at least he could answer. Because McGraw himself, big, rough, tough, unyielding, godlike McGraw was rarely out of the back of Paul's mind. Face it: I live in his goddam shadow; and unlike Diogenes, I am afraid to say, "Get out of my sunlight, Alexander."

He could see people walking, hurrying on the sidewalks below. Going home? Happily? Reluctantly? Angrily,

132

after a day of frustration? What difference? They are not a part of me; no one is a part of me. Not Patty, not Zib, nobody. I am me and—what was McGraw's phrase?— life has leaned on me this time and squashed me flat. And who cares, except me?

He found himself looking at the solid windows as if he had never seen them before. In air-conditioned buildings you aren't supposed to be able to open windows. It is partly at least to keep people from jumping out of them as they were supposed to have done back in Twenty-nine? Was he, for God's sake, even thinking of—that? Nonsense. You're playing to an audience—of one. Knock it off.

He walked back to his desk and stood for a little time looking down at the figures neatly written, impeccably aligned, like little soldiers marching along—where? To the edge of a high cliff, that's where—and then right over the edge. The sound of Pete Janowski's screams came to mind again, and the sickening *thunk* that had ended them. Once again the nausea rose. He fought it down with effort.

It was then that the phone had rung and he had stared at it for some time before he made any move to pick it up.

It was Zib's voice. "Hi."

"You." Paul said. "Hello." His eyes were still on the marching figures.

"That overwhelms me with its enthusiasm."

"Sorry. I was—thinking."

"I've been thinking too."

He and Zib, so much alike: her thoughts were of herself, his turned inward too. It was almost an effort to say, "About what?"

Zib's voice was carefully unconcerned. "I've been thinking that I'd like to be laid. Do you know any male who might be interested?"

Who arranged these things anyway? Who planned this juxtaposition of lighthearted bawdiness and tragedy, real tragedy? Sex was the last thing he was in the mood for now. Why couldn't the silly woman have chosen another time?

"Do I hear a bid?" Zib said.

133

And yet, why not, why the bloody hell not? Why not lose himself in her slim softness, listen to her sounds and smile to himself that he was their cause, find his own concentration, not on despair, but on pure sheer animal enjoyment? What better answer? "The bid was made silently," he said. "The hotel in twenty minutes."

Her voice was amused now. "You sound actually interested."

"Living," Paul said, "beats dying. And don't even try to figure that one out. Just come prepared for a romp."

Naked, relaxed, "I'm supposed to be having dinner with a writer who suddenly arrived in town," Zib said. "Nat didn't even question it. There are benefits to being an editor."

Paul was silent, staring at the ceiling. His mind, alive again, was probing strange, tortuous thoughts. What if—?

"Did you hear me, darling?" Zib ran her forefinger lightly down his chest. "Hmmm?"

"I heard."

"Then why so quiet?"

"I'm thinking."

"At a time like this," Zib said, "that is the hell of a thing to do." She sighed. "All right, you're a male chauvinist pig, so what are you thinking about?"

"Nat."

Zib frowned. Her forefinger was still. "What on earth for? What about him?"

"Why," Paul said, and suddenly he was smiling, decision made. "I think he's going to do me some favors."

"You're mad." Zib paused. "Why should he do you favors?"

"Well," Paul said, "he isn't even going to know that he's doing them." He reached for her then, and she came to him willingly. "Any more," Paul said, "than he knows that he lends me his wife on occasion. Like right now."

134

QUEENS

It was a modern insurance-company-built high-rise apartment building for middle-income tenants. Technically, the building inspector's income was above the upper limit, but, then, a considerable portion of his income was never reported.

The windows were closed and the air-conditioning made scarcely any noise. On the playground below children were playing, but their sounds were muffled, comfortably shut out. The building inspector was relaxed with a beer in his reclining chair, facing the twenty-five-inch color television set complete with one-button tuning, magic brain, and remote control, all housed in a Mediterranean-style console cabinet of vast brooding magnificence.

The inspector was in his forties, no longer able even to pretend that he could get into his Korean War uniform and no longer caring about it. "What the hell," he was fond of saying, "live it up and take all you can get because when you're gone there isn't any more. That's what I always say."

His wife was in her smaller reclining chair, also watching television, also drinking beer. She had worked hard beneath the sunlamp and with the application of several lotions to retain some of her early-year Florida tan. At supermarket and hairdresser's the neighbors always remarked it with envy. Her hair was red, matching her fingernails and toenails. "We're missing the *Family Fun Show*," she said.

The last speech in the World Tower Plaza had just ended, and the television cameras followed the celebrities down from the platform and through the concourse doors.

"Going up to the Tower Room," the inspector said, "to drink bubbly and eat little things on toothpicks." There was angry envy in his voice. "You see that one? That's Senator Jake Peters, friend of the people. Hah! He's been lining his pockets down in Washington for thirty years, more."

"Clara Hess is on the *Family Fun Show* today," his wife said. "She really turns me on. I saw her one day last week, Tuesday, no, maybe Wednesday it was. Laugh? I thought I'd die. She was doing that, you know, Women's Lib thing, really putting them down."

"And that one," the inspector said, "he's Governor Bent Armitage, a bag of wind if I ever saw one. And, look, there's pretty boy, Mayor Bob Ramsay, the All-American jerk. Why don't they have the guys there who built the building? Tell me that."

"What she said," his wife said, "was that it hadn't ought to be history, it ought to be herstory—do you get it? Oh, she was sharp, real quick, you never know what she's going to say next."

"There's Ben Caldwell," the inspector said. "When he comes around you're supposed to genuflect, you know, like in church. Well, goddammit, he puts his pants on same as me, one leg at a time, and I'll bet he's crooked as a corkscrew too. He'd have to be to get where he is. They all have to be. Nobody's that good and everybody's got his hand out."

"You'd like Clara Hess," his wife said, "you really would."

"Just who the hell is Clara Hess?" Rhetorical question. The inspector finished his beer. "How about another brew?"

"You know where it is."

"I got the last one."

"You did not. And you haven't even been listening to me or you'd know who Clara Hess is."

"Oh Christ, all right," the inspector said. He got out of his chair with effort and walked toward the kitchen.

136

"Don't touch that picture," he said, "I got a right to look at a building I built with my own hands."

"You didn't build it. You just watched."

"Same thing, ain't it? Who else makes sure they do it right?"

Or wrong, but those were the thoughts you kept submerged. Sometimes, usually at night, they surfaced, and those stupid childhood fears about God and Right and Wrong, like that, came out to torment you, but you were a grown man now, goddammit, and able to make decisions for yourself, and that childhood stuff was a lot of crap.

If there was one thing the inspector had learned, it was that there were only two kinds of guys in this world— takers and losers—and the inspector had made up his mind a long time ago which category he preferred.

The thing was that if you looked hard any place, *any place*, you saw that some guys had it and some, most, didn't. In the Army, when he wasn't much more than a kid, he learned how it worked. Some guys were always on KP or sent out on patrol, like that, always on somebody's shit list, born losers. And other guys always slept in nice warm barracks at headquarters and pulled jobs like company clerk where nobody shot at you. What do you want to be, a dead hero?

Building inspector now, same goddam thing. Some guys spent their lives doing just what the book said. And then what? A pension that wouldn't cover your ass, let alone give you the things everybody had a right to, didn't all those crooked politicians running for office say so?

So what if you let some subcontractor cut a corner here and a corner there, and you pick up a little extra for it? Who's hurt? And who's to know? That was the important question, because everybody had his angle, and anybody who told you different was either a fool or a liar, but the guys who made it were the guys who didn't get caught, and the others, the ones who did take a fall, they were the losers. Simple as that.

The inspector had opened a beer and was standing beside the oversize refrigerator-freezer drinking it. Funny, just looking at the Tower on the tube started up the thoughts.

Well, that job was finished now, but not really forgotten. A sizable piece of the inspector's life had been spent on that job.

"Harry!" His wife's voice from the living room. "Where's my beer?"

"Shut up," Harry said. "I'm thinking."

From any job you remembered some things, maybe one winter a whole series of days cold enough to freeze the balls off a brass monkey, maybe an accident like that big Polack falling off a beam and splattering himself all over the ground, or that kid killed on the subway on the way home from the job. You remembered, all right, and sometimes you thought about how and why things happened.

That Polack, for instance, Harry had always thought somebody pushed him; he was a big tough bastard and Harry liked to think that in this world that kind of self-reliant competent jerk always got what was coming to him.

That kid killed in the subway, now, that was something else, although the kid was a pain in the ass with his bellyaching about the change orders that kept coming through, and maybe if he'd lived, somebody would have listened to him and taken him seriously. Come to think of it, somebody was maybe pretty lucky the kid had been killed when he was. Harry had never seen it that way before.

Somebody. Not Harry. Harry had the signed change order to show if anybody ever asked why one of the safety circuits had been completely eliminated, and for all Harry knew, and never asked, the change order was for real at that. Harry didn't ask questions. Only fools stick their necks out.

But maybe somebody was real lucky the kid had fallen under the IRT express. Fallen? Harry had seen on TV how easy it was for somebody at rush hour to get a push at the wrong time, and who was to know? Maybe somebody wasn't lucky; maybe somebody was getting sensible, shutting up a kid who might cause trouble. Human nature being what it was, Harry wouldn't doubt for a minute that somebody might take that way to protect himself.

138

"Harry! Come here! There's something funny!"

Harry sighed and walked out of the kitchen. "I told you not to touch that picture. If your goddam Clara Hess is so great—" He stopped and stared at the massive television set.

The camera had zoomed in on the smoke plume high up in the building, and the announcer's voice was saying, "We don't know what it is, folks, but we've sent a reporter off to—here he is. George, what's going on? Is that smoke normal?"

In the living room Harry said, "Hell, no, it isn't normal. Something's burning somewhere and they'd damn well better find out where and do something about it." He sat down but did not push his recliner back. "What the hell goes on?"

"It looks like you didn't build it very good," his wife said.

"That'll be enough from you."

"If I see smoke coming out of my oven," his wife said, "I figure I've goofed on the cake. Where's the difference?"

"Goddammit, will you shut up!"

In silence they watched the fire engines arrive, the hoses snake across the plaza, smoke pour out the concourse doors.

Unseen George, breathless, came back to the microphone again. "The fire is on the fourth floor. We've just had a report. There are indications that the fire may have been set . . ."

Funny, the inspector thought, how all of a sudden his breathing was easier. A torch job, huh? Nothing at all to do with the kind of work buried in the walls; nothing at all to do with him. He leaned back in the reclining chair and had a long pull at his beer. He was smiling now.

"Torch jobs can be tough," he said. His tone was knowledgeable, his approach judicious. "But, hell, the way that building's designed, they'll have it out before Willie Mays could put one in the bleachers. They got automatic sprinklers and fire doors, and the air-conditioning takes the smoke away—" He shrugged. "Cinch," he said.

"The *Family Fun Show* is almost over," his wife said, "and you didn't bring me a beer. What kind of a gentleman are you?"

"Oh Christ," Harry said, and got himself out of his chair.

In the kitchen he took one beer from the refrigerator, changed his mind, and took out a second, opened them both. He finished the half-empty can in three long swallows, and walked back to his chair.

"There's still a lot of smoke," his wife said. "If your building is so great, why is that?" She took the beer can absently, drank deep. "Maybe we ought to have two TVs. Then you could watch what you want and I could watch what I want. How about that?"

"Jesus," Harry said, "do you know what this color set you wanted so bad cost? And that trip to Florida you kept nagging about all winter? You think I'm made of money?"

"All I said," his wife said, "was that if we had two TVs, then you could watch your ball games and your Monday night football games and like that, and I—"

"You could watch Clara What's-her-name. Well, goddammit," Harry said, "you got the whole week, every day, Monday through Friday—"

The picture on the screen suddenly wavered, shook. There was silence. Then, distantly, the sound of a hollow *boom!*

"Jesus," Harry said, "what was that?"

The announcer's voice, a little shaky, said, "We don't know exactly what has happened." He paused. "But I can tell you that the ground shook, and if I were still back in Vietnam, I'd say for sure that a mortar attack had just begun. Chief! Oh, Chief! Can you tell us what's going on?"

The microphone picked up crowd sounds now, an excited murmuring as at opening kickoff, the feeling of spectator enjoyment high.

"What was it, Harry?"

"How the hell do I know? Maybe somebody planted a bomb. You heard the man."

There was confusion covered by commercials. At

140

last the announcer said, "This is Assistant Fire Commissioner Brown, ladies and gentlemen, and maybe he can tell us what has happened. Commissioner?"

"I'm afraid I can't—yet," Brown said. "We know there has been something like an explosion down in the main transformer room in one of the subbasements. All electrical power in the building is out. There are two men dead down there and sabotage is being considered. Beyond that—" The assistant commissioner shrugged.

"Standby generators," Harry said. "What's the matter with the goddam standby generators?"

The announcer said, "What does the loss of electrical power mean, Commissioner? Lights? Elevators? Air-conditioning? Are all of those kaput?"

"That's what it means at least for the present. Now if you'll excuse me—"

As the assistant commissioner turned away, the long-range microphone caught Will Giddings and Nat Wilson standing together:

"If it was a short," Giddings said, "it ought to have gone to ground. Goddammit, that's how it's designed."

"Agreed." Nat's voice was weary. He had heard the point made several times. "Unless somebody altered it."

The voices were cut off. The screen showed a soup commercial.

"Harry!" The wife's voice was almost a scream. "Harry, for God's sake, what's wrong? You look like you seen a ghost!'

Harry tried to set the beer can down on the chairside table. He missed. It dropped to the floor and beer foamed out on the wall-to-wall carpeting. Neither of them noticed.

"What is it, Harry? For God's sake, talk!"

Harry licked his lips. His throat felt dry and filled with sour vomit at the same time. How could that be? He took a deep breath. He said at last in a low vicious voice, "All right. So all right. You got your goddam big color TV, didn't you? And your trip to Florida?" He paused. "Just remember that."

14

In the office the governor said wearily, "All right. There isn't anything for us to do right now except wait." So be it.

" 'When rape is inevitable—' " Jake Peters began. He shook his head. Then, "Where're you going, Bent?"

"I promised a report."

Frazee said, "Oh for God's sake! We don't know it's as bad as they say it is. Let's keep it right here in this room until we do know."

"Grover"—the governor's voice was sharp and the wolfish grin showed his teeth in a near-snarl—"I made a promise. I intend to keep it." He paused. "There is another point, and it is that those people out there have just as much right to all the facts as you have." He paused again. "Even more right because none of them could have had anything to do with what has happened."

"And I have?" Frazee said. "Now, look, Bent—"

"That," the governor said, "is something we will find out later. He looked down at Beth Shirley. "You don't have to come," he said.

"I wouldn't miss it."

There was still ample light coming through the tinted windows, but somewhere the waiters had found more candles and lighted them around the big room for cheer. It was, the governor thought, a setting for a pleasant, if pointless, cocktail gathering. But now with a difference. As he and Beth walked in conversation slowed and then stopped.

They walked to the center of the room, and there the governor signaled to a waiter to bring a chair. The governor stepped up on it and raised his voice. "In my younger day," he said, "I was used to soapboxes. This will have to do." Always start it on a light note—who had taught him that so long ago? No matter. He waited until the murmur of amusement subsided.

"I promised a report," he said. "This is the situation . . ."

Beth watched and listened, and thought, I have no right to be here. But would I change it if I could? The answer was no.

She looked around at the nearby faces while the governor was speaking. Most wore set smiles like masks; a few wore frowns of puzzlement, one or two of annoyance.

There was the young congressman, Cary Wycoff, whom she had met. Was that the expression with which he waited for a political opponent to finish his say on the floor of the House? He seemed tense, almost coiled, holding down angry words with effort. His eyes never left the governor's face.

There was Paula, Bob Ramsay's wife, tall, serene, smiling as she had smiled through a thousand social events and campaign visits. She caught Beth's eye and drooped one eyelid momentarily in a girlish gesture of intimacy. Obviously to Paula the situation was far from serious.

Directly in front of the governor's chair were the UN's Secretary General and its Ambassador from the Soviet Union. Their faces were expressionless.

Senator Peters, Beth noticed, had come out of the office and was leaning against a wall, watching the scene. A strange, earthy, involuted man, she thought. Over the years she had often come across newspaper and magazine pieces devoted to his accomplishments and idiosyncrasies. Now, meeting him for the first time, she found the reports all the more remarkable.

He was a bird-watcher of almost professional caliber, and his catalogue of birds to be found in the Washington tidal basin area was the standard. He had been a guiding spirit in the establishment of the Appalachian Trail, and he had walked its two-thousand-mile length. He read Greek and Latin with ease and spoke French and German—with an American big-city working-class accent. It was said that his mental collection of bawdy limericks was the largest in the entire US Congress. He was here now, as Beth was, not entirely, but at least partly, by chance.

Or Fate. Call it what you would. She was here, as he was, and it might not have been so. How often has one heard tales of the passenger who arrived at the airport just too late to board the airplane that crashed shortly after takeoff? The concept gave her a start. Was she, then, already accepting a foretaste of disaster?

She concentrated again on the governor. He was winding up his explanation of what had happened.

"The telephones are working," he said. He smiled suddenly. "That is how I know these facts. I did not make them up." There was no amused murmur—he had expected none—nevertheless, a little lightness was not out of place. His smile disappeared. "Help is on the way. Firemen have been sent up the stairs at each side of the building. It is a long climb, as you can appreciate, so we must be patient." He paused. Had he said it all? He thought so, except, of course, for an appropriate windup. "This," he said, "is not exactly the way this reception was planned, as I am sure you are aware. But I, for one, intend to enjoy myself while I wait for matters to be brought back to normal."

"And if they aren't?" This was Cary Wycoff, his words and his tone angry. "What if they aren't, Governor?"

The governor stepped down from the chair. "You are out of order, Cary." His voice was pitched low. "Justice Holmes made the point. I repeat it. 'The right of free speech does not carry with it the right to shout "Fire!" in a crowded theater.' That is precisely what you are doing. Why? Just to call attenion to yourself?"

The congressman flushed, but stood his ground. "The people have a right to know."

"That is a cliché," the governor said. "Like most clichés, it is partly right and also misleading. The people here have a right to know the current facts and that is why I have reported to them. They have no right, and I am sure no desire, to be frightened out of their wits by some loud young fool crying like a religious fanatic in Union Square about the doom that may be coming. Use at least some of the sense some people credit you with." He turned then to look for Beth.

She came forward and took his arm. "A fine rousing speech," she said, and smiled. "I will vote for you. You see, I am learning the ways of politics."

The governor covered her hand with his. He squeezed it gently. "Thank God," he said, "at least some people remember how to laugh."

She had expected to return to the office, which already she thought of as the command post. But the governor was in no hurry, and Beth understood that by his presence he was offering reassurance. Together they moved from group to group, pausing briefly for introductions where necessary and a few polite, apparently meaningless words.

To the secretary general: "Walther, may I present . . ." And then, "We have an Americanism, Walther. I think it applies here." The governor, smiling, looked around the room and then back to his small audience. "It is, I'll admit, a hell of a way to run a railroad."

The secretary general smiled in turn. "I have heard the idiom, and I am afraid I must agree. Is it not a Penn Central kind of—mess?"

To an aging actress: "There was a movie once," the governor said, "well before your time, I am sure. It was called *King Kong* and it featured a gigantic gorilla on the Empire State Building. I almost wish Kong would appear now. He would be a diversion at least."

"You're sweet, Governor," the actress said, "but not only was it not before my time, I had a bit part in it."

To a network president: "Do you think your people are giving us good coverage, John?"

"If they aren't," John said, "heads are going to fall." He was smiling. "We ought to be able to work it into a documentary on how civilization overreaches itself. We know how to build the tallest building in the world, but we're having trouble figuring out how to get people out of it. Isn't there, by the way, a battery-operated television set somewhere here? Or at least a radio?"

"Good thought," the governor said. "I'll see about it. But not," he added quietly as he and Beth walked on, "for public viewing. Those on the ground will be giving it the full treatment. They'll already have us doomed."

"Are we, Bent?"

Nothing changed in the governor's smile, but his hand tightened almost imperceptibly on her arm. "Frightened?" he said. His tone was easy.

"I'm beginning to be."

"Why," the governor said, "so am I. Just between us, I'd much rather be out in that high New Mexico meadow with a fly rod in my hand and a cutthroat trout, which they call out there a native, giving me a tussle." He looked down at her, smiling still. "With you," he said. "And if that makes me selfish and cowardly, so be it." He was about to say more when he was interrupted.

"This is outrageous, Bent."

A tall gray-haired corporate-executive type, Beth thought, and almost giggled when her estimate was verified.

"Why, Paul" the governor said, "I'll agree with you. Miss Shirley, Paul Norris—*J*. Paul Norris." And with no change in tone, "Outrageous is the proper word, Paul. Do you have any suggestions?"

"By God, somebody ought to be able to do something."

The governor nodded. "I quite agree." His smile brightened. "And there you have your answer, Paul. The Army has arrived." He pointed to two helicopters banking into position to circle the building.

They seemed so free, Beth thought, close but distant, impossibly removed from this—this confinement.

The governor's hand tightened on hers. "There's our diversion," he said quietly. "Now we can slip back to headquarters."

Senator Peters moved to intercept them. "I'll stay out here, Bent. If you want me for anything—" He left it unfinished, offer clear and without limit. "My role," he

146

said then, "unlike yours. You're the commander, the administrator, the organizer. My place is outside the chain of command"—he paused—"which is the way I like it."

"You seem," the governor said, "a little less unhappy with the human race than you were, Jake."

The senator looked around the great room. Slowly he nodded. "They're behaving very well. So far."

And so, Beth thought as they walked on, the senator felt too that foretaste of disaster. We're like something out of a Tolstoy novel, she thought: the gala ball before the disastrous battle—how ridiculous.

"Maybe," the governor said. (Had she, then, spoken aloud?) "And maybe not," he added. "We have built an entire civilization on the stiff-upper-lip principle. Others have different ways. Personally, I've never found breast-beating and hair-tearing and teeth-gnashing very attractive, have you?" He smiled down at her. "Rhetorical question. I know you haven't. Defeat—"

"Have you known defeat, Bent?" I want to know all about him, everything.

"Many times," the governor said. "In politics as in sports, you win some and you lose some. It doesn't make losing any easier, just a little more familiar."

Grover Frazee had a dark-brown drink beside him in the office. He said, "You spoke to the populace, Bent? You told them the unpleasant facts and you placed the blame squarely where it belongs?" The drink had had its effect.

"Where does it belong, Grover?" The governor perched on a corner of the desk. "That is a point I'd like cleared up."

Frazee waved one hand in a broad gesture of disclaimer. "Will Giddings came to my office with a cock-and-bull tale I didn't begin to understand—"

"Not quite, Grover," Ben Caldwell said. "You were lucid about it when you phoned me." He turned to the governor. "There are change orders in existence authorizing certain deviations from the original design of the building's electrical system. They came to light only today, and until now"—he gestured at the candles that were the

147

only lighting in the room—"we had no idea whether the changes had actually been made or not. Now we have to assume that at least some of them were made."

The governor said, "You knew they were potentially dangerous?" He was looking at Frazee.

"I'm not an engineer, for God's sake! Stop trying to pin it all on me. Giddings showed me the damn things and I told him I didn't understand them—"

"So," Ben Calwell said, "what did Will say then?"

"I don't even remember."

Some men grow in crises, Beth thought, some shrink. Frazee, the dapper jaunty patrician was already smaller than life size, and still shrinking rapidly. She felt a sad contempt for the man.

"You asked me," Caldwell said, "if I thought we should call off the ceremonies and the reception. If that was your idea, then you must have understood a great deal of what Giddings told you. If it was his idea, then you must have understood something of its urgency." Cold pitiless logic. "Which was it, Grover?" Caldwell said.

Frazee's hand of its own volition reached for the drink. He drew it back. "You said there was no need to call the reception off."

"Not quite." Caldwell's voice was cold. "I said that public relations was not in my line. A very different answer, Grover. You—"

The governor broke in. "The question was asked, Ben. Whether Giddings wanted the reception scrubbed or Grover merely wondered about it is largely immaterial. You are the technical man. Did you see the potential danger?" The question hung in the air.

"The answer to that ought to be obvious," Caldwell said at last. "I came myself. I am here, along with the rest of you." He showed an almost glacial calm. "No one could anticipate a madman down in the main transformer room. No one could anticipate the fourth-floor fire, which by itself might not have caused more than small unpleasantness." He paused. "But taken together, along with the design-change orders, which apparently were followed—"

148

He shook his head. "As I said before, a concatenation of errors."

"Leading how far?"

Caldwell shook his head faintly. "You are asking for an impossible judgment, Governor."

The mayor spoke up. "That," he said, "is precisely what he is asking for, Ben: a judgment, not a hard-and-fast answer."

Even Bob, her cousin, Beth thought, whom she had never considered one of the earthshakers, even he had this quality of command, of clarity in crisis, the total willingness to face facts which, in her experience, few men or women had possessed.

Caldwell nodded slowly. "Yes," he said. "I see." He looked at the fire commissioner. "Let's have a judgment from your people. Then let me speak again to Nat Wilson."

Assistant Commissioner Brown's voice was hollow on the telephone's desk speaker. "We're doing the best we can—" he began.

"That," goddammit," the commissioner said, "is no answer, Tim. I know already that you're doing the best you can. What I want to know is how much is that accomplishing and how does it look?"

There was hesitation. Then, "It doesn't look very good, to be honest with you. There isn't equipment anywhere that will reach up there, as you know. We're going in from the outside as high as we can, and we're going up inside—up the stairs. There are two men in each stairwell climbing to you, or trying to. They have masks—"

"The smoke is bad?"

"It isn't good. How long some of those fire doors will hold is anybody's guess, no matter how they're rated. If it gets hot enough—"

"I'm aware of it, Tim. Go on."

Brown's voice took on an almost angry note. "Wilson here, Caldwell's man, has tried to talk me into phoning the Coast Guard—"

"For God's sake, man, why?"

"They have guns that shoot lines out to ships in trouble.

149

And he thinks maybe, just maybe—" The voice was silent.

"At least Wilson is thinking," the commissioner said.

"He's got another wild idea—"

"Put him on." The commissioner nodded to Caldwell.

"Caldwell here, Nat," Caldwell said. "What is your thinking?"

"If we can get power in from the substation," Nat said, "I've got Joe Lewis working on it, then maybe we can jury-rig something for one of the express elevators." Pause. "At least that's what we're working on. We'll need some men—"

"Simmons can provide them."

Nat's voice changed. "Yes," he said. "I'm anxious to talk to Simmons. About a lot of things."

Caldwell turned back into the room. "You heard it," he said.

Nat's voice came again on the desk speaker. "The choppers can't see any way. With the tower mast there's no place for them to set down."

"All right, Nat," Caldwell said. "Thank you." He looked around the silent office.

The governor was the first to speak. "I've read about situations like this," he said. "I never expected to be in one." He showed his smile. "Anyone for parchesi?"

The time was 4:59. Thirty-six minutes had passed since the explosion.

15

4:58–5:10

Concrete and steel—insensitive? indestructible? Not so. The building was in pain, and the men climbing the interminable stairs could feel even through the fire doors the fever of the building's torment.

Firemen Denis Howard and Lou Storr paused for a breather on the thirtieth floor. Smoke was not constant, only the heat, and at this level the air was clear. They took off their masks gratefully.

"Mother of God!" This was Howard. "Do you feel like one of those mountain goats?" He was catching his breath in great gasps.

"I told you to stop smoking," Storr said. "See what it did for me?" His breathing was at least as labored as Howard's. "I make it ninety-five floors to go."

They breathed in silence for a time. Then, "Do you remember a poem in school?' Howard said. "It was about this crazy mixed-up kid who walked through some little town waving a flag that said 'Excelsior'?"

Storr nodded wearily. "Something like that," he said.

"Well," Howard said, "I always wondered just where in hell he thought he was going." He paused. "Like now." He faced the stairs again. "Let's get on with it."

They had carried the charred body from the subbasement covered decently with a stretcher sheet. The TV camera followed the body's progress to a waiting morgue wagon, where patrolman Frank Barnes stopped the stretcher, raised the sheet, and had a long careful look. To Shannon he said, "That's our boy, Mike." I could have kept him out, he thought. Self-incrimination, accomplishing nothing. He looked at the morgue attendant. "Does he have a name?"

"There's a name inside his toolbox—if it's his, that is."

Barnes looked at the toolbox, blackened from explosion but still recognizable. "That's the one he was carrying."

"The name in it," the attendant said, "is Connors, John Connors with an O." He paused. " 'Citizen of the World' is what it says after his name. A nut."

"The lieutenant," Barnes said, "will want to know."

"As far as I'm concerned," the morgue attendant said, "the lieutenant is welcome to the whole fried carcass. You know about radar ovens, instant cooking? That's what we got here."

Barnes went off to find the police lieutenant, whose

name was James Potter. The lieutenant listened, wrote the name down in his notebook, and sighed. "Okay," he said. "It's a start."

"I could have kept him out of the building, Lieutenant," Barnes said. "I could have—"

"Can you read cards through their backs, Frank? I can't. Did he wear a sign saying he was a nut carrying explosives?"

Barnes went back to rejoin Shannon at the barricades, feeling no better, while the lieutenant went to the construction trailer. There was a conference in progress, and the lieutenant sighed again, leaned against a drafting board, and waited for the conference to end. Patty was perched on a nearby stool. The lieutenant wondered idly what she was doing there, but did not ask.

"Two ways," one of the battalion chiefs was saying. "The stairs or, if you can work a miracle, an elevator." He was speaking to Nat.

"We're trying," Nat said. "Maybe it will work. Maybe it won't." He paused. "And maybe the stairs won't work, either. Maybe your men will get so far and find they can't go any farther because fire has broken through into the stairwell above them."

The battalion chief could think of another distinct possibility: fire might break through *beneath* his men, and that would be that. He said nothing.

"So the third possibility may be all we have," Nat said.

Tim Brown said, "The gun that shoots a line, and then what?"

"Breeches buoy."

Giddings was looking out the trailer window. "To where?"

"North Trade Center tower. It's the closest and the tallest."

All five men stared up at the soaring buildings. Their tops seemed to converge. Tim Brown said, "Sitting in a canvas bag with your legs sticking through, swinging in air a quarter of a mile above the street, a quarter of a mile!" Glaring at Nat.

Patty, listening, shuddered.

"All right," Nat said, and his voice was almost brutal, "which would you rather be—swinging in that canvas bag and scared half to death or being cooked to a cinder by a fire that won't stop halfway? Because that's the choice."

"Unless," the battalion chief said, "the stairs or the elevator."

Nat shook his head. "We can't wait."

Potter said to no one in particular, "Hobson's choice."

All five men looked at him.

"You can take any horse in the stable," Potter said, "as long as it's the one nearest the door." He took out his identification folder and opened it to show the badge. "If one of you has got a little time—"

Tim Brown said almost explosively, "All right! We'll get Coast Guard people here. Any other ideas?" He was looking straight at Nat.

The man is scared, Nat thought, and so are we all. "Not for the moment," he said, and moved to stand closer to Potter. "I don't know if I can be any help," he said.

Potter looked at Nat's badge. "Architect," he read. "Wilson." He paused. "A man named John Connors. Ring any bell?"

Nat thought about it. He shook his head.

"He," Potter said, "is the—charred one."

"The electrician?"

Potter's eyebrows rose. "You know about him?"

"The cops told me. The black cop. The man was inside, riding elevators. I heard him. I never saw him." Brief memory of that grizzly bear so long ago, also unseen.

At the far end of the trailer Tim Brown's voice said loudly into the phone, "I won't argue that it's unusual, Captain, and maybe far out as well. But we're running out of options." His voice dropped to normal tone, the words indistinguishable.

Potter said to Nat, "The other dead man—" He left it there.

"I don't know him," Nat said, "but I understand he was at the computer console."

Potter was silent, thoughtful. He said at last, "Could

153

he have—done anything if he'd been alive when the stuff hit the fan? Is that why he was clobbered?"

We are standing here, calmly talking about what has already happened, Nat thought, when what is really important is what is going to happen, to the building, to the people up in the Tower Room, those most important, unless somebody can figure out some way to get them down.

He was tempted to brush off the lieutenant's questions as beside the point. But they were not. You have to work both ways, he told himself, forward *and* back. Why? So that maybe, just maybe, this kind of thing could be prevented from happening again.

"I'd say yes," Nat said, "but that's just a guess. Almost any kind of trouble would show up on the console. Trouble ought to be taken care of automatically, but that's why there's a man there—just in case. He can override the automated systems, and maybe he would have had time to do something before everything went dead." Nat paused. "It seems likely that Connors, if that's who it was, *thought* the man at the console might be able to do something, so he took him out in advance."

Patty stirred on the stool. She cleared her throat. Both men looked at her and waited. "I don't mean to—interfere," she said.

The lieutenant said, "Lady, if you've got any ideas at all, give them to us, please."

Patty said slowly, "If he, the man Connors, even knew there was a computer console and that someone would be monitoring it, let alone thought the man could do anything—then doesn't that mean that Connors was familiar with the building and how it works?"

Nat was smiling now. "Good girl." He looked at Potter. "It means that Connors probably worked on the building, doesn't it? To know his way around?"

"And," Patty said, "Daddy's records will show if he worked for the general contractor. The subcontractors' records will show if he worked on one of their crews."

Nat said slowly, "I called him an electrician." He shook his head. "I doubt it. If he had been an electrician, unless

154

he really wanted to kill himself, he'd have known better than to mess with primary power. He might just as well have soaked himself with gasoline and touched a match to it. Better, he might have survived burns."

Patty shivered. Then she said, "I'll call Daddy's office and have them see if Connors' name shows up on a crew list." She stepped down from the stool, glad to have something to do to occupy her mind, which kept returning to the big helpless man in the hospital bed.

Nat watched her go. He was smiling.

And here came Tim Brown on his stork legs, red hair rumpled. "The Coast Guard's sending some men," he said, "and some equipment." He shrugged angrily. "They don't think it will work, but they're willing to have a look. The trouble is that the nearest Trade Center tower is probably too far away for shooting a line into the Tower Room, and unless they can do that—" He spread his hands. "No dice," he said.

Nat's face was thoughtful. "We'll just have to see," he said.

Paul Simmons was already in the midtown hotel room when Zib arrived breathless, her color high. She glanced at the television set. It was dark. So he doesn't know, she thought, he thinks nothing is changed. Then, "No," she said as Paul reached for her. "I didn't come for that."

"That is a switch. Then why the summons?"

Strangely, she felt almost calm. Perhaps resigned is the better word, she thought. Her voice was steady enough. "I have a message for you. You are wanted down at the World Tower building."

She walked to the television, switched it on. A picture sprang into instant focus—the plaza, the fire trucks and hoses, uniformed men, scene of controlled confusion. Zib turned the volume down and the room was still.

"Nat called me," she said. "He has been trying to reach you. Patty is with him down there and she told him I might know where you were."

"I see." Merely that. Paul was watching the silent picture on the television screen. "What's happening?"

"All he said was that they have fires in the building, that Bert McGraw is in the hospital with a heart attack, that they have a hundred people—he said trapped in the Tower Room—and he needs some answers from you." All? It was quite a bit to remember, but the words had been repeating themselves in her mind ever since she had hung up the phone after Nat's call.

"Trapped." Paul repeated the single word. His eyes had not left the screen. "That means no elevators. That means no power." At last he looked at Zib. "And just what answers does he think I can give him?"

He didn't say.

Paul wore a small quizzical smile. "Was that all he said?"

Zib closed her eyes and shook her head. The entire conversation clamored in her mind. She opened her eyes again. Paul seemed a stranger, unaffected, uninvolved. "He said, 'Where is the son of a bitch? If you don't know where he is, find him. And get him down here. On the double.' "

Paul said, "Well!" The quizzical smile spread.

"I told him," Zib said, "that he had never talked to me like that before."

"And?"

"He said it was a mistake, that probably he ought to have paddled my patrician ass." Like a little girl, she thought, a spoiled little girl given her way too long.

"As the British say," Paul said, "the cat seems to be amongst the pigeons."

Would she have laughed at the phraseology before? No matter. "This isn't really a time for witticisms."

"What is it a time for? Lamentations?" Paul glanced again at the screen, the tiny silent moving shapes. "There's nothing I can do down there. Nothing." He faced Zib again. "What's done, as Shakespeare might have said, is already done and not to be undone."

"You could try. They're trying."

"That," Paul said, "is the kind of platitude we're raised on. 'If at first you don't succeed, try, try again.' And they cite David the Bruce and his goddam spider. I think

156

it was W. C. Fields who put it much better, 'If at first you don't succeed,' he said, 'give up; stop making a fool of yourself.' "

Zib said slowly, "Have you any idea what has happened? Is that it?"

"How could I have an idea?"

"What you said about what's done."

"A figure of speech."

"I don't think it was. I think——"

"I don't give a tinker's damn what you think." Paul's voice was cold. "You're decorative and sometimes amusing, and you've very good in bed, but thinking isn't your forte."

Oh God, Zib thought, dialogue straight out of the magazine! Unreal. Escape fiction come alive. But the words were like a slap, not a blow. Where was real hurt? "You flatter me," she said.

"We agreed at the beginning——"

"That it was fun and games," Zib said, "Yes."

"Don't tell me you began to take us seriously?"

The bastard, she thought; he is actually pleased. "No," she said. "There was never anything about you to take seriously." She paused and glanced at the screen. "There is even less now." She faced Paul squarely. "You were the man on the job. I know that much. Paul Simmons and Company, Electrical Contractors. Did you skimp the work?" She was silent for a moment, thinking, remembering. "Once you told me that Nat was going to do you favors, only he wouldn't know it. Was that what you meant?"

"Silly questions," Paul said, "don't deserve even silly answers." He walked to the television set and switched it off. "Well," he said, "it's been nice. Don't think it hasn't." He walked to the door. "I'll miss this hotel and its cozy atmosphere." His hand was on the knob.

"Where are you going?"

"I think I'll go see a couple of men," Paul said. "And then I think I'll go home." He opened the door and stepped through. The door closed quietly.

Zib stood motionless in the center of the room. Unreal,

incredible: those were the words that came to mind. She tucked them away for later examination and walked to the bed, plumped herself down, and picked up the telephone.

She had no need to look up the number; after all these years the construction·office telephone number was familiar enough. And Nat was there. Zib kept her voice calm, expressionless. "I gave Paul your message."

"He's coming down?"

"No." Zib paused. "I'm—sorry, Nat. I tried."

"Where is he going?"

There was in his tone a quality Zib had never encountered. Call it strength, force, whatever; it dominated. "He said he's going to see a couple of men," she said, "and then he thinks he'll go home."

"Okay," Nat said.

"What are you going to do?"

"Have him picked up. Objections?"

Zib shook her head in silence. No objections. "He saw the television," she said. "And I told him what you had said." She paused again. "He said, 'What's done is already done and not to be undone.' Does that mean anything?"

Nat's voice was quiet but unhesitant. "Entirely too goddam much," he said, and hung up.

He turned from the telephone and looked around the office trailer. Assistant Commissioner Brown was there, and two battalion chiefs, Giddings, Patty, Potter, and himself. "Simmons," he said, "apparently has seen all he wants to see on the tube. I don't know if we can use him or not, but I think we want him."

"If you want him, we'll get him," Potter said.

Giddings said, "More important, if Lewis has done his figuring, let's get some men on the job and see if we can get power to at least one of those express elevators."

Nat snapped his fingers. "Simmons's foreman—what's his name? Pat? Pat Harris." He was looking at Giddings, and he saw that Giddings understood. To Brown, Nat said, "We need him and some men. Maybe they can do some good and maybe they can't, but we'll try." He paused. "But we need Harris for another reason. Simmons didn't put those changes in with his own hands. Harris had to know about them."

Patty cleared her throat. She was alone, a trifle diffident, but quite at ease in this man's world. To how many jobs had she ridden with Daddy? In how many construction trailers just like this one had she sat and twiddled her thumbs, waiting for technical discussion to end and a hooky afternoon's excursion to begin? How much knowledge had she absorbed unknowingly? "There is somebody else who would have had to know about the changes," she said. She paused. "The inspector who signed them off. Who was he?"

In the silence Nat said again, "Good girl."

Giddings said, "We'll damn well find out and get the son of a bitch down here. I know his face. His name—" He was silent for a moment. "Harry," he said. "Harry. I don't know his last name, but we'll find it."

16

5:01–5:11

Mayor Ramsay came out of the office in search of his wife. He found her alone at the Tower Room windows, looking out over the broad shining river. She smiled as he came up.

"So solemn, Bob," she said. "Is it really as solemn an occasion as Bent indicated?"

"I'm afraid so."

"You will think of something."

"No." The mayor shook his head. "Any thinking will have to be done by the technical people—Ben Caldwell, his man at the other end of the phone, or Tim Brown."

159

He paused. His smile was wry. "And any orders will come from Bent, not from me."

"It is your city, Bob."

Again denial by headshake. "There comes a time," Ramsay said, "when you have to admit that others are better men than you are. I'm not in Bent's class."

"That is nonsense." Paula's smile was gentle. "And you will only make me cross if you persist in thinking it. You are the finest man I have ever known."

Ramsay was silent for a little time, staring almost as if hypnotized at the river. "Bent threw something out this afternoon. He called this building just another dinosaur stable." He smiled at his wife. "There is the germ of truth there. Maybe I've been too busy running here, running there, patching this or that to see it."

"I don't understand, Bob."

"Where is the merit," the mayor asked, "in building the biggest anything? The biggest pyramid, the biggest ship, the biggest dam, or the biggest building? The biggest city for that matter. The dinosaurs were the biggest and it was their size that finished them. That is Bent's point." He shook his head. "No," he said, "quality and need ought to be the criteria, and need ought to come first. Do we need it? Is it possible? Those two questions ought to be asked at the beginning, and the answers written down in indelible ink in large letters so they won't be forgotten."

"Where have you strayed from that?" Paula said.

"I let the city stray from it. Is a building like this necessary? The answer is no. We have all the office space we can use. More. And I could have stopped it. Instead, I gave it every bit of help City Hall could give it. One more piece of—vanity, a building all the world would admire."

"And will, Bob."

The mayor opened his mouth, thought better of it, and closed it again in silence. In the end all he said was, "Maybe." There was no point yet in crying doom.

Paula said, "Thirty-five years is a long time, Bob. People get to know one another well." She paused. "I've been thinking while I stood here with you, knowing what

160

was in your mind." She smiled. "There are telephones. I think we might use one, don't you?"

The mayor frowned.

"I think we might call Jill," Paula said. "She was going to watch on television. She will be worried."

"Good idea." All at once the mayor was smiling again, the boyish smile the voters knew so well. "We'll reassure her."

"That," Paula said, "wasn't quite what I had in mind."

"Now wait a minute." The boyish smile faded, disappeared. "There's no need to panic."

"Not panic, Bob, but isn't it time that we stopped pretending there is nothing out of joint? Those helicopters out there—what good can they do? The firemen Bent says are coming up the stairs—" Paula shook her head. Her smile was gentle, unreproachful, even understanding, but it asserted denial. "The last mad dash to the top of Everest—why? What are they even hoping to accomplish?"

"Damn it," the mayor said, "you don't just—give up."

"I am not giving up, Bob."

"Maybe I misunderstood you," the mayor said slowly. "Just what were you thinking to tell Jill?"

"Mostly little things."

"Adding up to what?"

Paula smiled, mocking herself. The smile was quickly gone. She said slowly, "Adding up to 'au revoir.' I want to hear her voice again. I want her to hear ours. I want to tell her where in that big house she will find our own silver —Grandmother Jones's. I want her to know that there is some jewelry of mine, some you gave me, some that has been in the family for generations—that it is in the safe deposit box at the Irving Trust branch at Forty-second and Park and that the key is in my desk. I want to tidy up as many loose ends as I can.

"But aside from *things,* I want her to know that we don't think she has failed, even with her divorce! I want her to know that we understand that we heaped too much on her because there were always cameras and reporters and microphones, and that it has been hard enough for us, you and me, adults, to retain some kind of perspective, and that from the beginning it was probably impossible for her, a child, to see the world as anything but sugarplum candy—and all hers before she had earned any part of it. And you have to earn it or it is never really yours.

"I want her to be happy, to find her own happiness, and in that sense it will be a good thing if we are—no longer around because then she will have no shelter in which to hide and shiver and feel sorry for herself.

"But most of all, Bob, I want her to know what is true and has always been true—that she is very precious to us, wanted; and that now that we're up here in this ridiculous predicament, it is she we are thinking of, no one else. Maybe that will give her a little support, a little more—strength than she has so far managed to develop." Paula paused. "Those are some of the things I want to say, Bob. Are they—wrong?"

The mayor took her arm. His voice was gentle. "Let's find a phone," he said.

Cary Wycoff found Senator Peters leaning against a wall, watching the room. "You're asking it calmly enough," the congressman said. There was accusation in his voice.

"What do you suggest?" the senator said. "A speech? A committee hearing? Should we draft a bill or a minority report?" He paused. His voice altered subtly. "Or should we call the White House and lay the blame squarely on this administration, and then call Jack Anderson and give him the inside story?"

Wycoff said, "You and Bent Armitage—you both treat me as if I were still a kid, wet behind the ears."

"Maybe, son," the senator said, "that's because sometimes you behave that way. Not always, but sometimes. Like now." He looked around the big room. "There are a lot of silly people here who haven't the faintest idea what is going on. Have you ever seen panic? Real panic? A crowd gone wild with fear?"

Wycoff said, "Have you?" He ought to have known

162

better, he told himself: Jake Peters never waved an empty gun in discussion or argument.

"I was in Anchorage in sixty-four," the senator said, "when the earthquake hit." He paused. "Have you ever been in even a small earthquake? No? The fright, I think, is like nothing else. You think of the earth as solid, unchanging, secure. And when even it begins to move under you, then there is no security left anywhere." He made a small impatient gesture. "Never mind. I have seen panic, yes. And I don't want to see it again. Particularly here."

"All right," Wycoff said, "neither do I. What do you suggest?"

"That I move away from this wall," the senator said, and did so.

Wycoff opened his mouth in anger. He shut it with a snap.

"Don't jump to conclusions," the senator said. "I'm not having you on. Feel the wall. Hot, isn't it? I've been leaning there feeling it heat up. It's come along pretty fast. That probably means that heated air, maybe even open fire, is climbing up some of the shafts in the core." He glanced at his watch and smiled without amusement. "Faster than I thought."

"You ought to have been a scientist." There was disgust in Wycoff's voice.

"Aren't we, you and I? Practicing social scientists, that is?" The senator smiled, this time with amusement. "Not very damned scientific, I'll grant you, but we do try to measure the pulse and the blood pressure of the people we represent—and then act accordingly."

"And sometimes, maybe most times," Wycoff said, "not act at all."

"That in itself is activity. Which," the senator said, "is something it apparently takes a long time to learn, and some people never learn it. 'Don't just stand there, *do* something!' That's the usual reaction. Instead, sometimes, 'Don't do something, just *stand* there!' would be a far more sensible dictum. Do you remember when Mowgli falls in to the nest of cobras and they don't want

163

to hurt him, but they tell Kaa, the rock python, in effect, 'For Christ's sake, tell him to stand still and stop prancing around and stepping on us!' Hell's fire, boy, I don't like this situation a damn bit better than you do, but I can't think of anything to do about it, and unless or until I can think of something helpful, there is nothing to do without making things worse. So relax and watch the people. Where do you suppose Bob and Paula Ramsay are headed so purposefully? For the johns?"

Wycoff smiled. "As good a guess as any."

"Probably better than most," the senator said. "Right in the middle of a debate that has roused hackles on both sides of the aisle and filled the galleries with press and radio and TV people and just plain interested people, partisan people convinced the nation's future is at stake and maybe it is—right in the middle of it, the senior senator from Nebraska or Oklahoma or, yes, New York, leans over to his colleague and whispers something in his ear, and the press gallery takes careful note that something is about to happen. And it is. What the senior senator is saying is, 'George, I've got to pee or bust. It was all that coffee plus the bean soup. I'll be back before the windbag is even close to done.' And he stands up and walks solemnly out of the chamber. Everybody in the gallery thinks he's headed straight for the White House to have it out with The Man."

Wycoff smiled again. "What do you want for an epitaph, Jake? 'Exit laughing'?"

The senator shook his head. His expression was serious. "No. I'd like to feel that I had earned the proudest epitaph of all: 'With what he had, he did the best he could.' I think we might as well have a drink, don't you?"

Joe Lewis the electrical engineer said, "We can't know what's happened. Maybe the motors are burned out. Maybe the cable carrying power to them is gone. All we can do is bring in another cable from the substation, splice it in, and hope that there's enough of the rising cable left to carry power to the elevator motors." He lifted his hands and let them fall. "That's the best we can do."

164

"Let's get on with it," Giddings said. "Con Edison will give us all the help they can." He paused and stared at the sky where the great buildings seemed almost to come together. "Will you give me one good reason," he said, "why we thought we had to build the goddam thing so big?"

"Because," Joe Lewis said, "somebody else built a big one and ours had to be bigger. Simple as that. Let's go."

17

5:03–5:18

Zib was back at her desk at the magazine and unable to concentrate. It was late, but there were piles of manuscripts before her, all of which had been read and passed along as possibilities for purchase, and usually she found the reading of them at least an interesting exercise in judgment. Today, now, she found them pointless, even silly—what was the current phrase?—without relevance.

And yet that was not true. Without even looking at the pages, she knew that a good share, even most of the stories would deal with young women and their problems, and if that was not relevant, what in the world was? Because she was a young woman, wasn't she? And God knew it was plain enough at last that she had problems like everybody else.

Like everybody else. That was the phrase that hurt, because always she had considered that she was not like *anybody* else.

She had grown up as Zib Marlowe, a name that had meaning, and now she was married to rising young Nat Wilson of Ben Caldwell's firm. Those two facts alone were sufficient to set her apart. But there was more.

There was her job here, as fiction editor for one of the

few remaining national magazines, and she did the job well. There was the fact of her looks and figure, and an educated intelligence far above average. There was—oh, you name the criteria, and whatever they were you would find Ms. Zib Marlowe Wilson crowding the upper limits.

Except maybe in the old-fashioned virtues that used to be considered so important? How about those, darling?

Strike the question; Zib had answered it to her own satisfaction years ago, which was one of the reasons she was where she was.

And yet, paradoxically, it was right here at the magazine, that monument to upper-middle-class sophistication, that on occasion she found reason to wonder about the solidity of those chosen beliefs. There was, for example, that Meacham story a few months back that had caught her fancy and for which she had argued without success with Jim Henderson.

"Elizabeth, luv," Jim had said, "our readers are bright above average or they wouldn't be reading at all, they'd be sitting glued to the tube. But they are also wives and mothers worried about budgets and mortgages and the PTA, mundane matters like those. And most of them wouldn't know an identity crisis if it bit them. I'm not sure I would. They are the special salt of this earth, and I mean that as a compliment. Now take this navel-contemplating piece—"

"As you make abundantly plain," Zib said, "you are the boss. But this happens to be a beautifully written, sensitive, probing—"

"Piece of crap," Henderson said. He got up from his chair, walked around his desk, and sat down again. He was in shirtsleeves, long and bony and pitiless. "Sometimes I don't dig you, girl. You are a hell of a good fiction editor. Most times. Then some agent, probably Soames, who knows your weaknesses sends in something like this and you flip over it when you know perfectly well it isn't our kind of thing."

"Maybe it ought to be."

"And that is crap too, and you know it. You're being

schizo. Now send this back." He held the manuscript between thumb and forefinger, something unclean.

Zib, furious, marched back to her office and called John Soames. "I'm sorry, John. I liked the Meacham piece—"

"Let me guess, darling. Lord Henderson did not like it, and that is that. But whatever else did we expect? There was no way."

"Then," Zib said, "why did you send it to me in the first place?"

He was smiling. Zib could almost see it. And in the tanned face, beneath the graying hair and the glasses, crinkling the corners of his eyes, the smile looked very avuncular and English-professorish, very much the literary man at confident ease. "Just to show you the quality of fiction your magazine might run, if it chose. What else, darling?"

The day was already slightly out of focus, and seeing behind sham seemed easy. Strange. "You wouldn't waste your time," Zib said. "Or mine."

There was a short silence. Did the smile fade or perhaps let slip a little of its confidence? "I will level with you, darling," Soames said in a different voice. "I sent you the piece on the millionth chance that you might buy it at your splendidly exorbitant rates, one-tenth of which would have gone into my coffers as commission. Instead I will try to peddle it elsewhere, and maybe end by giving it away if anyone will take it. If my commission exceeds ten dollars instead of the hundred and fifty I would have had from you, I shall be mightily surprised."

"At least you're being honest," Zib said, although of course she ought to have known from the beginning how things were. "Tell me one more thing. In Jim Henderson's place, would you buy the piece?"

"Dear God, no! Certainly not. It is offensive, pretentious, flatulent. But as we agree, it does have a certain charm, and the literary establishment would make noises over it."

And why should she have remembered that so vividly now after all this time? Because, she thought, you never really forget the putdowns, you just tuck them off in a corner and hope they get decently covered with dust. Aloud, whispering, "What in the world am I doing here anyway? Answer me that, Elizabeth."

"Zib, darling." Cathy Hearn, associate editor, standing in the doorway. "How can you be so calm? The building that neat husband of yours designed is coming apart at the seams. It's on the radio *and* on Jim's desktop TV, and you sit here actually working! Honestly. Have you flaked out?"

Cathy, Zig thought, was a smalltown cornfed Midwest girl loving every moment of the big city. She was plump and perpetually worried about it; brighter than bright and forever trying to conceal it; as intimate with sex as a doe rabbit and yet forever exuding an aura of fresh virginity. "Maybe I have at that," Zib said.

Cathy perched an ample haunch on the corner of Zib's desk. "Trouble, hon?" She paused. "Man trouble, of course. It always is." She shook her head. "There are rules," she said. "If your man walks in and finds you balling someone else, he is supposed to say, 'Ah, pardon! Continue!' And if you *can* continue, *that* is savoir-faire."

Picture Nat in that role. No way. Face it, Zib told herself, you are married to a square, a real, honest-to-God, Herbert Hoover collar, McKinley morality, home-and-motherhood square. For a moment anger rose, flickered, and then died.

"Are you stoned?" There was concern in Cathy's voice. Zib shook her head. The long hair covered her face. She brushed it back angrily. "I don't even have that excuse."

"Then," Cathy said judiciously, "I'd suggest a witch-doctor, either the pill man or the shrink." She paused. Then, incredulously, "You aren't pregnant or any ridiculous thing like that?"

Again the headshake. Again the angry brushing motion. Why did she wear her hair long like this anyway? Why did anyone? Because it was the in thing to do? Because current fashion so decreed? How ridiculous. "I'm not pregnant. Stop worrying, Cathy."

"My problem," Cathy said, "is that I'm a mother at heart. I was a Four-H'er when I was a kid. Fact. I had chicks and lambs and calves coming out of my ears. And I worried about them. I canned vegetables and baked cakes and I just knew that one day HE would ride by on his white horse and scoop me up—if he could lift me—and we would ride off into the sunset to breed a family, and that would give me real scope for worrying. Instead, here I am, giving free analysis—"

"Cathy, go away."

It was Cathy's turn to shake her head. She brushed her own long hair back from her face with both hands. "And leave you here to meditate? No way. You stare inward long enough and you find you don't like anything you see, not anything at all. Your whole life is a living sham, a real mess. You've spent all these years trying to find out who you are, as they do in novels, snuffing around in the damnedest places, and what you finally do find is a little shriveled-up id that couldn't screw its way out of a loose nightie, that's what you find, and what's worse, what's far worse, the damn little thing is laughing at you." She paused for breath.

Zib said slowly, solemnly, "Yes, you're right. It is laughing at me."

Cathy was silent for a few moments. "You've got it bad, hon. You patrician types aren't supposed even to take a look at yourselves, let alone feel accountable for any troubles you may find. You—"

"Is that how you see it, Cathy?" It was her own voice, but it sounded like a stranger's, and it asked a question Zib had never even thought of before. "Is it?"

"It isn't that bad." Cathy was smiling, mocking herself, her exaggeration.

"But there is something to it?" Was that what Nat saw too?

"Look," Cathy said, "girlish discussions—" She smiled again. "We fought those out after Taps at Camp Kickapoo back when 'When are you going to start wearing a brassiere?' was the big question."

"I'm asking, Cathy," Zib said. "Tell me how it looks from where you stand."

Cathy hesitated. "You're backing me right up to it, aren't you?" She paused. "All right. It goes like this. I went to a country grade school and the local high with a student body of one hundred bused in—dirty word, but it wasn't dirty to us: it was the only way to get there—bused in from a hundred square miles of countryside. You went where? Miss This's or Miss That's? I went to a college you've never heard of. You went where? Vassar, Smith? Wellesley? Radcliffe? My father got partway through that same high school, only there was a depression then, and he had to quit to go to work at whatever he could find, which wasn't much, because Grandfather had been laid off by the railroad. Your father was Harvard? Or was it Yale? And maybe the Depression hurt you too, took you right down to your last yacht, I shouldn't be surprised, but your people knew that it was only a temporary embarrassment, and mine thought the end of the world, not the prosperity some people were talking about, was just around the corner. The basic difference between you and me is that you know whatever you do is right, because how could it be otherwise? And I have to wonder and worry every step of the way, because as far back as anybody knows the Hearns have been born losers, and maybe I've broken the mold, but maybe the genes are still there too, just waiting to pounce." Cathy paused. "That's the difference between background and cultural emptiness."

"I didn't know, Cathy. I never even thought."

"And the last thing I want to hear you say," Cathy said, "is that you're sorry."

"I won't say it." Zib paused thoughtfully. "You know Nat. You say he's neat. He—"

"He finally spit in your eye?" What was in Cathy's tone said far more than the words.

Zib looked up. "You've been waiting for it? Watching?" But how could it be that she felt no resentment?

"We haven't been making book in the office," Cathy said, "but we've followed the score as best we could."

She stood up from the desk. "What confuses me is that with what's happening downtown you're sitting here reading slush-pile gleanings."

So here at last was what it came to, the basic truth, uncovered. "I've been thinking about myself," Zib said, and found no pain in the saying. "I haven't even been thinking about what is happening downtown." She paused. "I guess thinking about myself is a habit I have."

"Could be," Cathy said, and walked out.

18

It was a neat little house in Garden City; green lawn, white petunias in bloom, a basketball backboard and hoop mounted on the garage door, an enormous television mast aimed at the city, clinging to the brick chimney and dominating the roof.

Mrs. Pat Harris answered the door in tight peach-colored jeans, matching sneakers, and a striped tank top. Her hair was in blue plastic curlers. She was young, attractive, and thoroughly conscious of it. "Well," she said, "this is a surprise, Mr. Simmons. You want to see Pat?"

"If I may." Paul wore his actor's smile and his easy manner.

"He's downstairs watching TV." The girl paused. "We thought you would be at the World Tower opening, Mr. Simmons. I haven't seen it, but I know it's going on. I have, you know, things to do around the house even when Pat's home. You go on down. He'll be awful glad to see you."

I doubt it, Paul thought, but the smile remained unchanged as he walked down the stairs into the paneled

171

game room. On the massive color television console screen the fire trucks crowding around the Tower Plaza looked the color of blood. The volume was turned low, and the announcer's voice was almost inaudible: "We have a report, ladies and gentlemen, that the fire is spreading inside the building. This entire disaster—because it is beginning to look like almost certain disaster—is incredible. Every safety factor known to architects—"

The set went black and the sound stopped all at once. From his chair Pat Harris said, "Welcome, Boss. I figured you'd be along." He laid the remote control on the coffee table and jumped up out of the chair. "Drink?" There was faint hostility behind the words.

"I think a drink would be a good idea," Paul said. He sat down and looked around.

There was a bar and a full-size pool table, a large Naugahyde-covered sofa and matching chair, a card table with cards and poker chips set out, a dart board on one wall, three darts in the bull's-eye.

"Nice place you have here," Paul said. He accepted his drink, nodded his thanks, tasted the mellow Scotch—Chivas Regal, at a guess, he thought. "Very nice," he said.

"Yeah." Pat Harris was a small quick man. His restless eyes watched Paul's face carefully. "Man works hard, he likes to live it up a little." Harris paused. "Just a working stiff," he said. "I do what I'm told."

Paul ignored the dark and silent television set, and concentrated on the man. "Do you intend to keep on the same way?" He said. He paused. "Doing what you're told?"

Harris lighted a cigarette and blew out a cloud of smoke. With the cigarette still hanging from his lip, he tore the match into small pieces; his movements were sudden and jerky. "I been thinking about that." He smiled quickly, without meaning. "Funny, I was just thinking about it when you come down the stairs."

Paul said slowly, carefully, "And what conclusion had you come to?"

Another huge cloud of smoke. Harris leaned forward to tap ashes into the coffee-table ashtray. He leaned back again. "Like this, you know what I mean, let's say, you know, work for a guy. He's a good Joe, treats you right, so you owe him, you know, something better than a kick in the teeth, don't you?"

"I think that is a reasonable viewpoint," Paul said. "A friendly view," he added.

"On the other hand," Harris said, "you know what I mean? a guy has to, you know, look out for himself. This is a dog-eat-dog world. You get yours or you get nothing." He paused, waiting.

"I think there is some cogency in that view too," Paul said.

"Big word."

And big words are a mistake, Paul told himself, because they seem to talk down. But it was too late to do anything but ignore the slip. "Go on," he said.

"The way I see it," Harris said, "you know, balance one against the other and try to see what's—right."

Paul nodded and sipped his Scotch. All at once it tasted foul and there was a burning sensation in his chest. Pure and simple tension, he told himself. "And," he said calmly enough, "how did you decide?"

Harris took the cigarette from the ashtray, inhaled deeply, and blew four large smoke rings in rapid succession before he spoke. "I hear Bert McGraw's in the hospital. Heart attack. I hear he may not make it." The restless eyes searched Paul's face.

"I can't say," Paul said. "He had a heart attack, yes." He waved one hand. "We were talking about your thought. Bert doesn't matter at the moment."

"That," Harris said, "is crap. If I thought I'd have that old man looking for me with blood in his eye—" He shook his head.

"Bert," Paul said, "showed me some change orders." His voice was wholly calm. "He asked me if we made the changes. I said yes, of course we made them, why should we not?"

Harris wiped his mouth. "Jesus! Now I know you've flipped."

Paul shook his head. Never mind the burning sensation. Never mind anything but this. "The change orders had surfaced," he said. "I don't know how, but Will Giddings found them. No matter what I said to Bert, they were going to tear into the walls to see for themselves. So the only thing I could say was, yes, of course we made the changes. Look at the signature: Nat Wilson, Caldwell's bright-haired boy. Should we question word from on high?" His voice underscored the last four words.

Harris stubbed out his cigarette carefully. Then he looked up again. "I don't know," he said. "You use big words and you make it sound okay, but I don't know." He stood up and walked across the room, turned and walked back to his chair. He dropped into it with an almost audible thud. "I'll level with you," he said. "You been a good Joe. I've worked for some crummy bastards, I'd just like the chance to kick their teeth in, but you're okay."

"Thank you," Paul said, and meant it.

"I'll tell you how it is," Harris said. "I got two things I can, you know, do. Two ways I can go. First"—he held up one finger—"I can go down to City Hall when this is over." He gestured toward the television set. "I can say, 'Jesus, if I'd of even guessed, I'd of told him to shove it.' You, I mean. 'But,' I can say, 'what the hell, he's the boss, and he's an engineer and he says the changes are okay and the change orders are signed by the architect and who the hell am I to argue any more than I did?' "

There was silence. Paul said without expression, 'Your only argument, Pat, was about how much it was worth not to argue."

"That's what you say," Harris said. "But that isn't, you know, what I say. I say I did argue, and I can come up with three, four guys who'll say sure I did, but you told me everything was okay, so I went ahead. And Harry, the inspector, signed the work off, so why should I even wonder about it?"

Easy, Paul told himself, easy. "And what is the—other way you can go?"

Harris was unable to sit still. He jumped up, crossed

174

the room again, and then turned but did not come back to his chair. "You told McGraw we made the changes because we had the orders with Wilson's signature on them. Okay, I can say the same. I can say you and I talked about them, wondered about them, but, goddammit, when Caldwell's office says you do something, that's fucking well what you do. That Caldwell, he don't mess around, the cold little bastard." Harris paused. "That's the other way."

"A very good way," Paul said.

Harris walked slowly back to his chair. He lowered himself into it carefully. "A couple things," he said. "Harry the inspector for one."

"Harry won't cause any trouble," Simmons said. "Or if he does, it will only be for himself." He paused. "You said a couple of things. What else?"

Harris's face was expressionless, the face of a poker player studying his opponent. "You remember a kid named Jimmy?"

"No."

Harris smiled faintly, scornfully. "No, I guess you wouldn't. He was just a kid, worked in one of my crews, went to engineering school at night." He paused and lighted a fresh cigarette. "He didn't like the changes that were coming through. Especially, he didn't like the change order taking out that primary-power safety-ground circuit. He said it was dangerous and he was going to talk to Nat Wilson about it." He paused again. "He wouldn't listen to me or Harry."

"I see," Paul said, and that was all.

"He didn't get to talk to Wilson," Harris said. "He had an accident instead. He fell in front of an IRT express at rush hour."

In the silence, "I see," Paul said again. "But why tell me? Is your conscience bothering you?"

Harris's smile this time was real and meaningful. "You might stand up at that," he said. "And if I back you up, I got to gamble that you won't fold and try to put it all on me."

175

"I'm not going to fold," Paul said. He sipped his whiskey. It tasted better.

"Just one more thing," Harris said. "What's in it for me?"

"You've already had yours."

Harris shook his head. "Uh-uh. I got paid for doing a job. I did it. This is something else."

Had he expected this kind of shakedown? Paul asked himself. Probably, he thought, because he felt no sense of outrage or shock, merely determination that the bargain would be a good one. He had no doubt of his ability to out-haggle this little man. "How much?" he said.

Harris was smiling again. "Now we're getting somewhere."

Paul went up the stairs alone. Down in the game room the television set was again turned on, Harris engrossed in the unfolding tragedy. To Mrs. Harris, who had taken out her blue hair curlers and now smiled fetchingly, "You have a lovely home," Paul said.

"Why, thank you, thanks a lot." There was genuine pleasure.

"Pat," Paul said, "is a lucky man."

As he drove away, a black-and-white police cruiser turned the corner toward the Harris home. Paul watched it in his mirror. It parked at the curb facing the wrong way, and two uniformed policemen got out and walked up to the Harrises' door.

Paul drove on.

19

5:13–5:23

Within the building's core, as in a chimney, heated air rising created its own draft, which sucked fresh air in through open concourse doors.

Outside the city's tallest fire ladders maneuvered uselessly; the problem was within, not without.

On floor after floor, above and below street level, sweating, panting, coughing, and sometimes vomiting firemen wrestled hoses and hurled water, tons of water, at the sometimes seen, but usually hidden enemy—fire.

In a thousand points within the walls of the building, ten thousand, material smoldered or burst into hesitant flame, grew in force and fury, or faded into mere glow and then nothingness from lack of oxygen.

But where, for example, plastic-foam insulation had melted, flues were formed and in them a new chimney effect reached down and out into open halls and corridors for fresh air to feed the blaze, and the growing flames themselves added strength to the draft.

Firemen Denis Howard and Lou Storr paused on the sixtieth floor. They stood for a time gasping, merely existing, while their lungs poured oxygen into their blood and strength gradually returned to their bodies. They looked at each other in silence.

It was Howard who approached the fire door, tried it, and found it free. He opened it cautiously and, as a blast of furnace air enveloped him, had a look inside. Then he shut the door quickly. "Let's go," he said.

Storr opened his mouth. He shut it again. Slowly he nodded. "Might as well." He paused. "Excelsior and all that jazz."

In the trailer Patty turned from the telephone and held out a slip of paper to Lieutenant Potter. "John Connors," she said. "He worked on the job months back. A sheet-metal man." She paused. "He was fired." She paused again. "The union made no protest."

The last sentence said a great deal, Nat thought. The firing was clearly justified or the union would have been up in arms. But what did that mean, except that John Connors had obviously been found wanting in some respect? There was no point in probing further into the circumstances of the firing. Connors himself had to be the

answer to the question of why he had come to the building today and done what he had.

Potter saw it the same way. "A sorehead?" he said.
"Maybe. You never know how deep resentment goes."

Patty was looking out the trailer windows at the plaza,
the dirty shimmering water now covering almost the entire
area, the hoses like spaghetti, the pumping engines, and
the crowds watching. "But," she said, "to do what he
did?" Her tone was incredulous. She turned to face the
two men.

Potter shrugged. "You never know." He tucked the slip
of paper in his pocket. "We'll try to find out."

Patty said, "Why?" Her chin was up. "It's done. It
can't be undone. And the man is dead."

"Let's say," Potter said, "that we like things neat and
tidy."

Nat, watching Patty, found himself thinking that there
was bulldog in her, more than a trace of her father's
stubborn pride. He thought of Bert McGraw and the
mobster forty-five floors above the street, a showdown
just as relentless and irrevocable as any scene in a
Western. There was no give in Bert; there was none in
Patty either.

"There has to be more to it than that," Patty said.

Potter sighed. "There is, of course. From each of these
—things we try to learn. Maybe some day we'll know
enough to stop crimes before they get started." His smile
was deprecatory, aimed inward at his own foolishness.
"That will be a day." He walked to the trailer door,
opened it, and started out. Then he stopped and turned.
"Luck," he said, and was gone.

At the far end of the trailer a walkie-talkie came to life.
"Seventy-fifth floor," a tired voice said, "and it's getting
hotter than the hinges, Chief. No smoke up here yet, but
I hate to think what's happening beyond these fire doors."

"Play it cool, boy," the chief said. "If you can't make
it, you can't make it."

Nat saw Assistant Commissioner Brown open his
mouth and then close it again in silence. The battalion
chief saw it too, and his jaw set in rising anger. "I'll not

178

deliberately throw good men away in a lost cause," he said, "no matter who is up in that building."

Commissioner Brown nodded wearily.

Nat said, "Are you sure it's a lost cause?"

"No, I'm not, and neither can you be sure it isn't. Inside the fire doors of that building we've worked men up twelve floors with hoses." The chief paused. "Near as we can tell there are a hundred more floors, each with their own fires, before the top is even in sight. I've spent twenty-five years learning my trade—"

"Nobody questions that you know it well, Jim," the assistant commissioner said, and there was temporary silence.

"Another thing," the battalion chief said, speaking still to Nat, "that electrical genius of yours. Drawing pretty pictures about how you string a wire here and a wire there and, lo and behold, an express elevator suddenly works."

"You don't think so?" Nat said.

"No, I don't think so!" It was almost a shout. Then, in a weary quiet voice, "But I'm willing to try rockets if anybody thinks they'd have the chance of a snowball in Hell."

The chief was silent for a few moments before he turned to look at the assistant commissioner. "You haven't said it yet, Tim, but you've been thinking it and I can't blame you. My district—just how in hell could a thing like this happen? We've got a building code. It isn't perfect, but it's too good to let this happen. For five—six years this building has been under construction in front of God and everybody, with inspectors and my people and heaven only knows who else watching every step." He stopped and shook his head. "I don't know," he said. "I just don't know."

The assistant commissioner looked at Nat. "You seem to know more about it than anybody else," he said, and left it there, implied accusation plain.

His first reaction was resentment; with effort Nat stifled it. He said slowly, carefully, "I'm beginning to find out some things about it, maybe put some of them together, not that that helps what you're trying to do."

Brown walked to the trailer windows and looked out, up. "If you didn't build them so goddam big," he said. There was anger in his voice, the anger of helplessness. He turned from the windows. "What in hell are you trying to prove anyway?"

"That," Nat said slowly, "is a good question. I don't know the answer."

"I think we've outsmarted ourselves," Brown said. "You know what I mean?" He walked to a chair and plumped himself down, a sad, helpless, angry man. "Look. I was born and grew up in a little town upstate. Tallest building in the county was two stories not counting widow's walks—no, the four-story Empire State Hotel over in the county seat. We had streams. With fish in them. And I can still taste the water that came out of our well."

Nat nodded. "I see what you mean."

"My grandfather took sick," Brown said. "He was in his eighties. The doctor came in the middle of the night, stayed until noon the next day. By that time Grandpa was dead." He spread his large bony hands. "That was how it was. You were born, you lived, you died. Oh, maybe there were accidents, sure there were, and illnesses we can cure today we couldn't even touch then. But there weren't any hundred-and-twenty-five-story buildings and there weren't a lot of other things too."

Giddings came up the trailer steps. His face was smoke-stained and his blue eyes were angry.

"My wife's uncle," Brown said as if Giddings had not appeared, "he's pushing ninety. He's in a hospital. Never mind what it costs. He can't hear and he can't see and he doesn't know anything that's going on. They feed him through a tube and he lies there, still breathing, his heart still beating, and his kidneys and bowels still functioning. He's been like that for three months. The doctors know how to keep him alive, if that's the word, but they don't know when to let him die decently. We're too goddam smart for our own good."

"I'll go with that, Nat said. He looked at Giddings and waited.

"Maybe yes, maybe no," Giddings said. "Personally, I think no. We haven't any idea what's happened in the upper elevator shafts. There's plenty of heat up there, too goddam much heat, we know that. The rails could be distorted—" He shrugged. "You name it and it could have happened by now. We should have told them to take the stairs—"

Brown said, "The doors wouldn't open."

"Break the goddam doors down."

Nat said, "I don't know. It was a judgment call and maybe I called it wrong."

"You didn't," Brown said. "Fire's broken out into one stairwell. Chances are the other will get it too. Then where would they be, out in the open, halfway down?"

"Maybe better than where they are," Giddings said, "trapped. And all because—"

"Because of what?" Nat said. He shook his head. "No one thing. Not even two or three things. A lot of things which shouldn't have happened, but did, all together. You and I ought to have caught on to what Simmons was doing, for one thing."

"He was too smart for us, he and that little bastard of a foreman."

"*And* the inspector," Nat said. "But a supervising inspector ought to have caught the changes too, and either didn't or let them go. That's another thing." He looked at Brown.

Brown nodded angrily. "And apparently we let some things get by we shouldn't. There are standpipes up there, but there's no hose, and by now there isn't any pressure either, because some of the pipes have burst from heat and generated steam."

"You didn't want this reception," Nat said to Giddings. "Frazee ought to have called it off, but you couldn't tell him why, so he didn't." He paused. "And nobody counted on a maniac getting past the cops and down into the mechanical basements to do God only knows what kind of damage before he killed himself. We knew somebody was inside. Maybe we ought to have insisted that the building be searched—"

"Floor by floor with an army?" Giddings said. "You know better than that." His temper had cooled.

"That's the trouble," Nat said, "I do know better than that. We could have insisted until we were blue in the face and nobody would have paid a goddam bit of attention." He looked again at Brown. "You have a big point," he said. "We have more knowledge than judgment." He gestured wearily to Giddings. "Let's go see whether they're ready to give it a try with an elevator."

"I want you here when the Coast Guard comes," Brown said. "It's your idea."

Nat nodded wearily as he walked out.

In the office off the Tower Room, "Sooner or later," the governor said, "we're going to have trouble, maybe panic." He spoke to the fire commissioner. "Just in case," the governor said, "I think we might round up four or five of those waiters, the young husky lads, and have them standing by."

"I'll take care of it," the commissioner said. He left the office.

"Grover," the governor said to Frazee, "why don't you go out and mingle with your guests." He paused. "And, goddammit, smile!"

"I'll go with him," Ben Caldwell said. The two men left together.

"And now," the governor said to Beth, "do you see how crafty I am? We're alone."

Beth said slowly, "Will there be a tomorrow, Bent?"

The telephone rang then. The governor put the phone on the rest and flicked on the speaker switch. "Armitage," he said.

"One stairwell is untenable, Governor." Brown's voice said. "The other may hold, but it may not too. My men aren't very optimistic, but they're still trying to reach you."

"And then what?" the governor said.

There was hesitation. "Get the door on that side open."

"And?"

More hesitation. Brown said at last, "I don't know what to advise, Governor."

"All right," the governor said, "let's look at the odds. One stairwell is already out. What are the chances—opinion, man; I'm not expecting anything else—what are the chances of all the fire doors on the other side holding long enough to get us down—to get *any* of us down?"

Brown's voice was reluctant. "I'd have to say almost nonexistent, Governor." He paused. "There are two other possibilities that seem to me better. Maybe Wilson and Giddings and the electrical engineer can get an elevator running." He paused again. "And the other is that somehow we can get the fire inside the building under control before—" He stopped. "Under control," he said.

The governor's face was expressionless. He stared, unseeing, at the far wall. "Then our chances are better staying here?"

"I—would think so." Brown hesitated. "There is one other chance, but it's wild. Wilson's idea. If the Coast Guard can get a line to you from the north Trade Center tower, and rig a breeches buoy—" The voice stopped, skepticism plain.

"We'll go for anything," the governor said. He paused, straightened. "Call your men back."

Brown said nothing.

"Did you hear me?" the governor said.

"Maybe," Brown said slowly, "maybe we'd better let them get on to you, Governor. Just in case. I'm only guessing about the odds."

"Call them back," the governor said. "There's no point in expending them in a lost cause."

It was, Brown thought, precisely what the battalion chief had said. He nodded weary, automatic acquiescence. "Yes, sir," he said. And then, "Two of them—they can't come back, Governor. There's fire beneath them."

"We'll let them in," the governor said. "We'll give them a drink and some snacks. That's the best we can do, and it is damn little." His voice changed. "All right, Brown. Thanks for the report." He hung up the phone. With no change of expression, "You asked a question," he said to Beth.

"I withdraw it."

"No." The governor shook his head. "It deserves an answer." He paused. He said at last, "I don't know if there's going to be a tomorrow, but I doubt it." There—it was spoken. "And I'm sorry about that for many reasons."

Quietly, "I know, Bent."

"How can you know my reasons?"

Her smile was faint, but real: the ancient all-knowing smile of Woman. "I know."

The governor stared at her. Slowly he nodded. "Maybe," he said. His broad gesture took in the office and the entire building. "I'm here," he said, "out of vanity, and that you always pay for. I love the hurrah. I always have. I might have been an actor." He smiled suddenly. "At any rate, there I am." The smile spread. "Exposed," he said.

"I like what I see."

The governor was silent for a few moments. "Maybe," he said at last, "with someone like you, the White House might not have been out of reach." He paused again. "What might have been." He straightened. "I'd far rather stay right here. but as I said, you pay for your vanity. I belong outside, moving around—" He shook his head in faint apology.

"May I come with you?" She was smiling still as she stood up.

Together they walked into the Tower Room, and there on the threshold paused to look around. The room was as before: groups forming. flowing; waiters and waitresses passing trays of drinks and hors d'oeuvres; conversation, even occasional sudden laughter, perhaps a trifle over-loud. But now there was a difference.

It is, Beth thought. like one of those party scenes on stage, in an opera perhaps or a ballet, an animated but patently false gathering designed to hold the audience's attention unti the principal come out of the wings.

She wondered if the governor had the same impression, and she saw from his smile that he did.

"Here we go on stage," he said.

The network president stopped them first. "It's getting hot in here, Bent."

The governor smiled. "Think of last summer when they closed down all power to three hundred thousand people at a time who had to do without their air-conditioners."

"Other people's miseries have never made mine feel much better."

"Nor mine really," the governor said. "On the other hand, when there is nothing you can do about it——"

"I've made it a practice always to find something to do about it. So have you."

The governor nodded. He was smiling his public smile, but his voice held no hint of amusement. "But not this time, John. Not now."

"We just wait it out?"

"For the moment," the governor said, "that's all there is to do." He and Beth moved on.

Mayor Ramsay came up, his wife with him. "Anything new?"

"They're trying an elevator. We'll know about that soon."

"And the firemen coming up the stairs?"

"Two of them," the governor said, "will get here. I sent the other two back."

The mayor's jaw muscles rippled. "Do you mind telling me why?"

"Because, Bob, the two who will get here can't go back. There is fire in the stairwell beneath them."

The mayor let his breath out in a sigh. "And that means the other stairwell isn't safe either, is that it?"

"I'm afraid that's it."

Paula Ramsay said, "We telephoned Jill." She was smiling at Beth. "She said to give you her best." She paused. "You were always her favorite." She paused. "Sometimes I thought you knew her better than I did and I resented it. I don't any more."

More words never spoken until this moment, Beth thought. Why? "I didn't know that."

"It doesn't matter now. The resentment is all gone. Jill——" Paula shook her head.

"She is young, Paula, so very young."

185

"And she'll be on her own now." She looked at the governor. "I'm not a noble woman, Bent. I'm an angry woman. Why are we here like this? Who is responsible? I asked Grover Frazee and—"

"Grover," the mayor said, "is both scared and drunk." There was scorn in his voice. "In a gentlemanly way, of course. Very Fly Club. What he said was, 'Now, now, my dear Paula, everything is going to be all right—I hope.' Or words to that effect."

"I want someone punished for this," Paula Ramsay said. "I am sick and tired of irresponsible, malicious people doing whatever they choose, calling it some kind of activism, and getting away with it. Whether those responsible for this are black or white, male or female, prominent pediatricians or university chaplains or priests or anything else, I want to see them punished." She stopped. "No, I won't see them punished, will I? But I want to know that they will be. Call me vindictive, if you will. Call me—"

"I call you honest, Paula," the governor said. "I'll admit that this particular situation is changing my views on crime and punishment too."

"But it isn't over yet," the mayor said. "You said so yourself. The elevator—"

"No," the governor said, "it isn't over yet." He thought about the breeches buoy and decided against mentioning it and raising hopes prematurely. "I don't like using football analogies," he said. "They make me sound like —someone else. I don't talk about game plans. But it isn't over until the final gun goes off. In the meantime—"

"A ladylike stiff upper lip," Paula Ramsay said. Her eyes were angry. "I am tempted to use privy-wall words, Bent. I mean that." And then, "Go carry on with your tour of reassurance." She paused and looked at her husband. "And we'll do the same. Can't let the side down, can we?" There was scorn in her voice.

The governor watched them walk away. The secretary general was approaching. "Between us," the governor said quickly to Beth, "I feel exactly the same way Paula does. And if that were known, wouldn't it just raise hell with my public image?" He smiled then at the secretary general, who carried a champagne glass in an easy practiced manner. "Walther, I don't think I've apologized before for this—melodrama. I do now."

"But are you responsible?"

"Only indirectly." The governor left it there, without explanation.

The secretary general said, "Have you noticed how quickly, how easily one's perspective changes? Until only a little time ago I was concerned largely with such matters as budget, unrest in the Middle East, problems of Southeast Asia, the ruffled feathers of a score of delegates on a dozen different issues, world environment—" He paused, smiling apologetically. "It reminds me of another time when only the here and now were important."

"When was that?" Beth said.

"During the war?" the governor said. "Is that when you mean, Walther?"

"For some months we lived in a haystack outside Munich," the secretary general said. "Our house had been— confiscated. I had been released from concentration camp—my wife managed to arrange it. We were six. Two children, my wife's mother, an aunt of mine, ourselves." His voice was quiet. "Once there was a chicken, a whole chicken." He shook his head gently. "I learned then what the here and now can mean. That chicken—" Again the gentle headshake. There was in his face, in his voice, compassion and understanding without censure. "It was for the children, but they had none of it." He paused. "When my wife and I were looking elsewhere, the two old ladies ate it. All of it, the bones were clean. So it is when—survival is the problem."

"Maybe," the governor said slowly, "if we could bring the squabbling sides of all your problems right here, now, put them in this situation, they would settle their differences in a hurry. What do you think of that as a solution?"

"Yankee ingenuity." The secretary general smiled. "I take it there is nothing new in our situation?" He nodded at what he saw in the governor's face. "I thought not. A

suggestion. Mr. J. Paul Norris is, shall we say, on the point of explosion. He is outraged"—again the smile—"well beyond my poor diplomatic powers to soothe."

"I'll talk to him," the governor said.

J. Paul Norris, the tall gray-haired executive type, glowered at them. "If somebody doesn't do something soon," he said, "I am going to take matters into my own hands."

The governor nodded pleasantly. "And do what, Paul?"

"I don't know."

"A splendid suggestion, entirely worthy of you."

Norris said slowly, "Now look here, Bent. I've had just about enough of you, in public and in private. You have a sharp tongue. You've always had it. And you use it to poke fun at all the things that have made this country great. You—"

"Among them," the governor said, "inherited wealth and position and what used to be known as privilege." He nodded. "I saw your name on a list not long ago, Paul. Your income last year was not far short of one million dollars, but you paid no income tax."

"Perfectly legal." A vein was beginning to show on Norris's forehead. "Absolutely within regulations."

"I'm sure it was, but a little difficult for a man earning ten thousand dollars a year to understand when he pays perhaps a twenty-percent tax."

Beth watching, listening, wondered what in the world the governor was hoping to accomplish by deliberately antagonizing the man even if it was justified.

"I don't give a damn about the man earning ten thousand dollars a year," Norris said. "He isn't worth consideration."

Beth smiled to herself. I see it now, she thought: it is pure diversion, waving a red flag to distract the man from the major problem.

"Do you know, Paul," the governor was saying, "our hypothetical ten-thousand-dollar-a-year man doesn't give a damn about you either, except as a source of annoyance. He thinks you and your kind ought to have been ploughed under years ago."

188

"You talk like a communist."

"It has been said before."

"You admit it then?"

The governor smiled. "I consider the source of the accusation. Those with far-left leanings consider me very much a part of the Establishment—which, together with your opinion and that of others like you, puts me just about where I want to be: very close to the middle." He paused. "Ponder those intangibles for a time." And then, his voice turning cold, "But don't even think of creating a disturbance in this room, or I'll have you tied up like a Christmas turkey with a gag in your mouth. Is that understood?"

Norris took a deep breath. The vein in his forehead was very plain. "You wouldn't dare."

The governor showed his teeth. "Don't try me, Paul. I only bluff in poker." He and Beth walked on.

A waiter with a tray of drinks stopped in front of them. "Thank you, son," the governor said. He handed a glass to Beth, took one for himself.

"How about it, Governor?" the waiter said. He kept his voice low. "They're saying, you know, that we're stuck here. For good. They're saying the fire isn't even close to under control. They're saying—"

"There is always 'they,' " the governor said, "and they are always crying doom."

"Yeah. I know. Like scuttlebutt in the Navy. But look, Governor, I got a wife and three kids, and what about them? I ask you, what about them?"

"Boys," the governor said, "or girls?"

"What difference does that make?" And then, "Two boys and a girl."

"How old?"

The waiter was frowning now. "One boy's eleven. That's Stevie. Bert's nine. Becky's just six. What're you giving me, Governor?"

"Becky is probably too young," the governor said, "but why don't you take both Stevie and Bert to the ball game Saturday?"

"That's tomorrow."

"So it is." The governor was smiling gently. "I may see you there. If I do, I'll buy you a beer, and a coke for each of the boys. How about that?"

The waiter hesitated. He said at last, "I think you're horseshitting me, Governor—excuse the language, lady." He paused. "But," he said, "I'll sure as hell take you up on it if I see you." He turned away. He turned back. "I like the first baseline." He was smiling as he walked off.

"He understands, Bent," Beth said.

The governor nodded, "I was stationed in London during the Blitz." He smiled. "You weren't very old then."

Beth's smile matched his. "Don't try to pull years on me."

"When it came right down to the crunch," the governor said, "the people took it. They didn't like it, but they took it. They endured and they didn't complain and they rarely panicked. People like that man. People Paul Norris isn't fit to—live in the same room with."

"Or die in the same room with," Beth said. "Yes. I agree." Her eyelids stung. "Maybe in the end I'll—panic."

"The end isn't yet." The governor's voice was strong. "And even if it does come, you won't panic."

"Don't let me, Bent. Please."

The time was 5:23. An hour had passed since the explosion.

20

5:21–5:32

In the trailer one of the telephones rang. Brown picked it up, spoke his name. He hesitated. "Yes," he said, "she is here." He handed the phone to Patty.

"I thought you would be there, child," her mother's

voice said. In her tone there was no hint of censure. "I am glad. Your father would have been glad." Silence.

Patty closed her eyes. She said slowly, hesitantly, " 'Would have been'? What does that mean?"

The silence on the phone grew and stretched. Mary McGraw broke it at last in a calm voice without tears. "He is gone." Merely that.

Patty stared out through the windows at the scene of controlled confusion outside and took a deep unsteady breath. "And I was here," she said.

"You could have done nothing." Mary's voice was gentle. "I saw him for a few moments at the end. But he did not see me or even know that I was there."

Tears were close. Patty held them back. "I'll come up."

"No. I am going home, child."

"I'll come there."

"No." The voice was strange, taut and yet controlled. "I am going to have a nice cup of tea. And a good cry." Then I'll go to church. And you cannot help me with any of those." Mary paused. "I don't mean to turn away from you. It is just that right now, with your father gone, I want to be alone. He would have understood."

Hesitantly, "I understand too, Mother," Patty said. We face our grief in our own ways, she thought; it was a new concept. There were many new concepts today.

"And you?" the mother said.

Patty looked around the trailer almost in bewilderment. And yet the answer was plain. "I will stay here." With Daddy's building.

There was a long pause. "Not Paul?" Mary said.

"Not Paul. That's—finished." Patty paused. "Daddy knew." And here in the midst of grief came renewed anger. She forced it down.

"Do as you think best, child." Pause. "God bless you."

Patty hung up slowly. She was conscious that Brown and the two battalion chiefs tried not to watch her, waiting self-consciously for her to give them their cue. Strange, how easily she understood that; how easily she understood many things about men like these, men Daddy had always dealt with, men unlike Paul. But I have no business being here, she thought. "My father is dead." She said it slowly, distinctly, and then stood up. "I'll leave now."

"Sit down," Brown said. His voice was harsh. In silence he got out his cigarettes, chose one, snapped it in half and almost threw the pieces into the ashtray. "Your father," he said. "I am very sorry, Mrs. Simmons." Through the fatigue and the strain he smiled, a gentle grimace. "He and I had our fights. We were bound to. He was a builder and by his lights I was a heckler, and we both had low flash points." The smile spread. "But a better man never lived, and I am glad he is not around to see—this."

Patty said slowly, "Thank you. I—don't want to be in the way." But I have no place else to go, she thought suddenly, it is as simple as that. And at last the enormity of being alone, wholly alone, bore in upon her. In an unsteady voice, "Thank you," she said again. "I'll try to stay out of the way."

The walkie-talkie crackled. "We're at the Tower Room floor, Chief." Denis Howard's voice, panting and dull with fatigue. "The smoke isn't too bad yet. We'll try to get the door cleared."

"What's the matter with it?"

"Oh, Christ, Chief, how can things like this happen?" Almost a lament. "There're big boxes, heavy boxes, some of them marked 'Fragile, Electronic Equipment,' and they're jammed so the door can't open from the inside. Where in hell were our people, letting anybody block a fire door like this?"

The battalion chief closed his eyes. "I don't know, Denis. I sure as hell don't know. All I do know is that if there's a wrong way to do something, somebody will find it. I've never known it to fail. And when all the wrong things happen at the same time—" He stopped. "Tear the goddam boxes apart." His voice was savage. "Get out of that stairwell and inside! There's your best chance."

Brown gestured wearily. The battalion chief handed him the walkie-talkie. "The governor has promised you a drink and some snacks," Brown said. "That ought to make your day."

There was no reply. The batteries in Howard's unit had failed from the mounting heat.

Nat was down in the black bowels of the building, moving partly by feel and partly by the eerie light of firemen's headlamps, claustrophobic in his mask and afraid that each breath would somehow be the last, drenched by water from the big hoses and fighting through smoke almost as through a solid substance. Giddings and Joe Lewis and two men of a pickup electrical crew were somewhere near, but for the moment Nat had lost them.

It was, he told himself, ridiculous that he should even be down here. Joe Lewis was the electrical engineer; Giddings knew as much about actual placement of panels and circuitry as anybody, including Nat himself. And yet here he was, unable to wait outside or, like a proper little prototypical architect, back at his drawing board, pencil in hand, head filled with abstruse calculations.

I don't belong here, he thought, and by *here* he no longer meant simply beneath this great building, but anywhere in this complex compartmentalized right-hand-doesn't-know-what-left-hand-is-doing megalopolis society where man was so far removed from actuality that a switch thrown miles away could cut off his light, his heat, his means of cooking or of keeping himself sane against constant din by playing the kind of music he could lose himself in. Or kill him by a radioactive mistake at some distant generator.

Oh, that was exaggeration, of course, but not by much. Here—

He was jostled suddenly by two firemen stumbling past in the murk, dragging a new hose. They seemed unaware that there had been any contact.

And that was another thing: the crowding even under the best of circumstances. Big city people were like turkeys in a pen. They seemed to prefer to be shoved and jostled and packed into impossibly small spaces. The subways at rush hour. The buses. The crowded ramps at Yankee Stadium. The Coney Island beaches. Times Square New Year's Eve. A Madison Square rally . . . By God, they enjoy it!

Thoughts flicked across the screen of his mind far faster than words could contain them.

A nearby voice muffled through a mask said suddenly, "If the motherfucker will—there, you bastard! Okay. Give me a light, goddammit!" One of the electricians.

Giddings was there, massive in the smoke. "If you can't move it, let me in." His voice too sounded unreal, distant and hollow.

"Look, mac, keep your goddam meathooks off this panel. You don't carry no union card."

Oh no! Nat thought. Not now! And yet it was so; ingrained, ineluctable. You staked out your own little territory and you defended it against all comers, friend or enemy. Why? Because that territory was you, manifestation of your essence; its violation assaulted your very soul. Shit. That was not how it ought to be. His anger had spread now to include the world in general.

Joe Lewis, standing close, said hollowly, "Hurry it up." He began to cough. "A man can only stand so much of this."

"Then beat it," Giddings said. "We'll finish it off."

In the smoke and near-darkness Nat saw Lewis raise an arm and let it fall in a gesture of defeat. His coughing was deep, wracking. He turned away, stumbled, fell, tried to raise himself, and failed.

Giddings said, "Goddammit—"

"Stay at the job," Nat said. His voice was sharp. "I'll get him out."

He knelt beside Lewis, turned him over on his back and raised him to a sitting position. Slowly, heavily, he levered the man over his shoulder and into a fireman's carry, took a deep breath, and managed to heave himself to his feet.

His legs were weak and even through the mask the taste of smoke filled his lungs, usurping areas of tissue that ought to have been filled with oxygen, creating a dizziness that would not go away.

He leaned forward against the burden on his shoulder and, half-walking, half-stumbling, headed off into the murk.

Lewis's body was limp, a dead weight. Nat could not tell whether the man breathed. He stumbled onto the first stairs and slowly, laboriously began to climb. One, two, three . . . there were fourteen steps to each level—why would he remember a thing like that now?

Thirteen, fourteen . . . level floor and then more stairs, and the smoke was in no measure diminished.

The next step would have to be his last—and he knew that it was not so. As in the mountains on a steep trail, the only thing to do was put your head down and concentrate on setting one foot in front of the other in slow rhythm. Ignore your breathing—if you can. Ignore the coughing that chokes you. Thirteen, fourteen—another level floor, and more stairs.

Once he stumbled over a hose and went painfully to his knees, was tempted to drop the body that hampered him —and managed to withstand the temptation. Get up, goddammit, get up!

He heard voices and knew them to be nothing more than sounds within his own head.

He stopped in the middle of a flight of stairs to cough and cough again, and then lurch on.

Ahead there was only blackness and smoke. And here was a door, closed—was it, for God's sake, locked as well? If it is, Nat thought, then I've taken the wrong stairs and we've both had it.

He lurched up the last two steps, and felt with his free hand for the doorknob. There was none.

The dizziness was near-nausea now, and thinking was almost impossible. No doorknob—why? Goddammit, you know the answer—what is it? You're the architect, aren't you? He leaned forward, pushing Lewis's limp body against the door. It opened suddenly and Nat almost fell through—into the smoke-filled concourse.

Out at last into the unbelievably sweet air of the plaza, freed from the claustrophobic mask—and here came two men in white to take the body from his shoulder, and someone else saying "Breathe this" and slapping a rubber mask over his nose and mouth.

He breathed deeply of the oxygen and gradually the

195

plaza came back into focus, the dizziness receded. Nat freed himself from the mask and went stumbling toward the trailer. His legs were weak as he climbed the steps.

One of the battalion chiefs grinned at him. "Like to join the Department?" he said. "We can offer smoke-filled outings almost every day, if that's the way your pleasure runs."

"Thanks much," Nat said. He made himself smile. It was a grimace. "But from here on I fight my fires in forests."

"Are you all right?" This was Patty, whom Nat had not even noticed.

He noticed her now, small, bright, at the moment concerned, genuinely concerned. Why? "Fine," Nat said. "Soon as I get my breath."

"You look," Patty said, "as Daddy used to say, like something dredged up out of the East River." She showed him an unsteady smile.

Brown said, "What about the elevator?"

Nat gestured wearily. "It may work. They're going to try it." There was no other way. Unless— "The Coast Guard is taking its time," he said.

Giddings came up the steps. Seeing him, Nat got some idea of how he himself looked. Giddings's face was freckled white where the mask had been. His forehead was black and soot colored his hair. His corduroy jacket was sodden and streaked. "What's funny?" Giddings said.

"A couple of chimney sweeps," Nat said, grinning still.

"And sweeps," Patty said, "are lucky as lucky can be. We'll hold that thought." And pray for luck in all directions, she told herself. Wherever you are, Daddy, God-speed!

Brown said, "Well?"

"If it goes," Giddings said, "it won't stop until the Tower Room unless—" He shrugged. "Oh, hell, unless almost anything. But the point is that we won't even know it's gotten there unless they tell us. Better get on the horn." He and Brown and the two chiefs moved toward the telephone.

Patty said softly, "Nat." What compelled her to this? Mere loneliness? She had no idea, but neither had she the strength to resist. "He's gone, Nat. Daddy. As big and strong as he was, he's—"

"I'm sorry." Nat took both of her small clean hands in his own. He looked at the results in dismay. "I'm sorry about that too."

"It doesn't matter." Patty made no effort to take her hands away. "Mother called. She saw him, but—he— didn't- -know—her!"

Nat squeezed the small hands. "Easy. Easy." What else was there to say? I'm no good at this kind of thing, he thought; all I know is things, not people. "I'm sorry," he said again. The words were inane.

Patty had caught her lower lip between her teeth. Her eyes were closed. When she opened them, they were bright but not tear-filled. "I'm okay." She paused. "Paul," she said then in a different voice.

"What about him?"

Patty drew a deep unsteady breath. "I told Daddy at lunch about Paul and Zib. I'm sorry, but I told him I was leaving Paul and I had to give a reason."

Nat squeezed the small hands again. "Of course." But where was pain in the knowledge, the concept that he had been cuckolded? Hadn't he cared to begin with? All along had he been fooling himself that he and Zib had what he had always thought of as a marriage when all the time it was merely a legal shakeup, no strings attached?

"Paul saw him after that," Patty said. "Paul was there when he had his attack." She was silent, watching Nat's face.

At the far end of the trailer the four men were clustered around the telephone. There were voices, words unintelligible. Here in a little area of isolation there was silence. Nat said slowly, "What are you saying, Patty?"

"Daddy being Daddy," Patty said, "he braced Paul with Zib. Isn't that how it had to be? Isn't it?" She paused. "And what do you think Paul would have said?" She paused, and then gave her own answer. "That you and

I were rolling in the hay too. Just to get even. Being Paul."

The silence surrounded them and time seemed to stand still. "I don't know," Nat said. But he did know. Paul being Paul—there was the operative phrase. "I don't know much about people," Nat said. "Why not give him the benefit of the doubt?"

Patty's head was shaking slowly. Her chin was set. "If that is how it was," she said, "then he killed Daddy." She paused. Her hands in Nat's were tensed. "And if I get the chance," she said, "I'll kill him. So help me."

Nat said quickly, "Patty—" He stopped.

Brown's voice was saying into the telephone, "You're sure? Goddammit, man, make sure!" He spoke to Giddings and the two battalion chiefs. "He *thinks* the elevator has gotten there. Thinks!" And then, again into the phone, "It is sure? Yes, Governor? Jesus, Mary, and Joseph!" A pause. "Yes, sir. We'll hang on." He cupped his hand over the mouthpiece. "The elevator got there. They're working the doors open now. How about that?" He looked the length of the trailer at Nat. "Now we can forget that breeches buoy nonsense."

Nat hesitated. Here, at least, he thought, he was dealing with a matter he could judge with some competence. "No," he said. "If the elevator works, fine. But let's have a backup, just in case."

21

Windows in the northeast quadrant on the sixty-second floor of the building were the first to shatter from heat. Heavy shards of the tempered tinted glass sprang out from the building as if from an explosion, glistened like icicles in their long fall, and crashed into the plaza. The crowd squealed and shrieked in its excitement.

"Move those barricades back!" a bullhorn shouted. "Back, goddammit!"

Patrolman Shannon put his hand to his cheek and stared unbelieving at the blood that instantly covered his palm and dripped between his fingers.

Barnes whipped out his handkerchief. He wadded it against the long clean cut. "Hold it tight, Mike, and head for that ambulance. You'll need stitches."

"Do you think," Shannon said, irrepressible, "that there'll be a Purple Heart in it, Frank? I've always longed to be a wounded hero."

"You have your wish." Barnes set about helping to move the crowd back out of apparent range.

The signs had disappeared from the plaza, but in the building's torment the Reverend Joe Willie Thomas saw opportunity for a message:

"It is the will of the Lord!" he shouted in that revivalist voice. "It is just retribution! Wickedness and waste, hand-in-hand, cheek-by-jowl, Sodom and Gomorrah repeated, I say!"

There were those who thought the comparisons apt.

In the plaza air there was a taste of ashes. Puddles of water on the pavement had spread into ponds, their surfaces dull with soot.

High up, impossibly high, near the building's gleaming tower, smoke roiled into the sky. Lower, on the opposite side of the building, more smoke oozed out and, wind-driven, curled around the structure like a smothering cloak.

Smoke still poured out of the concourse doors, but its quantity was lessened. Many in the crowd thought that the fire was being contained. It was not.

"Sooner or later," a Pine Street insurance underwriter in the crowd said, "it had to happen. I don't want to be quoted on that, but there it is. And, thank Heaven, we are not involved."

"Rates will have to go up."

The underwriter nodded. "No question. Losses have to be covered."

"What about the people up there?"

"That," the underwriter said, "is a good question. I don't know the answer. We insure things, not people."

22

5:32–5:43

The office off the Tower Room was again the command post, and the governor dominated the room. "What is the elevator capacity? Maximum? Even overloaded?"

Ben Caldwell said, "Fifty-five persons is the rated load. Another ten, perhaps, could be squeezed in."

"They will be," the governor said. He paused. He smiled then, without amusement. "Traditionally," he said, "women and children are first. Does anyone see a reason to flout tradition?"

"I do," Beth said, and there was silence. "You are the important people," she said then. "You are the ones who need to be—saved. Stop this silly chivalry and be practical."

Grover Frazee said, "Hear, hear."

"Shut up, Grover," the governor said. His tone was angry.

Senator Peters said, "All right, my dear, let's be practical. We've had our time. We've made what waves we could make, influenced what events we were capable of influencing." The habit of oratory was strong. He made himself stop elaborating the matter. "The point is," he said, "that the tradition isn't just from silly ideas of chivalry. It's grounded in that practicality you demand. You, not we, are the future of the human race. We manage its affairs while we live, but you see to it that there are those to replace us and you care for them until they are ready."

The governor said, "You are overruled, Beth." He smiled fondly. He looked around the office. "All the women," he said. "You, Pete," he said to the commissioner, "see to it. The rest of you help him. And hurry!"

Beth waited until only they two were left. "I'm not going, Bent. Not without you."

"Oh yes you are." The governor walked to the inner wall of the office. "Come here." He watched her approach slowly, wonderingly, and he took her hand and placed it flat against the wall's surface. She drew it away. "Hot, isn't it?" the governor said. "Not much more time, and I want you safe."

"I told you—"

"But I'm telling you." He lifted her chin with a bent forefinger and kissed her lightly. "I'm not going to make any speeches." he said. "For once in my life I don't have any words to cover what I think and feel." He was smiling gently. "And if that sounds unbelievable, well, this entire situation is unbelievable, but it has happened." He put his arm around her waist. "Come along. I'll see you off."

Still she held back. "Will there be a second load? You? The others?"

"We'll count on it. First we'll see you safe." Together they walked to the door and there they stopped.

Outside someone shouted, "What the hell do you think you're doing?"

There were other voices raised, and the sound of running footsteps.

"Wait here," the governor said and hurried out into the big room.

The scene had altered suddenly, drastically. Like ants around an uprooted nest, the governor thought, everyone seemed to be in haphazard frantic motion.

"Hold it!" the governor shouted. "Hold it!"

Some of the movement stopped. Faces turned in his direction. There was near-silence.

"What's going on?" the governor said. "We're supposed to be grown people, responsible people. Just what in blue blazes has changed that?" His tone flayed them all. "They've worked a miracle down below," he said, "and sent us an elevator. It—"

"That is the problem, Bent," Senator Peters said, his working-class big-city accent more marked than ever. "The elevator is gone, on its way down, and there's no way to stop it." He paused. "It has a passenger. One. Can you guess who?"

The big room was still, and all eyes watched him. I don't have to guess, the governor thought, I know. Aloud he said, "You tell me, Jake."

"Paul Norris," the senator said, "who else? J. Paul Norris."

The governor nodded slowly. Slowly he turned and walked back into the office past Beth as if she did not exist. He sat down at the desk, picked up the telephone, and flipped the desk-speaker switch. "Armitage here," he said. "The elevator is on its way down. It has one passenger. I want him held."

Brown's voice said, "Yes, sir." And then, incredulously, "Just one passenger?"

"That is what I said." The governor paused. "I want the district attorney apprised of the fact that the man deliberately stole the elevator. If the district attorney can see his way clear, I should like the man to be charged with attempted murder.' The governor paused again. "Witnesses," he said, "may be hard to come by. Tell him that too."

Brown said, "We'll send the elevator right back. If we can."

The governor nodded. "If you can," he said. "I understand." He paused. "You've done a superlative job, all of you, against apparently impossible odds. I want you to know that we appreciate it, all of us." He was staring thoughtfully at the telephone. "How long the telephone will last," he said, "is anyone's guess, I should imagine. I'm sure that somewhere up here there is a transistor radio. There always is. You can reach us with any information through the city's radio station. We'll stay tuned to it." He looked up then.

The mayor stood in the doorway. He was nodding. "I'll find a transistor," he said. And then, "Will they get the elevator up for another trip?"

"Governor?" Brown's voice on the desk speaker.

"Right here."

"The elevator is down, Governor. The man inside—" Brown paused. "He's dead, Governor. Burned pretty bad." His voice shook.

Nat Wilson's voice came on, weary but strong. "The heat in the core. There must be a blowtorch effect."

Ben Caldwell moved in past the mayor. "Masks, Nat?" he said. "Asbestos suits? Spray the inside of the car to cool it off—"

"No," Nat said. "One chance, and we blew it. We won't get that car up again. It's badly damaged and off its rails, so the rails must have distorted. We'll try another, but—" He left the sentence unfinished.

Caldwell blew his breath out slowly in a silent whistle. "I understand."

Brown's voice came on again. "We're still working the inside of the building," he said. "Floor by goddam floor. Sorry, Governor. Eventually—" The voice paused. "If only they didn't build them so big." Another pause. "What's left now," Brown's voice said, "is that wild idea of Wilson's."

The governor's face was expressionless. "Keep us posted," he said, pushed back his chair, and stood up wearily. "Time for another report." He started for the door.

"Do you have to, Bent?" This was Beth.

"My dear," the governor said, "if there is one thing I have learned in a long career, it is that people behave at their worst when they are kept in the dark. In the face of unpalatable truths they sometimes react unpleasantly; but when they aren't told anything, rumors start and panic is not far behind."

As before, the governor stood on a chair in the center of the big room. He waited briefly until all conversation

203

had stopped. Then, "The elevator reached the concourse," he said and waited.

There was a low angry murmur.

"The man in it," the governor said, "was dead from the intense heat in the core of the building." He paused again.

This time there was silence. He had his audience now.

"They are attempting to send us a second elevator," he said, "and if they are successful, there will be insulated clothing and breathing masks for those who ride in it." He raised one hand. "*If* they are successful in sending that second elevator. It is by no means sure that they will be."

There was hammering at the fire door on the far side of the room. The governor waited while the fire commissioner hurried to it, wrenched at the knob, and pushed the door wide. Firemen Denis Howard and Lou Storr lurched through.

Each carried a halligan tool, a long heavy bar hooked at one end, canted at the other. Their masks hung around their necks. In each face there was a bone-weariness plain to see. Their legs trembled as they walked forward in answer to the governor's beckoning gesture.

"Close that door," the governor said. Then, to the two firemen, "We thank you for coming."

Lou Storr opened his mouth, and closed it again carefully.

Denis Howard said, "Nothing at all, Governor. Just a stroll up a few stairs." He waved his hand in a grand gesture. " 'Theirs not to question why.' "

A male voice said, "Can we use the stairs? If we can, let's get at it."

There was silence. Howard, no longer grandstanding, looked at the governor, question plain.

"Tell them," the governor said.

Howard took his time. "You can use them," he said at last. "But you won't reach the bottom or anywhere near the bottom." He held out his hand. It trembled. "See that? There used to be hair." He ran his hand wearily over his face. "And I used to have eyebrows too, so I did." He nodded then. "You can use the stairs. You might even be alive all the way down to the hundredth floor—if you run fast enough."

The room was still.

"I promised you both a drink," the governor said. He looked at a nearby waiter: "See that they have them. Then bring them into the office." He looked around at his audience. "It is not good," he said. "But neither is it hopeless. We are exploring every possibility. I can't tell you more than that."

Cary Wycoff raised his voice. "What I want to know," he said, "no, correct that: what I demand to know is how did all this happen? Who is responsible?"

The governor waited motionless on the chair while the low murmur of agreement ran its course. Then, in the silence, "I suggest, Cary, that you appoint a Congressional committee to look into the matter. I will be happy to tell it all I know." He stepped down from the chair, offered Beth his arm, and walked neither slow nor fast back to the office.

Inside he dropped into the desk chair. "I think of myself," he said, "as a fairly patient man and a reasonable one. I even consider myself compassionate." He looked up at Beth and smiled without amusement. "Right now," he said, "I would cheerfully strangle Cary Wycoff. And my one great hope is that I will live long enough to spit on Paul Norris's grave." He paused. "If those sentiments are ignoble, then so am I."

Beth said, "If Mr. Norris had not stolen the elevator—" She left the sentence unfinished.

"True," the governor said. "None of you would have reached the bottom alive. And so I am glad it happened the way it did. But that changes nothing."

"I understand, Bent."

He caught her hand and pressed it to his cheek. "Little men," he said, "in scribes' caps and long pointed slippers. They write in the big book and then pull strings to see that everything works out as they have planned it." He shook his head. "I wonder sometimes if their motives aren't basically malicious. Do you believe in an afterlife, my dear?"

"I think so."

"I've never found it necessary," the governor said. "I've never found it necessary to believe in a deity either." He paused. "But I have gone through the motions of worship just as I have gone through the other forms of conventional behavior. And for the same reason: because it was expected of me. I wonder how many others do the same, but won't admit it." He paused. "If I could pray and mean it, I would pray to believe that you and I will meet again somewhere."

"We will, Bent."

"Beside a celestial trout stream? I think that would be my choice. Just in time for the evening rise." He dropped Beth's hand and sat up straight as the two firemen and the fire commissioner appeared in the doorway. "Come in," the governor said. "Sit down. Let's consider possibilities" —he paused—"as gloomy as some of them may be."

23

5:40–5:56

It was almost schizophrenia that had overtaken her, Patty thought, because one part of her mind had retreated into its own secret place to mourn; while the rest of her mind insisted on concentrating on the here and now, the tension that filled the trailer.

After talking to Ben Caldwell, Nat had walked back from the telephone to stand near Patty and stare unseeing out at the plaza and the tormented building. He said slowly, "The way they used to design them, the big buildings, they were so fire-resistant that the city actually reduced fire department coverage in high-rise areas." He turned then to look at Patty. "Did you know that?"

Patty made herself smile and shake her head.

"Thick walls," Nat said, "thick floors, windows that opened—you could get in and out. A fire could be contained. Now—" He shook his head. "Core construction is more economical: you can concentrate elevators, escalators, pipes, ducts, wiring, all the unproductive items, in a central shaft. That leaves more rental space. But when a fire breaks out, a big one like this—" He shook his head again.

"That blowtorch effect you talked about on the phone?" Patty said. "Like a chimney?"

One of the battalion chiefs standing nearby said, "Times, on a fire like this, temperatures in the core can be so high that firemen can only work for five minutes at a time, maybe less." He looked at Nat. "Blowtorch, you call it. More like a blast furnace." He pointed up toward the building's top. "If we get anybody out of there alive, it's going to be a bloody miracle."

Brown's voice angry on the telephone said, "Yes, goddammit, we want them in here! On the double! You think this is some kind of charade?" He slammed down the telephone and waved his bony fists in helpless rage. "The cops couldn't see what the Coast Guard had to do with a fire in a building. Seemed screwy to them, they said, so they took their time and then decided to check before they let them through the lines." He was glaring at Nat. "Do you think it'll work? Do you? That breeches buoy idea?"

Nat raised his hands and let them fall in a gesture of disclaimer. "Do you have any better ideas?"

"Those choppers," Brown said. "They're still sailing around, not doing a damn bit of good. That was your idea too."

"So was the elevator," Nat said, "and it could have killed fifty people instead of one." It would be a long time, if ever, before he forgot that.

Once in his fire-jumping days he had been dropped into an area where a forest fire, wind-driven, had altered direction without warning and trapped nineteen men in a fatal pocket. Their bodies lay stiffly in the fetal position, curled like snails, burned almost beyond recognition. That was a thing you remembered too. "What else can we do but try everything we can think of?" Nat said. "Because if we don't—" He spread his hands.

There was silence.

"Let's look at the possibilities," Nat said. "You can't reach them with anything. And they can't get down by themselves. Even if they had ropes, what good would they do? Middle-aged men and women trying to rappel fifteen hundred feet?" His voice was low-pitched, almost savage.

"Can the choppers do anything?" he said then. "The answer is no, not by themselves. You might be able to break some windows up there and transfer an acrobat to a ladder swinging from one of the choppers, but none of those people who went up there to drink champagne could make it. So what is left? That's the answer to your question. Shadrach, Meshach, and Abednego made it in Nebuchadnezzar's furnace, but it isn't going to happen here."

"Okay," Brown said, calmer now. "Don't get in an uproar. We'll see what the Coast Guard has to say."

"If it doesn't work," Nat said, "it doesn't work." He stared out the window again.

Patty touched his arm. "Is all this really Paul's doing?" Her voice was quiet. "Daddy said he wasn't sure and wouldn't badmouth a man until he was."

The envelope of change-order copies was still in his pocket. He took it out, shook the orders free on the drafting board. He watched Patty pick them up one by one, glance at them, drop them as if they were unclean. She said at last, "I'm not an engineer, but I do know a little." She was watching Nat's face. "Your name on all of these, but you didn't sign them, did you?"

"How do you know that?"

"Not your style," Patty said. "And don't ask me how I know, but I do." She looked down at the papers. "One of Paul's tricks, imitating handwriting. I used to think it was amusing." She paused. "Now," she said, "I think it's merely childish. And vicious." She was silent for a time. "Tell me," she said then, "what is the name for a woman who turns against her husband?"

208

"Admirable."

"I wish I could believe that."

Small and indomitable, Nat thought, willing to face facts squarely even when they hurt. How would Zib react in a similar situation? Probably just pretend that it was all a mistake that had never happened and walk away. But not this one. "You have my word for it," Nat said.

"Now," a new voice said from the trailer doorway, "what seems to be the trouble and what do you think we can do about it?"

He was a big man, broad, solid, massively calm—Chief Petty Officer Oliver, United States Coast Guard. He listened quietly while Nat explained, and together they went out of the trailer to stare up at the tops of the buildings—the square flat-topped north tower of the Trade Center and the World Tower itself, its shining spire almost touching the sky.

The chief looked around the plaza at the crowds, the sooty lakes, the writhing hoses and shouting firemen. "Quite a circus," he said, and squinted aloft again, measuring distances with his eye, his face expressionless. He looked at last at Nat, and slowly shook his head. "It can't be done," he said.

"You've got guns," Nat said, "and line—what you call a messenger line, no?"

"We've got it all," the chief said.

"And the distance, man, isnt all that great." Nat's voice was urgent, almost angry. "So it takes half a dozen tries. One line into that Tower Room is all you need, isn't it? We'll have the whole bank of windows on that side broken out. You'll have a target the size of a barn. You—"

"Down here on the ground," the chief said, "the wind is calm, or near enough. Up there—how high?"

"Fifteen hundred feet." The anger was suddenly gone. "I see what you mean."

"Blowing merry hell," the chief said. "It usually is aloft. See that smoke, how it lays out straight? That's what we'd have to shoot a line into—" He paused. "And there's no way we can get it there. Not at that distance."

209

Another bad idea, Nat thought, and blamed himself that he had not come up with a good one. Maybe there were no good ideas, but that in no way altered the fact of failure. Bitter thought.

"But," the chief said, "we'll give it a try." He paused. "We'll do the best we can—even if it isn't good enough."

For the first time on this disastrous day, Nat thought, he felt the first faint glimmering of hope. It was hard to keep triumph out of his voice. "We'll give you firemen and cops," he said, "anybody you need to go up on the Trade Center roof with you and help you do your thing. I'll see that the windows in the Tower Room are broken out and men are standing by to catch a line if you get it across." His thoughts were flowing now. "My boss, the architect, is up there. He'll find structure strong enough to fasten the breeches buoy line to and handle any strain. Then—"

"We'll try," the chief said. "That's all I can promise." He smiled suddenly. "But it'll be the damnedest gut-busting try you ever saw." The smile spread. "And who knows?" He gestured back into the trailer. "Get your people lined up."

The governor took the call and promptly sent for Ben Caldwell and the fire commissioner to hear the situation report.

"A Coast Guard crew," Nat's voice said, "is going to the roof of the north tower of the Trade Center. They'll try shooting a messenger line over to you—"

Caldwell interrupted. "That means breaking out windows on that side." He nodded.

"All of them," Nat said. "Every one. Give them as big a target as you can." He paused. "We're having the plaza on that side cleared of everybody. That heavy falling glass can kill."

"We'll start on the windows when you give the word," Caldwell said. He hesitated. "It's a long way, Nat, from that tower roof."

"We'll try. That's all we can do." And then, rather than dwell on possible failure, hurrying on, "As I under-

210

stand it, the gun shoots a weighted projectile carrying a light messenger line. When you get the line you haul it in on signal, and they'll have secured the heavier line to it. Two lines, actually: the heavy one to carry the load of the breeches buoy, and the smaller line that pulls the breeches buoy across to you and then back down to the tower roof." He paused.

"Understood," Caldwell said. He wore a faint smile.

"You're probably way ahead of me," Nat said, "but I'll go through it all anyway." Pause. "Make the heavy line fast to structure that will take a hell of a load, not just to a table or a chair." Another pause. "And I'd suggest that where the line goes through the window frame you make damn sure all the glass is gone. We don't want the line to be cut or frayed." Another voice spoke unintelligibly in the background. "Wait a moment—"

In the silence the governor said, "Your man, Ben—"

"The best," Caldwell said. "If it can be done, he'll figure out the way and see to it."

"They've cleared the plaza on that side," Nat's voice came again into the speaker phone. "You can start on the windows."

Caldwell looked at the fire commissioner. The commissioner nodded and made a circle of thumb and forefinger. He hurried out of the office.

Nat's voice said in a different note, "I don't know how many are hearing this—" He hesitated.

The governor said quickly, "This is Armitage. You can say whatever you want to say."

"Okay," Nat said. His voice was solemn. "It's just this. We don't want to get your hopes too high because it may not work."

"Understood," the governor said.

"But," Nat said, "if it doesn't work—" He paused. "Then, goddammit, we'll think of something else. That's a promise." Another pause. "All for now." He clicked off.

The office was still. Ben Caldwell, smiling faintly, almost apologetically, looked at the governor and Beth. "I've found," he said, "that Nat Wilson's promises can be depended on." The smile spread. "I find myself clinging to that thought."

"We all are," the governor said. "We can build buildings like this and invent governments and machines and set up systems that can't fail, but when it comes right down to it, there is no substitute for a man you can depend on." He paused. "Or a woman." He smiled then. "That sounds corny, doesn't it? But it wouldn't be corny if it weren't a basic truth."

From the big room came the sound of breaking glass and a growing murmur of voices.

The governor heaved himself out of his chair. "Show time," he said. "Let's bring everybody up to date."

Nat turned away from the phone and walked the length of the trailer to stand again beside Patty. "Big talk," he said. His smile was deprecatory. "But I couldn't just leave them—dangling."

"You'll think of something."

And what did a man say to that? He began to gather the change-order copies, stuff them back into the envelope. "We'll want the originals of these," he said. "If we can find them."

Patty said automatically, "Paul's office files."

Nat thought about it. He nodded. "You're probably right. We'll have them picked up. I'll talk to Brown." He was gone only a few moments, and then, compulsively, he was back to stand once more beside this small bright creature who did not know how to give up.

"How do you explain Paul?" Patty said. The feeling of schizophrenia was very strong: in its secret place that one part of her mind wept quietly; here her attention was on reality, life. "I mean," she said, "I know these things happen. But Paul?"

Nat had never considered himself knowledgeable about people, but he understood now that Patty's need was for someone to listen, occasionally to talk, but above all to try to understand. "You know him better than I do, Patty."

"Do I?" Patty was silent for a few moments. "I'm his

wife. We've made love together, laughed together, had our arguments, our hopes, our triumphs, our sadnesses—" She shook her head. "But know him? I don't think I do. I'm—lacking."

"Maybe," Nat said slowly, "there isn't very much there to know."

Patty's glance was shrewd. "You never thought so, did you?"

"He and I are entirely different. I'm a country boy."

"That's a pose."

Nat smiled faintly. "Maybe partly. But down deep it isn't. I can't complain—"

"Try."

Nat lifted his hands and let them fall. "I don't see things the way—city people do. Oh, I'm not trying to make myself out as a hayseed gaping at the tall buildings—"

Patty's smile was wry. "In Brooks Brothers clothes? Even dirty as they are? Hardly."

"But," Nat said, "an air-conditioned duplex apartment overlooking the East River, a house in Westchester or Fairfield, a yacht club on the Sound or a membership in the Racquet Club—these aren't living, to me; they're ridiculous attempts to make an artificial existence merely bearable." He smiled sheepishly. "That makes me sound like a bush-league Thoreau, doesn't it?"

Patty's smile was gentle. "What is it you want, Nat?"

"I'm an architect. Maybe that's it. What I want above everything else is space, room to move around in, distances you can see, mountains that make you feel small—"

"Room to breathe?"

Nat looked at the girl with new interest. "You do understand, don't you?"

"Is that surprising?"

"I guess it is."

"I've never been out in your country," Patty said, "and I'd probably be out of place—"

Nat shook his head. "Not you." He had said the same to Zib once, he remembered, but for wholly different

213

reasons. "You're—real," he said now. "That's a funny thing to say, I know."

"I'm flattered.

"Bert," Nat said. "You're like him in some ways, a lot of ways. When Bert said something, you didn't have to look it all over for booby traps. He said what he meant and he meant what he said."

"I'm more than flattered," Patty said.

From the far end of the trailer Brown said, "They're on the roof." A walkie-talkie was speaking hollowly. "Oliver wants the word when they're ready in the Tower Room." Brown held out the phone to Nat. "You'd better take over."

Nat nodded. "Here we go."

24

5:31–5:43

Paul Simmons drove back into Manhattan and parked his car in the basement of his office building. He started for the elevators and then changed his mind and walked out to the street and around the corner to a bar. It was dimly lighted and, except for the bartender, deserted. On the color television set behind the bar the World Tower writhed in smoke. Paul tried not to look at the screen as he paid for his drink and carried it to a corner booth. Thank God the bartender was not a talker.

So the cops had picked up Pat Harris. That was the first thing, and its implications were unpleasant. If that kind of pressure was on, then Pat Harris would think first, last, and always of his own neck, that was sure. The story he would tell would not be the one they had agreed on down in the game room, but the one he had threatened Paul with: Harris had wondered about the change orders, even questioned them, but Paul Simmons, his boss and an engineer, had told him to mind his own business and do what he was told. So maybe Harris came out of it not very bright, but neither was he apparently culpable. God damn Harris.

Harry Whitaker, the inspector with his hand conveniently out—what about him? In panic? Probably, because that was Harry Whitaker, but it would be well to find out. Paul maneuvered out of the booth and went to the public telephone.

Harry's wife answered and did not even ask who was calling. Her screech for her husband almost shattered Paul's eardrum.

Harry came to the phone at the double and his voice snarled, "Close the goddam door?" Then, into the phone, in a different tone, "Yes?"

"Simmons here."

"Oh," Harry said, "thank God! I've been trying to get you, but they said—"

"Now you have me," Paul said. His voice was cold. "What do you want?"

There was a significant pause. "What do I want?" Harry said in a new, wondering voice. "What do you think I want, Mr. Simmons? I want to know what to do."

"About what?"

The pause was longer this time. "I don't understand, Mr. Simmons."

"Neither do I," Paul said. The pause, he thought, would be almost interminable this time while the stupid oaf tried to think. It was.

"Look, Mr. Simmons," Harry said at last, "haven't you seen on TV what's happening? At the World Tower, I mean? There's fires, and people trapped up in that Tower Room, and there's no power! There's no power in that whole big goddam building! No electricity at all!"

"So?"

Harry's voice tried to sound amused. "You've got to be kidding, Mr. Simmons. I mean, you know; you and I know what must have happened. There isn't any other way. A primary short that wasn't grounded—I mean, what else could it be?"

"I don't know what you're talking about," Paul said.

Harry's breathing turned audible, harsh. "Look, Mr. Simmons," he said, and his voice lowered now, was carefully controlled, "you paid me. You know you did. You told me everything would be all right. and once everything was buttoned up, who would know we'd cut a few corners, who would ever know? You never told me anything like this could happen. I mean, there's two dead guys already, and some of the firemen they've carried out don't look too good, and what if they can't get those people down out of the Tower Room, how about that?" The voice paused and then took on new urgency. "If they can't get those people, Mr. Simmons, that's—murder! What do we do? That's all, tell me what we do!"

"I wouldn't know," Paul said.

"Look. you paid me!"

"I paid you nothing. I don't know what you've dreamed up, but leave me out of it."

"You paid me!" The voice was out of control now. "You paid me! How do you think I went to Florida on that goddam vacation?"

"I wondered about that," Paul said. "It did seem a little odd on an inspector's salary."

The pause this time was the longest of all. Harry's hoarse breathing was the only sound. Then, "So that's the way it is, is it?" he said. His voice was almost resigned. "Okay, Mr. Simmons. My name's on all the sign-offs. I'm the guy they'll come looking for. And you know what I'll tell them? Do you know, Mr. Simmons?"

"Tell them what you please."

"I will! I goddam will!" It was a shout, almost a scream. "You're fucking well right I will! I'll tell them what you paid me, right down to the last penny! I'll tell them you told me it was all right, not to worry, nothing could happen! I'll tell them I believed you!"

"But," Paul said, "nobody will believe what you say. Do you have any witnesses, and photostats of checks, anything at all to prove anything? That's what they'll ask.

216

They'll ask something else, too: 'Harry,' they'll say, 'aren't you making all this up just to try to save your own miserable neck?' And what answer will you give them to that, Harry?" Paul hung up and walked back to his booth, squeezed in, and sat down heavily.

Nat Wilson, he thought, Giddings, Zib, Pat Harris, and now Harry Whitaker; yes, and Patty herself, hadn't she gone over to the other side? So where did that leave him? Just how vulnerable was he? Think, goddammit. THINK!

He had told Bert McGraw that he had followed the change orders without question because they bore Nat Wilson's signature, which meant that Ben Caldwell's authority was behind them. So?

It was a good story, one to cling to. Let Harris and Whitaker say what they chose, nobody could prove anything. Or could they?

There were his files upstairs in his office, and if there was a real stink raised, as there probably would be, a special inquiry into what happened at the World Tower, there was little doubt that the files of Paul Simmons & Company would be subpoenaed. So?

Face it, Paul told himself, the files were entirely too revealing. Any competent cost accountant could with little trouble turn up the fact that up to a certain point in the progress of the World Tower job, Paul Simmons & Company had been floundering in financial quicksand; but that in a remarkably short time there had been a sudden turnaround and the ratio of costs to payments received had taken a sharp reversal. Simmons & Company had not only climbed out of the quicksand, they had marched to high comfortable ground where the living was easy.

And it would be no trick at all for Nat Wilson to tie the sudden change in fortunes to the issuance of the first of the change orders. Simple as that. Nat Wilson again.

Paul sat quite still, looking idly now at the color television picture. The camera was focused on the north face of the Tower Room, a closeup with a long-range lens. They were breaking the windows out. Glass shards fell like shining hail. Inside the room shadowy figures moved about without apparent purpose.

It was, Paul thought, like watching one of those crowd scenes from Bangladesh or Biafra or, for that matter, some unpronounceable village in South Vietnam—distant, vaguely interesting, but basically meaningless. Those weren't real people, they were merely pictures on a screen. There was no reality outside of one's own self—hadn't some philosopher postulated that? Well, that was the way it was. Paul returned to a study of his drink.

The files were bad, but still they proved nothing. He had followed the change orders, and because of the changes his fortunes had improved. People might suspect that there was a casual relationship indicating hanky-panky, but they couldn't prove it. What about that ITT flap in Washington when they had hastily run their files through a shredding machine in anticipation of a subpoena? There was a lot of suspicion, but no proof of anything, and who even remembered it now? Still it would be well to check. And one question remained: Where had the copies of the change orders come from?

He slid out of the booth and went again to the telephone, this time to call his office on his private line. It was late, but his secretary answered. Her voice was breathless.

"Ruth, honey," Paul said, "you sound uptight." A warning bell rang faintly in his mind. "What's up?" At least she would tell him the truth, stick with him. After all they had had together. Not so much since Zib, but what difference? A good-looking chick, Ruth, really stacked, very good in bed, *and* bright. "Anything wrong?" Paul said.

The breathless voice calmed a little. "It's just that—you *have* seen what's happening down at the World Tower, haven't you?"

"I've seen."

"And," Ruth said, "you know about Mr. McGraw's heart attack?"

"That too."

"He's dead."

"Is he now?" Paul began to smile. He bore the old man no particular malice, he told himself, but it was better, far better this way. "I'm sorry to hear it."

"Where are you, Paul? Are you coming to the office?"

That warning bell again. "Why do you ask?" He paused. "Have there been calls? Anybody asking for me?" Out of the corner of his eye he caught the change of television camera angle and he turned his head to look. The camera was focused now on one edge of the north Trade Center tower roof. Men were clustered there, some of them in uniform, and instantly he understood what they were about. Crazy, he thought, out of sight. Breeches buoy attempt? Nat's idea? "Well?" he said into the phone.

"No calls," Ruth said. "Nobody asking for you." She paused. "It's just that—I want to see you." She paused again. "That's all it is."

Still the warning bell tolled. "Is there anybody there in the office?"

"Who?" Ruth's voice sounded puzzled.

"I don't know. I'm asking."

"Nobody but me.

Paul let his breath out slowly. Just uptight, he told himself, jumpy. "Okay," he said. "I'm coming up. Get out the World Tower files for me. I want to look through them." He paused. "Okay?"

"Of course." Good-looking, stacked, *and* bright. "I'll have them waiting."

"That's my good girl," Paul said, and started for the door.

"You don't want another drink?" the bartender said. "Hell." He gestured at the television set. "You're the first customer I've had since that began." He paused. "Look at it. A fire. How can that be? Like, they got all kind of safety things, don't they?"

The wedding guest confronted by the ancient mariner, Paul thought, and found the concept vaguely amusing. "I wouldn't know," he said.

"Lots of nuts around these days, real screwballs."

219

The bartender paused. "You're sure you won't have another drink?"

"Another time," Paul said. "But thanks anyway." He walked out to the street. It was almost empty. Strange.

He did not remember it, but he had heard of another time when the total attention of the city was focused on a single event, and the streets, as now, were almost deserted. It was the play off game between the Dodgers and the Giants in a year he could no longer identify; and when, in the last of the ninth inning, Bobby Thompson had hit his winning home run, every building had emptied and people had capered in the streets, a city gone mad.

Now the city's focus was on not a baseball game, but a burning building.

The receptionist was long gone from her desk in his outer office. Paul walked past, into his own office. Ruth was waiting there, good-looking, stacked, *and* bright. And on his desk were the World Tower files, as he had asked.

"Hi, honey," Paul said, and closed the door. Then he stopped and stood staring, frowning, at the two men who had been standing behind it.

"This," Ruth's voice said quite calmly, "is Mr. Simmons. These gentlemen have been waiting for you, Paul."

The room was still. "John Wright, district attorney's office," one of the men said. "We've impounded your World Tower files. And we'd like you to come downtown with us to answer a few questions." Wright's voice altered a trifle, hardened. "Maybe more than a few."

"And if I refuse?" Paul said.

Nothing in Wright's face changed. "You won't."

Paul looked at Ruth. Her face was expressionless. He looked again at the two men. "By what authority—"

"We have a search warrant, Mr. Simmons," Wright said.

Paul looked at the pile of file folders. "You won't find anything—"

"Wrong, Mr. Simmons, we already have found a great deal. The originals of some highly suspect change orders, for example."

Paul's mouth opened. He closed it with effort. He looked at Ruth.

"They weren't destroyed, Paul," Ruth said. "I thought it better to keep them. That way I had them to make copies to send to Mr. Giddings." Her voice was perfectly calm, modulated. "I was sure he would be interested."

In the silence, "You bitch," Paul said.

The girl smiled then. It was a pleasant satisfied smile. "Perhaps," she said. And then, "You see, I don't like being used, Paul. I don't think many women do."

Wright said, "Shall we go, Mr. Simmons? We'll have a nice ride downtown."

25

5:56–6:09

One of the Coast Guard ratings whose name was Kronski walked with hesitant steps to the low parapet at the edge of the Trade Center roof. He put both hands on the structure and cautiously, fearfully leaned forward to look down. Hastily he backed away. "Jesus, Chief," he told Oliver, "you can't even see the ground! I never been this high in my life!"

"You've been in an airplane," the chief said.

"That's different." Kronski paused. "But I don't even like that. I ain't no paratrooper."

Standing well back from the roof's edge, Kronski studied the World Tower, the row of broken windows that was the face of the Tower Room.

At his feet was the riflelike gun to fire the projectile carrying the light messenger lines, which lay neatly coiled and ready in tubs.

"You got to be kidding, Chief," Kronski said. "That far, in this wind?" He shook his head. "No way."

221

Privately, Oliver agreed. It was even farther than he had guessed from the ground—five hundred, maybe even six hundred feet—and the wind was blowing half a gale. On the other hand he had offered Wilson assurances that they would try, and he was not going to go back on that.

Besides, he could see people over in that great goddam building and he could smell the smoke that was blowing toward him, and although this wasn't exactly the same as *fire at sea*, those three words that curdle any sailor's blood, it was near enough to start the juices flowing. *There, but for the grace of God, go I*, that kind of identification . . . "I didn't ask your opinion, Kronski," he said. "Let's get on with it."

Kronski shrugged and picked up the rifle, loaded it carefully. "Suppose we do get a line there, Chief," he said. "An' we get a breeches buoy rigged." He paused. He looked squarely at Oliver. "How'd you like to take a ride from there to here, up this high, in this wind?"

"Get on with it, Kronski."

Kronski nodded. He raised the gun to his shoulder and aimed high for maximum trajectory.

Into the walkie-talkie Oliver said, "We're firing the first try."

"Okay." Nat's voice. "They're standing by in the Tower Room."

"Poor fucking landlubbers,' Kronski said, "can get themselves into the goddamndest situations, can't they?" He pulled the trigger.

The light line rose shimmering from the gun's muzzle.

It grew in length, light as a contrail, glistening in the late sun.

Rising still, it reached in a graceful climbing arc for the row of broken windows, higher, higher until it was level with the tip of the communications mast itself.

And then it reached its apogee and, obeying the inexorable tug of gravity, began to fall, arching still, while the line paid out hissing from the tub.

They measured its reach and its fall with their eyes, and even before the head of the line dipped beneath the level of the distant windows, they knew they had failed.

"Shit," said Kronski.

Standing tall and broad and solid, massively calm, "Try again," the chief said. "We're not giving up yet."

The governor stood well back in the Tower Room, his arm around Beth. Together they watched the line rise shining and clean and bright, and for a moment there was hope.

Ben Caldwell's artist's eye first measured the failure. "Start thinking of something else, Nat," he said. It was a whisper, no more, but the senator heard it.

"Hopeless?" the senator said quietly.

"Probably," Ben said, "with that rifle. I think some of the shore stations have cannons, but how accurate they are—" He shrugged. "Getting a line aboard a ship the size of a freighter is one thing: all you have to do is land the line somewhere across the deck. Getting a line into these windows from this distance—" He shrugged again.

Grover Frazee, drink in hand, watched as if hypnotized, and when the line dipped sharply and disappeared beneath the winows his lips began to move without sound and the look in his eyes was not quite sane.

Someone in the big room had turned on a transistor radio. Rock music blared to a heavy beat.

"Oh, for God's sake," Mayor Ramsay said, "this is not the time for that kind of thing!" He too had watched the reaching line until it plummeted out of sight beneath the windows. "I'll put a stop to it."

"Leave it, Bob," the governor said, "unless you think psalms and prayer are more appropriate."

"I fail to see the connection."

"It's there." The governor's voice was weary. "The band played on the deck of the *Titanic* while it was sinking. Some people prayed." His voice sharpened but did not rise in volume. "Goddammit, man, some of these people are scared to death, and I don't blame them. Let them do their own things." His arm tightened around Beth's waist. "I'll get back to the phone." He hesitated. "You?"

"Wherever you go, I go," Beth said. "I—don't want to be alone."

On the phone, "Sorry, Governor," Nat's voice said. "It was a long shot. The chief is giving it another try, but—" He left the sentence hanging.

"Understood," the governor said. "The best you can—" He smiled suddenly at his own words. He shook his head. "Never mind." Pause. "The elevators are out of the question?"

"Too much heat," Nat said. "Distortion of the rails. Sorry about that too."

To Beth, the office seemed small, crowded, claustrophobic. Howard and Storr, the two firemen, had come in, along with Ben Caldwell and Grover Frazee and the fire commissioner. Beth had the insane feeling that she could smell fear and she looked around to try to identify its source.

The governor had turned from the telephone. He said to Howard, "You're sure the stairs are out of the question?"

"For a fact," Howard said. He looked at Storr, who nodded. "We're better off here," Howard said, "which isn't saying much, to be sure. Look—" He opened his hands in a mounting gesture. "You've seen a forest fire? Or maybe you have not. It starts small, usually. Somebody is careless with a campfire, a lighted cigarette, like that. Grass catches, then brush, then the lower branches of the big trees." He paused, with vivid gestures demonstrating how it was. "Up in the wee top of one of the big trees, say, there is a nest of little birds. Down on the ground and even in the lower branches of their big tree there is a fire, smoke and heat are rising, the flames are climbing branch by branch." He paused again. "But for a long time the nest is still safe." He shook his head. "Not forever, mind you, but for a time. Until the flames reach the topmost branches the little birds are best off where they are." One final pause. "Particularly," Howard said, "if they cannot fly."

The fire commissioner said, "This is a hell of a big tree. That gives us a little more time."

"For what?" Grover Frazee said. "Just to wait, knowing what's going to happen?" He stood up suddenly. "Well, I'm not!" His voice was rising.

In the doorway Mayor Ramsay said, "Sit down, man! Start behaving like a responsible adult."

In the silence, "You ought to have been a Boy Scout leader," Frazee said. "Probably you were. For God, for Mother, and for Yale? The old school tie and noblesse oblige?" He shook his head as he started for the doorway. "Don't try to stop me." He spoke directly to the governor.

"We won't," the governor said, and watched Frazee disappear around the corner.

The office was still. Beth opened her mouth, closed it again without a sound. The fire commissioner stirred uneasily. The mayor said, "We should have stopped him, Bent."

"A judgment call," the governor said. "I'll take the responsibility."

Fireman Howard said, "He'll never in this world get down those stairs, Governor."

"I am aware of it." The governor's face showed strain.

Senator Peters appeared in the doorway. He leaned against the doorjamb.

"A judgment call," the governor said again. "Maybe it was right, maybe wrong. I don't know. We'll never know. Decisions like that can be argued indefinitely."

"You are talking," the mayor said, "about a man's life, Bent."

"I am aware of that too," the governor said. "But what gives me the right of decision over another man's life?"

"Are you abdicating your position?"

"There, Bob," the governor said, "is one of the differences between us. I don't believe in the Papa-knows-best-in-all-matters theory. In areas of public concern I will take a stand. But what a grown man chooses to do, unless it directly affects others, is not my concern."

From the large outer room the rock beat was plain. A female voice rose suddenly in laughter, shrill, alcoholic, tinged with hysteria. Somebody shouted, "Hey, look! He's going out the door!"

"This is your total public at the moment, Bent," the mayor said. "And they are affected by Frazee. You can't deny that."

"That," the governor said, "is what makes it a judgment call. On balance I think the public is best served by letting him go. One more disruptive force—out of sight."

Senator Peters said mildly to the room in general, "Cold-blooded son of a bitch, isn't he?"

There was no answer.

The senator smiled. "But I'll have to go along with you, Bent."

The governor roused himself in the desk chair. "So what we have left," he said, "is the hope that somehow your people, Pete, are going to be able to contain the fire before it reaches"—he smiled suddenly—"the nest."

"Like I said," the commissioner said, "it's a hell of a big tree."

Ben Caldwell said, "Has anyone had a weather report? A good drenching thunderstorm would help."

Beth, watching, listening, could almost feel a storm in the air. Losing herself in memory, she thought of the approaching darkness as the thunderheads build. Then the first stir of the winds that mount, the first distant muttering of the storm. How often had she experienced it, and how many times, particularly as a child, had she resented the spoiling of a summer afternoon?

The drops at first would be large, heavy, widely spaced, while the lightning flashes came in faster sequence and the intervals between flash and thunderclap diminished.

One hippopotamus, two hippopotamus, three hippopotamus . . . counting the length of the intervals in seconds to estimate the distance of the flash until, with the center of the storm directly overhead, there was no longer any interval, flash and thunderclap simultaneous.

Then the heavens opened and the rain became a solid mass, sometimes with hailstones bouncing or rattling on windows and roof, and the gods themselves seeming to shake the universe.

And she had resented this? When now, merely because

of Ben Caldwell's two sentences, a thunderstorm suddenly represented hope of salvation? Incredible.

"A nice summer rain would be good," the governor was saying. He was smiling. "Do you know any rainmakers, Ben?"

The telephone made noises. The governor flipped on the speaker switch that all might hear. "Armitage here."

Nat Wilson's weary voice said, "The second shot was no better than the first, Governor. It wasn't much of a hope from the start, but we gave it the best try we could."

"Understood," the governor said. "We appreciate the effort."

"Brown wants to know if his two men reached you safely."

"They did. They are sitting here now." The governor paused. "Did the other two get back down?"

There was a pause. Brown's voice came on the speaker. "I'm sorry to say they haven't, Governor. They're on about the fiftieth floor. There's fire in the stairwell beneath them."

"Then send them back up, man. If they can still walk, that is."

"There is fire above them too, Governor."

The governor's eyes were closed. At length he opened them. "Brown."

"Sir?"

"Put Wilson on again." And when Nat's voice acknowledged, "I want a complete report prepared," the governor said. "Chapter and verse of this—comedy of errors. I want it made now, while some testimony can still be taken. No holds barred, no sensitivities pampered. Who did what or failed to do what and, where possible, why. As long as we are able we will keep you informed of everything that happens up here, every decision we make, every fact we find."

Plain on the speaker was a muttering voice in the background: Giddings rumbling protest.

"Tell whoever that is," the governor said, "that this is a court of inquiry before the eventual fact, and that if

227

properly done, this report may prevent further ridiculous episodes such as this one. At least I hope to God it will."

"I understand, Governor," Nat said.

"Let the facts themselves tell the story," the governor went on. "Grind no axes. They aren't necessary. I think under the circumstances there will be blame enough to go around." He paused. "Including blame among some of us up here for letting our ambitions get out of hand." He paused once more. "Is that clear?"

"Yes, sir."

"All right," the governor said. "We will put together—" He stopped at the sudden hush out in the big room.

Someone screamed, screamed again. It was contagious.

"Hold on," the governor said and jumped from his chair to rush to the doorway and look out. "God!" he said. "God in heaven!"

Someone had opened the fire door in answer to hammered knocks. Grover Frazee stood framed in the doorway. Most of his clothing had burned away. He was burned bald and blackened, his eyes were merely dark holes in the torment of his face. His teeth showed white in a rictus grin. Flesh from his upper body hung in ragged strips and the remaining leather of his shoes smoldered. He made one wavering step forward, arms partially outstretched, a bubbling rattling sound deep in his throat. And then all at once he collapsed face forward into a huddled, blackened, smoking heap. He made one convulsive shudder, and then no further move and no sound.

The big room was silent, in shock.

The governor said quietly, "Cover him up." His face was expressionless as he turned back into the office. A judgment call, he thought, and closed his eyes briefly.

26

It could not be happening—but it was. One by one the building's defenses tried to meet the attack and, failing, collapsed.

Lights blinked unseen in the computer-control console for a time, but when all power failed, they too went dead.

On floor after floor sprinklers went into action, their fusible metal links melted by the heat. But much of the heat was within the structure itself, unreachable by sprinkler spray, and when fire did burst into the open, gulping fresh air to fuel its fury, temperatures rose so rapidly that water within the sprinkler pipes turned to steam, and the pipes burst; and one more enemy attack had carried.

Within the building's core not one but a hundred, a thousand vertical crevices turned swiftly into chimneys, carrying heat up and concomitantly reaching down to suck in more fresh air, first to generate and then to support combustion.

Heated air rises—the statement is axiomatic—and super-heated air rises more quickly than air merely warmed. But heat can be transmitted by conduction as well: quickly through steel structure, more slowly but still inexorably through paneling and tiling and flooring, through ducts themselves, wiring and piping and curtain walls. And a fire once well begun becomes almost self-sustaining, raising temperatures above combustion levels, causing materials seemingly to ignite spontaneously. Prometheus has much to answer for.

Word had spread. The great building which was to have been a world communications center was now focus

229

for world communications of a different kind. Around the world it was known, and in some places the knowledge was received with pleasure, if not joy, that in the richest country on earth, in the newest, tallest building man had ever conceived, a peacetime catastrophe was in the making, and all the king's horses and all the king's men were helpless to cope.

Not quite.

They had covered what was left of Grover Frazee with a white tablecloth and left the body where it had fallen. The fire door was again closed, but to everyone in the room it was clear now that fire doors were only temporary protection. The invading enemy would break through in his own time. Unless—

"They are trying to contain the fire in the lower floors," the governor said. He was again standing on the chair. "That is our best hope." He had almost said *only* hope.

He no longer had a full audience. Over in one corner of the big room the transistor radio again played rock music. Half a dozen people were dancing, if that was what it could be called. Well, the governor thought, he had said it himself: it was either that or hymns and prayer. He ignored the spectacle.

"I am sorry to report that the elevator attempt failed." He paused. "Considering what happened to the first attempt, maybe that is just as well." Jesus H Jumping Christ, he thought, I am reduced to platitudes. He made himself smile suddenly. "I won't say that everything is ginger-peachy. It isn't. On the other hand, we are all right here for the present, and I for one intend to hold the thought that our fire-fighting friends will get here in time." He paused. "And now I am going to have a drink. After all, this started out as a reception."

He stepped down from the chair and took Beth's arm. "A drink," he said, "and somewhere to talk. I am tired of grinning like an idiot to show how confident I am."

With her, Beth thought, he did not feel that he had to dissemble. There was the miracle.

230

Together they walked to the bar, and then carried drinks to a deserted corner. The governor swung two chairs into proximity. They sat companionably close, their backs to the room.

It was Beth who broke the silence. "Thoughts, Bent?" she said.

"Gloomy and angry." The governor smiled suddenly, this time with meaning. "I'm thinking of waste. Regretting it. Hating it." He paused. "Mentally shaking my fists at the sky. Exercise in childish futility."

She could understand the feeling, even share it. She forced it aside. "When I was a child," she said, "and being punished, confined to my room"—she made herself smile—"I used to try to think of what I would most like to do, concentrate on that. What would you most like to do, Bent?"

Slowly, even perceptibly some of the tension flowed from him. His smile turned easy and gentle. "Retire from politics," he said. "I have the means and I have had the fun. That ranch out in New Mexico—"

"Just that, Bent? Nothing more."

He took his time. At last he shook his head. "No. You make me look at myself. I would hate total retirement." Again the meaningful smile. "I am a lawyer. I'd like to find out how good a lawyer I am."

"You would be good at anything you decided to do."

"But the fishing would always be there," the governor said, almost as if she had not spoken, "and I would see to it that there was always time for it." He paused. "And since I am painting a picture of Utopia, you would always be there too."

There was warmth in her mind, in her being. "Is that a proposal?"

Without hesitation, "It is."

"Then," Beth said slowly, "I accept with pleasure."

Nat walked to the door of the trailer and down the steps to stand on the plaza level and stare up at the immensity of the building. Until she spoke, he was unaware that Patty had followed him.

"All the people," Patty said.

Nat looked then at the huge crowd beyond the barricades. "Times Square New Year's Eve," he said. There was anger in his voice. "Goddam ghouls. Maybe we ought to burn people at the stake in public, sell tickets, make millions."

Patty was silent.

"We're all to blame," Nat said. "That's the first thing. I'm glad Bert never knew."

"Thank you for that." Patty paused. "And remember it. Others are involved too. Even Daddy. Everybody's had a hand in it, not just you, don't you see?"

He could smile then with effort. "You're a cheerer-upper." Unlike Zib, who tended to be stylishly downbeat. And that, he thought, was another of the big city's characteristics he did not like: the firm conviction that nothing was ever what it appeared to be; that there was nothing really to be for, only against; the ubiquitous you-aren't-going-to-make-a-sucker-out-of-me defense thrown up like a barbed-wire entanglement to protect the insecure inner compound; all of it in the name of worldly sophistication. Sophistry, perhaps, but not sophistication.

"What is going to happen to all those people, Nat?" Patty's voice was quietly intense. "Will they—" She left the question unfinished.

"They're hauling hose in and up," Nat said, "a floor at a time. Every step is a fight. There are one hundred and twenty-five floors to go."

"But what is burning? That's what I don't understand."

"Everything. Some of the offices have been leased. Furniture, carpeting, paneled doors, paper records—those are the first to burn. And that raises the temperature to the point where paint will burn and floor tiling and plaster will melt, and that in turn raises the temperature even more until things you wouldn't believe combustible start to go too." Nat paused. "I'm not a fire expert, but that in general is how it goes."

"Suppose," Patty said, "that the building had been occupied when this happened. Thousands of people instead of a hundred." She paused. "But numbers aren't really important, are they? If it were only one person, it would still be—tragic."

In the midst of her own grief over Bert McGraw's death, Nat thought, she could still concern herself with others. Maybe *because* of McGraw's death, the loss somehow making all men kin.

"What are you going to do, Nat?"

The question caught him off balance. "That," he said, "is what I'm trying to think of."

"No," Patty's voice was gentle now. "I mean when all of this is over."

Nat shook his head in silence.

"Will they rebuild?"

He had not even considered it, but the answer came loud and clear: "I hope not." Pause. "Just this morning," Nat said, "Ben Caldwell talked of the Pharos, the lighthouse that stood at the mouth of the Nile. For a thousand years, he said. That was how he thought of this building." He shook his head. "What is the word? Hubris: human pride that affronts the gods. In places in the Middle East they never finish a building. Always a few bricks or a few tiles are left out." He smiled down at the girl. "That's because a completed job is considered an affront. Man is supposed to strive for perfection, but he's not supposed to achieve it."

"I like that," Patty said.

"I'm not sure I like it, but I think I understand it. A man told me once that it was good every now and again for anybody to be cut down to size." He paused. "Let's go back in."

"Have you thought of something?"

"No." Nat hesitated. "But I can't stay away any more than you can." A new thought occurred: "What if you were not Bert's daughter," he said, "but just—married to somebody involved?"

"To you?" Small, brave, willing to face even conjecture, hypothesis. "Would I be down here at the building?" Patty nodded emphatically. "I would. Trying not to be in the way, but I would be here."

"That's what I thought," Nat said slowly, and wondered at the sudden pleasure the knowledge gave him.

Inside the trailer one of the battalion chiefs was on the walkie-talkie. His voice was the only sound. "You can't tell how deep the fire in the stairwell is above you?"

The voice that answered was hoarse with exhaustion. "I told you, no!"

The chief said almost angrily. "And below you?"

There was silence.

"Ted!" the chief said. "Speak up, man! Below you?"

The voice came at last, almost hysterical this time: "What is this, a fucking quiz show? We're going down. If we come out, I'll tell you how deep it was, okay? We're on fifty-two right now—"

"Inside," the chief said. "How about that? Any chance? You could break through the door—"

"The goddam door will blister your hand. That's what it's like inside. I tell you, we're going down. There's no other way."

Assistant Commissioner Brown took the walkie-talkie. "This is Tim Brown," he said. "Good luck."

"Yeah. Thanks."

"We'll stand by for word."

"Sure." And then, speaking aside, "All right. Haul your ass. Here we go." The walkie-talkie clicked dead.

The two battalion chiefs stood motionless, staring at nothing. Tim Brown's lips, Patty saw, moved gently. In prayer? Giddings wore a scowl and his blue eyes were angry. He looked at Nat and slowly, almost imperceptibly shook his head. Nat nodded faintly in acknowledgment, perhaps agreement. Patty closed her eyes.

It was not possible, she thought, and knew that it was. No dream, no nightmare this. There would be no sudden awakening, no rush of relief that the horror had fled with the morning light. She wanted to turn and run. Where? To Daddy? As she had run only this noontime for comfort, solace, understanding? But there was no—

The walkie-talkie in Brown's hand came to sudden hollow life. It uttered a scream and then another. And then there was merciful silence, and the trailer was still.

234

Brown was the first to move. He walked to the drafting table and set the walkie-talkie down very carefully, switched it off. He looked at no one. In a slow monotone he began to swear.

27

Paula Ramsay walked up to the two chairs in the quiet corner of the Tower Room. "I'm sorry to interrupt," she said, "but what's happening behind your back—" She shook her head. "I'm afraid I am old-fashioned."

The governor nodded, expressionless. "With the exception of Paul Norris and Grover," he said, "they've all done splendidly, so far. What can we expect?"

"Cary Wycoff is making a speech."

The governor cocked his head. He could hear the voice, not the words; but the tone, high-pitched, angry, almost hysterical, spoke volumes. "He's probably saying that someone is to blame and he is promising an investigation."

Paula Ramsay smiled faintly. "You have it exactly right, Bent."

"In a little while," the governor said, "Cary will lead a delegation demanding that something be done. God, how many delegations like that I've listened to!"

"People," Paula said, "are swarming to the bar. One of the waiters is sitting in a corner by himself, drinking from a bottle—"

The governor wondered if it was the waiter with three kids. He sighed and stood up. "What do you think I can do, Paula?"

Paula's smile was brilliant. "I am like Cary Wycoff, Bent," she said. "I think something ought to be done, but I don't know what." She paused. "And so I turn to you."

"I am flattered." The governor's smile sadly mocked himself and the entire situation. "There was a Mark Twain character who was tarred and feathered and being ridden out of town on a rail." The smile spread. "He said that if it weren't for the honor of the occasion, he would just as soon have walked. I'd just as soon sit right here." He glanced down at Beth. "But I'll give it a try."

He passed the closed fire door where Grover Frazee's body lay beneath a white tablecloth. The secretary general was standing looking down at the motionless shape. Slowly, solemnly he crossed himself, and then, seeing the governor, smiled almost apologetically.

"Since my student days," the secretary general said, "I have prided myself on my freethinking. Now I find that early beliefs do not die so easily. Amusing, is it not?"

"It is not, Walther. I find it almost enviable instead."

The secretary general hesitated. "I am beginning to understand," he said, "that you are basically a kind man, Bent. I am sorry I did not realize before."

"And," the governor said, "I always thought that you were, that anybody in your position simply had to be just a stuffed shirt."

They smiled at each other.

"In my country," the secretary general said, "where mountain-climbing is a popular sport, men tie themselves together with ropes for safety when they climb, and we have a saying: 'There are no strangers on a rope.' It is sad, is it not, that it requires a crisis situation before people come to know one another?" He paused. "Is there anything I can do to help?"

"Pray," the governor said without mockery.

"I have done that. I shall continue." Again the pause, polite, solicitous, sincere. "If there *is* anything else, Bent—"

"I'll call on you," the governor said, and meant it. He walked out into the center of the room and looked around.

Paula had not exaggerated. The bar was doing a land-office business; in the center of the room Cary Wycoff was making a speech; it *was* the waiter with three kids who was sitting by himself drinking from a bottle of bourbon; in the far corner the transistor radio was playing rock, and some of the younger people were maneuvering in spastic gyrations.

There was smoke leaking from the air-conditioning ducts now, but it was not yet oppressive; its acrid taste hung in the air. The governor sneezed.

Mayor Ramsay nearby said, "Good God, look at that!"

One of the younger dancers, female, was carried away. With a single motion she stripped her dress over her head and threw it from her. She wore minibriefs and no brassiere. Her generous breasts bounced with each pelvic lunge.

"It would have gone over big at the Old Howard when I was in college," the governor said. "Kitty would have enjoyed it." He smiled. "So would I."

Senator Peters walked up, "It's getting hot," he said, "in more ways than one."

Ben Caldwell joined the group. His face was expressionless. "More smoke," he said. "Until we broke out the windows, this was a more or less sealed system. Now—" He shook his head, smiling faintly to indicate that he understood there had been no other course. "I am still waiting for Nat Wilson's other idea."

Cary Wycoff let out a sudden wordless roar and shook his fists above his head. "Goddammit, have you all gone mad?" He glared at the governor's group. "Old men standing around at a tea party! Don't you even understand what's happening?"

The temptation was strong to reply in kind, shouting, gesticulating, charge and counter-charge until all sanity disappeared. The governor stifled the temptation. "I quite understand that you are having a temper tantrum, Cary," he said. "Are you going to hold your breath until your face turns blue? That is popularly supposed to get results."

Cary got himself under control with effort. A group had gathered behind him. The governor recognized a face here and there. They watched him cautiously.

"We've listened to you," Cary said. His voice was

237

calmer now. "We've behaved like little ladies and gentlemen—"

"All of you," the governor said, "except Paul Norris and Grover Frazee. They wanted action. You saw the results. Is that what you have in mind, Cary?" His voice now was cold and hard. "If you do, there is the fire door. It is unlocked."

Cary was silent, breathing hard.

"There is an alternative," the governor said. "We were just discussing the broken-out windows. You could jump."

Someone in the group behind Cary said, "There has to be some way, goddammit! We can't all be trapped here like rats!"

"And," Cary shouted, "that silly gesture of shooting a line over from the Trade Center tower. A token! That's all it was! Everybody knew it couldn't work!"

There was a general murmur of agreement. The governor waited until it subsided. The faces, he thought, were no longer polite, even deferential; they were the faces of a mob preparing to stone the police. Fear and the anxiety of helplessness needed no purpose.

"I am open to suggestion," the governor said. "We all are. Do you think I enjoy the situation?"

The blaring rock music stopped suddenly. The almost-naked girl continued her gyrations, lost in her own ecstasy, but the other dancers turned to watch the confrontation, to listen.

The governor raised his voice. "I'm not going to make a speech," he said. "There isn't anything to make a speech about. We're in this together, all of us—"

"Who's responsible?" Cary shouted. "That's what I want to know."

"I don't know, the governor said. "Maybe down on the ground they do, but I don't. Unless"—he paused—"unless we all are because we've come too far from our beginnings, lost touch with reality."

"That," Cary shouted, "is crap!"

The governor merely nodded. He was beyond anger now, into the calmness of scorn. "Have it your own way, Cary," he said. "I won't argue the point."

A new, quiet voice said, "What is your assessment, Governor?"

"Grave." The governor faced them all. "I won't try to fool you. There would be no point. We are still in contact with the ground by telephone. They know our situation. You can look down at the plaza and see the fire equipment, the hoses like spaghetti leading into the building. Everything that can be done is being done." He spread his hands. "Grave," he said again, "but not hopeless—yet." He looked around the room, waiting.

There was silence.

"If there is any change," the governor said, "I promise to let you know. That is damn small consolation, I realize, but it is the most I can give." He turned away then, and walked back toward the deserted corner, past the tablecloth-covered body without a glance.

Beth was waiting with Paula Ramsay. "We heard," Beth said. She was smiling gently. "That was well done, Bent."

"The next time," the governor said, "isn't going to be quite so easy." He felt old and tired, and he wondered if his subconscious was merely preparing for the end. He gathered himself with effort. "And there will be a next time," he said. "Panic comes in waves, each one stronger than the last." Well, all they could do was wait.

Chief Petty Officer Oliver had his twenty years behind him in the Coast Guard. He had served on shore stations and aboard cutters, in tropical waters and in the Arctic ice lanes. He had helped fish men from burning oil-covered water and plucked them from the decks of foundering vessels; and sometimes the men he had gathered in had been dead.

He had learned the long hard way that some operations are impossible. But a part of him refused to believe it, and all of him rebelled against failure of any kind.

Now, standing large and helpless on the roof of the Trade Center tower, staring across at the row of broken windows marking the Tower Room, so close, really, and yet so goddam far away, he was almost, but not quite, on the point of explosion from sheer frustration.

Kronski said, his voice weary, "So we shoot another line?" He paused. "You remember that poem? 'I shot an arrow into the air / It fell to the ground, I knew not where'? I'll bet that guy lost a lot of arrows that way. You want me to try another?"

"No," the chief said at last. Sheer waste, he thought, and that he could not countenance either. He stood motionless for a time, staring across the gap. There were people over there. He could see them. And he could see and smell the smoke.

Fire and storm: all of his adult life both had been his enemies. He had met them and fought them, and sometimes won, sometimes lost, but always before he had been able somehow to come to grips. Now—

He raised the walkie-talkie. "Oliver here," he said. "Come in, Trailer."

Nat's voice came on immediately. "Trailer here."

"It's no good," the chief said. His voice was heavy with disappointment. "The range is too long and there's too much wind against us."

"I see." Nat kept his voice carefully expressionless. Another idea gone bad. Think, goddammit! Think!

"We might as well pack it up," the chief said.

Holding the walkie-talkie in one hand, Nat pounded softly on the drafting table with the other. "Hold it a minute, Chief. Let me think." A plea, a hope.

The trailer was still. Brown, the battalion chief, Giddings, and Patty all watched in silence. You're grandstanding, Nat told himself, just playing to an audience— and despised himself for it.

And yet, something was crawling around in the back of his mind, and if he could get it out in the open— Goddammit, what triggered that feeling anyway? What—

Another idea gone bad, he thought suddenly. That was the key. *Another* idea—but what if two of them were taken together? Into the walkie-talkie he said, "We had a chopper up there early on, Chief." He made himself speak slowly, with unnecessary clarity, thinking it out as

240

he went along. "They couldn't find any place to land, so they couldn't do any good." He paused. "But what about getting the chopper back to take you and your gun over close to the building, close enough for you to shoot a line into the Tower Room? Then haul the line back to the Trade Center roof and start your operation from there?" Another pause. "Will that work? Is there a chance?"

There was a long pause. Then, in slow wonderment, "I," the chief said, "will be goddamned." He was grinning now, and the sense of helplessness had fallen away like a discarded cloak. "I don't see why it won't. Call in your whirlybird." He was looking at Kronski. "You're going for a ride, son. Just don't get airsick."

They called the governor from his secluded corner to the office. He listened to Nat's voice on the telephone speaker. "Will it work?" the governor said.

"We think it may." Nat's voice carefully controlling enthusiasm. "The chopper can hover and give the Coast Guard almost a point-blank-range shot into the Tower Room. You'll have to clear a good share of the room so nobody gets hit by the shot." He paused. "It may take a couple of tries, but it shouldn't be all that hard." I hope, he thought.

"We will see to clearing that whole side of the room," the governor said. "And we will have men standing by to catch the line. And then?"

"Make it fast to structure," Nat said. "There'll be strain while they carry the rest of the line back to the Trade Center tower. I'll be on the walkie-talkie to Oliver, the Coast Guard chief, and I'll also stay on this line with you. That way we can keep our signals straight." He paused. "When they have the messenger line on the Trade Center roof, they'll bend the heavier line to it. Then your men can start hauling in." He paused again. "But not until we get the word."

"Understood," the governor said. He was smiling faintly. "Your idea, young man?"

"We promised to think of something." Nat hesitated. "The only thing is, why didn't we think of it before?"

The governor's smile spread. "For years," he said, "I have been on the lookout for an idiot child of three I could hire to point out the obvious to me." He turned the smile on Beth. "But there are also times," he said, "when I manage to recognize a good thing as soon as I see it. Thank God." His tone changed. "What is the status of the fire?"

"Not good." In the two words there was finality.

"And those two men in the other stairwell?" the governor said.

Nat could hear again the screams coming over the walkie-talkie. It was my idea to send them in the first place, he thought, and knew that he would make the same suggestion again at need, because it was a chance that had to be taken. "They didn't make it," he said.

The governor watched Beth's eyes close. He said gently, "Neither did Grover Frazee. He tried to go down the stairs." His voice turned almost brutal. "What is the eventual butcher's bill going to be?" And then, quickly, "Strike that." He leaned back wearily and was silent.

The chopper pilot said, "Well give it a try." He shrugged. "How close I can get, I don't know. You get anywhere near these goddam tall buildings, and the wind—" He shook his head. "It blows in every direction at once, you know what I mean?"

The chief's face was expressionless.

"Look," the chopper pilot said, "I don't mean to make a big thing out of it, but if we bang into that building, it isn't going to do anybody any good, is it?"

The chief's head moved a fraction of an inch in acknowledgment of the point. His expression did not change.

"You know about Hell Gate?" the pilot said. "Water from the Sound coming in, meeting the Harlem River, those whirlpools, crisscross currents?"

"I know Hell Gate," the chief said. He had seen small craft completely out of control in Hell Gate waters, powerless to maneuver against the force of the currents, slammed against bridge pilings, against walls.

"Same thing in the winds around these big goddam buildings," the pilot said. He paused. "All I'm saying is that we'll give it a try, but I can't promise anything."

"Okay," the chief said. "Kronski, get into that thing."

"Thanks a lot," Kronski said.

Nat stood in the doorway of the trailer, looking up. Nothing yet. Waiting was the hard part—now who had said that? But it was true, and he had never realized it before. You have an idea and you set it in motion, and then you wait, and hope, because there is nothing else to do.

"It will work," Patty said. She smiled. "It has to."

28

6:24–6:41

With the windows broken out it was perceptibly cooler in the Tower Room, although, as some noticed with mounting alarm, the flow of smoke from the air-conditioning ducts was also increasing.

"Cause and effect, probably," Ben Caldwell explained again. "As long as this was a more or less sealed chamber, the flow of smoke, or air, through the ducts was limited. Now with the broken-out windows acting as vents—" He spread his hands and shrugged.

Henry Timms, the network president, said, "Then we shouldn't have allowed the windows to be broken." His voice was assured, decisive, and critical. "There was obviously little chance that a line could be shot here."

Caldwell said merely, "It isn't entirely black-and-white," and turned away.

He was an architect, a designer, and in his view life was rarely black-and-white. He detested even the word

243

compromise, but he was also aware that the accommodations it spoke for were all that made most enterprises possible. The choice here had been between the chance that a line could be shot from the Trade Center tower and the certainty that more smoke would be brought in. As far as the decision was concerned, he was happy to leave it to others. He could not have cared less.

He supposed that a majority of people in the room still entertained some hope. He did not. He was used to facing tangible facts, attempting to avoid them was exercise in futility. How deep the eventual damage to the building's structure was going to be he could not begin to estimate, but long before the damage was complete, everyone in this room was going to be dead. He had long ago resigned himself to that. And it no longer had the power to bother him because a large part of himself had already died.

This was his building, his vision, his soaring dream. And now it was ruined.

On whose shoulders lay the ultimate blame he had no idea. Nor did he particularly care. What difference whose hand had wielded the hammer that disfigured the Pietà? Oh, society might wish to take revenge, but nothing could restore the work of art.

In New York, in Los Angeles, in Chicago, in Pittsburgh and a dozen lesser cities he had his monuments, and they would stand long after he was gone. But this building was—*had been*—his masterpiece, and it was now beyond redemption; visions, calculations, compromises, labor, love, all the blood, sweat, and tears of the process of achievement—for nothing.

When he stood in his office this morning, the pile of change orders lying on his desk, Nat Wilson summoned, had he felt then the first intimation of disaster? Hard to tell; hindsight was always suspect. No matter. The disaster was now taking shape.

Senator Peters walked up, wearing his crooked smile. "Deep in reverie," he said. "Ideas?"

Caldwell shook his head. "Regrets only."

"That sounds like an invitation to a party."

Caldwell's tight little smile was expressive. "For this party, I am afraid, there will be no regrets."

"So I understand." The senator paused. "It doesn't seem to bother you."

"Does it you?"

"You know," the senator said, "I've been trying to find the answer to that for some time. I'm not sure." He made a deprecatory gesture. "Oh, I don't mean that I'm above any fear of death. I'm not. What I do mean is something entirely different."

"Such as?" Despite himself, Caldwell was interested. "Some kind of faith?"

The snator smiled. "Not in any established sense. I have always been a heathen. No"—he shook his head—"it's part, I suppose, of a lifetime of learning that some things can't be avoided, some battles can't be won, some decisions have to be accepted—"

"In a word," Caldwell said, "politics? The art of the possible?"

The senator nodded. "We're shaped by what we do." He smiled. "Bent couldn't shuck the habit of command if he tried. He's like a veteran airplane pilot, uncomfortable when anybody else is at the controls."

More and more interesting. "And Paul Norris?" Caldwell said. "Grover Frazee? How do you explain their behavior?"

The senator smiled. "I'll tell you a story about Paul Norris. At college he had a fine suite of rooms in Adams House. His bedroom window looked right out at the campanile of the Catholic church. Some of us had an idea and Paul went along. We mounted an air rifle on the window sill in a steady rest aimed at the bell tower. At midnight when the church bell struck twelve, we pulled the trigger and the bell struck thirteen."

Caldwell was smiling now, nodding, in this moment taken back forty years to youthful fervor. "Go on."

"We did it again the second night," the senator said. "A couple of Catholics who lived in Adams House attended Mass and reported that the good fathers were understandably puzzled, even mildly upset. There was

245

talk of a miracle." The senator paused. "The third night the bishop came over from Boston to listen for himself. We didn't disappoint him. The clock struck thirteen. Then we dismantled the steady rest and took the air rifle away."

Caldwell, smiling still, said, "But what about Paul Norris?"

The senator shook his head. "He wanted to keep it up. Night after night. He couldn't see that it was best left right there—a mystery. Among other unpleasant things about Paul, he was stupid, and I don't like to waste time arguing with stupid people." He paused again. "Although, God knows, a politician can't ever hope to avoid it."

Caldwell said, "You said *part* of your—acceptance was that some things couldn't be avoided, some decisions had to be accepted. What other parts?"

"I suppose," the senator said slowly, "that I have a sniggly feeling it's all for the best. Don't ask me how, because I can't give even a rational theory." He paused. "Do you recall," he said, "that in Athens, when things went wrong, the king had to die? Theseus's father threw himself off the cliff because the black sails on Theseus's ship indicated that things had gone wrong." His smile was apologetic. "Maybe we're a mass sacrifice? Ridiculous idea, isn't it?"

"To atone for what?"

The senator's smile faded, disappeared. "You do keep your nose to the grindstone, don't you?"

"If you mean," Caldwell said sharply, "the world's troubles, the troubles in this country, poverty, bigotry, that kind of thing—what have they to do with us? I'm not responsible for them in any way."

"A comfortable view."

Caldwell's gesture took in the entire room. "I'm not even responsible for these people's troubles. I just happen to share them."

The senator was silent.

"If you're thinking," Caldwell said, "that because I designed this building I am responsible for its failures, I deny that. The design was, and is, sound. I don't know all

246

that has happened to produce this end result, but it is not my design that is to blame."

"I think your reputation is secure," the senator said, "and that's the important thing, isn't it?"

Caldwell studied the senator's face for mockery. He found none. He relaxed a trifle.

"You asked me," the senator said, "how to explain Grover Frazee's behavior. I think I can in one word: panic." He too looked around the room.

In the far corner the heavy rock beat once more blared from the transistor radio. The almost-naked girl gyrated endlessly. Her eyes were closed, her movements erotically explicit; the world was shut out.

In another corner a mixed group was joined in song. The senator listened carefully.

" 'The Battle Hymn of the Republic,' " he said, "or 'Onward, Christian Soldiers.' With my tin ear I can't tell which."

By the bar the three rligious leaders who had participated in the ceremonies in the plaza conferred: the rabbi, the Catholic priest, and the Protestant minister.

"I can think of a good subject for prayer," the senator said. "It would have to do with deliverance from a fiery furnace. Nebuchadnezzar would have dug this scene, wouldn't you say?"

Caldwell said suddenly, "All right, I will have to admit that I share the responsibility. It is not all mine, but I share it."

The senator stifled a smile. "It doesn't really matter now, does it?" His voice was gentle.

"It does to me."

"Ah," the senator said then, "that's a different story."

"There is nothing fallacious in the design."

"I'm sure of it."

"Execution. There is where the trouble begins. When you turn the actual work over to others, you have lost control."

"It's a hell of a feeling, isn't it," the senator said, "when you have to turn over to somebody else something you've sweated over?"

247

There was a long silence. "In your own way." Caldwell said slowly. "you are a wise man. And compassionate You make me feel better, cleaner. Thank you." He started to turn away.

"Which group?" the senator said. He no longer stifled his smile. "Dancing song or prayer?"

Some of the perceptible tension went out of Caldwell's narrow shoulders. He half-turned and his smile was easy. "I may sample them all."

"Good for you." the senator said.

He walked slowly toward the office. alone. "And now, physician" he said almost whispering "heal thyself."

The governor was coming out of the office. His expression was inscrutable. "Come along Jake." he said "We've got good news I hope." He paused. "But if this try fails too, then I think we are really going to have panic. We may anyway." He paused again. "The traditional rush for the lifeboats or the exit."

The governor found a chair and climbed upon it. He raised his voice. "I promised news if and when there was any. Now I want your attention."

The singing died away. Someone turned down the transistor radio's volume. The room was hushed.

"We are going to try again to get a line into this room," the governor said. "This time--"

"More crap!" Cary Wycoff's voice dull with anger, tinged with terror. "Another sugar pill to keep us quiet!"

"This time." the governor said and his voice carried through Cary's. "they are going to try to shoot the line in from a helicopter." He paused. "I want this entire side of the room cleared so nobody will be hurt if the shot is successful." He beckoned the fire commissioner. "Have two or three men standing by to pounce on the line when it comes through the windows. Then—"

"When?" Cary shouted. "You mean if! And you know goddam good and well that it isn't going to happen." The words were almost running together now. "All along you've kept things from us. made your own decisions, your own little deals—" He took a deep shuddering breath.

"We're stuck here! Right from the start it's been a fuckup! Rotten clear through. the whole city government!"

From the crowd behind Cary Wycoff there was a low, angry murmur.

"Easy. Cary," Bob Ramsay said. He shouldered his way through the crowd to tower over Wycoff. "Easy, I say. Everything has been done that could be. and now this—"

"Shit' Give the voters that crap. don't give it to us. We're here to—die, man' And who's responsible? That's what I want to know. WHO?"

"I'm afraid we all killed Grandma." Senator Peters's voice raised enough for attention He faced Wycoff and took his time. "Ever since I've known you. Cary, you've had more questions than a tenement has rats. But damned few answers. only reactions. Have you wet your pants yet? You've made every other infantile move."

Cary took a deep breath. "You can't talk to me like that."

"Give me one reason why not." The senator was smiling. It was not a pleasant smile. "By your standards, I'm an old man. but don't let that bother you if it's violence you're thinking of. In the neighborhood I grew up in a ten-year-old kid would eat you for breakfast."

Cary was silent. indecisive.

"All of you." the senator said, "simmer down. The man is trying to tell you what to do. Now, goddammit. listen!"

Suddenly the governor was smiling. "I've said it all," he said. He pointed. "Look!"

They all turned. A helicopter was swinging toward the bank of broken-out windows, its staccato engine sound growing louder by the moment.

Inside the chopper: a man, Kronski thought, could spend a lifetime in one of these contraptions and never get his sea legs Boats. even small boats in heavy seas. move with some kind of rhythm. All this chopper did was buck and jump, and how in the hell the chief thought he could even hit the building, let alone the windows, he didn't know.

His stomach was bucking and jumping too, and he swallowed hard, swallowed again, and breathed deep in the cold air.

He could see faces now inside the Tower Room. They stared at the chopper as at a vision.

The pilot looked at Kronski. There was question in his eyes.

"Closer!" Kronski roared. "Closer, goddammit!" He bloody well wanted only one shot, he told himself, and then back to solid ground, or at least the solidity of that Trade Center roof.

The pilot nodded shortly. He moved his control stick as if it were a fragile thing that might suddenly break loose in his hand.

The building moved toward them. The faces inside were plainer. The bucking and jumping increased.

"Close as I'll go!" the pilot said. "Shoot from here!"

Inside the room people were on the move now, scurrying to one side of the room. A large man—it was the fire commissioner—was waving his arms to hurry them on.

Kronski raised his gun and tried to take a sight. One moment he was looking at the gleaming mast of the building, and the next moment what he saw was a row of intact windows below the Tower Room. The silliest goddam business he had ever engaged in. He raised his voice in a great shout: "Can you, for Christ's sake, hold this thing still?"

From inside the room they could see Kronski's strained face, and the gun he held, pointed, fired.

Against the chopper's bellowing clatter the sound of the shot was inaudible, but the fragile line itself was tangible for all to see. It shot twisting into the room, crashed against the far wall, collapsed in a writhing tangle on the floor.

The fire commissioner and three waiters pounced on the line and held it tight.

The helicopter lurched quickly away, paying out line as it went.

Someone cheered. It was contagious.

Patrolman Shannon, four stitches in his cheek beneath a fresh white bandage, was back at the barricade with Barnes. "You read about things like this," Shannon said. "But did you ever think you'd see it?"

His gesture took in the plaza, the hoses and scurrying firemen, the smoke pouring out of broken windows on the building's face, the plume of smoke near the tower's top, and now high up the hovering helicopter, tiny against the immensity of the buildings.

"An Irish ghoul," Barnes said. There was no rancor in his voice.

"There is," Shannon said, "nothing like a good fire. Nothing." He paused. "Oh, I know, Frank, I'm sounding like the bloodthirsty man I am not, but it is true. Why do people gather to watch? Because of the excitement of of the great leaping flames, a foretaste of Hell itself."

"How are you," Barnes said, "on a good juicy traffic accident? Bodies strewn around? Gore?"

"Oh, now, Frank, it is not the same at all. The one is man's little foolishness. The other, this, is something— grand! Look there. Flames showing halfway up the monster structure! Do you see?"

"I see," Barnes said. He paused. "And all I can think of is Götterdämmerung."

"Put that into English, you black rascal."

"Valhalla burning," Barnes said. "The home of the gods burning to the ground."

Shannon was silent for a few moments, still staring upward. "It's blasphemous," he said, "but I think I like it."

The telephone hooked on his shoulder and the walkie-talkie on the desk directly in front of him, "So far, so good," Nat said to the trailer in general. "They've made the messenger line fast inside the Tower Room. The chopper pilot is working back toward the Trade Center roof."

Tim Brown said, "God be praised!" He took out the half-empty cigarette package, looked at it, and in sudden decision threw the entire thing into the wastebasket. "I'll never have a better reason for quitting," he said.

Patty sat quiet on a stool, watching, listening, smiling proudly.

Giddings said, "Half the battle won. The other half—"

"Agreed," Nat said, his voice suddenly sharp, "but, goddammit, if we hadn't won the first half, there wouldn't even be a second half to try." Then, into the phone, "Yes, Governor?"

"Assuming it is going to work," the governor was saying, "what all is involved? Happily, I have never had to ride in a breeches buoy, so I know nothing about it. There is wind, considerable wind. Can a woman alone ride safely?"

"You stick your legs down through two holes," Nat said. You're inside a kind of sack. All anybody has to do is close his eyes and hang on." He paused. His voice was solemn. "But you do have a couple of things to work out, Governor. Who goes in what order—"

"Women first. We decided that earlier."

"Governor. The round trip, Trade Center roof to Tower Room and return, is going to take a little time. Say a minute. You have a hundred people up there, maybe half of them women. It's going to take the better part of an hour just to get the women across, and another hour for the men. That's a lot of waiting, and you'd better have the exact sequence—" He stopped at the sound of another voice in the office background.

The governor said, "Good for you, Jake." And then, to Nat, "Senator Peters has anticipated you. I was afraid

252

he was cutting out paper dolls. He is preparing numbered lottery slips instead."

Nat nodded. He smiled. "Good." He paused. "And somebody to enforce the sequence?" he said.

"That too is in hand." The governor's voice paused. "Two hours? That is your estimate?"

"Maybe less," Nat said. "But slow and easy is the way, the only—"

The walkie-talkie crackled. "Oliver to trailer," it said. "We've bent on the heavy lines. We'll pay them out as they haul in. Tell them to take it slow, easy. When all this heavy line is out, they're going to have a lot of weight to haul. More, because of the windage."

"Will tell," Nat said. "Hang on, Chief."

He spoke into the phone again. "All set, Governor. Tell your men to haul away, and be prepared for a load before they get the job done." He paused. "Good luck."

"Thank you, young man." The governor's voice was tinged with anxiety. "You will continue to stand by the phone?"

"Yes, sir. *And* the walkie-talkie."

"Bless you," the governor said.

Nat laid the telephone on the blotter and leaned back in the desk chair. He caught Patty's eye. She smiled.

Tim Brown said, "Will the structure stand? If it begins to collapse, we are going to have the damndest mess this city has ever seen."

"I think it will stand," Nat said. "If the fire gets completely out of control—"

"Man," one of the battalion chiefs said, "it *is* completely out of control. All we're doing is shoveling shit against the tide." He paused. "And losing men doing it."

"Then more windows are going to go," Nat said. "And that aluminum siding won't stand up indefinitely. But the structure itself isn't going to collapse."

"You're sure?" Brown said.

Nat shook his head. "My best guess," he said. "I can't do any better than that." His mind went off on a new tack. "With a forest fire," he said, "you pray for rain."

"Like they used to say in Boston," Giddings said.

"Spahn and Sain and two days of rain. How much good would it do here?" He spoke to the firemen.

One of the battalion chiefs shrugged. "It would help. It would give them up there"—his raised head indicated the Tower Room—"a little more time, I'd think." He paused. "But if they're already getting smoke—" He paused again. "Two hours is a long time."

Time was the essence, Patty thought. Time was the dimension against which all else had to be measured; within its framework, length, breadth, depth, those who waited their turn in the Tower Room would live or die. While we stand by outside that framework unable to help, she thought, and was reminded again of the vigil outside the Coronary Care Unit in the hospital.

She wondered how her mother was bearing up, and knew that at this moment Mary McGraw would be in church, on her knees, praying for the soul of Bert McGraw, and believing that her prayers would at least be heard even if not wholly granted. Faith has the power to move mountains? Maybe yes, maybe no. But certainly it did have the power to soothe and comfort.

And faith I have not, Patty thought for perhaps the first time with real regret. We have turned our backs on the old ways, many of us, but what have we taken in their place?

She was suddenly aware that Nat was watching her with concern, and she repeated the question aloud, wondering if he would understand.

"I don't think we've taken anything," Nat said. "We've substituted what we considered knowledge for belief and found that we don't yet know enough to make the substitution work. Maybe we never will."

His eyes searching her face asked a question, Patty thought, and she slid down from the stool to walk over and perch on the corner of the desk. "I'm all right," she said. "Honest. Mother said she was going home to have a nice cup of hot tea and a good cry. Mine will come later too."

"Tea?" He was trying to keep it light.

"I'm that old-fashioned," Patty said.

The telephone crackled. Nat picked it up. "Yes, Governor?"

"We've had one heart attack," the governor said. "It has set me thinking. I'm having a list prepared of names and addresses of all those up here. When it is ready, I'll have it read to you for someone to set down." He paused. "Just in case."

"Yes, sir." Nat cupped a hand over the phone. "Get a stenographer to take down names," he said to Brown.

Patty stirred herself on the corner of the desk. "Let me." Something, anything to do, she thought, anything that might in the slightest way help. Nat watched her; he was smiling approval. "I write legibly," she said.

Nat said into the phone, "We're ready for your list whenever, Governor." Again he leaned back in the desk chair, and smiled up at Patty.

"You did it," Patty said quietly. "You promised a new idea and you came up with it. I'm proud of you."

"It isn't over yet. Not by a long shot."

"I'm still proud of you. And however many people manage to get out will—"

The walkie-talkie said, "Oliver to Trailer. They've got the line over there. I want to make damn sure somebody knows how to tie a decent knot; a bowline is what I'd like. If that end pulls loose while somebody is between the buildings—" He left the sentence unfinished.

Nat said, "There are two firemen up there, and probably some ex-Boy Scouts as well—" He could not stifle entirely a triumphant sense of gaiety. "I'll see to it, Chief. Hold on."

He picked up the phone and spoke to the governor, smiling a little at the thought of a man used to dealing with the problems of eighteen million people now bothering to make sure that somebody had tied a knot properly in a piece of line. He listened. "Thank you, Governor," he said, and returned to the walkie-talkie. "Bowline it is," he said. "Rest easy, Chief."

"Then," the chief said, "tell them to haul away on the breeches buoy line. We're ready at this end." There was triumph in the chief's voice too.

In the building's core, already converted to one great flue, temperatures were climbing to welding-torch levels. A continuous blast of fresh air was sucked in at the base, driven upward by its own almost explosive expansion and accelerating to near the hurricane speed, acting, as the battalion chief had said, in the manner of a blast furnace.

Structural steel began to glow. Lesser materials melted or vaporized. Where, as on floor after floor, random spacing, superheated air burst out of the core into open corridors and turned instantly to flames, the heavy tempered windows lasted only moments before they shattered and threw out their shards to rain down on the plaza.

Aluminum panels curled and melted, the skin of the structure peeling away to expose the sinews and the skeleton beneath.

Like a gigantic animal in torment, the great building seemed to writhe and shudder, its agony plain.

From the ground, to those whose eyesight could make it out, the line dangling between the two buildings looked impossibly fine, delicate as gossamer. And when the breeches buoy swung loaded for the first time from the Tower Room and began its catenary descent to the roof of the lower Trade Center roof, it seemed that the canvas bag and the woman it contained were hanging free, suspended by nothing more than faith, defying gravity in a miraculous attempt to escape the rising blast-furnace heat.

Her name was Hilda Cook, and she was currently starring on Broadway in the new musical *Jump for Joy!*

She was twenty-nine years old, dressed in shoes, mini-briefs, and a mid-thigh dress tucked up now above her waist. Her long shapely legs dangled crotch-deep through the breeches buoy holes. She clung to the edges of the canvas bag with the strength of hysteria.

She had stared unbelieving at the number on the small square paper slip she had been handed from the empty punchbowl, and her first sound had been a squeal. Then, "It can't be!" Her voice was shrill. "I'm number one!"

The secretary general was conducting the drawing.

"Someone," he remarked, "had to be. My congratulations, young lady."

They had carried the heavy line on which the breeches buoy rode through the window and up to the ceiling where one of the firemen had broken through with his halligan tool to expose a steel beam around which they had bent the line.

Ben Caldwell, directing the operation, had made the point: "Unless we go to the ceiling," he said as if explaining a problem to a class of not very bright young architects, "the line will rest on the window sill and we will not be able to get the breeches buoy into the room. I, for one, would rather get into the bag inside than climb out the window to get to it."

Three men manned the lighter line attached to the breeches buoy itself, and Hilda Cook, swinging free within the room, said, "Easy, guys, for God's sake! I'm already scared spitless!"

As she rode through the window and away from the building's protection, wind buffeted the bag, the heavy line began to swing, and the sensation of falling was inescapable.

Hilda screamed and closed her eyes and screamed again. "And it was just about then, darlings," as she told it later, "that I wet myself. I really did. I'm not a damned bit ashamed to say it."

The wind was cold on her legs and it blew through the pulleys above her head with a banshee wail.

The rocking, swinging motions continued, the oscillations becoming wilder as she approached the center of the span.

"I thought I was going to die, I really did. And then I was afraid I wasn't! I screamed for the damned thing to stop! You know. Stop the world, I want to get off! But there was no way. No way! And when I was a girl, I didn't even like roller-coasters!"

She may have fainted; she was never sure.

"The next thing I knew, I was in Heaven! I mean the swinging had stopped, and the howling of the wind, and the biggest, strongest man I ever saw, darlings, just

257

plucked me out of that canvas sack like I was something coming out of a grocery bag. And he set me down on my feet and held me up or I would have gone flat on my face." Pause. "Was I crying? Darlings, I was bawling like a baby, and laughing all at the same time!" Another pause. "And all the big man said was, 'Okay, lady. It's all over now.' What he didn't know is that I still dream about it and wake up trying to scream!"

Nat watched from the trailer doorway until the breeches buoy had returned to the Tower Room and for the second time emerged loaded. "I make it just over a minute," he said. "At that rate—" He shook his head in silence and walked back inside to pick up the walkie-talkie. "Trailer to Oliver," he said.

"Nice going, Chief."

"Yeah, thanks." There was a pause. "But what?" the chief said.

The big man is perceptive, tuned to nuances, Nat thought "It's going to take a long time to get them all," he said. He paused. "How about a second line, two breeches buoys working at once?"

The big man was also decisive. "No dice. At the angle we shoot from, we couldn't get the lines far enough apart through those windows. Then in this wind they'd sure as hell foul each other, and we'd have nothing at all." His voice was calm, but tinged with regret. "I thought of it. But it won't work. We'll have to do the best we can."

Nat nodded slowly. "I know you will. Thanks, Chief." He put the walkie-talkie down.

For every problem there is not necessarily a solution—true or false? Unfortunately entirely too goddam true. One hour and forty minutes, he thought, that's all we need. All? Eternity.

Patty was at the desk, pencil and pad at hand, the telephone held to her ear by one hunched shoulder. "A-b-e-l, Abel," she read back into the phone. "Three twenty-seven North Fiesta Road, Beverly Hills. Next, Governor . . . ?"

Nat listened to the names as Patty wrote them down and read them back:

"Sir Oliver Brooke—with an e—Ninety-three E-a-t-o-n Square, London South West One."

That would be the British Ambassador, flown up only this morning from Washington.

"Henry Timms—double m—Club Road, Riverside, Connecticut."

Head of one of the major networks?

Howard Jones, US Steel . . . Manuel Lopez y García, Ambassador from Mexico . . . Hubert van Donck, Shell Oil Company, Amsterdam . . . Walter Gordon, United States Secretary of Commerce . . . Leopold Knowski, Ambassador from the USSR . . .

One name approximately every fifteen seconds. At that rate, it would take half an hour to list them all. Nat picked up the walkie-talkie. "Give us the names as you land them, Chief. We'll want to know who—may get left." He walked back to the doorway then and stood looking out at the plaza.

Firemen, police, gaping crowds. The orderly tangle of hoses and the sounds of pumping engines at work. Occasionally the booming voice of a bullhorn. The entire plaza was wet now, a dirty artificial lake. The tormented building still stood, of course, but in a hundred places smoke oozed out to obscure the no longer shining aluminum siding.

"Pretty, huh?" This was Giddings at Nat's shoulder. His voice was low-pitched, angry. "Circus day. When I was a kid, Fourth of July was a big deal. Fireworks shooting out over the lake at night. People came for miles to watch." He gestured at the crowds. "Like this." He paused. "Maybe you can't blame them, at that."

Nat turned to look at him.

"They've never seen anything like it," Giddings said. "Neither has anybody else." He made a sudden angry hand gesture. "That goddamn Simmons."

"He isn't the only one."

"Are you standing up for the son of a bitch?"

"No," Nat said, "for more reasons than you know.

259

But," he added, "neither am I letting the rest of us off the hook."

"We should have caught it, you mean?" Giddings nodded. "All right. We've agreed to that before. But which is worse, doing the dirty or failing to catch it? Answer me that."

It was a quibble, Nat thought, and found the question unworthy of answer. And yet he could understand Giddings's need to ask it. A man had to salvage what he could of his self-respect, didn't he? Didn't everybody do it every day in many ways—the games people play?

Inside the trailer Patty's voice said, "Willard Jones, Peter Cooper Village."

Who was Willard Jones? Or did it matter who he was? It was a name that belonged to a person, now living, maybe soon to be dead. Did he, Nat, accept that now?

Face it, friend, Nat told himself, you have known almost from the beginning how this was going to come out —and he thought of the nineteen bodies in that burned-over mountain clearing.

But for them I had no responsibility.

What difference? The question echoed in his mind.

No one could have anticipated that all electrical power would go out; anybody in his right mind would have said that it was impossible. But so was the grid blackout impossible that had crippled the entire Northeast a few years back. So were the *Titanic* sinking and the *Hindenburg* disaster, the wave of assassinations beginning with President Kennedy's, and the violence in cities only how many summers ago? Impossible, but they happened.

Logic, he thought suddenly, had nothing to do with it. Logic was for law, for stately considerations of fact, unhurried judgments objectively taken. Logic was not for him.

He, Nat Wilson, was what he felt, the subjective man, not the man with the computer mind. And what he felt was a sense of guilt that would not wash away—ever.

That he had failed to find flaws in the building's construction could be understood, explained, condoned, forgiven—but not by him. In the entire tangle of this day

260

he was inextricably involved, woven right into the fabric of events even if with some of them he appeared to have no real connection.

He had never laid eyes on the two firemen who had died screaming in the stairwell. Or the other two now in the Tower Room, probably no better off. But he had recommended that they be sent up the long stairs, and even though it had been within Brown's authority to ignore the suggestion, for Nat a sense of responsibility remained.

He had nothing to do with Bert McGraw's death. True? False? Logic said one thing, sensibility the other. Because as Zib's husband he had been insufficient, Zib and Paul had carried on their—thing. And somehow that had figured in McGraw's heart attack, if Patty understood it at all.

So where did all that leave him?

I am glad you asked that question, sir.

The hell I am.

Am I a jinx?

On the face of it, ridiculous. Involved, yes. Responsible, yes. Were not the two words, the two conditions intertwined? And if I am involved, responsible, then Ben Caldwell must also be drawn into the chain. And he is. He admitted as much in his office only this morning. Grover Frazee? Yes. Bert McGraw? Certainly. The list began to multiply with computer speed, its possibilities almost endless.

Then who was not to a greater or lesser degree involved, responsible? Incredible question, without answer.

He had welcomed Barnes, the black cop, to the lodge of blame. Now Nat thought: welcome yourself to the human race, friend; maybe now you are beginning to see what it is all about. Maybe—

"Nat." Patty's soft voice, almost pleading.

He looked down at her sad smile.

"The list is finished," she said. "Every name. Every address." She paused. "Somehow just by the act of writing them down, I'm—part of them. Can you see that? I probably don't know one of them, and yet I know them

261

all. I'm—" She shook her head. "I don't know what I am."

"Involved?" Nat said. His tone was gentle. "Responsible?"

The change in her eyes, in her face, was something to see. "You do understand, don't you? Thank you, Nat."

"Maybe I'm beginning to," Nat said.

30

7:02–7:23

Police Lieutenant Jim Potter sat with his captain and the chief inspector in the large quiet office. Potter had his notebook on his knee. He kept his voice purposely expressionless.

"John Connors," he said, "Caucasian male, age thirty-four." He paused. "Widower. No children. Occupation: sheet-metal worker when he worked, which hasn't been very often recently." He paused. "A history of mental disturbance commencing three years ago." He paused again, waiting.

The captain said, "What happened then?"

"His wife died." Potter's face was that of a poker player in a big-stakes game: totally expressionless. "She died in jail." Pause. "In the drunk tank." Again he waited.

The chief inspector said, "She was a lush?"

"She didn't drink."

"She was on drugs?"

"Just one." Potter took his time. "Insulin. She was a diabetic. They picked her up because she had collapsed and was lying on the sidewalk and they thought she was drunk." He closed the notebook carefully. "So they

262

tossed her into the drunk tank, and without medication she died."

In the silence the captain said, "Didn't she carry some kind of identification? Something to say she had diabetes?"

"Maybe." A little of the sad bitterness showed now in Potter's voice. "And maybe nobody bothered to look. The investigation after the fact wasn't very thorough. Connors was the only one who cared much, and he had gone off his rocker."

The big office was still. The chief inspector let his breath out in a noisy sigh. "Okay," he said. The word was without meaning. "But so he did have a grudge, and so he wasn't playing with a full deck of cards, why the World Tower building?"

"I'm no shrink," Potter said. "But the World Tower building was the last real job he had. He was fired. There's a connection, but maybe you have to be loony to see it. I don't know. All I know are the facts."

In a vague kind of way it made sense. All three men felt it. The Establishment had killed Connors's wife, hadn't it? The World Tower building was the brand-new shining symbol of the Establishment, wasn't it? Well?

They sat quietly, thinking about it.

At last, "Sometimes," the chief inspector said slowly. "I think the whole goddam world has gone crazy."

"Amen," said the captain.

In slow, almost interminable succession, the women were helped or loaded into the canvas bag, and their legs poked through the twin holes. Almost without exception their eyes were wide with terror. Some cried. Some prayed.

Paula Ramsay was number twenty-two. "I don't want to go," she told the mayor as they waited for her turn. "I want to stay here with you."

The mayor was smiling faintly as he shook his head. It was not his well-known campaign smile; this was the real man exposed. "I want you to go, and that is purely selfish."

"You, selfish?"

"I want you to go," the mayor said, "because I would

263

rather have you safe than have anything else in the world." The smile spread, even mocked himself. "Including the White House. Jill needs you."

"Jill is a big girl now. We agreed on that," Paula looked around. "Where is Beth?"

"In the office with Bent. Their little time together."

"I thought," Paula said, "that she was ahead of me."

The mayor could not remember when last he had lied to his wife. "I wouldn't know," he said, and stared out the window as the breeches buoy began its swaying trip back from the Trade Center roof.

The secretary general said, "Number twenty-one, if you please." There was no answer. He repeated the call.

"Hey," somebody said, "that's you. Here's your ticket."

The girl in the bikini briefs dancing in the corner stopped her automatic gyrations. She shook her head as if to clear it. "I thought I was forty-nine.' She giggled. "Funny." She waved her hand in the air and lurched forward, bare breasts bouncing, toward the loading window. "Here I come, ready or not."

"God," the mayor said. "She goes ahead of—anybody at all? Why?"

"You are usually kinder than that, Bob." Paula's smile was gentle. "The girl is drunk. And frightened." The smile spread. "The difference between us is that I'm not drunk."

"Or naked."

"Does it matter now?"

The mayor made an almost angry gesture. "I am stuffy enough or square enough to believe that some values—" He stopped suddenly. "No," he said in some surprise, "it doesn't matter, does it? We're down to basics."

"And my basic wish," Paula said, "is not to go but to stay--with you."

"You'll go," the mayor said. There was a new tone of command in his voice.

Together they watched the half-naked girl being lifted into the canvas sack. Someone tossed her dress into her lap. She stared at it in bewilderment, and then, as if only that moment realizing her nakedness, she crossed both hands over her breasts and began to cry. "What am I doing?" Her voice was almost a scream. "I—can't—!"

"Lower away!" This was the first commissioner, in command of the operation. "Hang on, sister, and you'll be home free before you know it."

The girl's shrieks were lost in the whistling wind.

The mayor took his wife's arms and walked with her toward the loading window. "Like airplanes and ship sailings," he said "there's never anything to say is there?"

They stood quietly. holding hands, watching the breeches buoy near the Trade Center roof reach it. They watched the chief lift the girl out of the canvas sack as if she were weightless. Her dress fell to the roof. The chief held her upright with one hand and picked the dress up with the other. Then he gestured toward the Tower Room and the breeches buoy began its return journey.

The mayor's wife watched it approach. "Bob."

"Yes?"

Paula turned to look up into the mayor's face. Slowly she shook her head. "You're right. There is nothing to say. You can't put thirty-five years into words can you?" She closed her eyes as the breeches buoy swung through the window and halted. swaying gently.

"Number twenty-two, if you please," the secretary general said.

Paula opened her eyes. "Goodbye. Bob."

"Au revoir," the mayor said. He was smiling gently. "Your words to Jill, remember? Give her my love."

The senator knocked and walked into the office. The governor was in the desk chair. Beth was perched on a corner of the desk, long slim legs crossed and swinging gently.

"Come in, Jake." the governor said. From the big room outside the mixed sounds of rock music and song blended in cacophonous counterpoint. From the bar came a sudden burst of laughter. "Sit down," the governor said. "I don't cotton to the bacchanalia either."

"I don't want to intrude."

265

"Nonsense." The governor paused. "You came in with a purpose, no?"

He had always seen deep, this Bent Armitage, the senator thought, which probably at least partly explained his success in public life. You did not go as far as he had gone without knowledge of your fellow man.

The senator sat down and stretched his legs wearily. "A long lonesome road," he said, and smiled. "The youthful bounce is long gone." He gestured toward the telephone. "Anything new?"

"I phoned down the lists," the governor said. "And then"—he paused, smiling—"I indulged myself by calling my daughter, Jane, in Denver." The smile spread. "I charged the call to the executive mansion telephone. That will give the auditors pause. Anyone you want to call, Jake? I'll let the taxpayers pick up your tab too."

The senator shook his head. "No one," he said. He stood up suddenly. "Do you ever doubt yourself, Bent? Do you ever wonder just what in hell use you have been to anybody?"

The governor grinned. "Frequently."

"I mean it," the senator said. He took his time. "When you're a kid just starting out—for me that was back in thirty-six, just elected to my first term in Congress—you look around and see the big ones, the important ones, the man in the White House, the Cabinet officers, names you've read about ever since you could remember—" He paused and plumped back down in the chair. He waved one hand. "You study their style because they're what you want to be." His smile was wry. "It's *in* today to talk about a search for your identity. That implies that there is already a you and all you have to do is be yourself." He shook his head. "What you're really doing is hunting for the character part you're going to play for the rest of your life, a very different thing indeed."

I have always doubted myself, Beth thought suddenly, but I was sure the reason lay in my own shortcomings. She watched the senator in wonder.

"So," the senator said, "you find the role you want and you learn it letter-perfect." He paused. "And it works. It's

266

convincing. First you're a bright young fellow. Then you're a comer in his forties, beginning to carry some clout. You reach fifty, sixty, and you've come a long way, but you aren't there yet. Do you know what I mean, Bent?"

The governor's smile was sad. "You're never *there*," he said. "There's always something just over the next hill, and the next. And when you reach it, it has changed too." He spread his hands in a gesture of dissolution. "What looked so bright and shiny from a distance up close is just sunlight on smoke."

"And so you wonder," the senator said, "just when you're going to make the final step that puts you where you've always wanted to be so you can relax and enjoy it and know that you've fought the good fight, done the job well, earned your rest and your place in the sun, lived out whatever crappy platitude you choose." He shook his head. "The answer is—never. That's why they don't retire, those old men in Washington and other places. They keep hoping that the time is going to come when they've done it all and they can rest content. And it isn't going to come ever, but you don't realize that until you face something like—this. And then suddenly you wonder why you ran so hard all your life, chasing something that never existed. Don Quixote, Galahad chasing the Grail—it's so damn futile!"

"But fun," the governor said. "Admit that, Jake. You've had just a hell of a time outsmarting, outarguing, outstaying the rascals who got in your way. Would you change it?"

"Probably not. And that's the stupidest part of all. We don't even learn."

The governor leaned back in his chair and laughed.

"What's so damn funny?"

"Your lament," the governor said. "It tucks its tail in its mouth and rolls like a hoop. Of course you'd do it all the same way. Because you're you, Jake Peters, *sui generis*. You fought and scrambled and bit, yes, and butted in the clinches when it was necessary—as I did— and you enjoyed every minute of it, wins, losses, and draws. You've been your own man, and how many can say that?"

"He wrote fiction in college," the senator said to Beth. "Bad fiction."

"And," the governor said, "you have the gall to admit that you enjoyed it all, but still find it futile? What more can a man ask than to be able to look back and say it was fun?" The governor paused. "You've probably left some things undone. We all have. But when you leave the restaurant filled to the brim with a good meal, do you spend your time regretting that you couldn't eat everything?"

"That," the senator said to Beth, "has always been his special touch: the homely analogy." He stood up. "As a philosopher, Bent," he said looking down at the governor, "you're no Santayana, but you may have made a point or two worth considering. I'll ponder them outside." He paused in the doorway to flip his hand in a vague gesture. "By the way, number twenty-one just went off." He spoke directly to Beth. "It was the naked chick. She thought—"

"I'm number forty-nine," Beth said, and made herself smile.

The senator hesitated, and then waved again as he walked out.

"And that," the governor said, "leaves us alone again for a moment at least. He smiled up at Beth. "So pensive?"

"All the things you said to him," Beth said slowly, "could apply as well to you, couldn't they?"

"Probably." The governor smiled again. "But the difference is that when you say them to yourself, you don't necessarily believe them."

"I think I understand, Bent." She was smiling too. "I hope I do."

"There have been times," the governor said, "when I have done things I am not particularly proud of, or allowed them to be done, which is the same thing, in order to achieve an end I thought worth the compromise. I know I am capable of deluding myself—at least temporarily. I think everyone is, and some not temporarily."

"I think you are a good man, Bent, in the best sense of the word."

"Thank you."

"I think you are a better, stronger man even than you believe. You are the one they come to. You are the one they listen to."

"Easy on that buildup, even if I love it."

Beth shook her head. "He said it, the senator. He said 'until you face something like this' you keep on—fooling yourself." She paused. "I am not fooling myself any longer. I hate what's happening. I don't want to die."

The governor took her hand. "Fair enough," he said. He was smiling gently. "Now tell me: what number did you draw? Was it twenty-one?"

31

7:23–7:53

To the west the sky had darkened and evening thunderheads were beginning to build. Giddings stood in the doorway of the trailer, watching. "A cloudburst now," he said. He looked over his shoulder at Brown, and shrugged. "A miracle? The Red Sea rolling back?" He shook his head and wiped the back of his hand wearily across his forehead. It left a black smear.

One by one Chief Oliver had called down the names of those safely across, and Patty had found them on the listings and checked them off.

Now, "This one," the chief's voice said on the walkie-talkie "doesn't know who she is, and I sure as hell don't."

Nat said, "Doesn't she have identification in her purse?"

"Purse?" The chief's voice was a roar. "She doesn't

even have any clothes on!" Then more gently in an aside. "All right, sister, it's all over now. You go with these cops. They'll take care of you." And to the trailer again. "We'll get you a name somehow." The walkie-talkie was silent.

Patty said, "Whoever she is, she's number twenty-one." She smiled up at Nat. "Thanks to you."

Nat pushed himself away from the desk suddenly and walked to the doorway to look up at the tops of the great buildings. Squinting, he could make out the breeches buoy, filled again, on its catenary journey down to the Trade Center roof.

Inside the Tower Room, he knew, three or four men would be cautiously paying out the guiding line lest the canvas bag careen madly down the slope, frightening its passenger even more than it now did, perhaps even throwing one clear to fall screaming the quarter of a mile to the plaza. Idly he wondered who was in the breeches buoy on this trip.

He turned and walked back inside to stand again near Patty. "How long do we have?" he said. "That's the question. How many are we going to have time to get out?"

"Maybe all of them," Patty said. She paused. "I hope." She paused again, studying Nat's face. "You don't think so?"

Nat shook his head in silence. He said at last, "I wish I knew what was happening. Up there in the Tower Room." He gestured suddenly. "Inside the core of the building. When it's all over, we'll study what's left, and we'll try to figure out just what happened." He shook his head again. "But that is no substitute for knowing at the time. That's why they put automatic recorders in commercial airplanes. If there's a crash and the recorder survives, it shows exactly what certain flight conditions were right up to the moment of impact." He paused contemplatively. "Maybe the computer control ought to be located well outside the building for the same reason." Something to think about. He was silent, thinking about it.

Patty watched and listened, the here-and-now part of

270

herself smiling inside. Daddy had never been very far away from his work either; she doubted that the good ones ever were. She said nothing lest she interrupt Nat's train of thought.

"This—mess," he said at last, "is going to change a lot of thinking. We've gone on blithely assuming that tolerances, mistakes would automatically cancel themselves out. This time they haven't. They've compounded themselves instead, and this is the result." He paused. "Think of the *Titanic*."

The analogy between the World Tower and the *Titanic* was strained. Only the fact of inevitable disaster linked the two, because the one setting for tragedy was strangeness and the other was everyday familiarity.

The *Titanic* was a ship crossing the ocean in a day when crossing an ocean was not at all the usual thing to do. Within that strange setting unknown dangers lurked; their existence could be accepted as real.

But this was a building, a known world, with differences only of degree, not of kind. You enter buildings and ride elevators every day—and nothing happens. This time something had happened, but it was beyond total belief that it could be as serious as some tried to make it out. The fact of the breeches buoy had allayed many fears.

Oh, there was still some singing, and some praying, and a few people drinking or dancing while they waited their turns at deliverance. But there is singing, drinking, and dancing every day, and praying every Sunday with no immediate crises in sight.

What was left of Grover Frazee was already forgotten beneath the white tablecloth. Paul Norris was merely a hearsay death. Singed eyebrows on the two firemen were scant proof that actual disaster was at hand.

There was the breeches buoy, and one by one women rode it across the gap between the buildings to safety. Still . . .

The fact of the matter was that of all the people in the Tower Room, only a handful understood and accepted not

271

only that catastrophe was in the making, but that it was inevitable.

Ben Caldwell understood and accepted. He needed no complicated calculations to convince himself; simple arithmetic sufficed:

One hundred and three persons had drawn numbers.

The round trips of the breeches buoy averaged very close to one minute.

One hour and forty-three minutes, then, would be necessary to evacuate the Tower Room.

With heat in the building's core already sufficient to distort steel elevator rails, would the Tower Room remain a sanctuary for one hour and forty-three minutes?

No.

So be it.

With far less technical knowledge the governor nevertheless understood and accepted the situation. "The need is for haste," he said to Beth, "but we can't hurry." He was remembering Nat Wilson's cautionary words.

It was becoming hotter in the office. The governor thought of Fireman Howard's analogy of the nest in the treetop: sooner or later the fire would reach it, and that would be the end of the nestlings. We are nestling, he thought, as unable as they to fly. The temptation was strong to hammer his fist on the desk in sheer frustration. He stifled it.

Mayor Ramsay appeared in the doorway. "Paula has gone," he said. "I watched her land safely—if that's the word." She had turned to wave. He paused, remembering. "Thank God for that."

"Good for her," the governor said. "And I'm happy for you, Bob."

Beth was smiling. "I'm glad," she said.

The governor said, "What is your lottery number, Bob?"

"Eighty-three." The mayor's voice was expressionless.

The governor smiled. "I'm eighty-seven."

"It isn't fair!" Beth said suddenly. "There are people out in that room who aren't worth any part of you! Of

272

either of you! And what is Senator Peters's number? I'll bet it's high too!"

"Easy," the governor said. "Easy." He stood up, took off his jacket and loosened his tie. He sat down again and began to roll up his sleeves. He smiled at Beth. "It's probably cooler out in the big room," he said, "but for now, at least, I prefer it here." He paused. "Unless you disagree?"

Beth hesitated and then shook her head slowly. Her lower lip was tucked between her teeth. When she released it, tooth marks showed. "I'm sorry, Bent."

"They're behaving very well so far, Bent," Bob Ramsay said. "I've been watching Cary Wycoff, and for the moment, at least, he is—defused. And I don't think anybody else is in his class as a rabble-rouser."

The last-moment rush to the lifeboats, the governor thought, or the inevitable jamming of the exits when flames appeared. He had never seen either, but he well understood that in sudden panic terrible things could happen. He said slowly, thoughtfully, "But it might be just as well, don't you think, to have barricades set up?" He gestured with his hands at right angles. "Some of those heavy tables set in place surrounding the loading area with room for only one person at a time to come through?"

The mayor's immediate smile was faint, bitter. He nodded. "And the opening guarded against gate-crashers." He nodded again. "I'll see to it."

"Maybe," the governor said, "we're seeing shadows." He paused. "But I'm afraid I don't think so." He leaned back in his chair and waited until the mayor was gone. Then, to Beth, "How do you walk the tightrope between cynicism and reality?" He shook his head.

"Is there going to be trouble, Bent?"

"We'll try to anticipate it."

"How?"

"Like this." The governor picked up the phone and spoke into it. Nat's voice answered instantly. "Everything," the governor said, "is going beautifully, young man. You and the Coast Guard have my thanks."

Beth smiled. It was lordly of him to make it *his* thanks; and yet it was also fitting, because from the beginning of the problems, it was one man. Bent Armitage. who had automatically taken charge and spoken for all. And so the imperiousness lacked arrogance and was thereby acceptable. More than acceptable. Beth's smile turned fond and gentle.

"Everything is orderly now," the governor was saying. "but when the pressure starts to build. and people begin to understand that maybe there isn't going to be time for everybody—" He left the sentence hanging, implications plain.

"Yes, sir," Nat's voice said. "I've been thinking about that too."

"Good man." The governor waited.

Nat said slowly, "We have the leverage, or the chief on the roof has, and maybe he'll do what I say."

The governor was nodding. "Which is?"

"We can issue an ultimatum," Nat said. "At the first sign of trouble we can put it that unless the process stays orderly, as you've planned it, we'll shut the entire operation down, because slow and easy, one person at a time, is the only way it can work. It may look simple, but it's touchy, and one mistake can spoil it for everybody."

The governor was nodding again. "And can you make the ultimatum stick?"

"If we have to," Nat said, "we will."

For the third time the governor nodded. "You may have to," he said. And then, "For the moment, that's all." He paused. "Bless you for standing by." He leaned back in his chair again and closed his eyes.

"Bent," Beth said. She hesitated. "Oh, Bent, why does it have to be like this?"

"I wish I knew."

"It's ridiculous," Beth said, "and I know it, but I can't help asking the big question: Why me? Why any of us individually, but most particularly why me? What have I done to be here, to meet you and then have it—like this?"

The governor was smiling faintly. "I've asked the same

274

question many times. He paused. "And, you know, I've never yet found the answer?"

The senator walked in. "I've just come to make a report, Bent. Bob is having tables moved into place around the buoy-loading area. Your idea, no doubt. And all is more or less quiet." He smiled. "So far." The smile spread. "Bob said you asked his lottery number." He took his time. "Well, I'll watch you both go. Mine is one hundred and one."

Beth closed her eyes.

"I've also been thinking," the senator said, "and lo and behold, a limerick came to mind fullblown:

"A nun from Biloxi, Miss.,
    Was seduced from her faith by a kiss.
She found that the cloister
    Was not quite her oyster,
And now she's called Madam, not Sis."

"I leave you with that thought." He was gone.

Beth was shaking her head, even smiling. "It isn't real," she said. "He isn't real. People don't behave that way at a—time like this. They don't."

"I don't think you have any idea how you'll behave," the governor said, "until you're there." He spread his hands. "And then it's too late to change."

Cary Wycoff had a glass of plain soda in hand. He sipped it slowly while he watched the heavy tables being maneuvered into position around the area where the breeches buoy came in through the window.

It was perfectly obvious what the purpose of the tables was. It was simply more of the same: entrenched privilege throwing up barricades to keep out the barbarians. Himself. And he resented it with fierceness and, at the moment, impotence, which made it even worse.

The lottery slip in his pocket was number sixty-five, which meant that fifteen males would go before him to safety. Bent Armitage, Bob Ramsay, and Jake Peters, he was willing to bet, would be among them. Oh, they would not be the first three; they were too canny for that. But they would have seen to it that they were close enough to the beginning of the line to be safe without being obvious in the bargain.

Cary resented the women's going first too. He had fought as hard as the next man, harder, for women's rights, but he did not really believe in them. Women were created weaker, usually less intelligent, altogether less useful members of the community except for the one function which they never let you forget they, and they alone, could carry out. And in Cary's view there were too many births anyway.

From a purely objective viewpoint, he, Cary Wycoff, was a far more valuable member of society than any of the women who had gathered in the Tower Room. He should, therefore, have preceded all of them across the chasm to the Trade Center roof and safety.

But to have gone first, even if he had been allowed, would have been to demean himself in the eyes of the stupid world, which thought with its stomach, more especially in the eyes of the stupid electorate, who kept sending him back to a very pleasant life in Washington. So there it was. Let the women go.

But the men, that was something different, and he was not going to stand idly by and watch fifteen—fifteen!—others go ahead of himself.

Bent Armitage and Jake Peters, those two in particular, had always treated him at less than his real worth; there was no denying that. Cary had another sip of soda while he thought about it. Then, "I'll show you bastards," he said softly. "You can't get away with it this time."

Nat put down the phone after his conversation with the governor. He was conscious that Patty watched him, frowning. "You heard what I said?" he asked.

Patty nodded. She kept her voice expressionless. "Would you do it? Stop the whole—operation just as a threat?"

"I don't believe in threats."

"I don't—understand."

276

"It doesn't matter."

"It does to me." There was that bulldog quality again; total refusal to sidestep unpleasantness.

Nat said merely, "We'll see what the chief says." He picked up the walkie-talkie. "Trailer to Trade Center roof."

"Roof here." The chief's voice. "The naked chick's name is Barber, Josephine Barber. And after her came Mrs. Robert Ramsay."

Nat watched Patty pick up her pencil and start searching the list. "Got it," he said. And then, "How's it going, Chief?"

"Slow. Steady. What we could expect. Twenty-two across in"—he paused—"twenty-three minutes flat. Best we could hope for." Was there faint belligerence underlying the words?

"Better than I was afraid of," Nat said. He paused again. "I doubt if it will happen before you have the women across. I hope it won't. But when the pressure really begins—"

"Trouble you mean?" Pause. "Important people, aren't they?" The chief's voice was unexcited.

"That," Nat said, "doesn't mean that some of them won't—panic."

Patty had found the two names and crossed them off. She sat now, pencil still in her small hand, watching Nat and listening.

"Yeah," the chief said, unexcited still. "Stripes on a man's sleeve don't necessarily mean too much." He paused. "You're getting at what?"

Nat told him what he had said to the governor. There was silence.

Then, "The way I see it," the chief said slowly, still unexcited, merely stating facts, "when you've got a command situation, men obey or they mutiny. If it's mutiny, you stop it right at the beginning or it gets out of hand. First sign of trouble, you let me know and we hold the breeches buoy right here until they line up again and stay in line. That way we may not get them all out, but we'll get some. Let them fall to squabbling and there won't be a manjack get out of there alive."

Nat nodded. "Long speech, Chief."

"Yeah. I don't ordinarily use that many words."

"But I couldn't agree with you more."

"We'll get along," the chief said. "You just pass me the word if there's trouble."

Nat laid the walkie-talkie down on the desk. He said nothing.

"So you two are in agreement," Patty said. She paused. "You knew you would be, didn't you?"

"Simmer down," Nat said. He could even smile and mean it. "What do you think Bert would have said?"

Patty opened her mouth and then closed it again in silence. Slowly she nodded. "Probably the same." Capitulation. "But I don't have to like it." Defiance flaring again.

"No," Nat said, "you don't." He pushed away from the desk and walked once more to the doorway to look out over the plaza.

It was a dismal, depressing scene. Thunderheads to the west had obscured the sun; the light in the plaza was smoky gray, the air soot-filled, acrid.

Firemen swarmed in the plaza—like scurrying ants in slow motion, Nat thought—and the perimeter of the area was an almost solid mass of fire equipment parked cheek-by-jowl, engines and pumps throbbing.

The entire plaza floor was a lake now. Cascades of water poured back out of the building, down the concourse steps—like spawning ladders for salmon.

A fireman lurched from the concourse, stumbled down the steps, and fell face down, his arms and legs moving weakly.

Two ambulance attendants rushed up with a stretcher, loaded him on, and bore him off.

Nat's eyes followed the stretcher to a neaby ambulance where three other firemen were standing, sucking oxygen from rubber masks.

Police manned the barricades. Nat could make out Barnes, the black cop, and, yes, there was his partner, the big Irishman, white bandage plain on his cheek.

Behind the barricades the crowds were orderly and strangely quiet, as if at last the enormity of the tragedy had reached them. In the crowd an arm was raised, pointing upward. Other arms followed. Without turning to look, Nat guessed that the breeches buoy was making yet another trip, one more person swinging to safety.

He felt no sense of triumph. That was long gone. Instead he blamed himself that this was all that they could do and it was not enough. What was it he had told Patty about the thinking in certain parts of the Middle East? That man was supposed to try for perfection, but he wasn't ever supposed to reach it? But that didn't make the fact of even partial failure any the more palatable.

He was not a religious man, but sometimes there were events—those nineteen bodies curled like snails in the smoking burned-over mountain clearing came to mind—that seemed to demonstrate a flaw, point a direction, and by the depth of their tragedy simply force a man to re-examine many tenets and thoughts he had long taken for granted. Too long.

If one result of all of these reexaminations was constant. even inevitable, it was determination that could be expressed in two words: never again.

Never again a *Titanic* blundering in the ice lanes.

Never again a *Hindenburg* filled with explosive hydrogen gas.

Never again if good men could prevent it a Hamburg firestorm, a Nagasaki, a Hiroshima.

Never again a fire like this in a building this size—

Correction: Never again a building this size. Didn't that make more sense?

Bigness for bigness' sake was never a solution. Remember that.

"I will," Nat said silently. "By God, I will!"

He heard a telephone ring in the trailer, and he waited for it to be answered. Patty's voice said. "Yes. He's here." And then, expressionless, "Nat."

She was holding the instrument out to him. "Zib," she said, and that was all.

Zib had left the magazine at the usual time, taxied home, and hurried into a scented bath. Luxuriating in the suds. feeling the tensions flow away, she told herself that everything was going to be all right. After that talk with Cathy she felt like a different person, able to see herself more clearly, and wasn't that the name of the game —know thyself?

And she had turned her back on Paul Simmons, hadn't she? Nat must have seen that from her telephone call telling him that Paul was not coming down to the building. It was a sharp cutting of the last ties. wasn't it? The symbolism was inescapable. And at heart Nat was a lamb. He hadn't really meant those harsh things he had said to her. He couldn't have. Nobody could. Not to her.

She sank deep in the tub, closed her eyes. and stroked one smooth sudsy shoulder and arm with her hand. What was that commercial on TV? "If he doesn't feel the difference, he has no feeling." That applied to all of her, didn't it?

Of course Nat would be tired when he got home. But not too tired. She had always had the power to arouse him. That was one thing the Women's Lib fanatics tended to forget, possibly because some of them. but not all, were rather unattractive pieces of sexual merchandise, and any subtle advances they might make would tend to be— what were that judge's marvelous words when he passed *Ulysses* as salable?—"emetic rather than aphrodisiac."

Zib's own qualifications in that direction were impeccable—as she well knew. And. given that headstart, in the constant underlying sexual struggle between herself and a man. any man there simply was no contest.

Men flattered themselves that they were dominant, waving their muscles and all that jazz. In many cultures. as Zib had learned in an anthropology course, polygamy was the norm. Polyandry. on the other hand, was rarely practiced. And that merely demonstrated how out of joint man's thinking was. because one woman could satisfy a dozen men, could she not? And a mere man was hard put to satisfy one woman. But, as the British said, there it was: man's thinking callused over by the ages.

She stroked her shoulder and arm again and decided that there was something to this bath-oil bit: her skin did feel smooth, soft, exciting to the touch. She stroked her breasts gently. Better and better. But, "Easy, girl," she said aloud, "save it all for Nat. Don't waste it now."

She got out of her bath, dried herself, and applied scent sparingly to throat, breasts, and belly. Then she put on the lightweight full-length white robe Nat liked especially, and the heeled mules he had given her and went into the living room to put music on the record player. It was then that she decided to call the trailer office.

On the phone, "Hello." Nat said.

And what had she thought to say anyway? "Hi." And she added inanely. "I'm home."

Nat heard the music in the background: "Scheherazade," the violin voice just beginning it theme. Scheherazade herself beguiling the sultan. Balls. "I guessed that."

"Darling. how is it going? I mean—"

"Great. Just great." Through the open doorway Nat looked again at the crowded plaza. He raised one hand to wipe wearily at his forehead and saw the grime from the subbasement on his palm.

Oh, he had known dirt before right here on the job, and he and Zib had even laughed together about the way he sometimes looked when he came home at night.

But this was different, as different as night from day, death from life. This was—

Zib said, "I—tried to watch on television. I—couldn't." She paused. "It's a mess, isn't it?"

"Understatement." Nat paused. "Did you want something?"

The hesitation in her voice was un-Ziblike. "Not really. I came home and—" She stopped. Her voice now was uncertain. "Will you be coming home?" She could not bring herself to add the single word: ever.

Nat was conscious that Patty was watching him. He tried to ignore her and could not.

"Darling, I asked a question."

"I don't know the answer." Nat hung up.

Zib hung up slowly. It was then that the tears began.

The telephone on the desk made noises. Nat walked quickly to it, picked it up, spoke his name.

The governor's voice said, "Only two more women to go. Then we start the men's lottery sequence." His voice said nothing in particular, but a faint warning was plain.

"Okay," Nat said. "I've talked with the chief. He says in a command situation either it's obey or mutiny, and if a mutiny begins—"

"The chief reaches for the nearest belaying pin and whacks the nearest head, is that it?" the governor said. There was patent approval in his tone.

"That's it," Nat said. "He knows his equipment and he's been through this before, and he says if disorder is allowed—" He paused, realizing he was speaking to one of the potential victims. Then he went on because there was no way to conceal the thought. "If disorder is allowed," he repeated, "the chief says nobody is going to get out alive. I'm sorry, Governor, but that's his message, and I have to agree with it."

"No apology necessary, young man. I agree with it too. Do you have any suggestions?"

"Yes, sir. A couple." Nat paused to gather his thoughts. "You might pass the word right now that at the first sign of disorder I'll tell the chief and he'll hold the breeches buoy on the Trade Center roof until people line up again. If anybody doubts that, have him get on this phone and I'll tell him."

"As long," the governor said, "as the telephone line remains in service."

"That's the second thought, Governor," Nat said. "We'll get right through to the city radio station. They've got to have a mike and remote equipment here. If the phone goes out, we'll go on radio. You've got a transistor radio up there?"

"Currently playing rock-and-roll," the governor said. He paused. "Agreed."

"If the phone is out," Nat said, "you won't be able to reach us. If there's trouble, just flutter a handkerchief at the window and the chief will call down to me. Okay?"

There was a short silence. "Okay," the governor said. Another silence. Then, "You think well, young man. You have done a superlative job. You have the gratitude of all of us." Pause. "That is just in case the opportunity to tell you in person doesn't arise."

"We'll do the best we can to get you all out," Nat said.

"I know you will. And thanks."

32

7:53–8:09

The lower forty floors of the building were now in shadow. Patrolman Shannon stared up at the smoking mass and shook his head in disbelief. "Do you see what I see, Frank? Up there the building is glowing!"

It was. Most of the windows had broken out because of the heat, and smoke poured through the empty frames. But through the smoke, in the darkened shadows plain to see, the building itself was faintly incandescent, and in the distorted air currents caused by its radiation the entire structure seemed to writhe.

"You're a praying man, Mike," Barnes said. "Better get to it." He paused. "It was a grand sight, remember? And all of these grand people came to watch."

High above them the breeches buoy swung out of the Tower Room again, by a trick of light glinting momentarily as it slid down the catenary curve toward the Trade Center roof. In the crowd all eyes watched. Shannon crossed himself.

"A cremation," Barnes said. "I wonder how many are thinking of that." He paused. "Or of Joan of Arc at the stake." For the first time his tone was angry. "We let the maniac through, Mike, and I for one will not forget it even though the man, bless him, said we were only members of the lodge."

"And," Shannon said, "whatever did he mean by that?"

"That the blame is shared, even though I don't know how or why. But I can guess. A—thing like this does not happen from one cause. Mrs. O'Leary's cow may have kicked over the lantern, but a thousand other things had to go wrong before Chicago could burn to the ground. It has to be the same here, although that is damn small consolation."

Shannon said nothing. He seemed unimpressed.

"There are people up there, man," Barnes said, "people like you and me, yes, I even saw a few black faces. And—"

"That what-you-may-call-it," Shannon said. "They're getting them out."

"They won't get them all out," Barnes said. "Not with heat that already makes the building glow. And do you know the worst of it, Mike, the hell of it?" He paused. "The best ones will be the ones to stay behind."

On the Trade Center roof Kronski said, "You're expecting trouble over there, huh, Chief?"

"Maybe. I hope not." The chief's massive calm was unshaken. Together he and Kronski caught the swinging breeches buoy, and the chief lifted the woman out.

She was sobbing, from fright, from grief. "Mein husband—"

"We'd like your name, ma'am," the chief said. "We're keeping a list."

"Bucholtz! But mein husband. You must bring him next! He is a very important man! He vill pay! He—"

"All right, lady," the chief said. "These cops will take care of you. We're trying to get everybody out." He gestured to the policemen who took the woman by both arms.

"Mein husband! He knows many important people! He—"

284

"One question," the chief said. "How many more women to come?"

Frau Bucholtz shook her head. "I do not know."

"You were number forty-eight," the chief said. "How many were there?"

"I think forty-nine. But I do not know. And I do not care. Mein husband—"

"Yeah," the chief said. "Take her away." He turned to watch the breeches buoy on its long climb back to the Tower Room.

Kronski said, "I seen a lifeboat once up in the Bering Sea." He shook his head. "Cold up there, you know what I mean, Chief? You been there."

"I've been there." The chief was pretty sure he knew that what was coming was some grisly tale he did not particularly want to hear, but he said nothing more.

"One of them coastal freighters," Kronski said. "Fire aboard. They'd lost their engines. Big seas, and the freighter began to break up. They took to the boats." He paused. "We got it all from one guy, the first officer. He lasted a little while. He was the only one.

"The thing was," Kronski said, "when they launched the boats, one of them capsized. Otherwise—" He shook his head and spread his hands. "You know what I mean, Chief?"

The chief said heavily, "I know what you mean." He paused. "So everybody tried to get into the other boat, isn't that how it was?"

Kronski nodded. "Right. They tried to beat them off with oars, the first officer said. No good. No fucking good. They kept coming." He was silent.

The chief's eyes were on the distant windows. He watched the breeches buoy swing through. In his mind was memory of the gigantic seas in those northern waters, the bellowing wind, and the cold—above all the bone-chilling cold. Men in open boats, he thought, or men trying to launch open boats, desperate freezing men. He kept his eyes on the windows, but he said. "And what happened was that they capsized the second boat too, isn't that it?"

Kronski nodded again. "Right. We got there less than an hour later." Pause. "Might as well have been a month. Only that first officer was still alive, and, like I said, he didn't last long." Another pause. "They might of saved maybe half—"

"But they panicked," the chief said, "and didn't save any. That's just the way it goes." His voice was savage, and his eyes were still on the windows. No handkerchief waving. Yet.

The governor walked back to the office and sank into the desk chair. He felt suddenly old, and tired beyond mere fatigue. It was as if in Beth's light presence he had spent these past few hours in the refreshing spring of eternal youth, knowing that it could not last, and yet half-believing that somehow it would. Now Beth was gone, the last woman out safely. At the final moment the governor had not been able to watch.

No fool like an old fool—he wondered who had first dreamed up that aphorism and in what circumstances. Probably some old gaffer mocking himself when the young chick he thought cared for him discovered that she preferred males of her own age after all.

Oh, it had not been like that with Beth. Given other circumstances in which choice was as free as choice ever was, the governor thought that Beth would have gone willingly, if not eagerly with him to that ranch in high New Mexico. Dream idyll—now where did that phrase come from? Dream stuff, pure and simple. And not to be.

But why not? The recurrent question that even Beth had asked. Why me?

Why couldn't the dream stuff have become reality? Why did lightning strike one person and not another? Why couldn't he have been allowed to live out what was left of his life in the peace and contentment he had planned, with the bonus of this new joy he had only today discovered?

If You exist, answer me that, Lord.

Feeling sorry for himself, wasn't he? Well, why the hell not? Down in that plaza there were a thousand people, maybe ten thousand who were going home when the show was over to do whatever they damned well chose before they went to bed, knowing that they were going to wake up in the morning. Oh, sure, most of them, in Thoreau's words, led lives of quiet desperation, but that didn't alter the fact that they had at least some freedom of choice, some options open, and he now had none.

Did any man ever die happy? That was the question. No, strike the final word. Did any man ever die *content?* The governor thought not.

Some men accomplished a great deal, some accomplished little or nothing—but no man ever accomplished enough.

Jake Peters had said the same, and he, Bent Armitage, had chided him for it.

All right he thought, all right! Cast up the balance. Things left undone, words unsaid, yes, but could any man say different? But no debts unpaid. And how many could say that' Pay as you go. Honest Bent Armitage. It sounded he thought like the name of a used-car dealer.

What of the knowledge and the judgment that would die with him? Well, what of them? Were they unique? Irreplaceable? Or was it just that he took such pride in them because they happened to be his?

Face it, he told himself as he had told the senator, you've had just the hell of a good time, haven't you? And what would you change if you had it to do over? Probably not a single bloody thing.

Except Beth.

Maybe he thought, if he had tried harder, he might have found her or someone like her before it was too late. Someone like her? Well, if he had never met and known the real article, he would never have known the difference, would he? My God, what a rationalizing machine the mind was!

Beth. At least she was down safe. He hoped. He wished now that he had stayed to watch, just to be sure. Well, it was easy enough to make sure.

He flipped on the telephone's speaker switch. "Armitage here," he said. There was no answer. He punched the disconnect buttons, punched them again. There was no sound. The phone was dead.

And now, he thought, we are truly alone.

The heavy line stretching from Tower Room to Trade Center roof supporting the weight of the breeches buoy was nylon, strong, flexible, flawless nylon. It was secured around a ceiling beam in the Tower Room, and the knot that secured it, a bowline, had been tied under the watchful eyes of the two firemen.

Because with nylon even a bowline, the queen of knots, has been known to work loose, the firemen had taken the added precaution of bending the bitter end of the line into two half-hitches around the standing part. The half-hitches showed no signs of slipping, and unless or until they did, the bowline had to hold.

But the beam around which the line was bent was steel, a part of the building's structure, major support for the communications mast that rose still shining into the waning sunlight.

Steel conducts heat well.

And nylon melts.

The telephone on the desk in the trailer made noises. Nat picked it up and spoke his name. The sound of his voice in the instrument was all wrong: it echoed. Like the governor, he tapped the disconnect buttons, tapped them again, and yet a third time. The dial tone sounded suddenly in his ear.

He dialed the Tower Room office number, dialed it again, and then hung up. "That's that," he said to no one in particular. "Their line's gone."

The buildings systems had been so carefully prepared, he thought, so cunningly designed, so expensively researched, and now one by one they were collapsing. *Were* collapsing? *Had* collapsed. There was something of finality in the death of the telephone.

He dialed again the number he had already called once, the city radio station. He was answered immediately.

"World Tower Plaza," he said. "Their phone line has gone. You're the only way we can reach them."

"We'll hold this line open. When you give the word, you'll talk right on the air."

"One thing," Nat said. "You have an automatic delay, don't you? So you can cut off foul language, that kind of thing?"

"You'll go straight on the air. No delay."

"Okay," Nat said. "Thanks. We'll stand by. He laid the phone on the desk again and picked up the walkie-talkie. To the chief on the Trade Center roof he said, "Telephone's out. If you get a signal, call me. I'll get on the radio."

"Will do," the chief said.

Nat leaned back in the chair and looked around the trailer. Tim Brown was there, one battalion chief, Giddings, and Patty. "You heard it," Nat said. He lifted his hands and let them fall. "What the hell is there to say?" he said.

"I have the feeling," the battalion chief said, "that something's going to happen, you know what I mean? That the alarm will go off, or I'll fall out of bed, or, you know, *some way* this goddam nightmare will end!" He paused. "Only it won't will it?" His voice was low-pitched, venomous.

Giddings's big shoulders moved restlessly. He looked at Patty. "Simmons is your husband," he said, "and I'm sorry about that." He paused. "But if I get half the chance, Im going to kill the son of a bitch with my bare hands."

Police Lieutenant Potter came in through the doorway. He looked at them all. "Anything I can do?"

No one spoke.

"That's what I thought," Potter said. He leaned against the wall. "If you don't mind, I'll stick around." He paused. "Though God knows why I bother."

It was Patty who said, "You found what you wanted about John Connors?"

"More than I wanted," Potter said. He told them what he had told the captain and the chief inspector.

None of the men in the trailer spoke. Patty said softly, "The poor man."

"I won't argue," Potter said. There was no bitterness, only sadness in his voice. Then, slowly, "I'm a rotten cop. My job is to find who's at fault." He shook his head. "Sometimes that's pretty easy. But sometimes, like now, it isn't." He pointed upward. His voice rose. "Those people up there—somebody has to be to blame for them, isn't that so?" He was looking at Brown. "Isn't it?"

"How the hell can I answer that?" It was almost a shout. And then, quieter, "It doesn't make sense. None of it. You've got a man who flipped because somebody let his wife die." Brown pointed at Patty. "She's got a husband who did things he wasn't supposed to do."

Giddings said, "And there's an electrical foreman and a building inspector who ought to be strung up by their"—he stopped and looked at Patty—"thumbs."

"Some of my men," Tim Brown said, "let things get by that they shouldn't have." He shook his head angrily.

"And," Nat said, "some of us ought to have caught mistakes and worse while they were going on." He was silent for a few moments. "One more thing." he said, "maybe bigger than all the others put together." His voice was solemn. "Just who in hell do we think we are, designing a building that size, that complicated, and that—vulnerable?"

It was then that the walkie-talkie came to life. "Roof to Trailer." it said.

In the sudden silence, Nat picked it up. "Trailer here."

The chief's voice said, "Something white is waving. You'd better get on the air. I have the breeches buoy and I'm holding it."

Nat took a deep breath. "Here we go," he said and reached for the phone.

33

Accounts vary; that of course is the norm. But in telling what happened there in the Tower Room, each survivor actually appears to have his own private version which holds him, if not heroic, at least blameless; and no amount of contradiction by others is even listened to. Perhaps that is the norm as well.

On one point there is agreement without warning, and by one of those freaks that were so much a part of this disastrous day, the air-conditioning ducts suddenly belched out quantities of hot acrid smoke. And that, like the pulling of a trigger, apparently set off the explosion.

This was the setting.

The transistor radio, tuned now to the city's own station, played quiet music. The women were gone now, and there was no more dancing.

In a corner of the large room Rabbi Stein, Monsignor O'Toole, and the Reverend Arthur William Williams spoke quietly together. The subject of their discussion has not been disclosed.

In the loading area behind the table barricades, Harrison Paul, conductor of the city's symphony orchestra, allowed himself to be hoisted into the breeches buoy and swung out through the window. He tried to keep his eyes closed, but the temptation to look was too great, and what he saw of the city beneath him from this terrifying and almost unsupported height made him violently sick. The storm music from the "Pastoral" Symphony thundered through his mind, he later recalled, as he clung desperately to the canvas bag, swaying and bouncing, positive that he was going to be killed. When at last he reached sanctuary, and the chief and Kronski together lifted him out of the breeches buoy, he dropped immediately to his knees to kiss the Trade Center roof.

He was the first man out, and for a time it appeared that he would also be the last.

The waiter with three kids was sitting on the floor now, still nursing his bottle of bourbon. The number of the crude lottery ticket in his pocket was ninety-nine. He had already decided that his chances of getting out safely were just about those of a celluloid dog chasing an asbestos cat through Hell. He did not particularly enjoy the bourbon, but he was determined that he was not going to panic; and he thought that maybe if he passed out, he wouldn't mind so much what he was powerless to prevent.

The two firemen, two waiters, the fire commissioner, and the secretary general were behind the table barricades. One of the waiters testified later that the room was quiet; that you could feel tension building particularly after the women were gone, but that everything seemed under control. "Until," he added, "the stuff hit the fan." There was surprise in his voice that it had been so.

Cary Wycoff was talking with a dozen men, only one of whom, another waiter, has been identified. His name was Bill Samuelson, and he had been at various times a longshoreman, a semi-pro football player, and a professional boxer of small accomplishment. No one else has ever chosen to admit being part of that group.

It was hot and getting hotter; on that point too there is agreement. The waiter from the barricaded area told it like this:

"It was funny. The wind coming in from the broken-out windows was cold and my hands were almost numb. But my feet were hot and the rest of me felt like, you know, like I was standing in a hot room in the gym, you know what I mean? Heat all around us, but still the cold wind, and that was what was so—funny, if you see what I mean."

Ben Caldwell and the Soviet ambassador were talking together about the architecture of Moscow and the nostalgia that always struck the ambassador whenever he saw in this alien land of America a Zwiebelturm, the onion-shaped tower of Eastern European design.

Senator Peters was at the west bank of windows, quietly watching gulls over the river and the harbor. For him there was never-ending pleasure and release from tension in watching birds, and sometimes even heart-lifting surprises as well, as when his eye and he had quickly counted thirty-five great birds in flight, heading south, their black-tipped white wings slowly beating and their long legs trailing to identify them beyond a doubt as the single remaining flock of whooping cranes, probably off their normal migrating path in order to avoid a storm, but still heading with that mystical knowledge and compulsion about which so little is known straight for their Texas nesting grounds. Now, watching the herring gulls wheeling and probably shrieking as well, free as the air in which they flew, he wondered as he had wondered infinite times before why man in his evolution had chosen to remain earthbound.

The governor was still alone in the office with the dead telephone and his thoughts. He could hear faintly the music on his transistor radio, but other than that the big room outside was quiet. The governor's thoughts were not.

Why had he not even tried to pull rank and place himself among the first of the men to ride the breeches buoy to safety? On the face of it, there was no answer that made any kind of logical sense. By now, or within a very few minutes, he could have been over on that Trade Center roof instead of sitting here at this stupid desk waiting—waiting for what? The answer to that was plain. He was waiting for the end to this tragic farce, but as a participant, not a spectator. How ridiculous could the situation be?

What thoughts a man allows hmself in private! Ignoble, craven thoughts, sometimes lewd thoughts, dishonest thoughts, warped, even mad thoughts: all of the mental brew the devil's cauldron can contain.

But they are only thoughts, and neither obsessive nor translated into action; and there is the difference between what men call sanity on the one hand and madness on the other.

So regardless of what he had done or not done through selfish use of power, he could wish that it had been otherwise. He told himself that he retained that privilege—and found that he was amused by his own hair-splitting. Amused. and not a little disgusted. He—

"So solemn, Bent." Beth's voice from the doorway. She stood quietly, a half-smile on her lips, awaiting his judgment.

The governor stared at her in wonder, gaping he thought. "Something happened to the breeches buoy?"

Smiling still, she shook her head.

The governor raised his hands. and then dropped them. It was near disbelief that he felt, colored by joy and sorrow. "You didn't go," he said. He paused. "I couldn't watch."

"I saw." She walked slowly forward.

"I tried to phone to see if you were—safe." The governor paused "But the line is dead " He roused himself from near apathy. "I wanted you safe." His voice was stronger, some of its old assurance regained.

"I know." Beth had reached the desk now. She perched on it as before. long legs swinging gently. She held out her hand and the governor took it, held it tight.

"You should have gone. damn it."

"No, Bent." There was calmness and serenity in her voice, her manner. "I told you I was not going to—make believe any more."

"I wanted you to live." He paused. "I still do." True or false? Damn the analysis anyway.

"I know. I made the decision."

"It was the wrong one." The governor pushed back his chair. "We'll—"

"No, Bent. I gave up my place. Even if I wanted to, there is no taking it back. When you step out, you go to the end of the line."

"Damn it—"

"Bent, listen to me." Her fingers squeezed his. "All my life I have been—decorative perhaps, maybe sometimes diverting, amusing, congenial, all of the things we are taught to be. She paused. "And useless." She saw objection forming on his lips and she forestalled it quickly. "Yes. Useless." She hurried on. "But these past few hours for the first time in my life I have felt that I was—doing something useful, not very much perhaps, but far, far more than I have ever done before."

"All right," the governor said, "so you've learned a few things while we've been trapped here. Then take that knowledge and go—"

"There is another reason, Bent. Shall I say it? Because it is not the kind of thing one says and is believed. But it is true." She paused, her hand now quietly resting in his. Her eyes were calm on his face. "It is that I would rather be here with you than be outside—alone again."

The office was still. Distantly, faintly, the music sounds reached them; but that was all. From the overhead air-conditioning duct a puff of black smoke appeared, spread, and settled slowly. Neither noticed it.

"What do I say to that?" the governor said. "I've been sitting here alone, feeling sorry for myself—" He stopped. "Damn it, it isn't right for you to be here! You—"

"Where I want to be?" Beth shook her head slowly. She was smiling again, with her lips, with her eyes, with all of her. "Dear Bent—" she began.

It was then that the first sudden sounds of strife broke out in the large room, voices raised in angry shouts, the din of furniture overturning.

The governor shoved his chair back and stood up. He hesitated only a moment. "Stay here," he said and hurried through the doorway.

It was a scene from bedlam played in a haze of black smoke. One of the barricade tables was already overturned and men like animals were forcing it aside, opening a passage, tearing at one another in their frenzy.

As the governor looked, the fire commissioner grabbed the nearest man by his jacket front, drew him close with a savage motion and drove his fist against the man's mouth. He released him and reached for another.

A waiter in a white coat, a large muscular man—it was

Bill Samuelson—crowded through the gap, slammed two punches into the commissioner's belly and pushed him aside to fall.

Cary Wycoff stood near the overturned table, free of the melee, his voice raised, screeching and as the governor trotted across the room Senator Peters, a candlestick in his right hand, poked Cary in the middle with it, doubling him over, and without pausing moved on to slam the candlestick against the big waiter's head. The man dropped like a poleaxed steer.

There was no sense, no pattern, only madness and confusion Someone punched the governor's shoulder; behind the punch was the contorted face of the network executive. All the governor could think of was a mad sheep, fear-crazed.

More smoke burst from the ducts, a choking, blinding, darkened mass, and the struggles within it seemed to rise in frenzied fury.

Someone screamed. It was unnoticed in the general din.

The governor raised his voice. "Stop it! Goddammit, stop it, I say!" He was shouting into a whirlwind. He lowered his head and charged.

An elbow bashed his cheek. He pushed on through. Here was the heavy line coming through the window. Here was the window itself. He clung to the line with one hand and leaned as far out as he could to wave his handkerchief again and again. Then he pulled himself back inside and tried to make his way out of the scramble.

Somewhere somewhere that radio still played music. The governor homed on it as a beacon.

He saw it sitting on a nearby table, and as he lunged for it, the table overturned. The radio skittered across the floor, playing still.

Someone slammed into the governor's side and he went down on all fours, and then with all of his strength dove forward and got the radio into his hands. Guarding it, holding it tight against himself, he worked out of the melee, and then in temporary peace, away from the struggle, he held the radio high and turned the volume full on.

Music blasted into the room. There was sudden silence. And then, at last, a giant's voice, Nat Wilson's voice roaring into the confusion: "NOW HEAR THIS! NOW HEAR THIS IN THE TOWER ROOM!"

There was a pause. Some of the sound of struggle was stilled.

"IN THE TOWER ROOM HEAR THIS!" the voice blared again. "THIS IS PLAZA TRAILER CONTROL. I DON'T KNOW WHAT'S HAPPENING UP THERE, BUT UNTIL IT STOPS THE BREECHES BUOY WILL REMAIN ON THE TRADE CENTER ROOF. IS THAT CLEAR? I REPEAT: UNTIL THERE IS ORDER AGAIN, THE BREECHES BUOY WILL NOT RETURN TO THE TOWER ROOM. IF YOU READ ME, WAVE SOMETHING WHITE FROM THE WINDOW."

The great room was silent, still. All eyes watched as slowly the governor walked toward the loading area, the radio still in his hand. He passed it to the senator, took a tablecloth from a nearby table, and, leaning out as before, waved it in the direction of the Trade Center roof.

The silence held.

"ALL RIGHT," Nat's voice blared suddenly. "ALL RIGHT! NOW RESUME YOUR DRILL. IS THAT UNDERSTOOD? RESUME YOUR DRILL OR THE ENTIRE OPERATION STOPS. WE'RE DOING EVERYTHING WE CAN TO GET YOU ALL OUT ALIVE. IF YOU COOPERATE, WE MAY SUCCEED. IF YOU DON'T, NOBODY GETS OUT. IS THAT UNDERSTOOD? NOBODY!"

The governor looked around at the faces, some of them bruised, some bloody. Bill Samuelson, the big waiter, was on his hands and knees, shaking his head. He looked up at the governor like an angry beast.

"Any comments?" the governor said.

There was no reply.

"IS THAT UNDERSTOOD?" Nat's voice roared.

The governor leaned out the window again. He waved the tablecloth. There was again that pause for transmission from rooftop to trailer.

Then, "OKAY," Nat's voice said. "STAY ON THIS
WAVELENGTH, AND RESUME YOUR OPERA-
TION. THE BREECHES BUOY IS COMING BACK.
BUT"—the voice paused—"AT THE FIRST SIGN OF
MORE DISTURBANCE IT STOPS AGAIN. I RE-
PEAT: AT THE FIRST SIGN OF MORE DISTURB-
ANCE WE STOP THE RESCUE." The voice was stilled.

The senator looked down at the radio in his hand. He
was smiling as he turned the volume down. Music began
once more to play.

The secretary general said quietly. "Number fifty-
two, if you please, number fifty-two."

One of the waiters not involved in the disturbance
moved forward. He had his slip of paper held tight in both
hands.

In the trailer Nat put down the phone and let his breath
out in a long sigh. Into the walkie-talkie he said, "Okay,
Chief? Do you think—"

"As far as I can see," the chief said, his voice still calm,
"you've made them knock it off. I'll let you know if it
looks different."

Nat put the walkie-talkie down. He looked around the
trailer.

Tim Brown said, "What an unholy stink there's going
to be. How many people were tuned in and heard that—
threat, ultimatum, whatever you want to call it?"

"It worked, didn't it?" This was Giddings.

"It worked," Patty said. She looked down at Nat and
smiled.

"Number fifty-three," the secretary general said, "if
you please."

Fireman Howard said, "What's your number?"

The secretary general smiled. "It is sixty." There are
seven more ahead of me."

"And I'm one of them," Howard said. "Fifty-eight."

The secretary general smiled again. "My congratulations." He paused. "It has been a pleasure working with
you."

"Maybe," Howard said, "we can have a drink together on that when all this is over."

"I will look forward to it."

The senator walked over to Cary Wycoff. The senator still held the candlestick in his hand. "The next time, Cary," he said softly, "I will crack your skull." He paused. "You can believe that."

She was sitting still where the governor had left her, perched on the corner of the desk, long clean legs swinging gently, calm blue eyes seeming to smile.

This, the governor thought, was how he would always remember her.

Always?

Always. Through eternity.

"You are leaving now," he said. He saw objection forming in her face and he attacked it immediately. "Yes," he said. "You are going. Because, my dear,' he said, "it is my wish, my plea, and if that sound stilted, I can't help it. At times like this you hide behind formality."

"Bent—" She stopped. Her eyes no longer seemed to smile.

"I will not end a long life with an act of craven selfishness," the governor said. He smiled suddenly. "That in itself is selfish I'll admit. I can't help posturing." He walked toward her and held out his hands. "Come along."

They came out of the office holding hands. The big room was subdued now, spiritless. The transistor radio played quietly; no one listened.

To the secretary general, "Number forty-nine was overlooked, Walther," the governor said "Here she is."

Cary Wycoff, watching, listening, opened his mouth and then closed it again in silence.

The room was still.

The secretary general smiled at Fireman Howard. "I was wrong," he said. "There were eight ahead of me."

Beth said, "Oh, Bent!"

"Goodbye, my dear." The governor hesitated. He

smiled. "Catch a trout for me some day." He turned away then and walked back to the empty office.

"Sixty-one!" The fire commissioner's voice.

"Sixty-two!"

Cary Wycoff started forward. The senator stepped in front of him. "I'm number sixty-five," Cary Wycoff said and held up his slip.

The senator merely glanced at it. He nodded and stepped back. "You would be," he said.

Within the giant structure the heat continued to rise. Floor by floor the incandescence crept up, following the evening shadows.

In the plaza it was almost completely night now, and standlights had been rigged. In their glare the moving men and equipment cast strange contorted shadows against the building, into the smoke.

Behind the police barricades the crowds stood quiet, no signs waving, no chanting, no voices raised.

Patrolman Shannon said, "It is a scene out of Hell itself, Frank."

"It is." Frank Barnes's voice was quiet, solemn. "Only the poor damned souls are hidden."

High above them, still in sunlight, the breeches buoy swung again down the catenary curve toward the Trade Center roof.

"You don't think they'll get them all out?" Shannon said.

Barnes lifted his shoulders and let them fall. "Even if they do, it's a sad day to remember." He paused. "For us all," he said.

"Seventy-six!" the fire commissioner said. His voice was hoarse from smoke and strain. He coughed, coughed again with a deep retching sound.

The senator turned from the west bank of windows. Breathing was hard and painful. He looked around the great room.

Over by the fire door the white tablecloth marked Grover Frazee's remains.

300

In a nearby chair a man the senator did not know, an elderly man, was slumped, head back, mouth and eyes open. As nearly as the senator could tell, he was no longer breathing.

Ben Caldwell lay in the center of the floor where he had collapsed. His body had curled itself into the fetal position. He made no movement.

The waiter on the floor held up his bottle offering a drink. He had a silly grin on his face.

"Thanks anyway," the senator said, "but I'll wait a little." His voice sounded strange. heavy. He straightened himself with effort and walked toward the office.

The governor was in the desk chair. He looked up, smiled, and coughed. When the coughing had stopped, "Sit down, Jake," he said. "What shall we talk about?"

Together the chief and Kronski hauled the man out of the breeches buoy bag. "Hold him up." the chief said, and added, raising his voice, "Oxygen over here!" He waved at the Tower Room windows and slowly the breeches buoy began its return trip.

"Seventy-seven," the chief said. He spoke into the walkie-talkie. "Name of Bucholtz. He'll need ambulance care."

He stood waiting then, large and massively calm, his eyes on the Tower Room windows, while Kronski paid out the breeches buoy guideline.

Here on the Trade Center roof from the beginning it had been cold. Now in the last slanting rays of the sun the evening chill worked its way into a man's bones. Kronski stomped his feet and beat his hands together. "Freeze the balls off a brass monkey." he said.

The chief showed no signs of discomfort. "Think of those poor bastards still over there," he said. "Heat enough, and to spare." And then, "Look!" For the first time his voice rose perceptibly. "Look there! It's coming out empty!'

The breeches buoy swung through the window. No hand held it back. Of its own weight it began the careening slide down the immense curve, faster, faster, swinging, swaying like a mad thing—

301

"Oh, Jesus!" the chief said. "That's done it!" He was pointing.

Like a snake the heavy supporting line slid through the window, its end whipping from the weight of the knots that still held, the line itself melted through from the heat of the beam it had been tied to. It fell endlessly.

"Stand clear!" the chief said, and jumped aside himself as the heavy line lashed viciously against its fastening on the roof. Then it was still.

The chief strained to see through the Tower Room windows. He held out his hand. "Binoculars." He studied the room through the glasses in silence and then let them dangle from their lanyard around his neck.

Slowly he raised the walkie-talkie. "Roof to Trailer."

"Trailer here." Nat's voice.

The chief's voice was expressionless. "The line has parted. You'll find the breeches buoy somewhere down below. It's empty."

Nat said softly, "Oh my God!"

"It doesn't matter," the chief said. "I can't see any movement over there. I think it's all over." He paused. "The best we could," he said. "It wasn't enough."

The time was 8:41. It had been four hours and eighteen minutes since the explosion.

Götterdämmerung.

Epilogue

They walked in silence in the evening chill, block after block, without destination, each deep in his own thoughts.

They stopped at last, almost as at an inaudible signal, and turned to look back.

The tip of the great tower caught the last of the day's light. Below, the structure glowed in gathering darkness. Like an ember after the leaping flames have died, it no longer seemed to writhe.

"The chief said it," Nat said. "The best we could and it wasn't enough. Maybe it wasn't the best we could." His voice was low pitched, savage. "Maybe——"

"It's done," Patty said. "Leave it there, and go on."

"On where?"

"Just on." Patty's voice was gentle. "Ahead, not back. There is no turning back." She paused. "It's all——behind us. All of it."

They began to walk again. Together.